I0675119

MIDNIGHT WORLD

VOLUME SIX

MIDNIGHT WORLD VOLUME SIX

1-800-DARKNESS

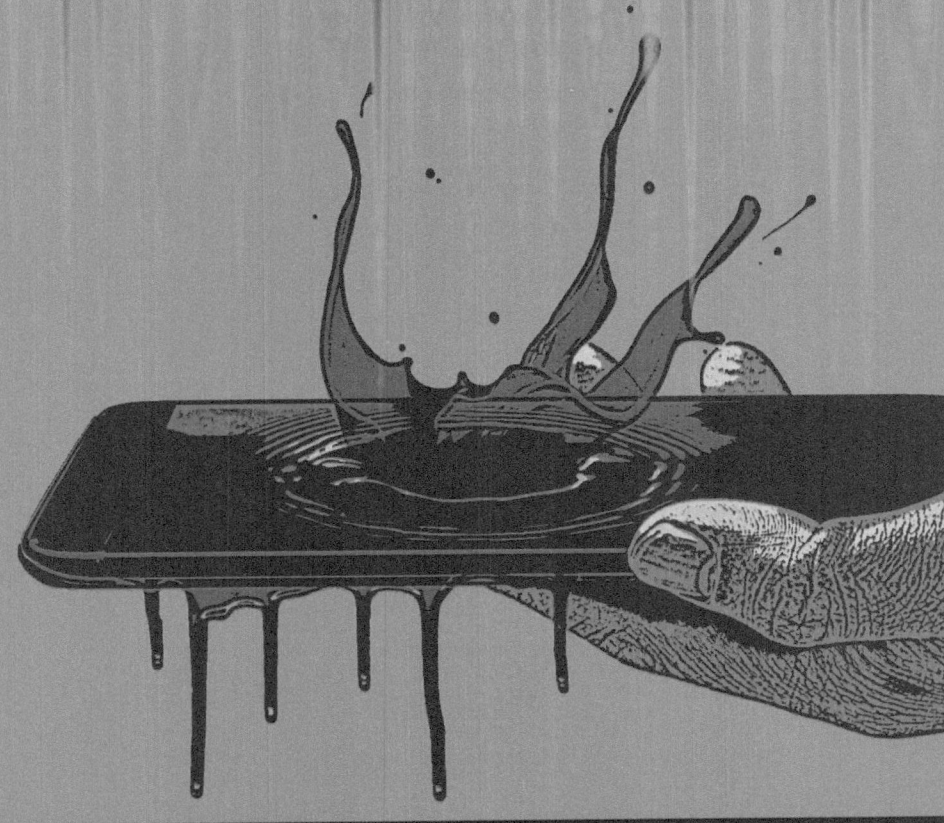

DALIVIA PLAUT

DARK PLOT
PUBLISHING

• • •

First Edition, October 2020
Story by Dalivia Plaut
Written by Dalivia Plaut
Edited by Ireland Lelisio

Copyright © 2020 Dalivia Plaut

All rights reserved.

ISBN: 978-1-7344831-2-3
Plaut, Dalivia, 1983—
1-800-Darkness
I. Title. Fiction. Dark Fantasy/Horror

ISBN: 978-1-7344831-2-3 pbk.

Cover Design by Low Key
Book Design by Dalivia Plaut
Cover Photograph by gremlin (istockphoto.com)

This is a work of fiction.
Names, characters, places, and incidents
are the products of the author's imagination.
Any resemblance to actual persons, living
or dead, is entirely coincidental.

Printed in the United States of America

Without limiting the rights under copyright reserved above, no part of this publication may be reproduced, stored in or introduced into a retrieval system, or transmitted, in any form, or by any means (electronic, mechanical, photocopying, recording, or otherwise), without the prior written permission of both the copyright owner and the above publisher of this book.

PUBLISHER'S NOTE
This is a work of fiction. Names, characters, places, and incidents either are the product of the author's imagination or are used fictitiously. Any resemblance to actual persons, living or dead, business establishments, events, or locales is entirely coincidental.

The scanning, uploading, and distribution of this book via the Internet or via any other means without the permission of the publisher is illegal and punishable by law. Your support and respect of the author's rights is appreciated.

• • •

Author's Note

The world presented beyond this page is a fictitious one, as are its characters. Any resemblance to actual persons, living or dead, is entirely coincidental.

MIDNIGHT WORLD VOLUME SIX:
1-800-DARKNESS

ROUGHLY seven thousand feet below a sun-baked boulder field along the southernmost rim of Snake Spine Canyon located in Crimson, Arizona, which, after geologist, Mel Dewing, discovered chalcocite containing rich copper deposits inside sulfite veins extracted deep within the earth, was home of one of the largest copper ore bodies in the world—estimated to be as large as Crimson Mountain—known as a "porphyry copper deposit," water droplets seeping from rock like a wrung-out sponge rained down into manmade tunnels like hot showers and sauna-like steam, which miners commonly referred to as "Lucifer's Hand," poured from deep pockets of the earth as though the devil was reaching out to touch those who had braved such a dark and unforgiving place where the only source of light came from the one glimmering from within the human psyche.

Chip Long, mine superintendent at New Frontier Mine, once told his men and women who made it his or her livelihood to descend into darkness, "When you're a mile below the earth's surface, anything could happen. And it wasn't a question of *if* it was going to happen, but rather a question of *when* it was going to happen. Down here, nobody could hear you scream—that is, except for the devil himself."

One of Chip's men, Xavier Chávez, son of a miner, knew the risks; his father had lost a good friend of his named Peru in the mines after a tunnel caved in on him, leaving rescuers to toil for weeks on end. After two weeks passed, it was no longer a rescue mission, but, more or less, a mission to salvage the remains of the trapped miners. Eventually, seventeen of the thirty-four miners were discovered. Peru was one of the seventeen bodies. As for the others, till this day, their bodies still remained missing. Every now and then, Xavier would think about those who came before him, like his father and his friend, Peru, who tragically perished, and tell his wife that he was ready—and most certainly, willing—to explore other career options and pursue a less dangerous path that would make him more "economically viable."

But a part of Xavier liked doing what he did.

It was in his blood, his namesake.

And he'd have it no other way.

☠

XAVIER, who was geared up in his hardhat, diggers, boots, and the safety harness that he wore each and every day on the job, placed a sign-in card on a board inside the office—which was mandatory for every person who entered the mine just in case the "inevitable" thing happened—rode an elevator-like cage down a narrow, nearly pitch-black shaft with two other miners, one of them being Chip, to a new tunnel, which, earlier, had been blasted from the method called block caving, which allowed gravity to naturally push manageable fragments of the deposit into a funnel inside the tunnel underneath that rich copper deposit.

With each shift lasting only three hours due to the extreme conditions, Xavier ran into a bit of trouble with the automated extractor right before he was about to take his break. He hollered at one of his colleagues, Terry Bannon, told him that he'd be right back, then checked out the problem.

When he arrived at the extractor, the teeth of the shovel were wedged underneath a massive boulder protruding from the ground.

Xavier closely inspected the boulder and realized he'd have to manually release the shovel from its stuck position.

As he tugged on the shovel, he witnessed a crack stretching between his feet.

Before he could even react, the ground below him suddenly collapsed into a dark pocket in the earth. The extractor was first to fall into the hole, then Xavier; however, fortunately for Xavier, the fall was no more than twenty feet.

He landed lightly, the pressure of the impact causing his bright orange hardhat to spring from the top of his head like a cork.

As the dust cleared away, Xavier inspected the damages, first, the extractor, which was overturned on its side and came inches from rolling over and squashing him, then, his injuries, only one of them, his right ankle, which he had twisted during the landing.

Xavier tried to stand to his feet, but he could barely apply any pressure to his ankle.

He shouted out to Terry, who, eventually, arrived at the hole.

"Xavier," he said from above, "are you hurt?"

"No," he lied. "I'm good."

He couldn't help but laugh at the fact that he had just faced death and dodged it by the skin of his teeth.

All he could think about was "Sweet Jesus" looking after him. The one—and only—savior came to his rescue yet again.

He motioned the cross over his head, chest, and shoulders, and pointed up at the gaping hole above as if Jesus Himself was looking down on him.

"Gracias."

Soon after Terry discovered his injured colleague below, a team of other men was quick to check on Xavier; however, they were extremely cautious to maintain a safe distance from the hole to keep it from further collapsing.

As Terry went to fetch a rope, Xavier inspected the inside of the dark cave-like hole.

Waving away dust and smoke, he limped around the extractor and shined the light along the jagged walls. Xavier could compare it to a large room, a din. The floor was covered in rock dust, which had the consistency of—sand? Even the air was somewhat dry, which was odd as well.

While scanning the rest of the cave with the flashlight, he caught a glint in the beam of the light. He redirected the flashlight back to the glint, inched closer to it, and mindful of his surroundings, picked up the hardhat from the ground.

He put the hardhat back on and made his way to the tiny flicker of light.

"Terry," Xavier shouted out, "I think I found something down here. . ."

Chip had now taken Terry's place and was monitoring Xavier.

"Try not to move around, Xavier—"

"—Chip, there's something down here!"

"What is it?" Chip asked while carefully leaning over the hole and shining a flashlight down below.

"I dunno," Xavier mumbled, as he arrived at the glinting object.

He kneeled down and shined the flashlight on a silver charm bracelet. As he pulled the bracelet from the ground, a misshaped skull rose from the rock dust and forced a frantic Xavier to backpedal away.

"Xavier," Chip shouted from above, "what'd you find?"

"It's a body," he said, trailing off.

He gathered the courage and closely inspected the skull, which was about the size of a baby's skull. He touched it with his own hand. The bone was incredibly soft, almost spongy. It was somewhat human. Yet, it was disproportionate. The forehead was much larger than any normal forehead, the chin much more shorter and narrower than any other human skull. Even one of the arms—the right one—was much larger, adult-like, opposed to the other arm, the left, which appeared half the size as the other one. He placed the flashlight on the ground.

With a handkerchief, Xavier dusted away the rest of the skeleton, which was the size of a young girl. As with the skull, the bones of her skeletal structure were soft and spongy. Xavier discovered a knife-like shard of black crystallized rock, similar to dark graphite, gripped in the skeleton's hand.

Using more force yet, at the same time, mindful not to break it, Xavier pried the black crystal from the hand of the skeleton and closely examined it.

He picked up the flashlight from the ground and carefully ran the beam along the black crystal.

"Holy Shit," he uttered, as he fell witness to an entire universe in the palm of his hands.

FOUR YEARS AGO

FROM the edge of the worn couch which, over the past couple of months, had become an exciting new game where checking underneath the cushions once a week was filled with more surprises than a daytime soap opera, Pan was watching controversial candidate, now president-elect, Richard R. Rhodes, aka the real-life "X-Man," who was constantly teased for his said-to-be supernatural power to hypnotize over half of the country—in particular, those voters who lived in and around the Rust Belt, as well as states who typically leaned blue—along the trail with his outrageous "sound bites" and constant "wall-to-wall" news coverage, giving his victory speech to an estimated crowd of two-hundred and fifty thousand red hat-wearing supporters at Cherry Hill in his home state of Tennessee when Brob suddenly blurted out from the other end of the couch, "This is some fucking bullshit! You really stepped in it now, 'Merica!"

"*Yeah,*" someone mumbled from the corner of the room, "*we're neck-deep in it now, aren't we?*"

Brob was wearing a special helmet that he only wore wherever he wasn't in the public eye. He worked at one of those big box stores. One day, a pallet fell on his head, cracking open his skull. Brob sued the company, got millions from the lawsuit; however, most of that money had gone straight to pixie dust.

Sitting in a recliner chair next to Brob was Skinny Gee— or just "Gee"—who was resting his head against his hand while, at the same time, shaking his head in a trendy theme of disgust. Gee here, a former user of dipping tobacco, as well as a "two-pack-a-day" smoker, lost his jaw after years of heavy tobacco use.

Replacing the old, rickety eclectic shaver of a electrolarynx, which was used underneath his metal mandible implant, for a portable handheld talk box stocked with over three million words, including the latest slang that was downloaded in a weekly update, Gee sounded off: "*Bollocks.*"

Which, he knew, sounded much better than "Gee golly."

The voice of talk box had a British accent and came with a "wide" variety of British lingo; however, at the time he upgraded to the talk box, due to a shortage in supply, the only other option was a talk box with a Wisconsin accent; and there was no way in hell he'd go for that.

On the TV, Taylor Swipe, whose song "A Christian Eagle" had become sort of an anthem—or rally cry—on The Trail, introduced Rhodes: "Now, ladies and gentlemen, without further ado, it is my honor to introduce to you the next president of the United States. . . "

"—Not my president," Brob chimed in.

". . . Richard R. Rhodes!"

"Know what the R stands for?"

"What 'Redneck'?"

"No," Skinny Gee said. "Remington."

"I wonder where he got that name?"

Skinny Gee said, "Certainly not from the painter."

In a sea of *red*, white, and blue—red, being the most predominant color—the crowd roared and waved their red hats, as well as their miniature American flags as Richard Rhodes and his wife, Karen, as well as their two children,

J.R., five, and R.J., seven, who were both dressed in matching tailored suits and red clip-on ties, walked out onto stage.

"Wow," Whiskers said aloofly from the corner of her puffy mouth, "if it isn't the two future serial killers. Soon, they'll have their own reality TV shows."

Whiskers, who had spent her entire life's savings on plastic surgery to make herself look like a cat—literally, as in the eyes, nose, cheeks, ears, teeth, even the whisker implants, all resembling the features of the common household feline—held up a bowl of milk (soy, of course) with both her hands, which were balled up into fists, or in Whiskers' case, her kitty paws, and licked up the soy milk with her normal human tongue. Or, at least she tried to. Considering a cat's tongue had a rougher texture, often compared to sandpaper, and was way more flexible, unlike a human's tongue, Whiskers was getting brown and spotty milk with tiny bits of cereal all over the armrest of the couch.

Pan found herself staring at Whiskers, more so out of amusement rather than repulsion. For Pan, watching not only her roommate, but also one of her fellow addicts from her recovery meetings lick up soy milk, which, for Whiskers, was as ordinary to her as a human sipping from an environmental-friendly straw, never got old. *Never a dull moment around this bunch.* However, a part of Pan couldn't help but hold in a laugh at how serious Whiskers was taking this whole "cat business." Who could blame her, though? For Pan, there was something incredibly special about being in the company of those who shared the same addictions that truly brought out a deep rawness in each addict's story.

According to Gwynne Banks's story, she was struck by a car while crossing the street after receiving a "WALK" signal. As her contorted, mutilated body lay in a puddle of blood in the middle of the intersection, Gwynne began to slip away; technically, her heart stopped beating for exactly one minute and thirty-three seconds before the emotional driver, who had been aggressively performing CPR on Gwynne, slapped her across the face in hopes to wake her up from death. When Gwynne came to, she actually believed, as devoutly as a Christian to Christ, that she was a tortoiseshell trapped inside the body of a twenty-four year old female named Gwynne Banks.

Pan often wondered if it wasn't getting hit by a car but rather pixie dust rearranging her brain, rewiring it, if you will, then, just for kicks, removing screws, adding new ones that didn't quite fit. After all, she drank catnip tea as an alternative to dust and in her own words, said it made her more "phlegmatic." However, Pan knew the tea had more of a placebo effect on her. She had done her research.

Whiskers pulled her face from the bowl and stared back at Pan with her wide cat eyes, "What?"

Pan rapidly shook her head.

"Nuttin'," she said and concentrated on the TV.

"I can't believe for the next four fuckin' years we're going to have to listen to this clown. I mean, how can these people," Whiskers pointed at the supporters in the crowd waving flags, "be so gullible? They have absolutely no clue what he's going to do to this country."

Jay, the most handsome one of the bunch, said from the corner of the room, "Let me guess: your *third eye*, huh?"

"You don't need a third eye to see who this man is—or isn't."

"Screw it, man," Brob said. "I'm moving to another country. Anybody with me?"

Brob combed his stringy black hair from his face and looked around the living room for any takers.

"You're just saying that, Brobby," Pan said.

"Canada? Who's down?"

"Well," Pan said and gripped the TV remote and just as Rhodes was about to address the nation, she flipped the channel to Cartoon Network, "you know you're right, Whiskers—"

"—Why'd you do that?" Jay whined. "I wanted to hear what he has to say?"

"Yeah," Brob said. "Turn it back."

"Why? You already know what he's gonna say, Brobby," she said. "Plus, all it's gonna do is make you upset, then, for the next hour, you're gonna continue on this 'moving out of the country' talk until you're blue in the face; but the fact is,

Brobby, you're not gonna move out of the country. So, please, do us all a favor: Don't be that person. It's unbecoming."

"What person?"

A "sore loser" was what Pan wanted to say, but she wasn't at all in the mood to hurt Brob's feeling. As she could see, Brob was already hurting. *What was the point adding more hurt?*

Next to Jay was Ogre, who was looking at Pan as if he was disappointed by her unwillingness to listen.

Silence grew between the group as *Animal Jack* was barking on the TV.

"Fine," Pan said and flipped it back to the speech where Rhodes was talking about "unifying" a nation after he had spent an entire campaign trying his best to rip it apart down the middle with his insensitive, xenophobic rhetoric for the sake of igniting enough passion out of voters in order to bring them to the polls.

If there was one thing she'd give Rhodes, it was his way of drawing out the best in people—and the worst.

But that time had come and past and absolutely nothing remained forgotten, especially the divisive words Rhodes used while running for the highest office of the country.

As tempers flared, Pan tossed the remote on the glass coffee table, which was littered with food crumbs and candy wrappers and empty potato chip bags.

She stood up from the couch and gave Brob the "screw you" eye on the way from the living room.

Inside the master bedroom, which she shared with Whiskers—Pan taking one side of the room while Whiskers taking the other side, her rather sparse side consisting of only a queen size mattress and a bin of kitty toys—Pan wiggled loose a small stash of pixie dust that she hid between the rough, crumpled pages of a raggedy-looking pocket sized book inside a compartment underneath the lamp on the nightstand. The book was old, obviously. At least centuries old from the ruggedness of the texture. She ran her fingers over the bumpy surface of a circular *sun*-like symbol engraved in the cover. In her other hand, she held up the baggie to the light. There wasn't enough to get high. She knew that the only way she'd be able to obtain a true high, the flying kind, she had to "re up" her drug supply; and if there was one thing she dreaded the most, it was paying an announced visit to her dealer.

The thought alone of having to visit that man—or whatever the hell he was—made Pan want to use even more. She licked the tip of her index finger as if she was using her spit as adhesive and picked up whatever glittery pinkish pixie dust was left in the very bottom of the bag and spread it along the top of her gums.

With the glow of the TV flickering the living room behind him, Jay stood at the edge of the bedroom doorway.

"What you think you're doing?" asked Jay.

The sound of Jay's voice caused her to flinch. She immediately crumbled the plastic bag in her hand and brushed away whatever dust was left on her finger.

"What does it look like I'm doing?" Pan asked more bitterly, as she struggled to look Jay in the eyes.

"I'll tell you what, Pan," Jay said, "we'll play a little game. Every time Rhodes says the word *train* you can punch Ogre in the face. It'll be fun."

"No thank you, Jay," Pan said while placing the book back into the compartment and closing it.

"Pan," Jay said seriously, "what about the past two weeks? It will all be for nothing. Please, Pan. Don't do this—"

"—I just want a little bump. That's all."

"A little bump? Right. A little bump turns into a big bump. Then, next thing you know, you're off flying in the clouds for the next three days."

"I can control myself, Jay."

"Pan—"

"—Jason," Pan said over Jay. "It's my life, not yours."

"You're so right," Jay said and held up his hands. "You are."

As the tension grew and Pan redirected her attention toward finding money, a voice said from behind: *"I'll call David."*

12

More irritable, Pan stopped, turned, and faced Jay.

"Oh yeah?"

Her cheeks were full of blood, eyes pulsing, breath shorter.

"Please don't make me, Pan."

"You call David and we're done. For good."

"You said that last time."

"This time, I mean it," Pan said, her expression dead-serious.

"If I was feeling like the way you're feeling right now, then I'd expect you to do the same."

"And how am I feeling, Jason?"

"I can't say exactly how you're feeling. Only *you* can," Jay said. "But I sure as hell can imagine you're feeling like you got something inside you trying to get out and the only way you can stop it is by going back to the vice that stopped it before. The one that nearly killed you, Pan. Listen, I understand you saw some things after the wreck—these other 'worlds,' as you've said. Shit that everyday people wouldn't want to see even if they didn't have a choice. You've been there. But, face it," Jay said and turned back to the group and pointed at each person—or animal—in the living room, "we *all* have."

Holding back a cocktail of emotions, Pan seethed, "You don't know what I went through."

"I'm not trying to argue with you," Jay said. "Let's watch some TV. If you want, I can rent a movie on-demand—"

"—A friend wouldn't call her sponsor behind her back," she said over Jay.

"Sure they would."

"What? Because you care?"

"Of course, I care. This is not you, Pan. This is the fuckin' brain candy talking. You know that, right?"

Pan didn't answer. In a way, she was done talking.

Jay stepped aside and went back to the living room to watch Rhodes's speech while Pan scrounged up whatever money she had stashed around the bedroom, as well as the rest of her apartment, including the seat cushions, for a gram of pixie dust. In the kitchen, she came across a check lying on the countertop. The check, which expired in two days, was from her insurance company, Omni Health, which had sent her the amount of money that they were going to pay for the hospital bill. The banks were already closed, obviously; however, she'd be lying if she said the thought didn't run past her mind. *What's the worse that could happen? People skip out on bills all the time.* Besides, *eating was so overrated. Worse case scenario: I could always bum some of those protein shakes from Gee. The guy has a large enough stock- pile to last him through two Armageddons.* She put aside the thought for the time being, placed the check inside the drawer, and after Brob was enabling enough to chip in a couple of bones at the very last second—which had drawn even more outrage from Jay—Pan barely had enough money to buy a gram of pixie dust.

As she was about to head out, she grabbed her phone on the coffee table. The phone only had three percent power left and more than likely, it'd probably die on the way to Apple Bottoms. She grabbed the phone charger lying next to several owner manuals, as well as a stack of DEV, Pro- Tips, and *Software Development For Dummies* books, which were scattered on top of her computer desk.

She plugged the phone into the charger and switched off the light to her bedroom and told the others that she was going on a "quick" dust run; however, once again, Jay urged the rest of the group not to condone Pan's actions.

In Pan's defense, Brob, the enabler that he was, argued that the dust was just for one night. "Considering the cir- cumstances," he said directly to Jay, "we could use it to take off the edge from, you know. . . "

He pointed at Rhodes, who had shifted his speech to- ward illegal immigration.

Pan searched the strongest person in the room. Clearly, it was Jay, mentally that is; however, she needed someone with more brute strength.

"Say, Ogre," Pan said, as she threw on a light jacket, "wanna grab some fresh air with me?"

Ogre shrugged, then nodded.

"Are you sure you want to do this?" asked Ogre.

"Is that a *yes* or *no*?"

The six foot seven inch tall Ogre stood to his feet and followed Pan outside.

"I won't be long," she said to the others.

Before Pan shut the front door behind her, Gee said through his talk box, "Be careful, darling."

"Always am," Pan said quietly, as the small hit of pixie dust suddenly sent a rush of euphoria through her body. The whites of her eyes brightened. She threw her head in a nod at Whiskers and said with a smirk, "If you use the toilet Whisky Poo, make sure to raise the seat."

Whiskers did her best to ignore Pan by focusing in on the snake oil salesman on TV. She knew it wasn't Pan talking but rather the dust.

"Better yet," Brob teased, pointing to the hallway with his thumb, "the crazy lady next door has a litter box. I'm sure she wouldn't mind if you used it—"

Whiskers opened her mouth, revealing her fangs. With both her pupils black and swollen, she hissed at Brob, who, in return, held up his hands in surrender for the sake of not getting scratched.

As Whiskers redirected her attention to the TV screen, she crossed her arms over her chest and then glared at Pan as she exited the apartment with Ogre.

On the way downstairs, the two bumped into Pan's landlord as he was taking out a bag of trash. She already knew what he was going to ask her before he even opened his mouth.

"I know, Frank," Pan said and held up her hand as if it was an impenetrable brick wall. "I'll have the money for you tomorrow. Promise."

"You said that last week, Pandora. Now, if you're not going to—"

"—Tomorrow," Pan said finally over Frank, who was killing her high.

The tone in her voice caused Ogre to step forward in defense. His presence alone caused "Mr. Buzzkill" to back away.

"If I don't have the rent money by tomorrow, you're out of here."

Pan left the apartment. Frank's comments had only made Pan's temptation to use again much worse. Not only that, of all the people to run into right now: Dexter the "Texter" Martinez, who was dressed in all black, no labels—in fact, whatever labels he had on his attire were either torn off or blacked out with a bold Sharpie—was hanging out on the street corner with a couple of his so-called "righteous" goons who were bored out of their brains and looking to "fuck up *shit*," shit as in like a monument of a historical figure or a museum or a passerby wearing an article of clothing that blatantly screamed to the Heavens, "Appropriation!"

Dexter shouted out at Pan, but she did her best to ignore him by continuing to walk.

"Where's your *pussy* cat?" asked Dexter, putting an emphasis on his favorite word in the English language.

Pan slowed down her walk, Ogre tempting to step in.

"Hey," Dexter continued, "why don't you tell that *pussy* cat to come outside. I have a little treat I want to give her."

"I'm sure it is *little*," Pan retorted, making sure to put an emphasis on a word that was destined to do more harm than good for her, especially on a night where she was jonesing for dust.

Dexter's goons snickered at her remark, which only made him more fired up.

"Why don't you come over here for a taste?" Dexter's confidence crumbled. He finished by mumbling under his breath, "*Bitch.*"

Pan rotated around, tightly squeezed her crotch, and seethed at him, "Pet this, Sticky Fingers!"

While Dexter and his friends were "*oh*-ing" and "*ah*-ing," she held back from Ogre from turning the teens into his human-pretzels.

After digesting what was intended to be an insult by Pan, several of Dexter's friends turned to Dexter and asked what Pan meant by the name; however, based on a certain "sticky" discovery last week inside a trashcan in Dexter's bathroom by one of his friends, it didn't take them long to figure out what Pan was insinuating, more like revealing.

"Forget about 'em," Pan said and continued walking on the sidewalk.

"So, where we going?" asked Ogre.

"Apple Bottoms," Pan said.

"Hold up," said Ogre. "You talking about the strip club?"

More laidback, Pan nodded.

Ogre, who was slightly terrified, replied, "What the hell are we gonna do at a strip club?"

"That's where Lil' Beelze is."

"Lil' Beelze? Who in the hell is Lil' Beelze?"

"He's one of the part-owners of the club. He also happens to be my dealer."

"You're getting dust from some guy who owns a strip club?" said Ogre, as if, by verbally running it back to Pan, she might reconsider using the money on the essentials, like food or having a roof over her head. "Sounds pretty sketchy—"

"—Aren't you the same guy who doesn't even do dust, yet he got Jay hooked on dust? The same spoiled guy whose rich father owns a chain of car dealerships across the entire East Coast?" Ogre didn't retort from Pan's comments. "So, now what? This guy's going to hand out advice to me?"

"You don't know me," Ogre said darkly.

"Let me ask you, Ogre," Pan said and stopped walking on the sidewalk. "Did Jason ever tell you why he got hooked on dust?"

Ogre shook his head.

"Nah," he said coolly.

As the north wind started to pick up from a cold front pushing in, Pan curled her hair around her ears and said to Ogre, "Two years ago, Jay's brother was accidentally shot twice in the chest during a Fourth of July celebration. Jay held his brother in his arms and had to watch him die while everybody else around them were celebrating. Till this day, they still don't know who shot him. Before the judge ordered Jay to take a recovery class to help curb the addiction,

he was one of the brightest basketball players in the entire
country. He always said basketball was an easy sport, *simple*; you put the ball in the basket, but for Jay, after he became a dust junkie, trying to kick the addiction was tougher
than any sport he had ever played. So, the next time, before
you open your mouth to criticize or speak about something
you don't entirely understand, you might want to save it for
your diary."

More impressed by Pan's fierceness, Ogre said calmly, "I
can see why you're so close to him. You know, because of
what happened to your—"

"—Don't," Pan snapped before Ogre could finish his sentence.

Pan glared at Ogre as if she was looking straight through
him.

In the corner of her eye, Pan suddenly witnessed her sister's face in the passenger seat of a passing car on the street.
She blinked away the face. The woman looked similar to
her but was *not* her.

"Sorry," Ogre said more compassionately. "Everybody
has their plights. For me, it's getting punched in the face.
Like I have any room to talk."

"By the way," Pan said and shifted the focus away from
her sister, "what do you get out of all of that?"

"For some," he said, "the pain is no different than a
drug."

Pan accepted Ogre's comment for what it was.

Then, they proceeded to Apple Bottoms, which was only
a couple of blocks from the apartment complex.

☠

THEY arrived at Apple Bottoms where there was a line of
people—mostly men— wrapped around the building. Pan
went straight up to Flattop, who was one of the two bounc-
ers standing at the front entranceway.

Flattop acknowledged Pan, who possessed a sort of local
status from her immediate connection with the two bounc-

ers. Without hesitating, Flattop unclipped the velvet rope along the stanchion and let Pan inside the club.

As Ogre was about to follow Pan into the club, Flattop closed the barrier and held out his hand. Pan tapped Flattop on the arm and said, "He's with me."

Flattop paused and carefully thought about whether or not he should let Ogre inside.

Eventually, after receiving a nod from the other bouncer, he let Ogre inside.

Together, Pan and Ogre walked into Apple Bottoms. First, Pan was greeted by a chubby, scraggly-bearded man named Rico who was overseeing the inside of the club from a booth above the cash register.

"Hey, hey, Pandora," Rico said jubilantly.

"Sup, Rico."

Without having to state her business, he flicked his head in a nod toward the back of the club and said, "He's in the back."

Once Pan was through talking with Rico, her palms became sweaty. She felt a bubble of nausea inside her belly and stepped outside her head for a moment in order to rid the thought of puking on the floor. *Once I do a little bump everything will be chill.* The more Pan concentrated on all that flesh surrounding her—an ass shake here, a titty jiggle there—the more her thoughts spiraled out of control. All she could think about was the dust, as though she couldn't walk through this place or even function properly for that matter, unless she had more dust in her system.

Pan and Ogre made their way through the club, passing several strippers who were working the pole and gathering tips, two others who were having a twerking contest to see who could make their butt cheeks clap the loudest, others giving lap dances in the darker recesses of the club. Others said hello and looked at her as if they were running into an old friend and followed with the curl of a smile.

Considering most of the club was rather dark, the only light came in sudden bursts from a flickering strobe light along the ceiling.

"Stay close to me," Pan said to Ogre, who was unable to hear Pan due to the blaring industrial-like synth wave music, which was intensifying that dark, steamy vibe. Ogre leaned in closer as Pan repeated herself once more.

With their sense heightened, the two cautiously shouldered their way through a crowd of rowdy college kids, who were burning away whatever brain cells they had left with an endless carousel of Fireball shots.

Still clinging to boyish attire with their baseball caps spun around backwards, several of the guys were throwing handfuls of dollar bills at the voluptuous stripper, Ms. Queen Apple Bottom herself, Serena, who put a new definition in having "too much junk in the trunk" with an ass so plump and holy that it was easily mistaken for implants. However, the boys in brands certainly weren't complaining; in fact, each one was left gawking as Serena twerked her ass through a rainstorm of crisp, coke-powdered bills. When Serena made it clap, it thundered.

Pan braced for any remarks but only received one, a soft and drawn out "Hey, gurl." Eventually, the two made it through the testosterone-driven chaos without drawing too much attention and located Lil' Beelze and his motley crew seated in a booth in front of a mirrored wall.

"*If it isn't Tinker Bell herself,*" a voice rose from underneath the mountain of flesh.

Lil' Beelze's face emerged from the bodies of two strippers. The top, as well as the top part of his scalp was covered in a tattoo of gnarly horns curling around the sides of his forehead. He wore an earring of an upside cross on his right ear. His clothing attire was minimal: black jeans that were so tight that looked painted on, which matched the black leather biker jacket with a set of metal spikes on the shoulder pads. The jacket was worn open, revealing his chest that had thousands of tattoos; however, each one consisted mostly of names, which, whenever asked, Lil' Beelze touted that they were the names of his "followers."

Pan stepped forward while Lil' Beelze rudely pushed aside the two strippers, as if they were objects.

"Long time no see, Pandora," he said, grinning.

Lil' Beelze noticed Pan's somewhat fidgety state.

"You should've taken my advice."

"And what advice was that?" Pan asked bitterly.

"*Once you have a taste of the dust, your soul starts to rust.* Didn't I tell you that before you came to me, Tinker Bell?" Eyeing Pan from head to toe, Lil' Beelze gave Pan a once-over. "You, my dear, look as rusty as a junkyard."

More paranoid, Pan said with her voice trembling, "I'm just here for a gram."

"Just a gram, huh?"

"Yeah."

Lil' Beelze leaned back in the booth. "The last time we saw each other, you said you were gonna quit the dust, Pandora, but I remember I specifically told you that you'd be back and now, here you are."

"I am," Pan said, as she started to lose patience with Lil' Beelze. "Just cutting back, you know?"

"Right." Lil' Beelze devilishly smirked. "And the only way to fix a broken record player that keeps skipping is to smash it with a baseball bat."

"Just a gram, Beelze."

"I would love to, Pandora, but I'm afraid I can't help you out. I'm only pushing pounds these days. I'm sure you can understand." He carried a dark twinkle in his eye when he said, "Cut out the middleman. It's nothing personal. It's just business. Of all people, you know my product is the best in the city, no additives, pure as a virgin, manufactured straight from '*The MW*,' unlike that purple knock-off *narwhal* tusk you call dust that my competitors be hustlin' on the other side of town."

Pan looked around the strip club and grew more fidgety. Lil' Beelze was first to acknowledge her fragile, shaking state.

"I'll tell you what, Pan. . ."

As soon as Pan directed her attention back to Lil' Beelze and saw that concealed darkness in his face, she knew exactly what he was going to ask of her because he had that same look when he asked her the last time she saw him.

". . . You work for me tonight and I'll give you your gram of pixie dust."

Pan's stomach turned to knots from the very thought.

Lil' Beelze said, as if he was trying to entice her, "We'll make it a new theme for tonight: '*Opening up Pandora's Box.*' And you'll be our main attraction. Just imagine for a second the star you will become. I'll get wardrobe to create the perfect look for you. Cute and innocent and yet, deep down inside, hiding a dark secret. You have the look, Pan. Cleopatra had the look as well."

Pan's skin started to burn from the sound of Lil' Beelze bringing up the subject of her sister.

"She knew it, too," Lil' Beelze said.

Pan finally responded, "My sister wouldn't have been caught dead in a place like this."

"Maybe not," he said, shrugging. "She was more head-strong than you. As I've said before, I've always had a certain 'thing' for your sister. More than some crush. When we were in school—"

"—I know," Pan interrupted, as Lil' Beelze drifted off into reflection and did so with glossy dark eyes. "You told me you used to shoot spitballs at her from the back of the classroom."

"In a way, I guess I was always searching for her to show me that look. *But you,*" he said and shook away the memory, "it's there. You may not believe you have it. I've been around plenty women and I know the look when I put eyes on it. You got it all right, Pandora. And believe me, once everybody finds out about you, you'll be the new sensation around town. Men, even women, will be shouting your name, begging you for more. You'll have them on their knees, Pandora, asking for your hand in marriage. I can make you famous. After all, what's every person's wet dream?"

Pan didn't answer the question.

Instead, Lil' Beelze answered for her.

"It's turning a broken angel, like yourself, into their own personal devil."

"I'm not broken," Pan said, as her chest tightened.

Revealing the two golden canines—his "bling"—underneath his wicked grin, Lil' Beelze shook his head.

"I like you, Panny. Maybe not entirely broken," he said and paused. "I'd say more like 'out of order.'" Another one of those wicked grins found its way onto his face once again. "So let's get you working again, Pandora. What'd you say?"

Darkness spread over Pan's face.

"Every time I come in this shithole, you're trying to get me to work for you," she said darkly. "Each time I give you the same answer. What makes you think my answer will be any different this time?"

"Like I said," he said with a glint in his keen eye, "you have the look."

As Pan thought about Lil' Beelze's proposal, Ogre touched her on the shoulder and said, "Come on, Pan. Let's get outta here."

Ogre was only thinking about the others who were waiting for her return with a gram of dust back at her apartment, which was a safe space where she could use and at the same time, be monitored by her peers.

Strangely, Pan was putting way more thought into what Lil' Beelze said than she'd ever thought she would. Ogre knew it was the small amount of pixie dust in her system doing most of the tinkering for her.

☠

AFTER Pan gave Lil' Beelze her answer—which wasn't exactly a yes but wasn't a no either—she excused herself to the bathroom while Ogre hung back and pulled out the gram of pixie dust that Lil' Beelze had given her free of charge from his own personal stash. She poured a couple of pinches worth of dust over the flattest part of the vanity, cut it into two fine lines with an old gift card from Café Cloud, dug out a crumbled Stop N' Shop receipt for two *Dark Cavern*^{TM} bars and a 22-ounce can of Tree Sap from inside her pocket, straightened out the receipt by unfolding it first and then running it along the edge of the counter, rolled it up, and snorted each line of dust through the rolled-up receipt. She jerked back her head while, at the same time, pinched her nose, as the pixie dust hit the very back of her throat, causing it to burn. Eventually, that burning mellowed to a cool, throbbing sensation. The drip hit her next, causing her to clear her throat and spit up a glitter-covered loogie covered in the sink. Soon after the dust settled, parts of her face went incredibly numb.

All of a sudden the left side of her body started to twitch. The muscles on her left arm, mostly her bicep, pumped like a spasm. She squeezed her arm and massaged the muscles until the spasms stopped.

Pan glanced at herself in the mirror and studied the dust coursing through the veins in her face, each one lit up like a 120-volt light bulb. She traced the lit veins past her eyes, which were much brighter. As the dust settled, each line of her face smoothed out as though the dust was shaving off years from her face, which was slowly fading into the hazy vanity light overhead. She was now wearing the face of an intruder, beautiful and deadly; and that manipulative intruder was starting to consume her body. She peered past the smooth, glowing flesh, past each contour of that pretty white skull, and stared into the void. In the darkness, she witnessed the dust underneath flashing like an electrical storm inside her brain.

Just as she was about to lose herself in the light, she readjusted her eyes and wiped away any dust she had on her nose. She took a deep breath. Then, exited the bathroom.

Once she made it back to Lil' Beelze, she noticed Ogre was gone; in fact, he was nowhere to be found inside the club.

"So," Lil' Beelze said, "have you made up your mind, Pandora?"

From the untrustworthy expression on his face, Lil' Beelze looked as if, in a way, he already knew Pan's answer before she even opened her mouth to speak.

"Where's Ogre?" asked Pan, as she continued to scan the club.

She caught a glimmer in the corner of her eye. She looked down and found a necklace on the floor. She kneeled down and picked up the necklace—which she knew was Ogre's necklace; however, when she stared at it, she couldn't help but notice the similarities in the necklace. She peered closer and realized it wasn't his necklace. It was her bracelet, the same charm bracelet she lost during the wreck. Each charm was accounted for, such charms including the "*compass*" charm, the "*unicorn*" charm, the computer "*mouse*" charm, the "*two hearts*" charm, the "*paw print*" charm, the "*letter P*" charm, the "*elephant*" charm, the "*tooth*" charm.

In a state of disbelief, Pan studied each charm along the bracelet.

But *how could this be?*

She was starting to feel the dust working its way through her veins; however, there was a tinglier feeling inside her body, as if the dust was laced with another drug. She closed her eyes, shook her head, and rubbed the backside of her eyelids as though she was rebooting herself. When she opened her eyes again, she witnessed Ogre's necklace in her hand, *not* her bracelet.

"What'd you did with Ogre?" Pan asked, clearly upset.

A voice among the noisy music said that Ogre had left, but Pan knew it was a lie.

She felt a darker presence looming over her. She looked up and saw Lil' Beelze standing in front of her. Slowly, the tattoos of those two horns on his head started to protrude from his flesh. The two horns were no longer tattoos but actual horns extending from Lil' Beelze's head. And massive horns, they were!

As a pendulum of fear and anger gripped her, she narrowed her eyes.

She stood to her feet; however, her body didn't stop moving upward.

She kept rising, as both of her feet started to lift from the floor.

PAN woke up on a leather couch with one helluva splitting headache.

She didn't own a leather couch nor did she know anybody who had a leather couch. Jay maybe, since he once commented that he liked the feel of leather.

As she rubbed away the blur from her red eyes, she didn't even recognize the environment. Even after a thorough study, the sticky couch she was lying on was foreign to her.

She carefully sat upright, which caused the pain in her head to intensify to the point where the living room started to spin. She closed her eyes, breathed deeply, and then opened her eyes. The spinning lessened and gave Pan a moment to make sense of where she was, how she came to be in a stranger's apartment, even what she was wearing, which was a white XXL T-shirt that ran down to her thighs.

In a sudden frenzied state, she searched for clothes, including her underwear, but didn't find any clothes scattered around the living room. She heard a noise in the other room. She checked it out. There, she found a strange man and a woman sleeping in the bed. She located her clothes on the floor next to the bed.

Trying not to wake the strange people, she grabbed her clothes, as well as her underwear from the floor and tiptoed out of the bedroom.

Suddenly, she heard a *creak* of a bedspring behind her.

She turned her shoulder, only to find that the man was repositioning himself on the bed.

As Pan slipped on her clothes and exited from the apartment, she still had no idea as to how she wound up on a couch in someone's apartment. Maybe she had met him at Apple Bottoms. She tried to attach the man's face to a memory but, as before, she found nothing.

Only pain.

☠

GROWING more anxious about not be able to remember the night before, Pan used the hand railing to walk down three flights of stairs.

When she made it to the front of the apartments called Village Square, which she knew were located on the *other* side of town, as in at least a good twenty minutes from where she lived, she couldn't help but notice the sunshine.

The sight of the bright blue sky and the crispness of the air triggered a memory.

It was overcast on the night she went to Apple Bottoms, and she remembered the forecast for the week and how her favorite, most trustworthy meteorologist on Channel 9— Bryan Showers, yes, that was his actual name—predicted that for the next two days it was going to be cloudy with an eighty percent chance of rain.

Has it been that long?

Pan forced herself to think and whenever she did, her head started to pound.

She soon confirmed what day it was with one of the residents, who, after telling her that it was Friday, stared at her as if she was from another planet.

Once Pan was made aware of the day, she immediately thought about what she was supposed to do on Wednesday, two days ago.

The only words that came out of Pan's mouth: "I'm fucked."

☠

AFTER bumming enough money from a nice man to catch a ride on a bus back to her apartment, Pan could feel the dread creeping through her body.

She sprinted from the bus as soon as the doors opened and hurried toward her apartment complex. She finally arrived at her apartment, only to be greeted by an eviction notice on her door. She walked to Frank's apartment and knocked on his door. He opened the door but only as far as the lock chain would reach. Through the crack of the door, he said what he needed to say, which was a short "sorry, it's too late," then closed the door before Pan had a chance to beg him that she'd have the rent money in his hands in the next hour.

Pan had no other option than to find a way into her apartment. With the help of a dumpster, she climbed up the fire ladder until she made it to her window.

Since the window was locked, she was left with no other choice than to kick a brick from the corner of the wall with her heel and use it to break the window.

Mindful of the jagged glass, she carefully snuck into her apartment.

She went straight to the check in the drawer. It had already expired, but she had to at least try and cash it. Her only hope was that the bank teller was in a forgiving mood. While she was inside, she grabbed a glass of water. Of course, that jerk, Frank, even cut off the water.

In a burst of rage, Pan threw the glass against the kitchen wall, causing shards of sharp glass to fly everywhere.

Among a whirlwind of thoughts, only one came forward and seized her attention.

Pan raced to her bedroom and snatched the phone from the charger.

The phone was dead.

"What?"

Pan rushed to the light switch and flipped it.

No light came on.

Then, she checked the time on the wall clock, which read "3:33."

The time sent another wave of rage thought Pan's body. She checked all the other lights in the apartment, but none of them came on.

Not only did he shut off the water, but he also cut her power.

"Goddamn it," Pan seethed.

Once she left the apartment with her dead phone and charger, she heard the sound of police sirens getting louder and heading toward her direction.

She ducked in an alleyway and from a distance, watched the two police officers enter through the front of the apartment. In her mind, Pan wasn't exactly breaking and entering since her belongings were still inside the apartment. With a little bit of wishful thinking, she assumed they were here for someone else. Although, in the back of her mind, she knew a certain someone—not to name any names—had called the cops on her.

She just knew.

At this point in time, she couldn't even utter his name.

All Pan could think about was his face and putting a hole directly through it.

☠

BY the time Pan arrived at the bank, she felt like death. She hadn't eaten anything all morning and she just wanted to lie down and close her eyes for an hour or two; however, she knew that if she didn't cash the check, then she'd be sleeping on the streets tonight.

There were only two bank tellers, both were occupied; however, one was being slowed down from having to converse amicably with a sweet old lady whose voice was raised to a near shout as she wanted to know the bank teller's life story.

While waiting behind six other people, Pan started to become unhinged.

All she could hear was that old, senile lady who kept repeating herself over and over, asking the same questions over and over in a vicious loop as though she was broadcasting it to seven continents via voice transmission.

The bank teller answered each one, loudly too, for the old lady was also hard of hearing. She even stopped counting money a couple of times to answer a question about her son, his age, and what her son did for a living as if it was her right to know his business. Apparently, the teller's son, whose name was Bret, worked as a construction manager; in fact, he was currently overseeing a new "E-Spand" project in Market Square. Not like Pan cared at all about the bank teller's son or anything, she fell into Bret's story, his life, and if he had any children. If so, was he a good father? Was he married, divorced, or separated? She had it stuck in her head—a sort of preconceived notion—that somehow this "Bret character" was an abusive father, in fact, a monster who ate worlds and on the side, treated his more than likely nonexistent wife and nonexistent children the same way he treated the very land that he was in charge of raping. Pan didn't know where such darkness had originated, how it had taken a man whom she knew nothing about, except for one) his profession and two) his mother working as a teller at As-set Bank, spun his life into what she only perceived to be true, then turned him into someone—or something—he was possibly, more than likely, not. All she could think about was Bret, "Bret the Rapist," as those close to him called him, the spawn of by a bank teller who had spent her entire career behind a pane of glass as if she was no different than a zoo animal handling bills covered in pixie dust and feces. *Bret*, you toxic waste of the synthetic world, you shit stain, you "little" puppet whose will was bent by his corporate masters, who was being paid vast sums of money to tear down the natural earth, smear it with cancer, and drive it straight into the darkness in order to build some brand new "one-size-fits-all" e-Mall for glutinous consumers who un-wittingly lived up to the very name they had been branded, putting the *consume* in consumer.

As Pan's thoughts spiraled out of control, she witnessed two other guys ahead of her in line.

One of them turned his shoulder, looked once at Pan, moved his eyes somewhere else, then looked back at her as if he had seen her before.

Immediately, Pan recognized the guy's face from Apple Bottoms.

While she mentally saw herself aimlessly flying around on stage—or *was it a dream?*—she witnessed his face in a dark crowd behind splashes of pink and blue lights. He was seated with these two other guys and they were all pointing at Pan and laughing at her.

The guy tapped his buddy or partner—she couldn't tell whether or not he was straight or gay—on the shoulder. The other guy turned his shoulder and glanced around the bank before shooting a quick eye toward Pan's direction.

Then, their heads dropped to the phone below.

They were watching a video on their phone and covering their mouths as they laughed.

Pan could hear the giggles and snickers.

Their whispers were like needles against her skin.

As her world started to spin out of control, Pan closed her eyes and breathed deeply. Which had helped before. But this time, it seemed to be making matters worse.

By the time she opened her eyes, a third bank teller, who had stepped from a closed room in the back of the bank, took her post and called out to Pan.

Relieved, Pan walked up to the bank teller and handed her the check through the narrow opening under the glass.

"I need this cashed please," Pan said, her voice slightly trembling.

"Absolutely," the bank teller said professionally.

As she looked over the check, Pan's heart started to beat faster.

Then, the bank teller moved her eyes upward at Pan and gave her a closed lip frown.

"Sorry," she said. "I can't cash this check. It's expired."

She held up the check and showed her an area below a date that read, "NOT NEGOTIABLE AFTER 90 DAYS."

Technically, it had been 91 days since she received the check.

"Please," Pan begged, "I was sick for the last two days—"

"—My only advice is that you contact your insurance company and *maybe*," she emphasized, "they can send you another check."

Pan rotated around and saw more people waiting in line. The line had tripled since she stepped forward.

"They're just going to give me the runaround," she said to the teller, who appeared as if she wasn't wavering from her initial position. "I'm begging you," she glanced down at the woman's name on the nametag, "Helen," she said, "if I don't cash this check, then I have nowhere to stay tonight. Is that what you want?"

"I'm sorry," the bank teller, Helen, said. "That's not my problem."

"It is your problem," Pan said, her voice growing louder. "All you have to do is cash the check and it will no longer be your problem."

The bank teller crossed her arms over her chest and remained stern.

"Please, Helen," Pan begged, lowering her voice. "Don't you recognize me? I was all over the news a few months ago. The woman who drove off the bridge? Ring any bells? Please. . ."

The bank teller's eyes flicked toward her right.

Before Pan could follow her eyes, a security guard approached Pan. He gently grabbed Pan's right arm; however, to her, she felt as though he was tugging at her arm.

She cried out, "Let me go!"

The security guard's hand tightened over Pan's arm; however, Pan suddenly jerked her arm away.

Calm and collected, the security guard pointed toward the front door.

"I'm going to have to ask you to leave, ma'am."

Pan resisted.

"This cunt won't cash my check," Pan said to the security guard and then she turned to the bank teller, "Why won't you cash my check, *Helen*? You cunt!"

Pan slammed the palm of her hand against the top of the counter in front of the bank teller, which caused the security guard to use force. He subdued Pan by grabbing both of her arms and manhandled her toward the front of the bank.

"If you don't stop, I'm going to call the cops. Understood?"

Pan finally surrendered.

Then, a thought came to her, a more strategic thought.

If I keep up, he'll call the cops, as he stated. *Which means I'll have a place to stay for the night.*

She wasn't at all thinking about money or how much it was going to cost for a bail or any of the legal charges she was about to face if she assaulted the security guard.

All she thought about was having a bed to sleep in.

She reacted and elbowed the security guard in the stomach, which caused him to pin Pan to the floor.

As the security guard secured Pan's arms behind her back and straddled both of his legs around her body, a flood of memories came back to her.

There, in those flashes of rough sex and violence and utter brutality, she saw other men, *not the security guard*, but many others, who were all undressed or in the middle of undressing and circling her, and several of them were pinning down her body to a bed in the back of Apple Bottoms. One had a shiny object in his hand, which was about the size of an average arm. She fell deeper into the memory and realized it was a golf club in his hand and they were performing sexual acts to her body, as well as inserting objects inside her, including that golf club. Among rising clouds of dust Lil' Beelze was sitting on a throne in the darkest part of the room while watching these men take advantage of Pan. The last images she had before she blacked out were a scaly tail slithering over her shoulder and moving down her chest and abdomen, then the faces. She looked up and tried to trace the origin of the tail; however, when she drew her eyes up at the faces above her, these men were no longer men. They barred their fangs at her. The drool dripped from their mouths and showered her face.

A bead of sweat rolled off the tip of the security guard's nose and dropped onto the side of Pan's face.

She flipped out from the feel of his sweat against her skin.

Pan cried out in horror, trying to squirm her way free from the monster; however, the security guard, some thirty-something who couldn't make it as a police officer, wasn't letting her go from his grip.

"Get off me," Pan said, as her chest started to tighten.

She pleaded for the security guard to let her go; however, the words became harder and harder to speak through her labored breath.

As the security guard—knowing or unknowingly—continued to smother Pan, the world around her started to spin out of control once more.

As a couple of other men in line broke through barriers and rushed to Pan's defense, her eyes rolled back in her head.

The world, as she once knew it, slowly turned black.

☠

PAN woke up to a bright overhead light.

One of the nurses, who was checking Pan's vitals, fetched the doctor from the hallway.

The doctor placed a clipboard under his armpit and approached Pan.

"Where am I?" Pan asked the tall smooth-faced man, who she assumed was a doctor based on his clothing attire.

Pan stirred around and suddenly felt a restriction against her arms. She took a glance downward and witnessed the restraints on her wrists.

"What is this?" asked Pan. "What are you doing to me?"

"Take it easy, Ms. Nikopoulos," the man, who called himself Doctor Cherkis, said to Pan. She was starting to get uneasy from his shady presence. "You had a panic attack, which caused you to lose consciousness."

"*Panic attack?*" The doctor's words alone infuriated her. A minor scare was what he really wanted to say; and if anybody knew that what Pan was experiencing, it was Pan herself. *Panic attack*, she thought to herself. *What a total bunch of bullshit?* "First," she said, as the anger rose inside her despite the sedatives she had been given through a drip feed, "I'm going to sue the bank. Then, I'm going to get that piece of shit fired."

"Are you referring to the security guard who restrained you?" asked the doctor, whom Pan thought came off as a smartass.

She ignored the doctor and looked around the emergency room. Everybody was going about his or her business in the ER as if her being restrained to a hospital bed was considered customary, dare she say, "normal."

Once more, she pulled at the restraints; however, it was useless trying to free herself. The restraints were on good and tight.

The doctor nodded at the nurse, who, in return, closed the curtain behind him.

Immediately, the doctor's cold mannerisms struck Pan the wrong way and for a moment, she questioned herself whether or not he was actually a doctor with a medical degree.

Once more, Pan tried to free her hands.

"Take it easy, Pan," the doctor said more calmly, as he stood at her bedside. He placed the clipboard on the tray next to the bed, pulled out a flashlight from the breast pocket of the white coat, and attempted to shine the light in Pan's eyes. At first, she flinched, then turned her head away; but after the doctor displayed the flashlight to her and specifically told her that he just wanted to "look" at her eyes, she moved the back of her head on the center of the pillow.

The doctor shined the flashlight in her left eye first, then pulled it away, then shined it back into the left eye and studied the reaction of the pupil. He moved to the right eye, did the same movement as he did with the left eye. Both of her pupils were still slightly dilated; however, the left one especially appeared to have two pupils, as though one pupil was starting to grow out of the other one.

Letting out a sigh, the doctor holstered his flashlight and overlapped one hand over the other and loosely held his arms along his waist in the shape of a letter v.

"With your permission, Ms. Nikopoulos, we'd like to run some blood work on you, but I'm ninety-nine percent certain as to what I might find," he said with a sense of glum coming over him.

"—What the hell does that mean?" Pan said abruptly but was cut short by the doctor's hand.

"Please, if you would, let me finish," he said sternly. "I'm not here to lecture you, Ms. Nikopoulos, *but* if I had to guess, that dust was laced with Renatafill and whoever gave it to you doesn't seem to care about your well-being." He lowered his head and looked closer at Pan. "Trust me. You're not the first person to wind up in the ER after coming off a dust binge."

How would some doctor, whom she had never met before, *know these things?*

Pan looked at him strangely.

"You're extremely lucky to be alive," he said directly to Pan, as if he could read her thoughts. "One of the police officers at the bank talked to several witnesses, who claimed they saw you snorting lines of 'pixie dust' at a nightclub last night—"

"—What? That's bullshit!"

"We contacted your mother, who was listed under your emergency contacts. We told her what happened—"

"—Where is she?"

"Where is who?"

"Who do you think? My mom."

"She said that she was tied up with work but she would be here as soon as she could."

"Of course."

"Your mother did us a favor by contacting a few people, including your sponsor, David Flores, as well as the people who you might've been hanging out with the night before your disappearance. They confirmed that you were relapsing and experiencing common 'drug-seeking' behavior—"

"Who said that?" Pan asked, sitting upright. "Was is Jason? Or, as it Brob?"

The doctor held out his hand, as if he was signaling for Pan to *stop* before she worked herself up again.

"That's irrelevant at this juncture," he said. "All that's important now is that we get you clean again. With that said," he grabbed the clipboard and unclipped a purple brochure, "I'm going to give you three options, Ms. Nikopoulos." First, he showed her the brochure of a treatment facility in Arizona called Golden Springs Rehabilitation Center.

"The first one: Golden Springs. You've probably heard of it through your meetings. If you haven't, I should tell you that it's quite an amazing establishment." Pan briefly glanced over the brochure before she placed it aside. "The other option is putting you on a drug called 'Quidaquin.'"

Pan had heard of that name, *Quidaquin*, but didn't know where.

"Right," Pan said, more dismissive. "Another drug. Makes total sense." Her voice was climbing with sarcasm. "You people make up some ridiculous disorder and put me on one drug. I stop taking that drug, which ultimately leads to my addiction. Then, *now*, you want to put me on yet another drug?"

"It's a fairly new drug on the market; however, based on all of the feedback, it's been known to show great results to those who have to be on it; in fact, the over day, I just recently saw a young man whom I treated last year. He's about your age. I asked him how everything was going. He told me he's been clean ever since I got him on the Q."

"So what? You want me to be a guinea pig? Is that it?"

"Well, Ms. Nikopoulos, the way I look at it, you only have these two options. The third and final option: You walk straight out the door and I'd say, in the next two to three weeks—but based on your recent behavior, I'd give you a couple of days—before you wind up back here. I go over this whole spiel with you again. We do this back and forth rigmarole for the next few months or so until, one day, you wind up back here," the doctor turned to the nurse behind him, pointed at her face, then his own face, "and these are the last faces you'll ever see. The fact of the matter, Ms. Nikopoulos: If you don't stop using, you're going to die. Simple as that. I see it all the time. Way too many times, if you ask me."

Pan thought about her options. Even though there was a force driving her out West, there was another force keeping her on the East Coast.

She looked up at the doctor and asked, "What was the second option again?"

PRESENT DAY

EVER since Pan started using the drug Quidaquin, she started to put on weight.

After the first year while taking Quidaquin, Pan went from a size 8 to a size 16 and did so without paying much attention in the mirror.

The second year she started to see the difference in her shape, as well as her stamina, especially when none of the clothes in her closet fit her anymore. Once she started shopping for a size 18 on retail store websites that she had never been on before, in particular, a website for plus-size women where all of the models, in regards to their physical shape, looked similar to her, she saw the changes in her body and wondered how she hadn't seen them before. For the rest of the year, she found a way to be content within her own skin; however, underneath, Pan didn't feel quite like herself and it felt as though someone had high jacked her mind.

The third year on Quidaquin was when everything went straight downhill for Pan. Not only did she decline physically, but also mentally. Doctors had warned her that weight gain was a side effect of Quidaquin. Once Pan kept putting on the weight—not just a few extra pounds that were manageable through self-discipline and diet but weight that was increasing dramatically every week—it had become apparent that something other than diet was going on with Pan.

By the end of the third year on Quidaquin, Pan couldn't even reach her folds when she bathed. Her whole body ached, especially her back. Food had become her new "go to" drug, which was triggered by mostly boredom or depression or both. Thinking about those blurry nights that she had spent at Apple Bottom sent her even farther down the rabbit hole. After a while, food was her *only* comfort. What added even more grief was the one time during a rare outing she bumped into one of her former dust addict friends on the street. Jay didn't even recognize Pan; worse, when he locked eyes with Pan, he displayed a look of utter disgust on his face. Later that day, after bawling for hours, she turned to her comfort. When she started to spiral out of control, she also turned to the Internet and became what was widely known as a "catfish," harvesting multiple fake profiles on social media websites, one of them going by the name of "Aerial," who was in a steady relationship with a twenty-something named Guy who lived in Washington. Aerial had shoulder-length dirty blonde hair—Pan making sure to put an emphasis on the *dirty* part—blue eyes, and weighed a buck twenty. Aerial was a librarian during the day, bartender at night. Or so Guy thought. Like a sexy villain in a movie. A "sexillain," as Aerial referred to herself. Guy had a pretty wild imagination.

By year four, she was up to seven hundred pounds and was continuing to gain weight, despite having cut out a lot of high-calorie foods from her diet. She used a walker at times, as well as a customized wheelchair to get around whenever she was out in public; however, leaving the house had become a rare and each time was nothing short of an "event." Even rolling out of bed or standing up from the futon was an issue for Pan. She put on an additional thirty pounds in a matter of two weeks. It wasn't until one night when she had a terrible nightmare where, in the not so distant future, she weighed over a thousand pounds. She was nearly the size of one of those heavy-duty trucks, like the ones she would see on those smash-mouth TV commercials during Sunday football, and the only way she was able to get around was via forklift. She woke up sweating profusely and feeling as if she had the rear tire of a truck spinning over her chest, as if the tire was stuck in a pile of flesh and it kept spinning and spinning and spinning until she could no catch her breath.

Pan's mother, Vivian, had no other choice than to intervene. She paid out of pocket for an aide to help her daughter with whatever she needed, including errands such as groceries, necessities, even helping Pan with everyday functions.

It had gotten *that* bad.

☠

VIVIAN showed up three and half hours late from the time she said she was originally going to arrive, which was eleven o'clock.

From the intensity of the car door slamming outside, Pan could not only see, but also hear obvious changes in Vivian's behavior and how visiting her daughter had turned into what she thought was a household chore. The sound of Vivian's footsteps were shorter and quicker as if all of her movements and actions once she found herself in the range of her daughter and her stellar ears were premeditated. Pan knew that one of the many reasons as to why her mom avoided meal times, such as eight o'clock, *eleven o'clock*, or seven o'clock, and how once she showed up, she'd only stay for no more than an hour, was that she couldn't stand to watch her daughter eat. Having been raised by a father, a "functioning" alcoholic—as in he needed a drink in the morning in order to function properly—who reminded her of the Zeus character she read about in books, it was no different than watching a person with a drinking problem, like her father, pounding down beers, one after another, only, instead of booze, it was a spread of platters, endless sides, and happy meals of food, as if somewhere beyond the flesh, he or she was bearing a black hole, an endless void.

As Pan's mother stepped inside the house, she displayed a fixed stiffness in her brow as if she had been primed to fight ever since she rolled out of bed—or in Pan's case, arrived.

Vivian checked on Pan, who was lying on the special bed in the corner of the bedroom, and asked how she was doing today and did so with a hostile tone.

Hardly able to look her mom in the eyes, Pan pouted and answered miserably, "Fine." Vivian knew the answer was clearly a cover-up to how her daughter was really feeling and had been feeling for the past four years.

With her arms planted over her hips, she stood over Pan and waited for her to give her something more, a follow up to the word that would explain how she was really feeling, but all she received was "Fine." All she ever received was a word that was anything but its true meaning.

"Okay," Vivian said shortly, grabbed the two paper bags of groceries from the living room, and stormed into the kitchen.

The crinkling sound of paper piqued Pan's interest, but only for a moment.

First, Vivian placed the bags on the kitchen counter and opened the fridge.

Pan knew what her reaction was going to be before she even let the expletives fly. The next sounds Pan heard were the *rustling* of bags followed by *thuds* of her mom throwing bags of frozen ice cream bars, as well as other junk food on the counter.

Finally, she heard her slam the fridge door, the *clinking* of glass bottles rattling around the shelves inside. She carried a frozen TV dinner of country-fried steak smothered in sausage and gravy into the bedroom and showed Pan the box.

"*What*—what the hell is this?" asked Vivian.

Pan shrugged.

"Food."

Vivian widened her eyes.

"Food?" she parroted. "This is *not* food, Pandora. Did Cary-Anne buy this for you?" Pan wasn't quick to respond. "I asked you a question. Did Cary-Anne buy this—"

"—Why does it matter who bought it for me?" Pan said, as her eyes watered.

"Pandora," Vivian barked and for a moment, couldn't even stand the sight of her morbidly obsessed daughter, who looked like nothing more than a stranger to her. She gathered herself by taking a deep breath, which only momentarily ridded the animosity that she had bubbling deep down inside her. The sight alone of her daughter and her confinement caused her to lose it once and for all, "You are on a very strict diet! You cannot be eating this *shit* anymore. Do you not know what it's doing to your heart? Do you want to die, Pandora? Because if you keep eating this garbage you'll be dead before you even reach the age of thirty. I mean, is that what you want? Do you want to die, Pandora?"

"Stop it," Pan said, more wounded from her mom's words.

"Believe me, Pan," Vivian said, trying to soften her tone. "I hate being the bitch around here. But I've about had it. I'm going to have a little talk with Cary-Anne when she gets here and if she continues to feed you this garbage, I'm going to find another aide." Vivian checked her watch, as she had been doing ever since she entered the house. "By the way," she said, her voice growing louder, "where is she? She should've been her by now."

"It's not her fault," Pan said, sniffling. "I made her buy me that."

"Quit defending her," she said shortly. "You're always defending her.'"

"*It's not her fault!*"

"Well," Vivian said, taking back by her daughter's behavior, "she knows better. That's all I have to say."

Vivian paused and looked over her daughter and her current state. She let out a sigh, a deep one that she had been holding onto for quite some time.

"Pan," she said, trying to chose her words wisely for they might come back to haunt her, "I'm sorry for lashing out at you. I just. . . *I want my daughter back.* That's all." Vivian took a couple of deep breaths, which calmed her down; however, beyond each feature of her face, like the center of her brow or the corner of her eyes, which had been pumped with Botox, Pan could see the frustration in her mom's face, the same frustration she witnessed during Cleo's funeral where Pan and Vivian filled her empty casket with Cleo's shoes, her favorite magazines and posters, and all sorts of memorabilia that was six feet deep in the cold earth. Everything that made Cleo "Cleo," all except for an actual body. "Listen, Pan, I have a friend who lives in Portland. She's a herbalist—"

"—You mean, your hippy friend?"

"She used to work at Golden Springs," Vivian said, referring to the rehab facility in Arizona. "Now, she works independently. I think she can help you, Pan. Can you give her a try? Please. For me."

"I don't want to," Pan uttered.

"Right now, it doesn't matter what you want, Pan. You need—"

"—Don't tell me what I need!"

Fed up, Vivian threw up her hands as if she wasn't even about to have a conversation with her daughter. Which, in most—if not, all—cases, would end up in a heated agreement driven by fire and fury where eventually Vivian exited stage right from the house feeling way more stressed out than before she arrived. She'd later thank the Academy in the car for her speculator performance.

Vivian stormed back into the kitchen where she restocked the fridge with the food that she had bought from the grocery store. Most of the food was fresh, not frozen. Fruits, including oranges, kiwi and avocados, as well as vegetables such as broccoli, spinach, carrots, cauliflower, and an assortment of leafy greens: all of which she placed inside the fridge. The only boxed food Vivian bought was several boxes of wild and brown rice. She placed them inside the pantry, which was heavily stocked with soda and other carbonated canned drinks to get Pan through the End of Days. Vivian poured out the soda in the sink and threw the empty bottles in the trash. The only drink she wanted her daughter to be drinking was water.

☠

LATER that night, Cary-Anne wheeled Pan into the living room and made sure she was positioned in front of the TV. She had already stayed an hour past her shift; however, she didn't like leaving until Pan was situated and taken care of.

As always, Cary-Anne listed everything Pan needed, which was within arm's reach, including the TV remote, phone, and bedpan—just in case.

"Call me if you need anything," Cary-Anne said, as she left Pan.

Pan didn't even say goodbye to Cary-Anne as she opened the front door. She was still upset by her mom's visit earlier that day.

"Pan," she said, thinking, "one day at a time. Remember?"

Pan could barely bring herself to nod.

Cary-Anne dropped her belongings onto the floor in the foyer before heading out and walked over to Pan, who was crying.

"What's the matter, Pan?" asked Cary-Anne.

"This is no way to live, Cary-Anne," Pan said, crying. "*Everything* hurts. It feels like I got something growing inside me, a cancer, and I can *feel* it spreading all over my body."

"Do you want me to take you to the hospital—"

"—I'm tired of living like this!"

Cary-Anne rubbed the top of Pan's hand.

"It's okay, Sweetie," she said. "I can stay, if you want—"

"—No. Just go. I'm tired of being a burden to everyone."

"What? Whoever said you were a burden?"

"My mom thinks I'm a burden."

"I'm sure she didn't mean it."

"She didn't actually say it, but I can sense it."

"Don't think that way, Pan. You're just tired."

"I know this all started ever since they put me on Quidaquin," Pan whined.

"Well," Cary-Anne said, "I'll get you a doctor's appointment first thing in the morning. How does that sound?"

Pan wiped away her tears and barely nodded.

"Pandora," Cary-Anne said more somberly, "can I ask you a question?"

Once more, Pan barely nodded her head.

"Did you take your medication today?" asked Cary-Anne. Before Pan could respond, Cary-Anne said sternly, "Don't lie to me."

Pan shook her head.

"No," she mumbled, then whined, "I don't like the way it makes me feel."

"I tell you what?" Cary-Anne said and paused. "How about I make you a cup of tea before I go? You'd be amazed what a warm cup of tea can do?"

"But I don't like tea," Pan said.

"*But* you haven't had my tea."

"What's the difference?"

"I make mine with love, darling," Cary-Anne said with a smirk.

"M'kay."

Cary-Anne excused herself.

In the kitchen, she put a pot of water on the stove and while she brought the water to a boil, she grabbed a cup from the cabinet, as well as a teabag of chamomile from the pantry.

As the water came to a rolling boil, she poked her head from the kitchen; and as soon as she noticed Pan distracted by flipping through the channels on TV, she tiptoed into the hallway bathroom. She crept behind Pan and grabbed the bottle of Quidaquin from the medicine cabinet. She removed one capsule from the bottle and crept back into the kitchen where she twisted open the capsule and poured the powdery medicine into the cup. To say the least, she was glad Pan chose capsules instead of tablets that way she didn't have to be sneakier than she desired to be when crushing the pill into a napkin with the butt of a saltshaker. The capsules were harder to swallow, too, even Pan often said so herself whenever she gagged while downing a capsule, which was followed with an extra sip of water; however, the doctor specifically recommended capsule-form because, in the past, patients were known to break the tablets in half and only take a half-dose when he or she should've been taking the "whole" dose.

The Quidaquin slowly sank into the warm water; then, she carefully stirred it around, trying her best not to make any *clinking* noises from the spoon hitting the sides of the teacup; however, she noticed that the medicine was still visible in the tea and left a dark ring on the bottom of the teacup. She raised the cup to her nose and breathed in the steam. She picked up a slight odor. She decided to add a little bit of milk, as well as a dollop of honey to help mask the taste of medicine.

Then, once the tea was prepared, she set the floral-patterned teacup on a saucer, let the tea steep for three minutes or so, which gave Cary-Anne plenty of time to side-chat with Pan from the kitchen, first asking Pan what was on the tube tonight, then Pan responding by running through a list of TV shows, including *Big Brother Redux* and *Luv Island*, then Cary-Anne following up as if she was oblivious and had never heard of such TV shows.

After four minutes had passed, Cary-Anne brought the tea to Pan.

"Here you go," she said and handed Pan the teacup and saucer. "Be careful," she warned, "it's a little hot."

Pan, who smelled everything she tasted, took a whiff of the tea.

"Not bad," she said and sipped from the warm tea.

She nodded her head as if it was her silent way of approval.

"Drink up," Cary-Anne said. "By the time you finished that cup, all of your troubles will melt away."

"'Kay," Pan said depressingly.

Cary-Anne checked her watched.

"Well," she said with a sigh, "I'm going to go now. Call me if you need anything."

Cary-Anne collected all of her belongings, said good night to Pan for the second time, and locked the door behind her with her own copy of the house key.

As the headlights on the car in the driveway cut across the living room wall, Pan took yet another sip of the tea. Her face turned sour from the taste of the tea. She spat it back into the cup and placed it on the saucer and set it aside on the tray right bedside the futon.

With the end of her tie-dyed T-shirt, Pan wiped her tongue as if she couldn't get rid of the taste quick enough.

She turned her attention back to the TV and flipped through all of the channels. She wound up on Channel 3, MWC, which, every Thursday night, aired old interviews by authors, musicians, actors, as well as forward thinkers.

Tonight's program was airing an interview with Doctor Riley, who, from the stretch of '94 through '95, had run a circuit of interviews on TV to promote a new book called, *World Next Door*. She was well known for her theory on the "Multiverse."

Pan listened to Doctor Riley talk for a few minutes—Pan was more drawn to those three long, jagged scars running along the left side of Doctor Riley's face—and for a moment, was tempted to turn the channel until the doctor referred to the very first time she experienced the so-called "Multiverse" after having choked on a piece of food. She talked about the experience as if she had lost her virginity. In the most articulate way possible, she explained it as falling *not* to the floor but "through" the floor. The inside of restaurant lowered, "like an elevator," and then she found herself in another world, as real as the one before her eyes, not inside her head, but real. The second experience happened when she was mauled by a wild Bengal tiger during a visit to India as her so-called "awakening."

Doctor Riley interrupted the interviewer before he could bring "science" into the conversation and provoked a question of her own: "*What if there was another world beneath our very own—another realm, if you will—one where its inhabitants gazed up at us the same way we gazed with awe at all of the stars among the Heavens? Ever since I was a little girl, the unbridled power of 'what if' had consumed my thoughts, as if the two words alone were part of a phenomenon as volatile as loose papers whirling in a windstorm that presented no origin, yet a sequence of events that shared an inevitable outcome based on how the material world had shaped my expanding mind. I always wondered about that 'what if' world and its 'what if' life forms: What would they think of us? Would they see us as their gods? Their saviors? Or were they canny enough to tap into our filtered armor and see us for who we truly were—their corrupters?*"

"*So,*" the interviewer followed, resting the side of his chin along the sides of his fingers, "*you're saying humans are to blame for the corruption in the world.*"

"*I'm not saying that humans are to blame per se,*" Doctor Riley replied. "*I'm saying human nature is to blame. Human nature and its vile interference with the natural world. From the dawn of mankind, we have been driven by a primordial force to connect and understand our surroundings and the nature all around us and in doing so we've managed to pass the torch. Overtime, however, as population of humans increased, so too did our need for understanding, which, inevitably, led to our willingness to reign. Now, we live in a society where flesh is king. Instead of rebalancing the scales by snuffing out corruption, we've tied our own nooses around our necks and reattached them to the fingertips of our sponsors. Imagine buying a bag of seeds and when you open the bag, every seed is bad, rotten. Do you eat them? Or, do you throw them away? Imagine a society where good or bad no longer exists; yet the lines separating good and bad are too blurry to distinguish. Eventually, everything that's good turns bad, and everything that's bad turns good. Who are we to say what's good and what's bad? We've become more concerned with our image and what we do to enhance that image instead of genuinely supporting a world where* every human *thrives. No question, ever since we discovered that we were not alone in this world, we've lived in the* 'Age of the Alpha,' *a society where social dominance has exploited our need for connection. To say, though, that we've never been this way would be ingenuous. We seek. We conquer, whether we like it or not. And eventually, given time and energy, we destroy. That's* the real *human nature. If anything, my second near-death experience only reinforced human's role in this world."*

"*Which is?*"

"*We are a disease,*" Doctor Riley said coldly. "*And how exactly do you stop a disease?*"

"*With a cure, of course.*"

"*And you ask what cure that may be?*"

"*You tell me.*"

Doctor Riley tapped on the side of her temple.

"*Self-awareness,*" she said, "*knowing that one day we're going to die and our actions will leave behind a mark for generations to come. We are nothing more than pebbles being thrown by those we yearn to become into a tranquil lake that bridges our world to the next. Based on our 'spin,' how hard we fall, or how far we travel, we ultimately create a ripple effect that resonates into the* next world. *The question: How big of a splash do you want to make?"*

"Let's backtrack," the interviewer said, shifting his weight, *"can you explain more about the incident in Boston at The Wicked Dish? How long would you say you 'blacked' out?"*

"My boyfriend at the time said I blacked out for at least twenty-seconds," she said, *"however, to me, it was more like twenty hours. I went somewhere else. Somewhere that shared the same similarities as our world, only one thing remained disparate: humans. They had reverted back to their most primitive form. That's when I knew* 'what if' *was only a conduit to the truth. Brand it. Advertise it. Slap it on a slogan. One thing remains certain:* 'The end is not end. Yet, it's only the beginning. And we are not alone.'"

Pan zoned out and thought about Doctor Riley's comments about this "other" world.

A shadow caught the corner of her eye.

She turned toward the dark kitchen and in the doorway, witnessed a dark figure lurching forward. Her pale face was barely visible from the bright glow of the TV flickering in the darkness; nonetheless, Pan knew each feature on her face; she knew each contour, each birthmark, each freckle, each blemish, each scar, in particularly, the inch-long scar on the top of her forehead. When she was nine years old, she had gotten that scar after using the living room couch as her own version of a vault. Her knee buckled in mid-jump along the armrest, causing her to flip over the couch and hit the top of her head on the edge of the brick fireplace. Pan, a proud tag-along who was six years old, remembered that day as if it was yesterday. In those months following the 2000 Summer Olympics in Sydney, Australia, which were considered a difficult time for a parent who was raising a daughter, many young girls wanted to become world class gymnasts, not because their parents pushed them toward gymnastics but because of US Olympian Tiffany Kibbler, who won the gold medal that year. Of all the Olympians, "Tiff" had a way of attracting the youth through cartoons, cereal commercials, and clothing advertisements on TV. Pan wasn't a Tiffany Kibbler fan; in fact, Pan wasn't at all interested in athletics or the country's obsession with athletes. The only person she looked up to was her older sister. She was basically her sister's shadow.

"Cleo?" said Pan. "Is that you?"

"Hello, Pan," she said from the dark kitchen.

"What are you doing here?"

"Is that some way to greet your sister?"

Pan frowned.

"Hey," she said, more glum.

"Hey," Cleo responded.

"Am I dreaming?"

"Does it feel like you're dreaming?"

Pan shook her head.

"No," she said.

"Well," Cleo said, smirking, "then I guess you're not."

The tears brimmed underneath Pan's eyelids.

The haze from Quidaquin started to wear off, bringing Cleo's face closer to the light. Pan picked up a strange vibe from Cleo. She'd be lying if she said that the thought didn't cross her mind, but she questioned whether or not this person she was talking to was, in fact, her older sister. After all, why would she cling to the darkness of the room?

With her voice trembling, Pan asked, "What you want from me?"

"What do you want from yourself?" she turned the question back toward Pan. "Isn't that the reason why you stopped taking the medication, because you were curious about what would happen?"

Pan didn't respond.

"As hard as you try, Pan, you cannot erase me. I am here to stay—"

"—You're *not* my sister," Pan cried.

"What makes you so sure I'm not?" asked Cleo.

"My sister was afraid of the dark," Pan said clearly.

The glow of the TV glistened in Cleo's dark, maddening eyes.

As Cleo—or the imposter who was pretending to be Cleo—stepped back into the darkness of the kitchen, that pale glow of the TV changed color and warmth.

Pan heard the words *don't ssstare at it* hissing in the darkness.

With the warmth pressing against the side of her face, Pan turned toward the TV and no longer witnessed a TV. Instead, she fell witness to a large campfire.

The beat of the orange flames replaced that flickering glow of the TV.

Circling around the fire were strange, disfigured faces, young faces she could tell.

"What happened next?" one of those faces repeated.

Pan snapped from her trance.

"Where was I?" asked Pan.

"You were talking about the song on the radio, the one you heard right before the accident."

"Yes," Pan said, shaking off the daze. "I was singing the song 'Me Too' by Meghan Trainor—"

"**—You mean, *we* were singing the song 'Me Too' by Meghan Trainor.**"

She heard Cleo saying next to her.

Startled by the sound of her sister's voice, Pan corrected, "Right. We were both singing the song when all of a sudden a car veered across the center lane and forced me to swerve off the road—"

"**—Probably some effing moron texting and driving,**" Cleo said.

"The car plowed straight through the guardrail, I remember. The next thing I know, we're headed straight toward a river below. The drop must've been at least twenty stories. At least."

"**Hold up a sec,**" Cleo said over Pan. "**We must have two completely different versions because that's not how I remember it. We were clearly hanging from the bridge for quite some time before the car tipped over.**"

"We were?" Pan uttered, as she tried to visualize the moments leading up to the fall.

Turned off by her sister's resilience, Cleo copped an attitude with Pan and in the most exaggerated way possible, rolled her eyes and then smacked her gums as if she was a cartoon.

"Yeah," she said, her voice drawn out. "Don't you remember?"

That tone. Pan didn't hate much. Seldom did she ever use the word. But she hated the tone her sister would often use whenever she was feeling like the Queen of All Bitches. The king's bitch. The bitch of state. Her Bitchesty.

She puts the itch *in bitch.*

Cleo always had a way of throwing the ball back onto Pan's court after making her feel so little and stupid. Pan couldn't help but wonder how much Cleopatra sounded like Mom, who was notoriously known for her innate ability to display the same condescending behavior to both her daughters, mainly Pan; however, very rarely did Vivian ever press the tip of her stiletto against Cleo. It's like that old saying: "If you step on a snake, don't expect it not to bite."

"I remember the wreck," Pan said finally, "*then* falling like I was in slow motion, *then* everything got chaotic once the car hit the water."

"Well," she said more superiorly, "it happened. How about this?" she suggested, as she moistened her lips. "Why don't we rewind for a sec, go farther back in the story, start with *why* we're driving clear across the country to being with."

As always, Pan protested with her silence.

Here we go again, Pan thought.

CLEO'S VERSION

We were driving to Reno to reunite with our biological father whom we met on Ancestry.com. *Actually, it was me who came up with the idea.* His name was Kirk, but our mom referred to him mostly as 'Jerk. She hardly talked about him, but whenever the subject of 'Kirk came up, she'd try her best to avoid that convo. I don't know all of the details. But what I know for certain is that only a couple of months after Pan was born, the man ran out on our mom. She said that he was going through issues. He was a drinker. He couldn't handle the responsibilities of raising a child, let alone two of them. Since our mom had grown up around a father, who was also a drinker himself—What is it about some men who just can't get enough alcohol? She told me she gave him an ultimatum. Clearly, he chose Jim and Jack over our own mother. A couple of years after Kirk ran off, our mom met a man named Truman. He said he was named after the writer, not the president. To me, I never looked at him as a stepfather or a man who was trying to fill someone else's shoes. To me, Truman was my father. *Maybe to you, he was. You weren't around him in the afternoons when you were too busy hanging out with your friends, trying to retain your perfect image.* So, one day, Pan decided to go on Ancestry.com. I heard some of my friends doing it for shits and giggles. So, immediately, it sounded intriguing. We filled out the form and whatnot. A couple of weeks later *we* found him, our long lost father, Captain Kirk. So, we said, 'What the hell?' Right. Well, let's backtrack, I had to do a little convincing, considering Bubble Girl over here hardly left the crib. I leave the house. Okay. Sure you do. *Like you would know what I do when you're not around, Bitchosaurus.* So, it was official. Pan and I were finally going to go on that road trip we had always been talking about. *You mean, that road trip you've always been talking about. You just want to drag me along because none of your friends would go with you since most of them are either getting married or have jobs and families.* To say I was excited about the trip would be an understatement. Pan was excited as well. I was. Strangely. So, we told ourselves, 'Reno, here we come!' The first two days went by so fast. We stopped in front of the road signs at each state line and took a selfie. FYI, Selfie 101: Always take a selfie in front of the light; if you're outside, the best light is going to be the *sun*light. Thanks for that pro tip.' Now, can you do us all a favor and speed it up a little? I don't think they're interested in advice on how to take a proper selfie. Hey, it's my story too!

PAN'S VERSION

Your story is missing several key details, Cleopatra. I hate it when you call me that. First off, we didn't stop to take selfies. *You* stopped to take selfies while I waited in the car. Which makes me start to wonder your real intentions as to why you wanted to go on this road trip so badly in the first place. The whole time it was as if you were planning each stop in order to take a photo of yourself and post it on your Insti.' Let's face it, *Cleopatra*. The whole trip was about you—you always make it all about you—when, in fact, the trip really should've been about reconnecting with Kirk. **That's not fair.** Not fair? Secondly, the first two days didn't go fast—maybe for you—but not for me. You were complaining the whole time. You wouldn't listen to a word I had to say and whenever I tried to actually talk' to you, you changed the subject to whatever made *you* more comfortable. I don't like talking about what's currently fashionable. I don't like talking about all of the crap on the Internet, who said what to whoever, or who fucked who, or did this or that. **Complaining? Excuse me. You were the one who was complaining, Ms. 'My stomach hurts-I'm hungry. Now, if you don't mind, I would like to finish my story please before you ruin it like you always do.** *Bitch.* **After Day Two on our journey out West, we had ourselves a break-through. Sure. At times, we were at each other's throats but I think we started to bond after we nearly got kidnapped by some psycho road rager who was literally the dude from** *Hitchhiker.* **If it weren't for your impressive driving skills—** thanks—**then both of our heads would probably be mounted on the wall somewhere like hunting trophies.** What was it exactly you said to that guy to tick him off? **It was what you said, not. . . Me? Ah yes. Don't you remember? You complimented the guy's trench coat, but apparently he wasn't too fond of your sarcasm.** *She said that, not me. While I was at a pump filling up the tank, she stuck her head out the passenger window and said, 'Nice coat, Draven.' The name was obviously a jab at the stranger. Since Cleo was a woman who constantly referenced scenes from movies or recited popular movie quotes— when she wasn't off Columbusing around the world, she watched a lot of movies on a portable DVD player in her downtime—the comment clearly came from her mouth, not mine.* **All he needed was clown face paint and he'd fit the part.** About a mile down the road I saw the same car that the man was driving in the saw the same car that the man was driving in the side-view mirror. He was closing in. . . and fast! It was like a car chase out of the movies. He pulled up beside us, inches, and shouted through the passenger window, 'Is that gasoline I smell?' which, now that I think about it, was a line straight out of the movie, *The Crow*. I knew we were both in big trouble. You nodded at the fuel gauge on the speedometer and noticed the needle dropping from F to E. You glanced in the rear view mirror and saw the trail of gasoline. He must've punctured the gas tank when we both went to use the restrooms behind the convenient store. Like I said, if you hadn't been quick to react, that psycho's face would've been the last face we'd see before he turned us into wall decorations. It was like you knew *exactly* what the dude was going to do before he even did it. He suddenly turned that POS he was driving toward us and tried to ram us off the road. If I was driving, I would've swerved and more than likely, we'd hit that telephone pole head on and we'd be roadkill. Instead, you hit the brakes. His car fishtailed right in front of us. He swerved out of the way of the pole, but the car ended up barreling over into a ditch on the side of the road. Good thing for us there was a repair shop two exits away. The mechanic was nice enough to fix the leak in just a couple of hours. And that wasn't even the most insane part of the day. The mechanic's name was Eric. And, not only that, the guy was totally into you. You saw the way he was looking at you. *But you, Cleo, you managed to screw up my chances to meet a decent guy. As always, you find a way to shatter my confidence by pointing at my flaws and giving me pointers on how I should wear my hair, only to steal the spotlight as soon as Eric handed me the car keys. You know my buttons and no coincidence there, know the right moments when to push them.* But, of course, you were too chickenshit to talk to him. I can't believe that you actually started to open up to me during those couple hours of waiting. Some guy, who was clearly in the wrong for what he did— even though what *you* said to him was uncalled for—you mean, what you said—whatever. We go through a traumatic event. You finally share to me the reason why you dropped out of Creston last year, which lead to a meaningful conversation about our trust issues, then, once Mr. Nice Hair re-enters the picture and it's so obvious he's way more interested in me than he is you, you go straight back to your usual annoying self. By the way, I thought we were still on my version of the story where—get ready for it—while you were grabbing yourself a *Dark Cavern*™ bar and Slam energy drink inside the convenient store, I cut myself a deal with *Road Warrior* to chase our asses all around the state of Texas, which, in return, would help us reconnect. What better way to get closer to someone than sharing a near-death experience? Don't act like you didn't know. You saw us talking when you stepped out of the convenient store. That's when you made the comment because, straight up, you jelly.

Cleo's face slackened into a blank expression.
"**Run that by me again. You did what? You mean. . .** "
Pan suddenly burst out laughing.
Eventually, after falling for the joke, Cleo laughed as well.
"**Not funny,**" she said. "**Not funny at all.**"
"Admit it. I had you going for a moment."
"**Okay. You got me. Now, can I continue?**"
Again, Pan's silence was her protest.

CLEO'S VERSION

Like I was saying before *Joker* over here tried to dim my shine, Pan had her chance with a cute, very smart guy who was very 'hands on, but blew it because she's just a big normie. Okay. I'm a normie? Says the one who basically mimics everything Danielle does. That's not true. Danielle takes a trip to Belize with her rich boyfriend who has so much money he doesn't even know what to do with it. Then, what do you know? Three weeks later, you're in Belize. **I booked that trip long before her.** Danielle goes hiking in Flagstaff. A month later you go hiking in Flagstaff. Danielle spends an entire week in Italy. Sure enough, after draining nearly all your money from your savings, three months later, you're taking selfies along the canals in Venice with some Italian dude you probably just met. **Least I'm not a hermit like you.** That's your only comeback? *Day Three*, **I arrived into New Mexico. I stopped at a hole-in-the-wall taco stand called Julio's. Every time I pass through New Mexico, I have to grab the tacos al pastor. Julio's are out of this world. He marinates the pork in tequila. Adds just enough pineapple. To die for.** *Straight up.* I see what you're doing. So, I'm no longer part of your journey.' Is that it? *Go ahead. Continue to ignore me. Why don't you tell these nice folks what happened while you were scarfing down your 'famous' tacos al pastor? She doesn't. And I know she won't because the way she treats my medical condition is reprehensible. First, I was diagnosed with acid reflux, which I managed on my own through years of meditation and change in diet. Then, after the first year of college, when I was feeling super stressed out, I went through this stage where I had a hard time swallowing my food halfway through eating a meal. It felt as if the food would get stuck directly in my chest. Doctors called it a 'hiatal hernia.' It's where the stomach literally pushes up into the diaphragm. They always have a label for something, but to me, I called it 'hell' and it was all brought on by people like Cleo and how, after she inhaled her food, she'd rush me, causing me to eat faster than I should, thus sending me straight to a world of regurgitation. Try swallowing your food, only to have your stomach reject it as if it doesn't want it despite how hungry you may feel. She's fully aware of my poor stomach; knows exactly what closes me up. Yet, anytime she's feeling like watching a show, she'll pull the same shit my mom used to pull when I was younger. She'll hover and linger and wait for me to take the one bite that will stick to the bottom of my esophagus and for the next hour or so, cause all kinds of havoc and sap all of the energy from my body. I remember this one time I wasn't eating the way all the other young girls were eating, so she stopped at McDonalds, drove through the drive thru, bought me a Big Mac, and then she wouldn't pull out of the parking lot until I downed the entire burger. I know, later, it will cause my problems—more mental than anything, just the thought of getting married to a man who's a faster eater than me and having him find out the hard way that his wife has a tendency to regurgi-*

tate her food like a fly *gives me chills and makes me want to never get married to another life form. Cleo's so insensitive. Only those who lack understanding of issues are forged by a cruel world where dominance is the only motto to living. She thinks it's fun to rush me while I'm eating. Sometimes, I'd like to shove my foot right down her throat and watch her squirm and gag. Then, maybe, she'll know what it's like to feel completely powerless.* **So, after I left Julio's, I decided to pay a visit to the White Sands. I've always wanted to see what all the fuss was about. It's. . . it's not at all what I expected.** *Your typical Cleo. Ms. Center of Attention who, after the first smell of blood, wears her heart on her sleeve. The emotion is extra heavy on her face. She knows what she did to me. So, she does what she always does: She turns it against me.* Sorry about what I said about Danielle, all right?

In the heavy silence, Cleo started to tear-up.

"It was wrong for me to bring up her name," Pan said sympathetically. "The truth is I'm the one who's jelly. I've never had a close friend like you had with Danielle. Once, maybe I did, but that was so long ago that I can't even remember. In a way, I was always destined to be alone. You, on the other hand, are the opposite. I'm not saying it's your weakness—"

"—See," Cleo blurted out, **"that's the difference between you and me, Pan. You think by me wanting to be with someone else is a weakness, whereas I think it's what makes us human. Humans need connections as much as they need air to breath."**

Pan said with slight annoyance, "I said I'm sorry. Geez."

Cleo sobbed for a while before she used a similar tactic Pan used to protest.

PAN'S VERSION

Despite all of the drama, it was fair to say *we* were having a good time whether or not a certain someone didn't want to admit it. I believe it was those few hours we spent at the Grand Canyon that brought us closer. Then, of course, once we left the Grand Canyon, I somehow got lost. I never get lost. **Hey, I always say it's the best way to travel. The best way to get where you need to be is not knowing where you need to be.** We went so far out of the way. That's what I get for relying on my phone. Of course, for some reason, my shitty GPS stopped working and it kept rerouting me somewhere else. I can't even remember the last time I used an actual map, you know, one made out of paper. The guy who sold it to us was a creep, wasn't he? **Yeah. I know how much you like those creepers.** It's like they're attracted to me. **You can say that.** After we crossed into Colorado, we decided to stop at Sharptooth Mountain Park to stretch our legs. Do you remember how loud it was? **You mean nature? It was loud, wasn't it?** Like nature was having itself a giant orgy. We wandered through a couple of trails and ended up at a gorge. We stood over the edge of a cliff and watched the river running below. The sound of the water was loud as well, yet, it was so tranquil. So, that brings us to how we wound up here. We left the park and continued on our journey to unite—and reunite—with our biological father, Kirk. Throughout the entire trip, we saw all these Richard Rhodes signs either on the side of the highway or in people's front yard or on the billboards. Then, once that Approved Advertisement' came on the radio, I nearly flipped my shit. The guy couldn't get the clue. He didn't give a fuck-all about people. Yet, he wouldn't go away. He was like a ghost haunting America. Every time I saw his face, I couldn't help but go on these long-winded rants until I was *blue* in the face. Fortunately, your song came on afterwards, which rid any thought of Richard Rhodes. As we were driving over a bridge, we were both singing along to the song 'Me Too' and getting our swerve on when, all of a sudden, some *dog ran out into the road*. It all happened so fast. One second, we were having so much fun, then the next thing, we were falling to our deaths. Everything was hazy when we hit the water. Both of my shoulders were completely yanked out of socket. Never have I experienced so much pain when I swam to the surface. I could literally feel my shoulder rubbing against bone. It's a good thing that you rolled down the windows right before we crossed the bridge. **Always do.** I know how you are and all of your superstitions. Once we surfaced, the river carried us downstream. The water became rough. I tried to swim toward you, but you were too far from reach. As I struggled to stay afloat, I sank underneath the water for a moment. Once I resurfaced, you were nowhere to be found. Then, the sound of water became louder as I was being carried down the river. All I could think about was *waterfall.* I was heading straight to a waterfall—a big one, too, based on how loud it was. I hoped that you somehow managed to swim to the shore. At that point in time, all I was thinking about was survival. My arms were heavy. I couldn't reach the shore in time. That's when I basically gave up and let the water carry me wherever it was going to take me. Once I reach the edge of the waterfall, everything slowed down again, like the moments when we were falling from the bridge. Before me was a vast valley. The clouds above were as massive as mountains from the storm that had recently passed. They were parting ways, revealing the blue sky and the sunbeam shooting down. I fell for at least ten stories. Once I hit the water— yet again—the impact knocked me out. When I cracked open my eyes, I was blinded by this bright light shining down on me. *But* it wasn't the sunlight. It was this Lazarus' light coming from a large, bulky device in the back of a truck—Light of Lazarus,' as I've heard it being called several times since I've been here. *Oops. Here it comes.*

Beyond the firelight, the dark, shadowy faces in the night darkness shouted, "The Light of Lazarus! The one true light! The light of. . . "

. . . *all life*, Pan thought. *Yes. I get it already.* She couldn't help but stop and acknowledge those Gabrielites for a moment, as well as their commitment to the special light every time the three specific words *Light of Lazarus* were mentioned.

She delved back into the story as to how she wound up in such a strange town called Gabriel. *I woke up on the shore like a beached whale. Two people were standing over me, one of them a young girl named Kazlauskas Inc. and the other, a rather short stocky man named Cupid. The dark-faced man asked the girl,* "Any crossers with her?" *She replied,* "No. Not that I'm aware of." *As soon as I found the strength to stand on my feet, I realized that I was somewhere else. Cleo was nowhere to be found. Or, was she?*

"I was extremely worried about Cleo," Pan said. Then, "Kazlauskas Inc. here informed me that she was abducted by some clan called. . . well, I don't. . . "

All of a sudden, the name of the clan slipped her mind.

Pan's eyes drifted in thought. The more she thought about the name, the more it fell deeper into the blackness of her thoughts.

"**I wasn't taken by The 1999 Star Cruisers**," said Cleo, as she rolled both her eyes. "**Where in the hell would you come up with such a ridiculous idea?**"

Not my idea, Cleo. Your idea.

All of a sudden, a darker thought crept into her thoughts as if somehow it was starting to consume her.

Although I know for certain that little freak show stole my charm bracelet—you mean, my charm bracelet—I was the one who bought it for you, didn't I? She found the bracelet on the river-bank after they shined that light on us. It slipped from your wrist and the little freak show snatched it when you weren't looking.

As Pan turned her eyes toward Kazlauskas Inc., who was sitting on the other side of the fire, Pan drifted deeper in thought and remembered young Kazlauskas Inc., *not* the one Cleo had described, telling her about this so-called clan and how they were known to kidnap or at times, wrangle up "strays," referring to Cleo and Pan or any others who crossed over to the other side, then sell them to a ruthless organization who went by the name the "High Order" in order to obtain a higher knowledge, or "enlightenment," as Cupid simply put it.

Cleo capped off the gesture by smacking her gums.

"**Whatever.**"

CLEO'S VERSION

Not too long after the incredible expandable water toy who happened to be named after the makers of a popular candy bar and fairy boy found you on the shore, they found me farther down the river. *Kazlauskas Inc. and Cupid's disfigured appearance isn't what I'd call photogenic, more of a carnival act, neither is the rest of the townspeople for that matter. However, the notion that Cupid was actually named after the god of love was somewhat comical. That is, if Cupid aged thirty years, put on a beer belly that protruded under his undersized T-shirt, shaved once a week, became a heavy smoker, and developed, in any god's terms, a winged dysfunction. According to Kazlauskas Inc.'s explanation, the real reasons as to why Cupid cut off his wings, leaving only two small nubs where two wings used to be, was that they no longer worked and they hung from his back like wet blankets and after a while, Cupid was sick and tired of looking at those limp things. Talk about a hopeless romantic. I've heard rumors about small, sleepy towns located in the middle of Bum Hole, Nowhere, such as Gabriel, getting involved in incest and all kinds of icky stuff, like rituals and sacrifices. The fact they worship three children called the Underlings as their gods was one of the first of many red flags. Maybe that's why they look like they way they do, the features on their faces disproportionate, their abilities mutant. Cleo's tells them 'everything leading up to that was a blur. That being swept away by a raging river. There's one thing I can relate to Cleo: Ever since I arrived here it seems like everything has been a blur.* All I remember was thrashing around the water, then I hit the shoulder on a boulder in the bottom of the river after I fell from the waterfall, then I was sucked into a black hole at the bottom of the surface, like a funnel of some sorts, then I remember floating around a cold, thick blackness. Only instead of waking up on the shore, I'm clinging to a rock in the middle of the river. The water was much different, too, murkier, heavy, like sludge. After I found what little strength I had left, I manage to swim to the shore. That was when I saw *these* two characters coming to my rescue. They told me that they found you and that you were okay. They did? Yes. For the trillionth time, Pan, *they* did. *But there was someone else. A man. He was injured. He couldn't walk on his own.* Once I was able to walk on my own, they collected their fishing stuff and I hopped in the back of their rusty truck and we rode down a foggy dirt road through the woods where every tree was stripped bare by what looked like a fire and the only life forms came in warped shadows. *I won't forget what she said to Cupid: Where's your halo? I hadn't felt so humiliated in my entire life. And* I won't forget the sounds all around me. There were no sounds, not a single bird chirping, no insects, no animals. Nothing. Everything was silent. When we made it to the highway, the sky was different as well. Dark red and eerie, like the morning of a bad storm. Strangely, though, I knew it wasn't going to storm. A part of me knew the storm had already passed. I thought maybe we wound up all the way back in New Mexico, or maybe Utah or even somewhere in the Midwest. I soon realized we weren't in any of those places. We were somewhere else, something strange. . .

Pan lost herself in her sister's words, her "version" of the story, and given the situations that had occurred, started to believe her.

What if my version was all wrong?

What if I was *confusing it with a dream?*

Or, what if *Cleo's version was the only version?*

But what about the one man who was injured? Pan could see the man's face as if she was looking at him in real-time. He was a cave diver from Arkansas, had an accent so thick it sounded foreign, also had a rugged handsomeness to him as if he could've played a lead role in any American Western. He said—or claimed—that he was taking photographs of an underwater cave which he referred to as the "Devil's Throat" when all of a sudden he felt a force tugging him into a crevice. He compared the pull to a rip current. Pan, too, had felt a similar force twice as the man described: once when she was driving over the bridge, then another time once she hit the water after plummeting from the waterfall. The name was what seized her attention the most: "Devil's Throat." She had heard of the name before in the news.

She read it in the headlines but, among the cross-chatter of her thoughts, couldn't quite put a story to the name. Then, as she was about to lend the man a hand, a great silence rushed through the woods, she remembered. When we were about to help him to his feet, the fisherman—Cupid—started acting fidgety and he insisted that we leave him alone. Before Pan could even question him, the cave diver was pulled into a narrow opening underneath a boulder. He struggled for a bit, but he was sucked into the hole as though he was being sucked into a vacuum. *His entire body violently folded inward like a lawn chair.* His head, hands, and legs were the last parts of his body to be sucked into the hole and when they did so, they ballooned outward as if, any moment, they were ready to pop.

Pan fell deeper and deeper into "Cleo's version" until finally she was reliving the story as if it was her very own.

"As you said earlier, this place doesn't share the same rules as the world we come from," Cleo said. **"This place is special."**

☠

THE fisherman with two worn down nubs protruding from the back of his shoulder blades asked them for their names.

Cleo was first to speak: "I'm Cleopatra," she said and pointed at Pan, "this is my little sister, Pandora."

"Pandora What?"

"Excuse me," Pan uttered, speaking over Cleo.

"You have a last name, don't you?"

"Pandora Nikopoulos," Cleo said for Pan.

"How you spell that?"

More upset from the way her sister was speaking for her as if she was a mute, Pan said louder, "N-i-k-o-p-o-u-l-o-s. Nikopoulos. What's your name?"

"Cupid," he said.

"Cupid *What?*"

"Well," he said blandly. "Just Cupid." He pointed at the young girl who was throwing pebbles into the sludgy river. "That there is Kazlauskas Inc."

Normally, such a tongue twister of a name would've drawn way more attention than a name like Cupid; however, Pan was somewhat disturbed as to why this stranger "Cupid" wanted to know her last name and even weirder, how to spell it.

She retorted, "What kind of name is Cupid?"

"Easy, Pan," Cleo said and walked to the back of the truck.

"Come on, Kaz," Cupid waved at the young girl and said that they were now leaving.

To the left of Pan, she heard what sounded like a man groaning in the woods.

☠

AFTER riding for a few miles down a desolate highway through a flat countryside, which had the similarities of Indiana yet slightly similar to New Mexico with jagged mountains underneath dark, stormy clouds at a distance, they passed several cars, mostly older models, ones she hadn't seen since she was a child.

Pan shot weary glances at each driver inside each passing car and was completely stumped by their inhuman appearance.

As Pan redirected her attention forward, she saw Cupid and Kazlauskas Inc. leaning forward and looking up at the sky through the windshield.

Cupid pulled the truck underneath an overpass and from the sliding window, instructed Pan and Cleo to get out.

As Cupid parked the truck, Kazlauskas Inc. stepped outside and hurried to the tailgate where she waved Pan and Cleo toward a recess underneath the bridge.

In the corner of her eye, Pan witnessed the shadow speeding across the road. She heard the sound of what she thought was a drone; however, it was way higher in pitch, like an amplified beehive.

Nursing her injured shoulder, Cleo gingerly stepped out of the truck.

The noise coming from above grew louder and louder, nearly deafening, and forced Pan to help Cleo up the ramp while Cupid and Kazlauskas Inc. closely followed behind.

"What are we running from?" asked Cleo.

Cupid immediately shushed Cleo and pushed the two up the ramp.

Together, the four hunkered underneath the bridge while more of those same shadows zipped across the road, as well as the open field.

"*They* can sense us," said Cupid, as he escorted Cleo and Pan farther into the recess.

Pan turned to Kazlauskas Inc., who had shrunk down to the size of a toddler in the very back of the dark, dusty recess.

She couldn't help but notice Kazlauskas Inc. and her sudden change in size. She had gone from the average size of a teenager to the size of a girl who looked as if she could barely walk on her own. Even those raggedy clothes still remained the same size and were loosely hanging from her body.

"How the hell is she able to do that?" Pan asked Cupid, who, in return, placed his index finger over his mouth, signaling for Pan to be absolutely quiet.

Once more, Pan glanced at Kazlauskas Inc., who was trembling in fear.

"Wait till *they* pass," Cupid whispered to Pan.

"They?"

Before she could further question the seemingly dire situation, Cupid pressed his index finger against his lips once more, but this time exercising more urgency.

It was easy enough to see the fear in Kazlauskas Inc. considering her age, but to see it in Cupid's eyes was something else entirely for Pan.

The sky above darkened like a cloud, thus causing the area under the bridge to darken as well.

As the buzzing sound intensified past the overpass, Pan felt a cold, staticky gust of wind hit the side of her face. In the corner of her eye, she caught a massive creature, which was about the size of a human, swooping down and landing behind Cupid's truck. The creature looked similar—if not, identical—to a mosquito. Of course, considering its size, it clearly was *not* a mosquito or at least not like any mosquito Pan or Cleo had ever seen. Its proboscis was nearly the size of Pan's arm. When fully stretched out, its wings could cover twice the height of her body. It hunched over the tailgate and ran the end of its proboscis along the bedding; then, after a speedy inspection, it flew away.

Soon afterwards, that harsh buzzing sound lessened.

The light brightened slightly. Eventually, those sounds faded away.

"All clear," Cupid said, breathing a sigh of relief.

"Now, can you explain what those things were?" asked Pan.

"They are carriers of a virus that has recently plagued our town. Other towns within our county have been hit hard, Finnegans and Fielding, Castaneda, Huxley, Mann, Outpost 13, all of them are now hot spots. It's only a matter of time before it spreads to the city of Leatherwood—"

"—You're talking about mosquitoes?" said Cleo.

"The *Culexx* with two x's," he said. "Mosquitoes on steroids."

"What about you?" Pan said, nodding at Kazlauskas Inc., who was starting to return to her normal size. "How are you able to shrink like that?"

Kazlauskas Inc. bashfully shrugged her shoulders.

"I dunno," she mumbled.

"You don't know? Seriously?"

"You have to realize," Cupid said before Pan lost her cool, "in this world, we don't have any rules, not like in your world."

Finally, Cleo asked the inevitable question: "Where are we?"

"Gabriel," Cupid then corrected, "well, technically we're still on the outskirts of Outpost #7."

"Are we in another country?" Pan followed.

"No," Cupid said bluntly. "More like another world."

"What do you mean 'another world'?"

"I promise I can answer any question you want," Cupid said. "Right now, we need to move. They'll be back. And next time, they'll be in a greater numbers."

"The mosquitoes?"

Cupid hesitated.

"If that's what you want to call them, then, yes. The mosquitoes."

Pan and Cleo inched down the ramp; Kazlauskas Inc. shouldered by the two and hopped into the passenger seat. Lastly, Pan and Cleo used the tailgate to step in the back of the truck. Then, as soon as they were seated, Cupid drove away.

☠

ONLY a few miles of riding through the flat countryside, they drove past what appeared to be a cornfield, which gave off the odor of a corpse. The crops were rotten and infested with what looked like disease. Behind the dead, rotten stalks Pan witnessed three tentacles flailing around in the air. She tapped Cleo on the shoulder and pointed to the cornfield, but the tentacles were no longer visible.

Cleo shrugged off her sister's paranoia for she was more concerned about the town they were approaching.

They passed the sign for "GABRIEL," which was constructed of a mound of painted black rocks. Seven of the rocks were painted white with the letters G, A, B, R, I, E, L painted in red.

Pan couldn't help but pick out each and every detail of her surroundings. She had driven through towns such as Gabriel; in fact, she had driven through similar countrysides. However, each detail wasn't quite right, yet slightly. . . off, as if it was a poor imitation of "her" world, as if those who had built these roads or threw up these buildings had done so without any blueprint, but rather solely based on a memory. Even the road they had been driving on for the past few miles looked as if a child haphazardly poured asphalt through the rough terrain, didn't even bother to smooth out the surface or the edges of asphalt before it dried, painted a couple of red lines, *not yellow*, in the middle of the road. The same went for the buildings, which sat crookedly along their foundations: each building was very similar to everyday buildings that she saw everyday in her world, but, on the other hand, weren't. The only way Pan could put it was that they, like the roads, the bridges, or even the signs, were *off.*

For Cleo, however, Pan knew the easiest way to explain what they were experiencing was with a movie. This one being *Beetlejuice.* Cleo mentioned to Pan how much it reminded her of that movie. Cleo only shared this with Pan because Pan knew it was how Cleo tried to make sense of situations, especially ones that were all but foreign to her, by comparing it to a movie. She felt that, like those two characters who were portrayed by Alec Baldwin and Geena Davis, they were stuck between worlds, living and dead.

Pan teased, "I don't see any sand worms yet."

Cleo wasn't at all amused by Pan's humor.

Curious, yet at the same time, skeptical, Pan drew her attention to the cooler-like container next to the wheel well. She cracked open the lid and took a peek at Cupid's so-called "catch of the day." She immediately gagged and covered the bottom half of her face from the horrendous stench, which reeked of a warm turd baking in the sun. Most—if not, all—of the ice was melted inside the cooler. The surface of the water was rather oily and left a swirling array of bright colors, including pinks, purples, and blues, along Cupid's "catch," which appeared as if it was scraped off the road instead of being fished out of the river. The texture of the mollusk-like creature reminded Pan of a jellyfish, only it was bumpier, like gooseflesh. It had a lot of tentacles; however, Pan couldn't quite count how many since most of them were either bundled up or knotted. What struck her the most was its eye, as well as its vaginal similarities. It had only one, like the eye of a cyclops, swollen, rather elongated, and protruding along the center of a vulva-shaped head, which rested underneath a cap-like hood—or *was it a fin?*

A part of Pan sure hoped it was a fin.

Repulsed, yet more so intrigued by the sight of what she assumed was a creature fished out of the river, Pan gently elbowed Cleo in the arm, nodded her head at the cooler, and whispered to her to take a look inside.

Startled by Pan's interest, Cleo didn't bother to question her sister. Instead, she did as Pan asked, looked inside the cooler, and then, following a similar reaction as Pan, immediately pinched her nose and recoiled from the sight of the slippery, smelly creature inside the cooler.

"What is that?" mouthed Cleo.

"Look at the head," Pan said. "Doesn't it look kind of like ah. . . "

"A what?"

"You know?"

Cupid glanced in the rear view mirror, causing Pan to close the lid.

As Cupid turned his attention back to the road, Pan turned to Cleo with what could only look like a guilty expression on her face.

She had no words, and even if she did, she didn't even know where to start.

As they rode past several houses, Pan and Cleo witnessed the pale, disfigured faces behind the windows: faces creeping past the edge of curtains while others gawking at the two sisters with wide glassy eyes. Neither Pan nor Cleo saw anybody outside, no children playing, no adults doing any yard work or repairs to the shoddy-looking houses. Each Gabrielite appeared quarantined inside their homes.

Pan glanced inside the cab of the truck and saw Cupid checking a wristwatch that was pulsing with a soft white light.

Thinking it might've been one of those digital watches, Pan peered closer at the watch; however, she saw no time, no numbers, no minute or hour hand either, just a light pulsing like a heartbeat.

Cupid tapped Kazlauskas Inc. on the shoulder and showed her the wristwatch thingamajig. Then, turned to Pan and Cleo and cracked open the back window.

"We have to make a pit stop," he said over his shoulder.

"Sounds good to me," Cleo said, turning his sights to several houses where, strangely, that same pulsing white light on Cupid's watch was pulsing behind the windows of each house.

The light, Cleo noticed, was also coming from the inside of buildings. It was a white, bluish light, angelic, like the soft glow filter she had seen being used in the 1970's movies during a flashback scene. It reminded her of a time when she was young and how she and Pan would go to the pool during those hot and humid summers. Pan used to wear goggles; however, Cleo always lost hers and thought they were distracting and a burden to carry around, especially when she was having so much fun in the sun. She'd swim with her eyes open, even while under the water, and when she'd surface, her vision was blurry, especially when she looked at the light.

Pan followed Cleo's eyes and she, too, recognized the light.

"When I woke up next to the river," she said quietly to Cleo, "they were shining that same light down on me."

Cleo read the name engraved along the side of the device next to her.

"*Lazarus*," she whispered, then turned to Pan, "What do you think it means?"

"I dunno."

They drove past a church-like building that was missing a cross; however, in its place was a wooden circular symbol with three lines positioned upward. Pan thought it looked like a sun rising—or setting—along a horizon with the lines being sunrays shooting into the sky. In the very front of the building, she saw three bronze statues of what looked like children.

As they made it to the Main Street of Gabriel, Pan saw the *same* symbol on a bumper sticker on the back of a parked car, looking exactly the same way she saw it on top of that building, with a circle and three lines, the first line slightly slanted left in a sixty degree angle, the second line straight, the third line slightly slanted right in the same sixty degree angle.

Immediately, Pan began to worry while Cleo became unusually quiet.

Usually, she'd be talking her head off, throwing out movie quotes and jokes about Gabriel.

Not a peep from her.

☠

THEY arrived at Gulps.

Cupid and Kazlauskas Inc. were first to exit the truck, then Pan, who helped her sister out of the truck. Cupid suggested that they come inside and wait, if they liked, since it wasn't entirely safe to be outside because of, you know, the "giant mosquitoes." Pan and Cleo tagged along and followed Cupid and Kazlauskas Inc. inside Gulps, which, surprisingly, had the traits of a convenient store. They had aisles of snacks and refreshments. Pan felt at home.

"Watch your step," Cupid said, pointing at a couple of beige colored circles of what looked like the spill of a milk-shake on the floor. Next to the spill was a yellow "Caution" sign indicating a wet floor.

Cupid mentioned to them that he had to pick up a few supplies before heading back home, including a bag of ice. Which, in a spur of the moment, prompted Pan to bring up that "strange smell" in the back of the truck. Not to point any fingers. But the crusty turd muffin coming from the cooler.

"Yeah," Cleo said bluntly. "It smells like a fart." Then, mumbled under her voice, "Or better yet, a queef."

Wearing her best mean face, Pan elbowed Cleo.

"Queefs don't smell," she whispered.

She couldn't even believe she was saying the word *queef*.

"Some do," Cleo said.

Immediately, Pan shushed her, trying to put an end to the topic of smell.

Pan's veiled attempt at asking Cupid what that creature was inside the cooler didn't go over so well.

"Must be coming from the plant," Cupid said plainly and made his way to the front of the store where a featureless-looking clerk escorted him to a secret room.

While Cupid was off doing who-knows-what, Pan and Cleo moseyed around the store, checking out a shelf of candy bars called LiverSticks. She read the ingredients on the back and sure enough, it was actual liver. Pan dropped the candy bar in disgust and made her way to the back where she found a refrigerator full of Type A Negative bottles.

From behind, Cleo asked, "Is that what I think it is?"

"Blood," Pan murmured.

"What the hell is this place?" asked Cleo.

The clerk, whom she heard Kazlauskas Inc. refer to as "Wax," returned to the front counter with Cupid, as well as the supplies that he needed: a bag of ice and a Mason jar filled with a white cream said to be a special ointment extracted from a rare hepa-pod, which was on the verge of extinction.

Listening to the sound of Wax's gravelly *phlegmy* voice from across the store seized Pan's attention; in fact, she couldn't ignore his voice. She inched closer to the front of the store. Cleo followed closely behind. As soon as Pan stepped past a shelf of more organ-flavored snacks and laid eyes on Wax's face underneath the bill of the cap, she covered the gasp with her hands. He wasn't at all human—his face, that is. He had the body shape of any average man; however, underneath the raggedy jumpsuit and burgundy baseball cap, his gooey skin was moving.

She moved her eyes from his face and inspected his hands, which were gooey as well. The cuffs around his sleeves were stained with his own dripping skin.

Wax removed the rag from the breast pocket of the jumpsuit and wiped away that loose skin falling from his brow and then pocketed the soggy rag. Strangely enough, the skin kept oozing, then falling like sweat beads, then once it hit a surface, for instance, the countertop, the skin started to mold and harden.

Hence why they called him "Wax."

Made sense.

But *not really*, Pan thought.

She realized where that wet spill from earlier had originated.

"The hot weather does this to me every time," he said, as if he was explaining himself for Cupid and Kazlauskas Inc., who were well-aware of his "condition"—if that was what you called it.

"We're most definitely not in Colorado anymore," Pan uttered to Cleo.

Kazlauskas Inc. voluntarily expanded in size in order to touch the shard of a chalky black crystal inside a squared glass case next to the cash register while, at the same time, sneakily grabbed an air freshener in the shape of a mushroom from a clip of "magical" fresheners on a wing stack in front of the checkout counter.

Once Kazlauskas Inc. slipped the air freshener inside her back pocket of her sweatpants, which were starting to rip down the rear seam from the change in her size, Pan knew the move was what she observed as a distraction.

Without realizing what Kazlauskas Inc. had done, Wax slapped her hand and told her no touching. The slap left behind a smudge of his thick, gooey skin along the top of Kazlauskas Inc.'s hand.

"Sorreee," she uttered, as she shrunk back to her normal size.

Cupid placed the bag of ice next to that jar of cream on the counter. The bag of ice split open, causing a couple of ice cubes to spill out onto the counter.

Wax attempted to gather the rest of the ice cubes, but Cupid stopped him.

"Not so fast, Wax," he said, holding out his hand. "I got it."

One of the ice cubes slid from the counter and landed next to Pan's foot.

Pan picked up the ice cube.

At first, it looked and felt like any other ice cube; however, the sensation on the edge of her fingertips intensified. The ice cube was no longer cold, yet it was sharp and prickly. Pan held the ice cube to her face and saw hundreds of parasitic creatures squirming around inside the ice cube.

As the ice starting to melt into that same colorful rainbow-like water that she saw inside the cooler along her fingertips, her skin started to become more translucent.

Pan immediately handed Cupid the ice cube and dried her fingers along the side of her pant leg. The outer layer of her skin peeled away like an open blister; nonetheless, her skin did return to normal.

Must've been some kind of reaction to the water.

"Thanks," Cupid said. Then, introduced Pan and Cleo to Wax, "Found them by Raven's Gullet."

"Pan," she said to Wax. "My sister, Cleo."

Cleo said hello; however, Wax hardly acknowledged her.

"Tourists, huh? Passing through or just passing away?"

Wax laughed by himself, whereas Cupid and Kazlauskas Inc. remained dead serious—no pun intended.

Pan had an inkling as to what Wax meant by the comment.

Over the awkward silence, Cupid gathered the rest of the ice cubes and paid Wax with a handful of teeth, varying in size and shape. Among the teeth, human as well as animal, Pan spotted what looked like the fang of a snake.

Once Cupid paid for the bag of ice and that "special" ointment, he pinched Kazlauskas Inc. on the arm and told her to put back the air freshener.

Over his shoulder, he said to Pan, "Please excuse Kaz here. She has a knack for taking things that don't belong to her."

Pan felt as though her attention was being physically—and mentally—pulled back to the black crystal with the same force surrounding a magnetic field; however, she fought through the attraction and couldn't help but notice the product on the wall behind Wax. After all, it was "pixie dust," or at least, that was what the label had read.

Pixie dust?

No joke.

Cupid recognized Pan's interest in the dust.

"Like what you see?" Wax said to Pan but didn't expect any reply from her. "Grounded down from the horn of a unicorn. It works too," he said to Pan before she could follow up, "in case you're wondering."

"What do you mean 'it works'?"

"Well," he said, "pixie dust worked before the virus." He nodded at the fully stocked shelves of pixie dust on the wall. "Now I wouldn't really call them a best seller. Before the ZOMBA virus, pixie dust allowed us to fly. Yes. Like in those movies you watch. But now, *they* own the skies."

"The mosquitoes?"

"Yes," he said and shot a glance at Wax, "the mosquitoes."

"In a way, though, the virus has been for our own good. It has grounded us, made us more appreciative to what we have in front of us instead of what's below us."

Pan nodded at the black crystal and asked, "So what's that?"

"That there is a piece of resin leftover from the gods, which was pulled from *your* world," Cupid said.

"My world?"

"It is said to have the power to foresee the future of those who come in contact with it. Which, ultimately, allows those who come in contact with it a chance at immortality. I know. Pixie dust. Gigantic mosquitoes. Deadly virus. A tiny sacred *rock* that can see your future. It's a lot to take in. Me," Cupid said, pointing at himself, "I don't personally believe in some of the stuff I hear around here." He flicked his eyes toward Wax behind the counter and winked his left eye; however, to Pan, it came off more as if his eye was twitching and he had an eyelash or grain of dirt stuck behind an eyelid and he was trying to flick it out. "Not to mention any names, but I think there are some corrupted folks who find any opportunity to take advantage of the more weak-minded."

"—Like you have any room to talk, Limp Wing," Wax said abruptly, as part of his mouth broke apart and dripped along the collar of his jumpsuit. "How can you criticize something that you've never tried?"

In an instance, the part of his mouth that had fallen from his mouth regenerated and reformed along his lips, as well as the one side of his chin, as if he had an endless supply of skin—or wax?

Cupid shook off the insult and swallowed what, to Pan, appeared to be a dark shade of despondency behind his face.

"Before the virus, you'd have folks lined up around this entire building, waiting to buy dust. Now, as you can tell, it's like a ghost town around here. Everybody has sort of given up on hope."

Hope?

Cupid said, more soberly, "Whether the resin works or not, in a way, it made folks more. . ."

Pan waited for Cupid to finish the sentence.

Cleo said, "More what?"

"More present," he said thoughtfully.

Wax grinned at Pan.

"Why don't you give it a try, *Pan?*" he said. "I'll cut you a discount. What'd you say?"

"You know she doesn't have any loot."

"Hey, some of us still have to make a living around here."

"Maybe next time," Cupid said and made his way from the store. "Be seeing you around, Wax." He waved at Kazlauskas Inc. "Come on, Kaz."

Cleo eventually left with Cupid and Kazlauskas Inc.; however, Pan wasn't so quick to follow. Instead, she crept over to the shard of black crystal mounted like a museum piece inside the glass case and once more found herself being "pulled" into the black crystal. In that trance, Pan envisioned herself lying on the floor of a dark living room with the glow of a television screen flashing on her face; however, she couldn't even recognize herself, mainly her body. In her right hand, she was holding a knife and staring at a stranger inside the refection of the blade. Just as she was about to use the blade on herself, she bolted upright.

☠

PAN suddenly yanked herself from the vivid memories, as though she was actually experiencing them outside the threshold of her mind.

Was it really the Quidaquin that was suppressing these memories?

As the memories grew stronger and more brighter and vivid and forced Pan to reconcile her time spent in Gabriel with an image here of a car ride from Gulps to Cupid's house or an image there of Cupid removing that smelly river creature from an ice cooler, Pan couldn't take it any longer. Her thoughts were spinning. *Her world* was spinning. She so desperately wanted them out, the memories—if that's what they were and not something else entirely. She just wanted to go back to the way it was before, when she didn't remember.

Using every single muscle in her body, she reached for the TV remote, which had fallen on the floor. Once she was able to reach the remote, she turned up the volume to drown out voices from the beyond, only to hear a much gentler voice, a soft-spoken one from one of those depressing commercials about abused and mistreated dogs that aired mostly during Christmas time direly pleading for her help and, of course, money.

"For just a dollar a day you could help Charlie find a home!"

It got every time. But, she told herself, not tonight.

Once the sickly images zapped away in a bright flash and the TV screen went dark, the reflection in the screen displayed not only herself but also someone else, a scruffy-looking man with a belly so large and round that he looked pregnant.

Startled by the reflection, she turned to her immediate left and without thinking uttered the name, "Cupid?"

Nobody was standing in the corner of the living room. She turned back to the reflection in the TV. He was gone.

Once more, she turned to the same spot where he was standing. Nothing.

Pan was more confused by the name, where she had heard the man, why she even uttered the name. Her thoughts raced. Once more, she found herself in spin city.

Unable to think straight, Pan maneuvered herself from the futon and managed to stand on her own. Just standing up was taxing enough for Pan. Her breath, labored. She only had twelve steps to the bathroom where she saw the Quidaquin bottle lying on the vanity. At this point, twelve steps was like twelve miles.

Exerting all of her strength, Pan made her way to the bathroom.

Halfway to the bathroom, she had to stop by the dresser to catch her breath. She used the dresser to lean against.

"You can do this, Pan," she told herself.

She continued to move forward.

Only five steps left.

Four.

Three.

Two.

By the time she made it the bathroom, she was completely gassed. She could hardly stand on her own two feet. She worked up quite a sweat, too. The thought alone of that strange-looking guy from the convenient store and his dripping skin made Pan more uncomfortable. Not only was she sweating from exerting herself, but she was also sweating from the anxiety. She leaned up against the side of the vanity and took a moment to catch her breath and relax. She turned on the faucet, ran warm water over both of her hands, which helped calm her breathing.

Then, she switched over the water to cool, placed a washcloth underneath the faucet, and soaked it with water.

She placed the cool, damp washcloth on the areas of her body where she was sweating the most, including her forehead, her cheeks, the back of her neck, then her armpits, her folds.

Once she was able move again, she grabbed the bottle of Quidaquin from the vanity. She opened the bottle, took out one capsule, and placed it in the center of her palm; however, she never popped it or swallowed it. Yet, she just stared at it.

After debating whether or not to take the Q-capsule, Pan threw it against the mirror and cried out in great agony.

As the pain settled, she listened to the wind over her labored breath.

To her right, a curtain was blowing around like a mane of lush hair from the wind blowing through the open window.

Once more, she drifted off into a trance, but this time, she was back in a small town called Gabriel.

FOUR YEARS AGO

PAN wondered to herself if these Gabrielites were the real monsters instead of the monsters they were hiding from.

Where would such an idea originate?

A voice pulled her from her thoughts.

"Pan?"

Pan pulled herself from the open window of the living room and turned to the voice.

"You sure you're not hungry?" asked Cupid.

At the kitchen doorway, Cupid was holding a plate of bunkfish, which didn't smell nearly as pungent as it did in the ice cooler; in fact, it smelled like any other fish that was well seasoned.

As though its smell was imprinted inside her nasal cavity, all she could think about was the bunkfish prior to being charred over an open flame and how there was absolutely no chance in hell she was going to eat something that smelled as if it was scooped out of a toilet.

Pan held up her hand.

"I'm good," she said and looked around the dark living room where the only means of light came from an old lantern.

Cupid cut the bunkfish in half and brought one half to his son, Enoon, who was lying in a bed in one of the bedrooms next to the living room. According to Cupid's story,

Enoon, who, at times, was lucid while other times he would blather away and not make any sense, had recently been bitten by the "Culexx."

When Pan had pressed him, he also referred to the Culexx as an "experiment" gone wrong. "I know. Let the madness begin, right?" There was no truth behind Cupid's statements, yet they were merely conspiracy theories.

Pan couldn't help but overhear Enoon in the other room. She swore that she heard two voices, not just Enoon's but someone else in the room as well.

Disturbed by the two different voices, she decided to occupy her mind by focusing on the visuals. As though it came natural, Pan roamed around the living room, snooping through whatever she could find. Which, first, happened to be a closet. She cracked open the closet and found various coats, which were raggedy and covered in a red dust. One coat in particular stood out the most. It was translucent, as if it was made out of plastic. She reached out to touch the texture and as soon as her fingertip grazed the sleeve of the coat, it suddenly flickered like an old bulb; however, the light was similar to that light she saw back on the river, as well as the light behind the windows of the other houses.

The sudden burst of light caused Pan to remove her hand from the coat, thus causing the coat to dim and return back to its normal translucency.

She heard the floor *creaking* behind the door. She closed the closet door and saw Cupid standing right next to her. She flinched from Cupid's presence.

"Didn't meant to scare you," he said.

"No," Pan said, searching for reasons as to why she was snooping around his closet. "I thought I heard someone in the closet."

"You heard someone in the closet?"

"Okay," Pan said, surrendering. "You caught me. I was just being nosy."

"I know you were. I get it. You're still freaked out a little."

"It's that obvious, huh?"

Cupid pointed to a chair.

Pan followed Cupid back into the living room. She didn't take a seat, though. Instead, she walked to the window where she saw more flickering light, this time coming from a fire. She peeked outside where Kazlauskas Inc. was sitting alone in front of a fire pit. The glow of the flame flickered over her face. Feeling Pan's dim presence, she looked up and locked eyes with Pan.

"Don't worry about her," Cupid said from behind. "She's much tougher than she looks."

Pan asked Cupid if his son Enoon had any brothers or sisters.

He didn't.

Which prompted Pan to follow up by asking Cupid if he had any friends over. Again, he didn't.

It was just him and Cupid and, of course, Kazlauskas Inc.

Cupid walked up to Pan and stood next to her and together, they watched the fire burning in the backyard.

"The fire repels them, you know, the mosquitoes, that is."

"Your world doesn't seem so different than mine."

"It had its similarities," he said. "Yes. Of course."

She nodded at Kazlauskas Inc. "What's her story?"

"Kaz?"

Pan nodded.

"Right," he said. "You noticed, huh?" Referring to Kazlauskas Inc.'s interest in Pan. "Let's just say she's not used to strays. She might not look like it, but like the others, she's extremely curious about your world."

"What happened to her?"

"I found her out there, in the woods, all alone, no home. She had no family, no friends, no one. So, I took her in. Gave her a home. She helps out around the house."

"How is she able to change her body like that?" Pan asked.

"That's a good question," he said. "You should ask her, but I wouldn't guarantee you that she'd give you an answer that will make any sense."

Struck by a sudden state of confusion, Pan looked around the room.

Cleo was nowhere around.

Cupid said that she stepped outside for a minute to clear her head. Pan didn't remember her sister saying anything about stepping outside and even if Cleo did, Pan would certainly join her.

No way I'd leave her alone, she thought, *with those monsters out there.*

"Where's your bathroom?" asked Pan.

From the corner of her eye, she caught Cupid reaching for a small object, thin and pencil-like, from a drawer. The move was rather quick and if she blinked, she would've missed it.

Once she turned her eyes toward Cupid, he straightened up and placed a hand behind his back as if he was hiding something from Pan.

Looking at Pan suspiciously, Cupid told Pan it was just down the hallway, to the left. He specifically told Pan, in fact, he couldn't emphasize enough that the restroom was on the "left."

With her legs stiff and heavy as though she had been sitting for hours without stretching, Pan exited the living room. Not only was it nerve-racking to be inside a stranger's house, but it was also enthralling to be caught in the middle of a situation, possibly dangerous, where she had no idea what was going to happen next. Her mother, Vivian, was a strict parent of conservative background, an untrusting, cynical woman who had often warned her daughters of situations such as these.

Feeling Cupid's lingering presence behind her, Pan waited till she was halfway down the hallway before she shot a quick, innocent glance over her shoulder. Cupid was gone from her line of sight.

To the left was the restroom, a poorly managed one at best and looked as if it hadn't been cleaned since the fallout that Cupid often spoke of. To her right was a normal-looking boy's bedroom with juvenile furniture and posters of swimsuit models hanging on the wall. At the very last second, Pan hooked a right into the bedroom and saw what she assumed was Cupid's son, Enoon, lying on a bed in the corner of the room. His head was rolling back and forth along the pillow, as if he was having a nightmare. His face appeared emaciated, cheeks sunken in, eye sockets dark and hollow, and his forehead dripping wet with sweat.

Pan could hear two voices, one of them coming from Enoon, who was groaning in agony, then another coming from underneath a tattered comforter, a weaselly, voice snickering and whispering in tongues.

More curious to uncover what was wrong with Enoon, Pan inched farther into the bedroom. She noticed the same cream that Cupid had bought at Gulps on the side of Enoon's neck and upper chest.

Suddenly, Enoon cracked open his eyes and turned to Pan.

His breath became rapid, his chest pumping up and down, up and down like a piston.

"Who'ah you?" Enoon asked feverishly, his beady eyes riddled with panic. "Wh'ah you want from me?"

"My name is Pan," she said softly. "I'm not going to hurt you."

"Why you here?" Enoon said, his voice louder.

Pan couldn't take her eyes off Enoon's left side, which was slightly moving. She thought maybe it was his elbow underneath the comforter; as she looked even closer, she realized it was a protrusion.

"Are you okay?"

Enoon, who must've been around the age of eight years old, had both of his frail hands tightly gripped on the ends of the comforter as if he was holding onto the handlebars of a rollercoaster.

As she stepped closer, she heard a whispering voice coming from underneath the comforter. She studied Enoon's lips, which weren't moving.

Once she realized that Enoon wasn't alone, she saw a third hand, a redder and rawer hand emerge from underneath the comforter, crawl up the side of Enoon's neck, then grab hold of the nape of his neck as though it was trying to pull Enoon underneath the comforter.

A hand grabbed Pan by the shoulder, startling Pan.

"*What you doing in here?*" a voice said from behind.

Pan rotated around and saw Cupid standing with both of his hands planted on his hips. The center of his brow was curled inward, showcasing two deep, narrow trenches across the lower half of his forehead.

"I was just. . . "

Pan pointed at Enoon, then his hands, two hands, *not* three.

"You were just leaving," Cupid finished.

"I must've gotten turned around."

"What part of bathroom on the left do you not understand?" Cupid asked, as he escorted Pan from the bedroom. He showed her the bathroom across the hallway.

Pan stepped into the bathroom and just as she was about to close the door behind her, she noticed Cupid wasn't leaving until she closed the door.

"You gonna watch me pee too?" asked Pan.

Disgusted by Pan's tone, Cupid shook his head.

"Just make sure you flush twice," he said. "I've been having trouble with the piping as of lately."

"Got it," Pan said shortly and closed the door behind her.

She was immediately hit by a god-awful smell. It wasn't like any bathroom she had ever smelled before. Most shit smelled about the same. This, however, it had the smell of death, like the human body had been turned inside out. Along a filthy vanity, she found a couple of imported toiletries, including a bottle of hand lotion, which was spotted with dark stains and streaks that closely resembled dark mud—Pan hoped it was only mud—and a bar of soap covered in pubic hairs.

Too repulsed, Pan didn't bother using the toilet or any of the imported toiletries. She waited a couple of seconds before she flushed the brown-colored water.

Then, as she stepped out of the bathroom, she heard a noise coming from the outside. She walked to the door at the end of the hallway and tried not to make a sound as she carefully opened the door.

The noise was coming from the back of the garage.

She crept inside the garage and closed the door behind her the same way she had opened it.

Yet again, she heard the same noise and pinpointed it to a shelf of rusty tools and hardware.

As she inched closer to the shelf along the wall, she couldn't help but notice an old blanket covered in dark spots on the ground.

Distracted by the blanket, she changed course and checked it out. She peeled back the blanket, which was folded in half. Inside the blanket she witnessed what looked like a severed arm in a pool of brownish colored blood. The smell nearly knocked her over. She covered her nose and examined the insect-like arm, which, after a thorough study, she concluded to be the same arm that belonged to one of those gigantic mosquitoes.

Startled by more of that same racket coming from the shelf, Pan drew her attention away from the bloody blanket.

To her left, Cupid was standing by the doorway.

"Pan," he said, surprisingly more cautious than angry, "come back inside. It's not safe."

"Is there something you're not telling me?"

"I don't know what you're talking about."

"What's one of these creatures doing in your garage?"

Cupid immediately noticed the blanket, which was open.

"*Pan*," he whispered with urgency, "*come back inside. Now!*"

"What are you hiding, Cupid?" asked Pan.

"I'll explain later," he said and followed by waving Pan inside the house, "for now, just please come back inside."

Pan was startled by yet another racket, this time louder and more violent and coming from a black coffin-like crate perched against the other side of the wall.

Overwhelmed with curiosity, Pan decided to check out the noise while, at the same time, Cupid urged her to come back inside the house.

Expecting a Culexx to suddenly pop out and give her one helluva jump-scare, Pan opened the crate without thinking twice. She braced herself. No Culexx. No scare. The crate was empty.

More relieved, she closed the crate, only to find a dark figure looming before her.

The mosquito-looking creature, which was missing one of its arms, pounced on Pan! She defensively threw up her arms to shield her face from its assault. Its power was doubled her own. The impact had forced her backward, causing her to land on her back. Pan grabbed whatever she could find within her reach, which was a jerrybuilt shovel and swung at the creature. The creature wasn't at all fazed by each baseball-like crack at its body. One of its wings, however, appeared crippled and badly injured while the other one, which was torn down the middle, fluttered around and prevented it from flying.

Once more, the creature attacked Pan and chased her around the garage until it leaped from behind a shelf and planted the end of its proboscis directly into her neck like a vampire sucking her dry. It managed to drain at least an ounce or two of her blood before she saw yet another dark figure in the corner of her eye.

An incredible large figure!

Before Pan could turn to see who—or what exactly—it was, the creature was suddenly flung in the air. The spear penetrated the center of its thorax, the velocity of the spear sending the creature against the farthest wall where it was pinned up like a crucified exhibit.

While grabbing hold of the area of her neck that was turning red and starting to swell, Pan noticed Kazlauskas Inc., standing in front of Cupid on the other side of the garage. Her right arm was incredibly veiny and muscular and was the size of a brutish bodybuilder. The arm was so thick and massive that it was nearly the size of her entire body. Eventually, the arm shrunk and returned to normal size.

Cupid brushed past Kazlauskas Inc. and rushed toward Pan to check on her condition.

"I feel dizzy," she said, staggering.

Cupid caught Pan before she collapsed and eased her limp body to the ground where she sat lazily with one hand holding her upper body upright while the other one constantly rubbing the edge of her brow as if she was trying to massage away a dizzy spell. He kneeled next to her and waited to catch her if—or when—she should pass out.

She said unsteadily, "What the hell just happened?"

"You were bit," Cupid said.

"*What*. . . what was that thing?"

Cupid said hesitantly, "It was same one that bit Enoon. I thought I killed it. I guess I was wrong."

Initially, the next follow up question for Pan would've been "Why didn't you bury it or dispose of it? *Why save it?!?*"

Instead, she turned more outwardly and focused on the throb along her neck.

"What's happening to me?" she asked Cupid.

Her breath was labored; everything about her was frail and panicky.

"Just relax." He turned his shoulder and told Kazlauskas Inc., who was still standing in a state of disbelief, to grab a blanket and that special "cream" that he used to treat Enoon.

Cupid was well aware of Pan's breathing. Once he had seen it before with a stray whom he found wandering through Gabriel: a gunshot victim named Treble who couldn't quite understand his situation and had trouble understanding that he was no longer in a world where such faculties existed. Over a full moon Cupid watched that gunshot wound on Treble's head grow wider and wider throughout his brief time with Treble, first starting out as a tiny red speck in the middle of his forehead, then as night fell, that speck growing redder and bloodier until it was a gaping gunshot wound.

"I'm having trouble. . . catching my breath," she said shortly.

"This is going to be difficult to understand, Pan," Cupid said somberly, as he let out a deep sigh, "but it's all in *your* head. The breathing part, that is. There's no easy way of putting this. Your being, your soul," he struggled to even utter the words but when he did so it brought him great relief, "your *new-me*, as we call it, it's reacting to the parasite."

Kazlauskas Inc. returned with a blanket. She handed it to Cupid, who, in return, unfolded it and carefully placed it over Pan's shoulders.

"My what?"

"New-me," he said. "Soul. The you in what makes you. . . *you.*"

I knew it, she thought. *I am dead.*

"Not dead," Cupid said with clarity as if, oddly enough, he could read Pan's thought. "You're just stuck."

"I told you you shouldn't have used Lazarus on her," Kazlauskas Inc. griped over Cupid's shoulder. "Didn't I?"

"Zip it, Kazy!"

Pan somewhat gained more control over her breathing— or lack of breathing. *The device in the back of Cupid's truck*, she thought, *the Lazarus Light.* She retraced her footsteps back to the moments she wound up on the riverbank. Cupid was shining a pale bluish light on her. But what exactly were his intentions?

"What is she talking about?" she asked Cupid.

Her feverish body was shaky. Her face more flush, the bite more swollen.

"To put it as plainly as I can," Cupid said, struggling to find the right words, "the Light allows you to. . . "

"To what?"

"It allows you to interact with us. We feel more comfortable if you're like us opposed to, you know, walking through walls, closed doors, or worse," he tapped on his head, "getting inside our minds."

Bemused by his comment, Pan insisted that he further explain himself. She asked him for the "no bullshit" version.

"Once," Cupid said methodically, "we decided not to use Lazarus on this one stray who wandered into Gabriel. Miles was his name. *Miles Straum.* I'll never forget that name. So sneaky," he said in reflection. "Anyway, apparently, he had himself a crosser—"

"—Crosser," Pan said feverishly. "What's that?"

"Think of it as a companion, a sort of 'tour guide,' if you will. The crosser can be your best friend or worst enemy. Most of the strays who come here without crossers end up staying here. Just the way it is. Miles ventured away from his crosser and *apparently*, thought it'd be fun to get inside the locals' heads and start screwing with their minds. He had an agenda all right."

"Which was?"

"The same agenda that all frustrated young men have on their minds, which is to undermine everything they don't agree with. Fortunately for him, his crosser found him, brought him back to his world. If there's anything we took away from the incident, it's awareness. Being more aware of who comes into Gabriel. So," he let out a sigh, "does that answer your question?"

"No," Pan said, lacking the energy to retort. "Not really." She remoistened her lips and cleared her throat. She started to see two Cupids before her. Then, three. She drunkenly dropped to her elbows before she rested on the ground.

Cupid bunched up the blanket underneath her, preventing her head from lying on the ground.

Pan asked more dizzily, "How can we get back to our world?"

Cupid paused, thinking more about Pan's usage in wording, in particular, the word *we*. After Enoon was bit, Cupid heard his son using that one particular word every now and then.

"I know this one crosser," Cupid said and for the time being, pushed aside the one question, which was on his mind. "Goes by the name Creach. I can't promise you that she'll get you where you need to be, but she'll try."

"Creach?" Pan said, as she started to fade. Her eyes bobbed around like pinballs against the sockets of her skull. "What kind of name is Creach. . ."

Pan's eyes suddenly rolled in the back of her head. She fainted. Cupid was there to grab her head before it hit the ground. In doing so, an object fell from his back pocket and hit the ground with a *clinking* sound. A burst of life shot through Pan's body, causing her to power through the gray haze. She concentrated on that clinking sound, then pinpointing it. Her eyes drunkenly followed Cupid picking up the object from the ground. It wasn't a pencil. It was a syringe filled with that same brownish liquid she found pooled over the blanket.

Once more, her eyes rolled in the back of her head.

Everything went dark, as if she had internally flipped off a light switch.

Cupid nodded at Kazlauskas Inc. and told her to grab Pan's legs.

Together, they carried Pan back inside the house.

PRESENT

PAN woke up to the squeak of Cary-Anne opening the front door.

She checked the time on the clock on the nightstand and saw that it was seven o'clock on the dot. Cary-Anne was literally like clockwork.

After shaking away the thought of what happened to her fours years ago, Pan attempted to roll out of bed. Cary-Anne dropped her belongings and rushed to her aide. Pan brushed her away.

"I need to do this on my own for once," Pan said, as she struggled to sit upright.

She tried several times to roll out of bed. Eventually, after much frustration, Pan managed to sit upright on her own. She took a moment to catch her breath.

"How'd you sleep last night?" asked Cary-Anne.

Pan shrugged.

"Not good," she said and grimaced and grabbed her left side.

"Is it still bothering you?"

Once more, Pan shrugged.

Then, over the silence, nodded.

"I can call the doctor if you want," Cary-Anne said, which was met with Pan shaking her head.

"If it's not better by tomorrow," Pan said, "then I'll go."
"You sure? You said that last time, Pandora."
"Yeah," Pan said straightforwardly. "Promise."

☠

ABOUT an hour before lunch, which normally started around eleven o'clock since most of the restaurants closest to her house didn't serve lunch until ten-thirty, Pan was binge watching the entire third season of her favorite dramedy *4 Reelz* on the streaming service, Shh! The show was centered around four family members of the Reale Family: *the father*, Emilio Reale, a wealthy movie producer who spent most of his time away from the camera in a million-dollar beach house in Malibu with the girlfriend-of-the-week and throwing what were known as the most epic parties that'd make a carnival look like an appetizer, if compared a three-course meal; *the mother*, Esther Reale, an inmate of San Anita who already put in six years of a twenty-five year stretch for third-degree murder; *the* hundred and one year old *grandmother*, Mamma Chiara, a well-admired chef who immigrated from Italy to New York City when she was seven years old and made her living from a popular cooking show called *Cooking With Chiara;* the stepsister, Kennedy, a real estate agent who was the daughter of Emilio's second wife; and finally, *the star of the show*, Emilio's rebellious *daughter*, Gigi Reale, a struggling film projectionist who, unlike Kennedy and her humbled background, grew up privileged, yet, after three years in high school, rejected her comfortable life in order to make it on her own as a screenwriter. After Kennedy moved back home from Nowhere, Texas, to Los Angeles, Gigi moved in with her stepsister in a cramped apartment in Beverly Hills. Most of the show revolved around Gigi's life and her frustrations with the movie industry, as well as her job at a less-than-perfect movie theatre struggling to survive during a constantly evolving society where widespread streaming services were slowly, in Gigi's own words, "murdering" movie theatres. The two sisters argued a lot about various issues, either old ones or recent, trendier ones on the news; however, at the end of each show, somehow the two managed to find common ground, despite their stark differences in opinion. After many headlines surfaced from one of the cast members making some off-the-cuff comments about upcoming governor, Avanti Washington, the show was cancelled halfway through filming the fourth season due to what studio execs called "creative differences."

Pan had seen episode three, which was called "Peanut Butter and Jelly." The New Pan, who had been taking a Q-capsule everyday for the past four years, wouldn't have thought anything of the scene when she came across it. If anything, the New Pan would've found it more comical than relatable.

In the episode "Peanut Butter and Jelly," as Gigi, who was scheduled to work on the opening day of the new blockbuster, *Cybersaurus*, which had been sold out ever since its first trailer debuted back in spring, and Kennedy, who was holding an important open house that she had been planning for the past week and a half, were about to head out to work, the two happened to rush out of the living room at the same exact time, thus causing them to get stuck between the doorway. As hard as the two tried to force themselves free, their attempts were unsuccessful. Kennedy would try wiggling herself free—of course, being the drama queen she was, she'd make several insidious jabs at Gigi while doing so—and then Gigi, the quirky anti-social character whose morbid sense of humor drew stocked laughs from a so-called audience, would try kicking herself free—of course, it wouldn't be Gigi without her own share of more personal attacks at her stepsister. Eventually, they gave up and accepted their fate. They were both stuck. Like that rare moment when a basketball got stuck between the rim and backboard. As *4 Realz* had a tendency to do—which was an unearthing comedy from the most serious situations—the two sisters were left to duke it out until they reached the very cornerstone of their personal, yet, at times, trivial gripes.

Most of the episode took place with the two sisters stuck in the doorway, trying to work out their issues. The one issue weighing heavily on Gigi's mind was the fact that Kennedy wouldn't dare let Gigi ask out one of her guy friends, Clark. Kennedy was extremely protective of Clark and knowing Gigi's wild history with men, would find any opportunity to steer Clark away from Gigi by making up the worst traits, like for example, she never used nail clippers to trim her toe nails—which was a lie, Gigi used garden shears (audience laughter)—yet, instead, Gigi chewed them off. Her attempts had an opposite effect and Clark ended up liking Gigi even more based on how unconventional Kennedy had made Gigi out to be.

Toward the end of the episode, Gigi and Kennedy worked through their trust issues. Kennedy gave Gigi her blessing to ask out Clark. Still stuck between that doorway, one of Kennedy's friends, Shay, who was stopping by the apartment to drop off a DVD, found the two sitting on the foyer floor, shoulder-to-shoulder, stuck between the doorway like a human wedge. As Shay reached out her hand to pull Kennedy, Gigi slipped out on her own. Realizing that Gigi could free herself at any time, Kennedy was absolutely furious, as in that "fire and fury" kind. The show always ended with a freeze frame. What better way to end the episode with a freeze frame of Kennedy snarling at Gigi as she leaped at her with both hands curled like hooks, ready to choke the life out of Gigi.

Audience laughter.

Roll credits.

Fade to black.

By the time Pan finished watching the episode, she found herself drifting off into a memory where Vivian was making a comment about the wide doorways in the house. She said it about a year or so ago while she was helping Pan clean out old clothes and accessories from Pan's bedroom. She was carrying an oversized box of childhood stuffed animals packed inside a cardboard box from the bedroom. She couldn't help but mention the doorways throughout the

house and how they were built much wider than any tradi-
tional-sized doorways.

"*Thank God that whoever built this house,*" she said with her
breath labored, "*had an appreciation for wide doorways.*"

As Cary-Anne stepped into the living room and asked
Pan if she had any suggestions for lunch, Pan knew she was
going to push her mom's "menu" on her whether she liked it
or not. As soon as Pan asked for fried chicken, Cary-Anne,
in her own subtle way, suggested grilled chicken. The two
went back and forth, Pan suggesting one food while Cary-
Anne returning with another.

Eventually, Pan broke down Cary-Anne with her unwillingness to eat any of the more healthier food that her mom
had bought her yesterday and convinced her to pick her up
some Eddie Macs.

Cary-Anne suggested a couple of places close by.

On the verge of temper-tantrum, Pan demanded Eddie
Macs.

"I'll start eating better tomorrow," Pan said, pouting.

"No more after today," Cary-Anne said dourly. "Okay?"

"Yes," Pan said. "Okay."

☠

WHILE Cary-Anne left to pick up fast food at Eddie Macs,
which happened to be located on the other side of town,
Pan took the opportunity to search the house. She looked
under things, electronic devices, appliances, and whatnot.
Even tore apart items, including ripping the feathers out of
the couch cushions.

By the time Pan went through every nook and cranny of
the house, she could hardly stand, even with the help of the
walker. She knew that if she sat down she probably
wouldn't be able to get back up again.

Completely wiped from the physical excursion, she sat
herself down against the overturned couch and decided to
rest for what she told herself would only be a moment.

As she leaned her head back against the corner of the
couch, she noticed the ceiling fan above. She peered closer

at the light fixture underneath the fan and couldn't help but notice a wire protruding next to the frosty glass covering.

After some struggling, she managed to stand to her feet. She grabbed a stepladder from the closet and positioned it underneath the fan. She removed the fixture and yanked on the wire, which revealed a camera inside the ceiling fan. The lens of the camera was mounted between a small, narrow opening in the fan. Pan remembered an electrician stopping by not too long ago to repair the ceiling fan. She specially remembered that whenever she flipped the ceiling fan on it'd trigger the breaker and cause the power to cut off inside the living room. Most importantly, she remembered how strange the electrician was. He was not only staring at her, which wasn't at all uncommon, but he was also watching her. He'd frequently mention his parents whenever he talked, as if, in a way, they had control over him and what he said.

Doctor Cherkis, Pan thought. She remembered the conversation she had with him after he prescribed her Quidaquin. It was Doctor Cherkis who referenced Pan to that non-profit organization, RESET, who, essentially, provided Pan with a new custom-built house. Ever since Pan moved into the house, everything went straight downhill for her.

As though she was right on cue, Cary-Anne arrived with Pan's food.

Which was cold.

Cary-Anne dropped the bag of Eddie Macs on the floor from the sight of the destruction inside the living room.

Her mouth was open, but she had no words.

Which, Pan knew, was all an act.

FOUR YEARS AGO

BEYOND the flames, the hazy reflection of Cary-Anne's gawking expression faded in the living room window and was replaced with a blurry face that appeared featureless, as though the face was moving back and forth at a breakneck speed while a photographer was snapping a photograph and the resulting image had what was known as a ghosting effect. The individual—Pan knew he or she was young based on lack of confidence, insecurity, and fidgetiness—was standing over her shivering body on a thick comforter next to the living room window and staring down at her with shaky black eyes. Pan refocused away from Kazlauskas Inc., who was sitting with other shadowy-faced Gabrielites by the fire and redirected her attention toward the stranger danger standing behind her.

In the hallway outside the living room, Pan heard Cupid talking to one of the locals, who had a voice as deep as a well. Among those words, she heard Cupid telling the local that *the reaction was quick*; then he heard *quicker than Enoon.*

"She's still a traveler, Que," the local said.

She heard other words—at least, she thought she heard—words like *narcissist* and *crossing over.*

The two voices turned softer.

Next, she heard footsteps.

Then, the *thap, thap, thap* of snapping fingers at the other end of the room!

"Shim," Cupid whispered. "Out! Now!"

Pan watched the young stranger's reflection dart away from the room, leaving only a fuzzy, fading silhouette in the mirror.

She tried to remember how she wound up here, in the living room, but it felt as if she was hungover and couldn't find a legit timeline, only bits and pieces, like an image of Cupid's son, Enoon, lying in bed.

As Cupid entered the living room and Shim exited left, Pan rolled over to her side until she was facing the hallway. She grimaced slightly from the soreness on her side. It felt as if the left side of her body had been hit by a truck and her entire side pulsed with a heavy pain. Cupid approached Pan.

"He wasn't bothering you, was he?" asked Cupid.

Pan acted as if she didn't know what Cupid was talking about.

"No," she said dumbly.

"Well, if he was, I apologize. Shim's never seen a stray before."

"Why do you keep calling me that?" asked Pan.

"What? *Stray*? Don't take offense. It's just a term we use around here. It's nothing personal."

Pan rolled back on her other side where there was less pain and looked outside. There had to be at least a dozen locals and each one of them was whispering and skittishly shooting worried glances toward the living room window.

"Forgive me for the audience," Cupid said from behind and closed the curtain on the window. "As you can tell, word travels fast around here whenever there's a stray in town. Don't you worry about 'em. They're just curious. That's all."

"Who are they?"

"Mostly locals," he said shortly. "Residents of Gabriel. A few from the town over, Castaneda, who are just passing through."

He kneeled down to Pan's level and asked how she was doing.

"I'm burning up," she uttered, as she glanced at the Mason jar of cream in his right hand. "What happened to me?"

"You were bit by a Culexx."

"I was?"

"Yes."

Once more, Pan glanced at the Mason jar. She noticed the difference in the color, which was much lighter in tone than the other cream he bought at Gulps, as well as the texture of the cream, which was much smoother, less clumpy, like lotion.

"It's the fever," Cupid said.

"So, what the hell does that stuff really do?" she asked.

"It helps slow the spread of the virus," he said and held up the jar for Pan. "If I can slow the spread, then I can bring down the fever. May I?"

She lifted her hand and attempted to feel the red, swollen area along the left side of her neck, which was partially covered with a blanket, but Cupid redirected her hand and told her not to touch it.

"Is it a rash or something?" asked Pan.

Cupid opened the jar.

Immediately, Pan noticed the hint of sweetness while sniffing the cream.

"Not exactly," he said and placed the lid aside. "More like a growth."

"A growth? You mean like what? A tumor?"

Cupid was hesitant to answer.

"Sort of," he said unsurely.

This time, Pan tried to sit up and look at the "growth." Cupid grabbed Pan by her good shoulder and told her to relax. Pan was too weak and exhausted to fight Cupid, who followed by scooping out a dab of so-called "hepa-pod cream" with a tongue depressor and showcasing it to Pan.

"It's for your own good, Pan," he said with untrusting eyes.

Pan allowed him to spread the cream along the side of her neck. Not like he was giving her any choice. At first, the cream was surprisingly cool on her skin.

"It may burn just a bit."

Which it did.

Pan did her best to ignore the burn. Eventually, the burn subsided and the left side of her body felt somewhat numb.

As Pan lay down on her back, she started to relax. She didn't know whether or not it was the cream. But she did feel somewhat more relaxed than she did before Cupid applied that hepa-pod shit.

"Tell me, Cupid," Pan said thoughtfully, "you part of a cult?"

Cupid laughed.

"How you mean?"

"When I was in Enoon's room, I saw a symbol of a sun on his wall. I saw the same symbol a couple other times while we were riding through town."

"You mean The Trinity."

"What's their deal?"

"Many of those in Gabriel worship The Trinity as gods and consider them as the holders of The Light."

"And I take it you don't believe in this Trinity?"

"Once," Cupid said sorrowfully, "maybe. Eventually, though," he said more bluntly, "I came to my senses."

Cupid stood up, walked to a drawer along the wall, reached inside the bottom drawer, and pulled out a raggedy-looking book. He handed Pan a book that bore that same symbol of a sun with three lines projecting outward. Cupid called the book the *First Light*. Pan cracked open the dusty *First Light* book and after skimming the first couples of pages, realized that it wasn't at all different than a book she had once read when she was a young girl. That book had many versions, but she simply called it *The Bible*. And those lines, which she thought were sunrays, were children, three underlings called "The Trinity."

The so-called Genesis of the story started out similar to the Bible's Genesis, albeit with a slight twist. She flipped halfway through the book and being the fast reader she was, skimmed over the filler and managed to catch only the juicy parts: *"The white coats scoured the site of explosion that had paralyzed Maven,"* and *"collected a shard left behind from The Darkness,"* only to later use it in a secret government project called *"Project Third Eye."* The *"white coats found ways to release that ancient Darkness,"* first *"experimenting it on rats, curing"* rats from all *"ailments."* One day, a *"white coat became obsessed with the black shard"* and *"used it on his ailing wife"* without anybody knowing. *"The wife survived."* After recovering from ovarian cancer, *"she* (the wife*) gave birth to triplets called 'underlings,'"* which would later be known as *'The Trinity.'"*

"Interesting read," Pan said and handed the book back to Cupid.

"Keep it," he said. "Maybe it'll come to use one day."

"You sure?"

"Positive—yes."

"Thanks," she said softly, as she ran her finger along the rough texture of the book.

Over the quietness, her eyes lit up with surprise and the thought alone of her sister nearly stole her breath away.

"Cleo?" she uttered. "Where's Cleo?"

She turned toward Cupid, causing the cream to rub off on the blanket.

"Try to keep still," he said, using his hands like a guardrail to keep Pan from sitting up. "You have to let the cream dry."

"Where's my sister, Cleo?"

"I'm sorry," Cupid said. "Who?"

"Cleo," she said louder. "My sister!"

"I don't know what you're talking about, Pan—"

"—What don't you mean? Where is Cleo?"

Cupid scooped more cream onto the tongue depressor, which, after a second and more thorough study, Pan realized was the severed scaly toe of what appeared to be a reptilian creature—possibly an alligator—attached to the end of a wooden stick like a popsicle. As Cupid was about to apply more cream to the areas that Pan had rubbed off, his face slackened. For a moment, he actually flinched from the sight of Pan's shoulder.

Pan immediately recognized the shock rippling through Cupid's face.

"*What*?" she said while filling up with panic. "What is it?"

Cupid was hesitant to respond.

"Cupid?"

In return, Cupid shook his head with mild disgust and discreetly leaned away from Pan.

"It's nothing," he said. "Just let the hepa-pod cream do its magic."

"No," Pan protested. "I want to see it."

Cupid cleared his throat.

"I'm afraid that's a bad idea. It's in your best interest not to—"

"—I want to see!"

Her voice overpowered Cupid and left him with no other option but to show Pan the site of the bite.

Cupid rushed to the bathroom where he grabbed a grimy, cracked handheld mirror and brought it into the living room. He was cautious to hand Pan the mirror and before he committed himself, he warned Pan about what she was about to see and that she must keep calm; otherwise, it would only make her condition much worse.

Pan didn't even give a second's thought to Cupid's advice as she snatched the mirror from his hand, arched her head away from the bite, and aimed the mirror at the area between her neck and shoulder. Pan gasped in horror from the reflection of an ear—or many ears, due to the cracks in the mirror.

"What the hell is that?" asked Pan, as she searched for the best angle by tilting and turning the mirror.

Cupid didn't respond.

While keeping her eyes on one particular piece in the mirror, which happened to be the largest section, a triangular piece that gave her the most detail, she lowered the mirror closer to her neck until she had a clear view of the ear. She picked at the ear with her other hand, even played with it a little by flicking the tip of the ear up and down, up and down.

Surprisingly calm by the discovery, Pan asked, "Is that what I think it is?"

"Please, Pan," Cupid said carefully. "Don't freak out."

"I'm not," Pan said, trailing off.

All of a sudden, the thought hit her—again!

"Just try to relax, Pan."

Pan puckered her face as if she was trying to hold back the emotion.

"Where's Cleo?"

"Like I said, Cleo is not here," Cupid said more patiently. "This may be difficult to understand, but you are now a host and the parasite inside you is trying to manipulate your thoughts, showing you things that aren't there—"

"—But Cleo was with me."

"Maybe she was," Cupid said and touched the side of his temple, "but in your mind. It was just *you*. Your new-me. No one else."

"New-what?" Pan uttered. "I don't understand."

Cupid consoled Pan and suggested that she step outside and meet the locals—he was tempted to tell her, "grab some fresh air to clear your head," but he caught himself.

As Pan delved deeper into herself, her legs grew incredibly numb as if, for a moment, they no longer belonged to her.

☠

As Pan told her version of the story, she could *feel* Cleo rolling her eyes as if Cleo was ultimately showcasing disapproval to the rest of the locals who were gathered around the fire.

Pan dismissed Cleo's gesture and searched for what she was going to say.

"A few days before you went missing," she said finally and recalled the past events, "I was sitting on the edge of the pool with my feet dangling in the water when my phone rang. I looked down at the phone, and I saw your number on the screen. I contemplated whether or not I should answer. I almost didn't. I knew you weren't the type of person to call me because you wanted to talk. You hardly ever called me—"

"—**Not true.**"

"And whenever you did," Pan said over Cleo, "you usually called to ask if I wanted to go on a trip with you because the truth is that you had nobody else to go with you."

Not only that, you think you're better than me; you use me, deep down inside though, you don't care about me, only calls whenever you have no one else to talk to. The truth is I always came second to you.

So not true.

I killed you hundreds of times in my mind. Electrocuted in a bathtub—you always had a way of singing while bathing. You said the acoustics of a bathroom made you sound like Mariah Carey.

They did.

The list goes on and on: burned by the blow dryer; strangled by an electrical cord; pushed off a water slide; choked to death by gramma's famous falafel; run over by an eighteen wheeler while riding *my* Big Wheel that you always hogged; gauged by a Barbie Doll; bludgeoned in the back of the head with a croquet ball; trampled by Staley High Bull-dogs during a Friday night football game.

Countless times, I sent you to the grave. Yet, each time the phone rang and I saw your number, it was like you kept rising from the dead.

Again, Pan could *feel* her eyes rolling.

"The more the phone kept ringing, the more I kept wondering where Danielle went this time. What excursion prompted you to plan your next getaway: Back to Belize? The Ozarks? Sharkman's Cove? Orange Hill? I was even tempted to go on Danielle's phony InstiGarbage page and scroll through her most recent posts of her latest 'vacay.' It was an hour before lunch and there was nobody hanging out at the pool, except for Nurse Ratched who was sunbathing on the other side of the pool and shooting daggers at me while deliberately mouthing every insult in the book under her breath. Vegas from Apartment 213 hadn't showed up yet for his weekly dip and I was still searching for the right starter that would open up our overdue conversation. So, I picked up the phone. Sure enough, I was right."

I wondered why, of all people, you would want to invite me. *What was your real agenda?* You felt as if I always ruined all the fun for you, that I never had a good time, was a party pooper, always complaining, always finding some excuse to be miserable: "that" person. I heard once from Mom about Kirk and his behavior toward her, how he always complained. Yet, behind Mom's back, he'd go off with his drinking buddies and have the time of his life. *Yet*, he'd never allow her to have any fun. So, *immediately*, I was skeptical.

"'The last one for a while,' you said. This time, you were asking to go white water rafting in Colorado. You said how much fun it'd be even though you knew that I wasn't much of a good swimmer and how I *hated* getting into any body of water that wasn't super chlorinated. The last time we talked, I told you about a story involving someone I knew from my junior year and how water went up her nose when she was rafting and a couple of days later, she was hospitalized due to a brain-eating bacteria. You know how much that story freaked me out. Yet, you asked me anyway. Either you did it out of spite or you forgot, like you always do, like everything I say goes through one ear and out the other. You never listen."

"I do to."

"You tried to convince me that it'd be for my own good," Pan said over Cleo as if she wasn't allowing Cleo to respond and whenever Cleo did manage to retort, it was no more than three words. "The thing is you hated water, too. Worst than me."

"You lie—"

"—Yet, after I declined your adventurous getaway, you still ended up going. You were going to go regardless of what decision I made; in fact, you didn't even want me to go with you. You knew what my answer was going to be. Yet, you went ahead and asked me anyway as if you were looking for someone to fight with that day because you were sick and tired of fighting with yourself. I won't forget what you said to me right before you hung up on me." Pan paused, thought carefully about that time leaning over the pool and listening to her sister throw all kinds of expletives at her, most of them beginning or ending with the word *bitch*. Then, finally, once Pan was left bleeding out from insults, Cleo went for the final kill. Those four words resonated inside Pan as she stared at the wavy reflection of herself in the water. *"You're dead to me."*

You're one to talk. "Bull! What a bunch of bull! I never said that—"

"—But you did. And that was the last time I talked to you. Face it, sis. We never got along. You were bubbly, outspoken, the sociable one who craved attention and would dominate a conversation by only talking about herself. I was the introverted one who'd rather spend an evening curled up with a book opposed to hanging out at parties. But *you*, you just couldn't accept that. Could you? I was never good enough for you. You wanted me to be more like you. But the fact: I wasn't you. And I was just fine with that."

Cleo made an airy noise with her mouth, as if she was dry-spitting.

"Are you still talking?"

You're just like her, Pan wondered, especially the part where she completely blotted out everything post-first sentence.

In those final moments, Pan ran through the timeline of the story as to "how" she wound up in Gabriel. Cupid had discovered her alone on the riverbank. Cleo was not there; in fact, she never was. Riding through the countryside, stopping at Gulps, or driving into Gabriel in the back of Cupid's truck: Cleo was a mirage of a thought, a figment, a conjuring inside her head. Whatever Cleo had said either at Gulps or in the back of the truck, Pan had either said or thought. Cleo's actions were instead Pan's actions.

Pan visualized herself entering Gulps with both Cupid and Kazlauskas Inc., then, after momentarily losing herself inside the grip of the black crystal, exiting with Cupid and Kazlauskas Inc.

"You're not my sister," Pan said darkly.

"**Whatever, Two Face,**" Cleo said, smirking.

As Pan fought through the heavy restraint of the parasitic passenger weighing on the left side of her body, she moved her eyes downward toward her feet. The imitation that was Cleopatra attempted to take back control over Pan by forcing her eyes upward at the fire. Pan overpowered Cleo. Her entire body was drenching wet, her hair stringy, her face dripping with murky river water.

To Pan's right, Cupid was telling her to come back inside the house. He advised her to get some rest.

Pan ignored Cupid and focused on her feet, which were submerging in thick mud. Pockets of water bubbled to the surface. Her feet continued to sink until the water reached her shins. She felt a sudden pressure pressed against her body as if even the air itself was pushing against her. Her breath was shorter; the ends of her fingers became tinglier. The tingle rushed up her arms, shoulders, then down her chest.

As Pan sank deeper and deeper into the wet mud until she was neck deep, she felt a balled up fist beating against her chest like a hammer. Her body convulsed, then jolted upward. She was met by a burst of sunlight first, then the worried face of a man in his mid-sixties. He was wearing a yellow helmet, as well as a matching life vest. Behind him was a red kayak rested along the riverbank.

The kayaker sat Pan upright and rubbed the center of her back.

"That's it," he said reassuringly. "You're okay. Just breathe."

Pan did as the kayaker said and breathed in through the nose, out through the mouth. Her lips were blue and bloodless. Blood streaming down the sides of her face.

Once Pan caught her breath, she gathered the rest of her surroundings. From the sound of the rushing water next to her, to the birds chirping in the trees, to the blue skies above her, it looked and *sounded* like home again.

The kayaker shook Pan on the shoulder.

"For a sec," he said, smiling, "I thought I lost you."

Pan combed back the stringy, bloody, soaking wet hair from her face.

"Where am I?"

Then, said, "Sharptooth River."

"What world?"

The kayaker puckered his face in a "huh" expression.

"Earth?"

PRESENT

WHILE Cary-Anne was going number two—or so Pan thought, based on a) Cary-Anne's more than usual coffee consumption due to oversleeping, which led to b) Cary-Anne's breakfast, which consisted of fast-food, more than likely Dempsey's, Burger Inn, or Sandwich Shack, which brought on c) Cary-Anne rubbing her belly throughout most of the morning, which, finally, inspired d) Cary-Anne "quickly" excusing herself to use the bathroom—Pan took advantage of what little time she had left and rummaged through Cary-Anne's purse.

As soon as Cary-Anne flushed the toilet—Pan knew she had at least another flush left—Pan dug out a company card inside the inner pocket.

The card read "Neuvak Corporation."

As predicted, Cary-Anne flushed once more.

Pan put the card back in the purse and walked back to the futon where she sat down and watched the rest of episode nine of *4 Reelz*.

☠

MOST of the day was a complete haze for Pan.

Apart from spending most of the day keeping a close eye on her aide, who, without Pan's consent, scheduled an appointment with Doctor Cherkis tomorrow after she witnessed Pan making a grimace, she put together the missing pieces of what happened four years ago. She couldn't believe it had been that long. *Four* flipping *years*. Where did the time fly? Pan tried her best to hide the pain in front of Cary-Anne. She thought it was best not to argue with Cary-Anne. She thought it'd only make it harder to do what she needed to do.

Instead, Pan complied and went along with Cary-Anne.

Once night fell and Cary-Anne ended her shift, Pan hobbled past the "Doctor Apt." reminder on the fridge. She fixed herself what she thought was going to be her last supper: a plate of leftover fried chicken, which she heated up in a microwave, steaming hot collared greens and baked sweet potatoes with a side of hot glazed donuts that she had stashed away late last night. She even planned to peel and eat the skin off the chicken. There was nothing tastier than eating the skin of fried chicken.

The food did not require a knife, but Pan grabbed the sharpest one she could find in the holder. She placed the food on a tray and took her food back to the living room, ate, and savored each bite.

Once she was finished with her dinner, she sat in silence. Not once did she ever turn on the TV or even contemplate watching TV. She turned to that knife, which was lying on the table. She picked up the knife and ran her fingertip along the edge of the blade to feel its sharpness. She pulled up her T-shirt over both her saggy breasts.

Pan could still feel it moving around inside her as if it was slowly growing on its time, not Pan's, stealing every precious moment of her day, manipulating her, and at times, resisting each move Pan made by sending waves of stabbing pains throughout the left side of her abdomen. It was either slithering around underneath her folds or beating its pointy fingers along her ribcage like a xylophone or tugging at her nerves, bunching them up like spaghetti, or gnawing at her bones or pushing and reshuffling her vital organs around as though it was playing a wicked game with Pan. Once and for all, Pan turned the tip of the blade to herself and aimed directly at the protrusion along her loin.

As she was about to thrust the blade into her flesh, Pan pulled up the image of Cleo's face in her mind as if she could now easily access it at any time.

Then, Pan cut away.

☠

IN the darkness, Pan heard birds *chirping* and *tweeting*.

The chirps and tweets synchronized to the repetitive sounds of beeping.

Pan cracked open her eyes and followed the sounds to a heart monitor next to her bed.

The number on the machine skipped a couple of points, shooting up from 78 to 85. The beeping sound increased slightly.

"Where am I?" she mumbled.

Her mouth was parched, the words like sandpaper rubbing against her throat.

"What happened?" she asked the dark, blurry figure standing at the doorway.

The lanky dark figure stared at Pan and just as Pan's eyes started to focus, it stepped out of the room.

"Who are you?" Pan asked groggily.

The words became harder and harder to deliver. Each one was heavy, sluggish, and brought on a stabbing, choking-like pain.

Moments later, another figure stepped into the room.

Pan realized it was a hospital room; however, everything appeared somewhat larger in size. The heart monitor was the first indication, then the TV mounted in the corner of the room, then that uncomfortable bed, then the mesh of cords and tubes attached to her body, then, finally, the nurse.

"Welcome back to the land of the living," she said, holding Pan's hand.

"What. . . " The words were so dry that she couldn't even spit them out.

The nurse grabbed a Styrofoam cup with one of those twisty straws.

"Here," she said, as she held the cup to Pan's face, "a little sip of aqua."

Pan didn't question what was in the cup. The nurse helped nudge Pan's head forward, as she maneuvered the end of the straw into Pan's mouth. Pan took a sip of the "aqua." The sip, like the words, was heavy. She could feel the liquid sliding down her throat and entering her stomach. Nonetheless, the words came out more fluidly.

"What happened?" asked Pan, as she cleared her throat.

"Lucky for you," the nurse said, as she placed the cup on the tray and stood by Pan's bedside, "you have a guardian angel looking after you. A good Samaritan found you wandering around on the side of the road. You were pretty banged up. You had several lacerations on both your arms and lower abdomen. You had a laceration just above your right eye. It was deep enough to require some stitches. He thought maybe you were struck by a car, maybe a hit-and-run."

Pan raised her arm, which was attached to an IV, and ran her fingers over the area above her right eye. She felt a bandage first. Then, she ran her finger along the cheekbone of her skull, which was still tender.

"Give it time to heal," the nurse said.

As Pan drew her attention back to her arm, a rush of panic suddenly flooded her body. The size of her arm and hand was much different. Her breathing was different as well; and each time she spoke, she felt as if she was no longer carrying around a load. Her eyes moved down her body. The panic was tight now. All up inside her. In her chest. Her throat. Her head. To her left, all of those machines were getting louder, that *beeping* sound faster.

The nurse looked closer at the heart monitor.

"Pandora," she said, reading Pan's BPM, "I need you to relax." She leaned closer to Pan and asked motherly, "Can you tell me what's bothering you?"

Pan was touching and studying every inch of her body as if she was somehow trapped inside a suit of flesh that did not belong to her.

"What happened to me?" asked Pan, as her heart rate increased. "What world is it?"

"World?"

Pan continued to study her body, her arms. They no longer had flab hanging underneath her biceps. She pulled off the blanket and lifted up her gown. Her abs were flat. She no longer had burdensome folds of flesh.

"As I've said, Pandora, you were found injured on the side of the road," the nurse said patiently, "a man brought you here to Peach Street Memorial."

"Mirror," Pan said, holding out her hand, "do you have a mirror?"

"Please, Pandora," the nurse said and deliberately let out a sigh, "I need you to relax."

With her voice raised, Pan asked once more as if she wasn't going to ask it again, "Where's a mirror?"

The nurse reached into her pocket, pulled out a compact mirror, and handed it to Pan. Pan immediately opened the mirror and looked at her face in the reflection. She was her old self again, as in she looked the same way she did four years ago. Except for one minor discrepancy.

"My eye," Pan said. "Why is my left eye brown?"

Her once green eyes were always the two features of her body where she felt the most confidence. She was the most proud to have those three letters GRN on her driver's license. She received many compliments on her eyes. She believed that the only thing she and her mom had in common were their eyes. Cleo, on the other hand, had gotten her eyes from their biological father, Kirkland, whose eyes proudly matched the color of his skin.

"Right," the nurse said and hung her head for a moment. "I assure you Doctor Berzins will explain everything."

"I don't understand," Pan said, the mirror lowering from her face.

"Pan, can you remember anything?"

Pan combed her thoughts and searched for answers. She had nothing, only a flickering image of herself sitting in front of what looked like a campfire.

She made an attempt to answer the question, but her words turned to mush.

"Give it time," the nurse said. During the pause, she pointed at her nametag and read her name to Pan, "Name's Maya. Doctor Berzins will be in here shortly. For the time being, is there anything you need that I can get you?"

Pan drifted off for a moment.

"No," she said and started messing with the IV along the top of her hand.

Maya separated Pan's hand and told her to leave the IV alone.

"You were severely dehydrated," she said and held Pan's hand. "I know how irritating it can be, but it's for your own good, okay."

As Maya was about to walk away, she was sidetracked by a thought.

"Oh yeah," she said, rotating around. "Your mother was here earlier, but you were out of it. She told me to call her as soon as you woke up. Is there anything you want me to tell her?"

"No," Pan said again.

Maya walked back to the bed and showed Pan the nurse's button on a corded remote dangling over the handrail.

"If you need *anything*, just hit that button. Okay?"

"Yeah," Pan said, trailing off.

Maya smiled and left the room.

☠

PAN heard a *knock* on the door but was too exhausted to open her eyes.

She drifted off for what felt like a few hours; however, by the time she finally woke up, Vivian was staring down at her.

Startled by her mom's presence, Pan wondered how long she had been standing by her bedside.

Wearing the look of a woman who appeared more frightened than comforted by her daughter, Vivian held Pan's hand and asked her how she was doing.

Pan broke down and told her that she didn't know where she could even begin to answer that question.

"Pan," Vivian said, as the disappointment appeared in her face, "I talked to a detective earlier today. He wants to talk to you whenever you're able. He said he has a few questions he'd like to ask you."

"Detective?" Pan furrowed her brow. *The blood*, she thought, as she noticed only a couple of cuts along her arms and legs. *Was it mine?* Or, someone else's? "Why does a detective want to talk to me?"

"There was some damage to a bus stop," she said to Pan. "They found some blood on the shattered glass. They're still trying to find footage. The reason why they're so interested in talking to you is because you were found not too far from the scene."

"I remember crashing through glass," Pan uttered, as she searched deeper into her thoughts. "Everything is foggy before and after that."

Pan suddenly heard yet another *knock* on the door.

Vivian awkwardly removed her hand from Pan's and clutched the hand railing alongside the bed.

The doctor first nodded at Vivian, as if they had already spoken to one another.

Pan pointed out the white coat that he was wearing. She couldn't stop staring at that white coat.

"Sorry. I didn't meant to disturb you, Pandora," he said, drawing his attention to Pan. "My name is Doctor Berzins. How are you feeling today—"

"—What happened to me?"

"As Maya had already explained to you, you were found on the side of the—"

Pan said more fiercely, "It still doesn't explain how I lost over six hundred pounds in one day."

Vivian rubbed Pan's forearm.

"Honey," she said, "six hundred pounds? What are you talking about?"

"Just the other day I weighed around seven hundred and fifty pounds. Maybe even more than that. Now, I'm back to the same size I was four years ago. Please explain to me how that is even possible? Not to mention, my eyes are a different color."

"Pandora," Doctor Berzins said mildly, "what I'm about to tell you may very well come as a shock to you, but you probably came as close to death as anybody would in your condition."

The word alone *condition* infuriated Pan.

"Condition? What's my condition?"

"What I do know for certain, Pandora, is that you ingested a cocktail of over-the-counter sleeping pills that could've easily killed you and if we hadn't found you when we did, then you wouldn't be here talking to us. That's the hard truth. To be blunt, the only explanation I can give you is that you had a mental breakdown."

For someone who was in a line of work that thrived off long, complex words attached to words like *syndrome* or *disease*, his vague usage of words, like mental breakdown, sounded as if the doctor didn't have a clue how to diagnose Pan or her condition.

"What about my weight?"

"What about it?" the doctor said in a snarky tone, as he overlapped his hands over one another. "When you arrived here, you were the same weight as you are now."

Pan had absolutely no words; in fact, even her thoughts were sparse. Just the thought alone of losing all of that weight in such a short period of time sent waves of heat flashing through her body.

"What about my eye?" asked Pan.

"It is extremely rare, but the iris is known to change color whenever the nerve pathway from the brain to the eye has become disrupted from blunt force trauma and in your case, a possible fall." Then, *how does that explain both eyes, smarty pants?* "Unfortunately," he said, carefully delivering his words, "the damage may be permanent."

"What does that mean?" Vivian asked over Pan. "Will her eye color eventually return to normal?"

"Most cases," he said grimly, "it's unlikely. I can refer you to an ophthalmologist. For the time being, he or she may recommend wearing contacts."

"I'm not wearing contacts," Pan said.

The doctor had no response for Pan. He gave her more of a "you're shit out of luck" type of shrug paired with a facial expression that Pan was almost tempted to open-hand slap.

AFTER a series of survey-style questions and satisfactory ratings and formalities, which were all a part of the tedious process of being discharged from Peach Street Memorial, Pan was super-relieved once the orderly stepped into the room with a wheelchair.

Pan said that she could walk, but Vivian insisted on having the orderly wheel her out.

Speaking through the corner of her mouth, she teased, "Who would pass up the offer to be carried out like the queen consort?"

He was *kind of cute*, Pan thought. She admitted to herself that the notion of being wheeled around, if only for a short while, intrigued her.

The orderly, whose name was Kyle, helped Pan into the wheelchair; and once she signed her signature on the discharge form, she was a free woman.

Kyle wheeled Pan from the hospital room.

On the way out, Doctor Cherkis was talking to a nurse at the other end of the hallway. Pan had seen the doctor's face before but couldn't quite pinpoint when or where, even though that *where* part was a no brainer.

The doctor keenly turned his eyes toward Pan, kept them there in a cold gaze, then walked the other way.

Pan jarred the many questions she had bouncing around her head and focused on her surroundings.

Vivian excused herself for a moment.

"Geez Mom," Pan whined, as she fiendishly bounced her leg against the foot rest, "you act like you enjoy being here."

As one of her many nervous ticks, like chewing her nails or cracking her jaw and knuckles, Cleo used to bounce her leg a lot. Pan didn't understand why, all of a sudden, she was bouncing her leg.

Vivian told the two that she'd meet them in the lobby.

"You can't stand it here, can you?" Kyle said, as he wheeled Pan to the elevators.

"You're very perceptive," Pan said moodily.

"I'm not a fan of this place either."

As Kyle wheeled Pan down the hallway, Pan couldn't help but notice all of the dark and empty hospitals rooms. They passed one room, which was occupied with a couple of janitors. One of them was pulling the blood-soaked sheets from a hospital bed while the other one was mopping up a puddle of blood.

"Frankly," Kyle said over Pan's trance, "it gives me the creeps."

Pan only caught that one word *creeps*.

"Then why you work here?" she asked, looking forward.

"Well, every now and then, you get to meet beautiful women like yourself."

"Wow," Pan said, unimpressed. "Is that a line?"

"Not a line," he said shortly with a smirk on his face. "Just an observation." Kyle received nothing from Pan, who couldn't even remember the last time a guy had given her a compliment on her appearance. Somewhere behind her blank expression, the corners of her lips were rising into her cheeks in what appeared to be a smile.

They arrived at the elevators.

Kyle was first to push the down arrow.

As they both waited for the elevators to arrive, Pan picked out her mom from behind a crowd of nurses. She was talking to two men, one being Doctor Berzins and the other one a tall man who was dressed in an all black suit. The top button of his shirt was unbuttoned. Pan thought he looked like a more refined version of a minister, one of those televangelist types who flew around in expensive jets paid for by his flock and profited from selling God. He was wearing Wayfarers, which Pan thought was unusual since they were indoors. He had a round gray spot about the size a quarter, which appeared to be a birthmark, in his finely trimmed beard.

The *ding* of the elevator pulled Pan's attention forward. Before her the elevators doors were opening.

Pan redirected her attention back the strange man talking to Vivian at the end of the hallway. Several nurses were obstructing her line of sight.

As Kyle wheeled Pan into the empty elevator, she noticed a sign on the wall, displaying the different floors.

The name of Floor 13, which was the floor she was currently on, was crossed out with a piece of tape.

The words *Under Construction* were written in a black Sharpie.

Kyle pressed the L button.

Which she assumed was Lobby.

She closely inspected the other numbers along the panel. There weren't any. None. Only two buttons, the L button and then a blank button that had a lock next to it. The only way it appeared to work was through a key.

As Kyle talked about a book with the name *March* in the title, Pan zoned out. She slightly rotated her head to the right. In the reflection of the metal wall, she spotted the ring of keys attached to a string hanging from a clip on Kyle's waistband. *Why would you need a key to access that floor?*

As soon as the question reached the tip of her tongue, she was startled by yet another *ding.*

The doors opened to a narrow hallway.

Pan didn't recognize the area until they rounded a hallway and arrived at the lobby.

"Just a short cut," Kyle said, as if he could predict what Pan was going to say before she even said it.

The sight of the lobby triggered a memory. She spent two weeks in the hospital, mostly coming and going after her grandmother went in for a simple procedure called an upper gastrointestinal endoscopy and wound up on life support due to a bacterial infection that nearly killed her. The more she thought about it, the more she started to question her own memory. Wondering whether or not it was a dream. Or, if it really did happen.

As Pan kept to herself in front of the receptionist desk, Vivian finally arrived.

"Who were you talking to back there?" asked Pan.

"I had a couple of questions for Doctor Berzins."

"No," Pan said. "Not him. The other guy. Who was he?"

Caught off guard by the question, Vivian said hesitantly, "What other guy?"

"The black one," Pan said bluntly, as if her mom only identified by color.

"Right," she said, as if, for a moment, she had what she'd call a human moment. "That's the hospital administrator. He's a nice man. He just wanted to ask me how your stay went and if there was anything he could do for us—"

"—And what'd you say?"

"What do you think I said, Pan?" Vivian asked more strictly. "I said everything went well."

"*Well,*" Pan said, thinking, "why didn't he ask me? I mean, wouldn't it make more sense to ask me?"

Trying not to make an outburst in front of Kyle from Pan's persistent grilling, Vivian clenched her teeth. She said sharply, "It wasn't like I was planning to talk to him, Pandora. He was just trying to be nice. That's all."

"Okay," Pan said, trailing off.

Kyle wheeled out Pan from the front of the hospital and the two waited by the curb while Vivian fetched the car.

She should've felt a weight lifting from her shoulders as soon as that fumy air hit her face.

Surprisingly, the weight felt heavier.

☠

AFTER a few minutes of riding in silence, Pan lazily rested her head on the passenger door and stared at herself through the side view mirror. She was more fascinated with the color of her eyes and how one of the irises was brown.

"What happened to my father?" asked Pan.

Surprised by the question, Vivian knew she was referring to Kirkland instead of Callum. Ever since Vivian and Callum were married, Pan never ever referred to Callum as "father" or "dad." He was just Callum, the man who was present.

"Your father, Kirkland," Vivian said, gaining more confidence, "he died last year. Liver cancer. I'm sure you were aware he was a drinker. I guess his drinking days caught up with him." The comment didn't draw any reaction from Pan. Which caused Vivian to look over at Pan several times to make sure she was all right. Pan continued to stare at the ghost in the mirror. "Pan," Vivian said more directly, "I was going to tell you—eventually. Before the car accident I knew you were trying to reach out to him. *But*," she said, sighing, "after your accident, you never spoke a word of his name. I hoped maybe you made your peace and moved on with your life." Once more, she took her eyes off the road and shot a longer glance at Pan. "So why are you asking me about your father, Pan?"

Pan sat up more straightly and shrugged.

"I dunno," she said. "I was just thinking about him."

"I'm sorry I didn't tell you about him sooner, Pan," Vivian said while glancing back and forth from the road to Pan.

"You hated him that much, didn't you?"

"No," Vivian said, as sorrow came over her. "I didn't hate him. I just. . . "

"What?"

"I gave up on him."

☠

THE rest of the ride home was quiet.

As soon as Vivian pulled the car into the driveway in front of Pan's house, Pan perked up from the sight of the house.

"I live here?"

"Four years ago, a generous individual anonymously paid for the house, had it furnished, you didn't have to make a single house payment. The word *lucky* is an understatement. You were blessed."

"I don't feel blessed," Pan said depressingly. "Why in the world would some stranger buy a house for me?"

"There are decent people out there, Pan," Vivian said, as she studied the confusion on Pan's face. "People who want to help out others without the publicity. Personally," she said from the corner of her mouth, "those who help out others in front of the camera are doing it for *other* reasons."

"It just doesn't make any sense. That's all."

"It doesn't have to make any sense." Vivian placed her hand over Pan's and said more friendly than motherly, "Doctor Berzins told me it'll take some time for your memory to come back."

"Who are you again?"

Silence formed inside the car.

Vivian glared at Pan, who was holding back the laughter.

"That's not funny," she said seriously.

"It is, a little," Pan said, as Vivian cut the engine.

She walked around the car, opened the passenger door, and as she was about to assist Pan from the car, Pan waved her away and said, "Not like I'm crippled."

Vivian stood back, watched and waited for Pan to stand on her own, and then, once Pan was able to walk on her own, she led the way. She opened the door for Pan. Pan stepped inside the house and surveyed the living room. Like the exterior of the house, the interior was similarly, if not, more foreign to her.

☠

WHILE Pan and Vivian were eating garden salads for lunch at the kitchen table—Pan mostly picking at hers—Vivian's purse chirped. She stopped eating, reached into her purse, and pulled out an iPad.

"That's must be Allen."

"Who? Your slimy lawyer friend who I talked to at the hospital?"

"Don't talk about Allen like that," Vivian said, her tone bitter. "Believe it or not, but it's my lawyer friend who's working his butt off trying to get your butt off the hook. If worse comes to worst: you may have to pay for the damages."

"That's the most butts I've ever heard you say in one sentence."

"I thought you couldn't remember anything."

Pan shrugged and pushed around the grape tomatoes inside the bowl of iceberg lettuce.

Vivian opened her iPad and clicked on the email Allen had sent her.

"It's the surveillance video from the corner of 3rd and Harkam," Vivian said, as she opened the link and watched the video clip.

Pan moved her eyes from the salad and carefully watched her mom watch the video.

"So?"

"You wanna watch it?" asked Vivian.

"Should I?"

Vivian sighed.

"Yes," she said, placing the iPad on the table. "You should."

Pan reached over and grabbed the iPad. She played the video clip, which was thirty-seven seconds.

In the video, she was stumbling over the sidewalk along a fairly quiet intersection.

"I don't remember any of this," she said while watching. "I look like a baby taking her first steps."

"Keep watching," Vivian said, as she, too, carefully watched Pan and her reactions to the video.

In the video, she staggered and tripped over her own feet and crashed directly into a glass pane of the bus stop.

Pan cringed from the sight of the fall.

"Luckily, there was nobody waiting for a bus," Vivian said, "otherwise, you could've been looking at a lawsuit."

Pan stopped the video and slid the iPad toward Vivian.

"Yeah," she mumbled and hung her head. A dark, devilish grin flashed along her face. She said sardonically, "**We sure are glad that didn't happen.**"

Unaware of the grin, Vivian immediately noticed the change in Pan's behavior and how she had gone from depressed to super-depressed.

"Are you okay?" asked Vivian.

Pan thought carefully about the question.

Then, responded: "Even when I try to remember what happened on the day, I only get these flashes, certain tastes and smells. And it all feels like the past four years of my life have been one on-going nightmare that I can't wake up from even if I try." With tears brimming in her eyes, she turned to Vivian and asked, "Why can't I remember what happened to me?"

Vivian reached across the table and grabbed Pan's hand.

"It'll come back to you," she said, tightening her grip. "Just give it time."

☠

PAN walked Vivian to the front door and said her goodbyes.

Vivian said she'd stop by tomorrow and check on how Pan was doing.

After Pan watched Vivian drive away, she walked back into the house.

As she was making her way into the kitchen, she stepped on a sharp object in the carpet. A sudden pain shot up her big toe, causing her to recoil. Pan lifted up her foot and pulled out a tiny shard of glass, which was embedded in the carpet.

She held the squared piece of glass close to her face and closely inspected it. Then, she kneeled down to the carpet and found yet another piece of glass below the coffee table, which was made out of oak; however, she was more intrigued by the smell of the carpet. She leaned down for a closer whiff. The carpet had a fragranced smell, as though it had recently been cleaned.

As she sat upright, she also noticed the sales tag hanging from the bottom of the futon. She yanked off the tag, which appeared brand new. She ran both hands over the fabric covering the futon and strangely, it appeared new. She moved toward the fold of the futon. Normally, she should've found crumbs or coins, anything that had fallen in the gritty wrinkles of the fabric. She didn't find anything. She stood up and studied the other furniture in the living room.

For some reason, Pan thought the furniture looked larger in size, as if she was the only feature of the living room that didn't quite fit.

☠

LATER that afternoon, when Pan was using the restroom, she came across yet another item that made her question what had really happened to her.

As she reached for a square of toilet paper, she noticed the capsule behind the toilet in the warped reflection of the toilet paper holder. She finished her business and did so in a rush, then flushed the toilet, then slipped her pants back on.

She squatted down in a tight space next to the toilet and used the end of the plunger like a hockey stick to slapshot out the capsule.

Once the capsule was within reach, she picked up the capsule, which had the letter "Q" on it.

Instead of flushing the capsule down the toilet, she decided to pocket it.

☠

RIGHT before Pan was about to fix herself a healthy TV dinner that Vivian bought for her earlier that morning, she found herself wandering from the kitchen to the bedroom for no apparent reason. She stepped into the bedroom and found herself looking around. She completely forgot what she was doing in the bedroom. She pulled her attention to the bedroom doorway, in particular, the width, and found herself studying it.

She walked over to the doorway and closely examined it.

"I don't remember these doorways being so wide," she said to herself.

Over the sound of the running air condition, she heard Vivian's words inside her head: *I just want my daughter back.*

Pan froze.

Was it a dream?

Or was it the other?

She leaned toward "the other."

☠

THE strange man in black, whom Pan had witnessed talking to her mom and Doctor Berzins at Peach Street Memorial, exited from a parallelogram-shaped building numbered "36" inside a heavily-guarded business park occupied by a crew of heavily armed security guards attired with orange and burgundy uniforms that had the letters "NC" written on a badge worn over the sleeve.

With a small blue ice cooler in his hand, he made his way through a parking lot until he finally reached a black Crown Vic.

Once he stepped inside the car, which was as hot as an oven from the Arizona heat, he placed the ice cooler in the passenger seat and cracked open the windows to air out the car. He removed the black shades from his cloudy grayish eyes and wiped the sweat from the top of his brow with a handkerchief.

He paused mid-wipe and felt a chilly presence in the backside of the car.

All of a sudden, a burst of Lazarus Light shined throughout the inside of the car.

Once the brilliant light dimmed to a soft, computer monitor-like glow, Cupid, who was wearing the Lazarus coat, revealed himself in the backseat.

"What's in the cooler?" a voice asked from behind.

"If it isn't my favorite crosser—"

"—Ex-crosser," he said and nodded his head at the strange bearded man sitting in the driver's seat. "Hello, *Narcissus*. So, what's in the cooler?"

The strange man, Narcissus, used one of his strongest senses to pinpoint Cupid's exact location.

His nostrils flared.

"None of your damn business," Narcissus said. "That's what."

"Very well," said Cupid, as he stared at the storm clouds in Narcissus's eyes. "So, how'd you know it was me?"

"I can smell you from a mile away, Lover boy."

"Amazing," he said cynically, "even a blind man can detect me. You know, I really thought I could maneuver my way around your world without getting spotted. Was I wrong? Lately, it's been slightly more challenging considering people now all have a camera in their possession and would jump at any opportunity to capture something, let's say, foreign to your world."

"Right," Narcissus said. "Big Brother. Who can blame them?"

"I see you're still doing all of Neuvak's dirty work. When you finally gonna realize those people don't care about you? Never have."

"Unlike you, Cupid," Narcissus said, "I don't let my personal feelings get in the way of an impersonal job."

"Yeah," Cupid said more arrogantly. "That's because you're not human."

"You don't know what's going on, do you?"

"Should I?"

"Someone," he corrected himself, "*something* is picking off members of the Board of Directors. Five now just in the last month. Last week, one of the board member was sent home after complaining of a sore throat. Out of precaution, he took the afternoon off; and a few hours later, his body was discovered about two miles from his house by a delivery truck driver. He dropped dead on the street, no warning at all. Just a sore throat, as he said. His wife mentioned that he went out for a jog around the neighborhood to help sweat out the sickness. Now, I have to contain the situation before it gets out of hand."

"Well, it shouldn't be a problem for you."

Narcissus didn't respond to Cupid's comment.

Then, in the wake of the silence, Cupid decided to make up his own theories, sort of fill in all those blanks: "Sounds like a disgruntled employee getting back at those in charge."

"Hardly," Narcissus said, as he was in no mood to hear Cupid and his soapbox lecture. There was something about the summers in Arizona that made him as irritable as a toothache. He'd cringe at those who flippantly disregarded it as a dry heat. "So you're here to collect, am I right?"

"That's right," Cupid said. "So, you got it or what?"

"Yeah," Narcissus drawled, reached into the glove compartment, and pulled out a small jar carrying a toxioplexus. "I got it."

Narcissus handed the jar to Cupid.

"I can't believe it survived in the heat."

"*This?* It'll survive in any condition."

"You really think it works?" Cupid said, looking over the toxioplexus.

"The snake worm will absorb the parasite," Narcissus said. "*But*," he emphasized for Cupid, "make sure you remove it after the infection is gone."

"How will I know?"

"You'll know."

Once more, Cupid looked over the toxioplexus.

"I'll take your word for it."

"By the way, how's he doing?"

"Not good," Cupid said grimly. "It's spreading faster. How about the girl?"

"Which one?"

"Pandora."

"So far, so good."

"Does she remember anything?" asked Cupid.

"I thought you didn't care."

"I don't," he said callously.

Narcissus flexed his right ear. "You know, you're not any good at lying, Cupid. I know you've been checking up on her? Don't bother," he said before Cupid could return. "I can't hear the lie in your voice."

"I just—she seemed different from the others."

Narcissus backtracked to Cupid's original question.

"As far as we know," he said, "no. Not that much. For all she knows, it was all a bad dream. But I'm sure, you already know that."

Cupid said more casually, "If my memory serves me correct about your world—or, at least what I remember of my time spent in your world—a bad dream lasting four years isn't a bad dream. That's hell."

"And that place you now call home isn't any different?"

Ignoring the comment from Narcissus, Cupid said, "So, that's it. The project was considered a success?"

"According to Berzins, he thinks so. Say," Narcissus said, as if the idea just sprung to mind, "I might have another job for you, a big one, if you're interested."

"No chance in hell." Cupid smirked. The Lazarus Light suddenly brightened and shot like a knife-like glare through the car. "See you around, Narcissus."

"Yeah" Narcissus said, as he moved his cloudy grayish eyes to the rear view mirror as if he was undisturbed by the blinding light. "See ya."

Cupid faded away inside the glare, which could've past as the sun reflecting off a metallic surface. Eventually, like Cupid, the glare faded.

To the naked eye, the back door appeared to open and close on its own.

Narcissus placed the black shades back on his face, started the ignition, and drove away.

☠

JACK anxiously waited inside the stolen minivan with a Virginia license plate that appeared as if it had been recently—and suffice to say, poorly—screwed-in based on the wear and indentations along the corners of the plate, as well as fresh circular-shaped etching around the holes from where the bolts that secured the plate to the bumper had been stripped and replaced with brand new ones.

The parallel parking appeared rushed or done by a driver who wasn't familiar with the city or all of the above. The minivan was parked with the front left end slightly protruding outward into the street. On the other side of the minivan next to the sidewalk was an old, rundown twelve-story building that consisted mostly of small businesses, one of them being a heavily-trafficked jewelry store run by "Billy Bling," his real name William Steinman, whose clients included A-list celebrities, elites, and top tier athletes.

As the windshield wipers sloshed back and forth, Jack stared at the handful of customers who were waiting on line. Some with umbrellas while others braving the downpour by doing the whole popped-collar jaded gumshoe gesture with their heads sunken between their shoulders like a frightened turtle. They were standing in front of *Sal's* Bagels, a popular bagel shop that had its roots firmly embedded in New York. Sal's had been around since The Great Depression. Several investors tried multiple times to persuade, even, at times, coerce Sal into franchise by tempting Sal to start up his own chains across the country or expanding his brand by offering him a spot for his famous bagels in the bread aisle of every grocery store. Sal had five shops, one for each borough. Except for the one in Brooklyn, which shared space with a laundromat simply called "The Mat," each shop had its own building.

The sound of shouting made Jack more alert.

Appalled yet, at the same time, incredibly frightened by the bombastic chatter on the sidewalks, both in front of the building and the other across the street, between the two heated New Yorkers who were about to swap bullets, Jack rolled up the window to drown out the noise.

"*Are you ready?*" a phlegmy voice said from behind Jack.

"After driving clear across the country, I think I deserve an explanation as to what's really going on here," Jack not only said, but demanded. "What is it that you're not telling me?"

Jack turned his eyes toward the rear view mirror and shot a glance at the dark slender figure sitting in the back of the minivan. The grayish, wrinkled face was covered in the shadows of a hoody. Which, for Jack, had only made the situation worse, especially after having seen her face, then having to witness it in a darker, moodier light.

"In time, I promise I'll tell you everything—"

"—*Star*," he said, tightening his fists over the steering wheel, "I'm losing my patience here. You have to give me something. Anything. . . "

Star, the dark damsel in disguise, remained quiet. Both of her beady black eyes—which were much farther apart on her face and nearly touching the sides of her temples—lit up a hazy gray color from the headlights of a passing car.

"Listen, Star," Jack said, his voice calmer, "I know a lot of plastic surgeons, good ones, who can take a look at you."

"Are you going to help me or not, Jack?"

"I wouldn't have driven this far if I wasn't. This Billy guy," Jack said, trying to block out the noise outside, "he knows I'm coming, right?"

"He does."

The shouting across the street intensified.

One of the men had his hand behind his back, as if he was about to brandish a gat.

"We're running out of time, Jack," Star said to Jack, who turned his bloodshot eyes from the man on the sidewalk to the rear view mirror.

"All right," Jack said, giving up. "You sure you don't want to come in with me?"

"No can do," Star said. "Warrick has eyes everywhere."

"He's that dangerous, huh?"

"I wouldn't exactly refer to Warrick as a he." Jack managed to get out one word from his mouth, which wasn't a word at all but more so an incoherent utterance, before Star cut him off, "Even though Warrick may be wearing the body of a human, trust me, Jack, Warrick is anything but human. But if it makes you feel more comfortable referring to Warrick as your own kind, then so be it."

"You mean, *our* kind," Jack said sharply.

Star ignored Jack, especially his passion.

"Take the most dangerous entity in the world and multiply it by ten. That's what I'm up against."

"What *we're* up against," Jack said, less sharp, more doubtfully.

"Right."

"So what the hell does he," Jack paused and corrected, "Warrick want?"

"What every asshole who can't handle their own shit wants," Star said more upfront. "*Control.* He could've just stopped by sacrificing that poor girl for his little experiment, got his magic medicine, and been done with it." She shakes her head from the very thought of his plan. "That wasn't good enough for him, nothing ever is. He wants complete control over people, to bring people back into a world where they lack free will. Does that remind you of anybody, Jack?" Star asked but didn't expect an answer from Jack. "Just imagine an entire world under one..." Star paused in a similar fashion to Jack and thought extra carefully about her next usage of words to explain this tyrannical-type of character whom she was so tempted to refer to as, not a thing, but something far less relative than an inanimate object,

"... *man's* control. Worse case scenario, if that was to happen, 'if,' that's not a civilization anymore, Jack. That's a puppet show."

"Then, we can't let that happen. Can we?"

"The world doesn't belong to Warrick, Jack," she said. "It *never* will. This world, this land, it doesn't belong to anyone. Never has. I'd like to think that we were put here to take care of the world, not destroy it."

"In an ideal world, yes," Jack said unsurely. "I'd like to think so too."

Star said solemnly, "The world doesn't have to be ideal, Jack. The world was never intended to be ideal. But if it's a fraction of ideal, I'll take that any day of the week." Under the brim of the hoody, she moved her beady eyes up at Jack. "Of all people, especially one who makes a living repairing the human heart, you should know this better than anyone."

With heavy eyes, Jack glanced through the rear view mirror and didn't even follow up on what Star was telling him. He already made up his mind about Star, already had ever since she snatched him while he was on the way to the hospital and forced him inside a car with her what felt like a millennia ago.

"Before I do this," Jack said, as if he wasn't leaving until Star gave him a tidbit as to why Star looked the way she did, "I need to know. Is it true about what happened to you? The news said—"

"—You actually believe the news? What are you really trying to ask me?"

"Star," he said confidently, "did you die?"

"I'm here talking to you, aren't I?"

"After Mandy's death," Jack started, as he took a moment to drift off in reflection. Buried within that reflection was a bottomless rage, which had made the lines along his brow run longer and deeper. The thought alone of Mandy, the savagery of her brutal passing, and how that opportunistic jackass in the White House had completely smeared the memory of her with a serious of tweets, all to benefit his own prejudice against fangs, caused the emotion to simmer inside Jack. "It's weird," he said, "but part of me felt as if she wasn't dead, yet she was somewhere else; and at times," Jack paused and laughed at the images in his head, "she'd stop by the house just to fuck with me either it be switching on a TV or tilting a picture frame or reorganizing the fridge or even, writing me messages in a steamy window. She was never going to forgive me for what I did to her, for what we did."

"That sure doesn't sound like the Doctor Jack I know."

Jack's eyes filled with tears.

"We had a good thing between us, you and I did. Was it real?"

"Of course, it was real."

"I'm sorry I wasn't there for you before, you know—"

"—Before I lost my shit."

"I should've been there."

"You were," Star said. "In a way."

Jack inhaled deeply through his nose, as he wiped away a tear from the corner of his eye. He cracked open the door.

"Are you forgetting something?" asked Star.

Jack closed the door.

"He'll only accept cash," Star said, as he pulled out the briefcase from underneath the seat and handed it to Jack.

Jack asked, "How much is in here?"

"Trust me," Star said. "You don't want to know."

While holding the briefcase against his body, Jack reached for the door handle. Just as he was about to pull on the handle, he paused and turned to Star.

"Why me?" he asked.

Star said bluntly, "You're the only one I can trust, Jack."

☠

JACK ran through the rain until he reached the door next to Sal's. He walked inside and rode the grimy elevator to the seventh floor.

Keeping a tight grip over the briefcase, he made his way to Room 710.

Outside, two well-built security guards were standing in front of the door.

One guard ran a metal detector over Jack's clothes while the other one patted him down for any weapons.

Once Jack was cleared, they escorted him inside the jewelry store.

There, Jack met Billy Bling, who was standing behind a case full of diamond rings and necklaces.

"You must be Doctor Jack Sender," Billy said and shook Jack's hand.

Without wasting anytime, Jack asked Billy, "Where is it?"

"Right," Billy said. Then, sarcastically, "The *magic crystal*. Right this way."

Jack followed Billy back into a dimly lit private room where he had the black crystal sitting on top of a display case.

"Here she is," Billy said, as he picked up the shard of black crystal and held it up in the light.

Jack placed the briefcase on the countertop.

Being the businessman he was, Billy didn't waste anytime either. He opened the briefcase, revealing all of those Benjamins inside. There had to be at least two mill inside. At least.

"That's a lot of money," Jack said, clearing his throat.

Billy laughed and said to Jack, "You're telling me. Saving the world has its price, my friend."

DOCTOR Berzins stopped by his office to make a couple of calls before calling it a day.

As he stepped inside his office, he was greeted by Vivian, who was standing with her arms crossed in front of a window overlooking the city of Atlanta.

"Ms. Nikopoulos," he said, surprised, "how did you get in here?"

Vivian snapped, "Why does one side of her look more like Cleopatra? What did you do to her?"

The doctor hung his head from the question and after collecting his thoughts, closed the door behind him,

"I thought we had an agreement, Ms. Nikopoulos," he said, as he cautiously approached his desk. "I told you it wasn't going to be easy. Didn't I?"

Vivian didn't respond.

"Eventually, she'll come around. And so will you—"

Scowling, Vivian faced Doctor Berzins, "She's not my daughter, is she?"

The doctor held out his hands.

"I'm aware it might be a lot to take in right now, considering what you had to endure for the past four years," he said. "But I assure you she is *your* daughter."

☠

THE pizza guy happened to arrive as soon as Pan stepped out of the shower. She didn't even know where the time had gone. One minute, she was jumping in the shower to rinse off after a jog around the neighborhood. The next, she drifted off and found herself inside another place, talking to a man with bulky shoulders. He called himself "Cupid."

As Pan rushed out of the shower and threw on some clothes, she called out to the pizza guy and told him that she'd be out in one minute.

On her way out of the living room, she bumped into the dresser, knocking the lamp to the floor.

During the impact, the bottom of the fixture broke apart, revealing the tiny compartment underneath the lamp. The corner of a book was protruding from the bottom part of the fixture. Pan kneeled down and pried a raggedy-looking book from the lamp.

The front of the book had a symbol of a sun with three lines projecting outward. Pan had seen the book before, but she couldn't quite tell where.

☠

AFTER spending the last three weeks living a hermit-like life, Pan decided enough was enough. She packed extra light and managed to fit four to five outfits inside a travel

bag—six or seven if she mixed and matched. Then she hit
the road like a warrior, first by making an impromptu visit
at a tourist site in Louisiana called the Swamp Park where
she spent an afternoon riding in a boat full of tourists and
picking out alligators along Louisiana's bayous; then after
exhausting herself by soaking up the wild life, she headed
West. She stopped multiple times: local family-owned restaurants—"dives"—where she tasted local cuisine; rest stops
to relieve herself; convenient stores to refuel. She spent the
night in a hotel three times during the trip, once in Missis-
sippi, then another night in Texas, then another night in
New Mexico. Her memory started to come back to her
when she drove through the Land of Enchantment. She
stopped at a hole-in-the-wall gas station to fill up both her
tank and her belly. It was there, at Zed's Supplies, when
she was taking the last bite of a *Dark Cavern*^{TM} bar and as
she was about to toss the wrapper in the trash, she noticed
the maker of the popular candy bar below the ingredients.
If it were any other day of the week, she wouldn't have
looked twice at that name, Kazlauskas Inc.; however, the
sight of the name triggered a memory, buried miles deep
inside her and locked away by the chains of time.

When Pan crossed into Colorado, each and every detail
of the road, the surroundings, including road signs and businesses along the highway, were familiar. She had been here
before. In a way, Pan felt as though she was chasing after
her own ghost.

Once she reached a steep bridge that towered over
Sharptooth River, the very same river where her sister,
Cleo, had gone missing, she knew—at least, a part of her
did—that her sister wasn't missing.

On the contrary, a part of Cleo was found.

And still alive!

Guided by a lost memory, Pan turned the car around
and drove to Sharptooth Mountain Park, which was empty
that day, not a single car in the parking lot. She told herself
that the rest of her journey would be traveled by foot. So,
she did.

Carrying only the book that Cupid had given her, she took her time exploring the vast wilderness, marveling at the life pulsing throughout its lushness, basking in its wave of comfort, and trekking through unbeaten trails until she wound up in a familiar spot underneath the waterfall where the water was calm. She walked to the edge of a rock and peered into the water below where she witnessed a reflection of a dark figure standing directly behind her.

Not frightened, instead, rapt by the presence, Pan kneeled down for a closer look at the reflection and realized it was her sister, Cleo.

In a state of euphoria, Pan was swift to rotate her shoulder as she scanned the woods behind her. Cleo wasn't there. Pan wasn't expecting to see her sister, but part of her wasn't entirely convinced.

Pan turned back around and watched the reflection slowly fade into the water. As she sat back upright, she saw the water rippling in the middle of the pool. A pale arm inched its way to the surface. Graceful in manner, the hand of the arm meticulously waved Pan into the water. Pan found herself laughing at the sight of the hand. *It can't be real, can it?* She carelessly shrugged her shoulders.

With the book *First Light* gripped in hand, she placed her foot into the water and while doing so, the hand slowly submerged.

"I can't believe I'm doing this," Pan said to herself.

She placed the book on the top part of a rock, which was dry, and walked farther into the water. Each step became heavier and heavier the farther she walked into the water.

By the time the water reached her waist, she was trudging forward. She wasn't even thinking straight. She wasn't even thinking at all. She was merely seizing a moment, one where its outcome remained in uncertainty.

As she moved farther and deeper into the water, the questions would eventually resurface. A part of her knew that she would discover the answers in a place called Quidaquin County.

KEY waits for a response as he watches Nevaeh dress.

In spite of his attempts at convincing her to stay home for the night, the girl's already made up her mind.

Who can blame her?

As Key points out, she takes up after her momma.

"It's final, Key," she says more harshly to Key, who's lying in bed. "I'm going out whether you like it or not. And believe me. . . " she stops midway through dressing, squares up to the bottom corner of the bed, does this cute gesture where she shifts all her weight to one side of her body, her hips tilted upward like a seesaw, which really has Key turned on, and as his Baby's been known to do whenever the mood strikes her, uses both of her hands like a magician to convey—or conceal—her emotion, "we can bicker for an hour or so, distract Alexa from doing homework, but it sure as hell ain't gonna get us anywhere, is it?"

"You underestimate her," Key says, moving his eyes to the ceiling. "Alexa's got the focus of a samurai. The way she wields that pencil like a katana."

Emotion builds to the point where it floods over Nevaeh, which, surprisingly, makes Key harder.

Nevaeh eyes the growing bulge in Key's pants and rolls her eyes.

"You and I both know that what's going on out there is much bigger than the both of us, Key," she says, forcing Key's eyes elsewhere.

With both hands intertwined behind his head, Key arches his upper body forward and rests against his elbows as he glances at a small VHS/TV set perched on Nevaeh's dresser.

On the grainy screen, the cable news is replaying the footage from earlier that afternoon in the small town of Conoma, La Verite Valley, where four of eight police officers, who were charged last year and had been awaiting trial for the beating of a Los Angeles resident, Antwain Chaquille Grady, who is best known by his peers as "Straight A," are exiting with an entourage from the courthouse. The verdict is in: "*Not guilty* on all counts." Outside the rowdy courthouse, the mobs are standing shoulder-to-shoulder in full force, one lining the sidewalk, the other lining the street, both sides expressing how he or she truly feels about those four police officers, now considered "free men." The sides are split down the middle. One side is "pro-cop" and more or less, condones the brutality inflicted on Antwain Grady, who was left with several broken ribs, a shattered eye socket, which led to the loss of vision in his left eye, fractured arm, many cuts and bruises, flesh along his chest seared, beaten. The other side is outraged as it should be, and feels as if justice did not prevail, never was going to prevail based on a stacked jury and a broken system and everything in between; and the end result was, indeed, not only a miscarriage of justice, but also a prime example of how poorly American citizens, in particular, young black men, regardless of their background, were being treated in a country where a word like *equality* didn't exist; in fact, those who are in favor of the conviction by the fullest extent of the law, believe Antwain Grady was nothing more than a subject who was playing a role in part of a greater, more malicious pattern that had been going on for decades, even centuries.

"Nothing's ever gonna change," Key mumbles to himself. "Soon they'll find themselves another race to pick on. They always do." He switches off the television and moves his eyes back to Nevaeh, who's leaning in close to a standing mirror and picking out an eyelash from the corner of her eye. She finds the eyelash, blows it away, and finishes dressing. He loses himself yet again as she maneuvers her hips into a pair of blue jeans. He reaches out and grabs Nevaeh by the wrist, trying to pull her back to bed. "Come on," Key begs. "I have a bad feeling about this, Baby. I tell you what. Tomorrow, we can take Alexa to the lake."

"The lake sounds good and all, Key, but it ain't gonna change my mind from going out tonight—"

"—Baby," Key says, sitting more upright, "I'll stand by you in whatever you choose to do, but to say I'm cool with you going out with, of all people, Jada on a night like tonight, I'd be lying to myself."

"What's wrong with Jada?" asks Nevaeh, her tone shifting.

"Don't give me that, Nevaeh," Key says more defensively. "You know how she gets when she's around other people. Not to mention her long-standing history with cops. She's like a magnet for trouble."

"I dunno why you ain't sticking up for her. You've had your run-ins with the police."

"Of course I have, but she's known to blow up, Nev. You know it—"

"—Don't even start," Nevaeh says, as she throws on her last article of clothing, a black windbreaker worn underneath a purple and yellow LA Lakers T-shirt. "You can go somewhere else with all of that bullshit. Jada be like my sister to me and her name won't be talked about negatively in my house."

"Then, who's gonna watch Alexa?"

Nevaeh says over her shoulder, "I can always drop her off at my parents'."

"You can't be turning them into your own personal babysitters, Nev. Besides, your Pops has his hands full as it is."

"He don't mind," she says, primping. "Anyway I think he likes having Alexa around while he works. But. . ." she glances at the reflection of Key in the mirror, ". . . she likes being with you more."

"She does, doesn't she?" he says, drifting off.

"She practically talks about you all the time. You're good for her, Key."

Silence forms between the two.

Key rolls out of bed and holds Nevaeh from behind while she does some last second primping in the mirror. He breathes in Nevaeh's scent and licks his lips.

"I can't lose you, Nev," he says, kissing the side of her neck.

"Whoever said you was."

"I can't lose Alexa."

"You ain't."

She feels the bulge pressed up against her backside.

"You really are something tonight," Nevaeh says, impressed. "Whatchu been feeding that creature?"

"Come on, Nev," Key begs. "Alexa needs her momma tonight."

"Oh please!" Nevaeh says, rolling her eyes in a well-demonstrated exaggeration. "I think someone else needs *this* her momma tonight."

"Maybe so," Key says, more quietly.

"She listens more to you, than me. You know?"

Key moves his hand underneath her arm and reaches for her breast.

"You know I need some, " he sings the words of Marvin Gaye, "*Sexual Healing*, Baby."

"Nice try, *M16*," Nevaeh says, grabs hold of his hand, and redirects it somewhere else. Her eyes flick downward at Key's crotch-region below and says with contempt, "I'm afraid you gonna have to unload that weapon somewhere else tonight, Mr. Machine Gun, cuz there *Ain't No Mountain High Enough* to keep me from going out tonight."

"So it's like that, huh?"

Key smacks his gums and leans away from Nevaeh.

"Don't give me that. . . "

Nevaeh mimics Key's gum-smack.

Waving off Nevaeh, Key leaves the bedroom and walks into the living room where the TV is airing the same news footage from earlier that afternoon. Those four cops who were charged but not convicted walking out of the courthouse with mass chaos following their every step. Chants of *"No Justice, No Peace"* or *"Justice For Straight A"* simmer underneath commentary like background noise. The cries and screams all share a common theme, which has been heard too often over the years. Those who stand with law enforcement and solely believe the opposition is the doings of a mob provide their own personal opinions to news reporters, who strategically seek out those who would only inflame the situation.

Sitting at the kitchen table that bleeds into the edge of the living room, Alexa, undistracted by the TV noise, is drawing a picture with a crayon.

The sight alone of Alexa intrigues Key and how, despite what's going on in the city, she maintains a keen warrior-like focus on the drawing before her.

As Key checks on Alexa, he stops halfway into the living room. A headlight in the corner of his eye pulls him toward the front door where he sees a car pulling up in front of the house. There, he notices Jada's red Oldsmobile Cutlass Supreme parked outside.

With all of her windows rolled down, she's blasting the song "Disco Inferno" by the 1960's soulful, super group known as The Trammps. From her exuberant, pre-party-like glow to her singing along "Burn baby burn!" Jada appears unfazed by the powder keg-like situation in the city.

Dressed for a night out, Nevaeh exits from the bedroom and kisses Alexa before she leaves the house.

"She's not coming in?" asks Key.

"What?" Nevaeh returns. "So you can try to talk her out of it?"

"Why you doing this, Nev?" asks Key, growing more agitated.

"I told you, Key, I ain't doing this right now," Nevaeh says, as she heads to the front screen door.

Jada sticks her body out of the driver side window and shouts at Nevaeh, telling her to get moving and that "What you waitin' on, Nevaeh? We got ourselves a city to burn!"

"Nevaeh," Key says more fatherly, "you're gonna get yourself killed. Is that what you want?"

"Jada is just being Jada," she says reassuringly. Then, lowers voice so Alexa can't hear. "You know she ain't gonna do shit."

"So that's it, huh?" Key says, losing his stance. "So, there's nothing I can do that'll change your mind?"

"Quit be so dramatic, will you?" she says, grabbing Key by the hand. "I'm only going out for a couple of hours—"

"—You don't need to do this," Key says with defeat in his face.

Nevaeh places her hand along the upper part of Key's chest and rubs a small starfish-shaped scar left behind from a gunshot wound, which is partially exposed underneath the white tank top.

"I do, but I understand why you don't want me to go. And that's okay." She kisses Key, but Key doesn't kiss her back. "I promise we'll go to the lake tomorrow morning cuz I know how much you love going to the lake to feed them Mallard ducks." Smiling, she shakes Key's arms, as if she's trying to shake—more or less—cast the drama out of his body. "A'ight, *Malle*," Nevaeh says. "When we get back from the lake, I'll drop Alexa off at Pop's studio. You can drop off that book that he's been bugging you about for months." From the corner of Nevaeh's mouth, she says in side-thought, "—You know how he be about his books. After that, Alexa can hang out with her Paw-Paw while me and you take care of some beeswax." Her eyes trail downward and stay pinned to Key's nether regions before finding there way back to his eyes. "It'd be worth the wait. Promise."

"A'ight," Key drawls and finally, returns a kiss on Nevaeh's lips.

Nevaeh says her goodbyes to Alexa firstly, kissing her two peace-loving fingers and blowing a kiss to Alexa, Key secondly, only giving him a wave goodbye. She exits from the house and greets Jada with a hug outside the idling Cutlass Supreme. All the while Key watches the two ride away into the fading daylight, that soulful jam "Disco Inferno" shaking the very concrete of the street.

Once Nevaeh is gone from view, he walks back into the house and grabs the paperback, *New Harlem At Sunrise*, from the edge of the coffee table. He brings the book into the kitchen where she checks on Alexa and that drawing.

Key asks her, "What do you got there?"

"A drawing," Alexa says shortly.

"Yeah," Key says, grinning. "I know it's a drawing, but what is it a drawing of?"

"It's the Nowhere Land," Alexa says and with her purple crayon, shades in a lanky figure standing on top of an orange-colored hill.

"*Nowhere Land*, huh?" Key points at the figure on the top of hill. Alexa has gone through nearly the entire set of crayons to fill in his tie-dye like attire. "And who is this person here?"

"That is Lollipop Man," she says. "He is a protector of all people. Today, he is going to help Don Juan find his way back to his family. Paw-Paw said that he's going to create Lollipop for me."

"Did he now?"

Key studies the drawing of the countryside with rolling orange hills. Standing in front of a green two-story house is yet another figure, this "Don Juan" character who is wearing much darker attire and appears no brighter than a shadow. Above the figure are swarms of flying creatures, which look like black birds.

"Lollipop Man," he says out loud while studying Alexa's colorful character on top of the hill, as well as the upside down rainbow that he casts from his bright smile. "So, you come with that idea on your own?"

"I'm drawing it, aren't I?"

"You sure are." Key decides to take a seat next to Alexa at the kitchen table. "Not bad for ah. . . How old are you again?"

"Six."

"Six? What? That can't be right. Swear I thought you were much older than that."

"How old did you think I was?"

"I was thinking more like, I dunno, ten or eleven."

"No," she says, her voice drawn out.

Key studies Alexa and that cool, calm, and collected aura about her when she focuses her mind on one thing, such as a drawing. He moves his eyes toward her neck and can't help but study those deep, wrinkled-like marks around her neck from where she was nearly strangled to death by the umbilical cord when she escaped Shelly's polluted womb and entered the world, only to, many years later, be gazed upon by yet another. Key notices Alexa watching him through the corner of her eye while she continues to draw, moves his attention away from Alexa, and turns his focus back toward the drawing. He points at all of those dark, winged, scribbly creatures flying above the shadowy man—or "Don Juan."

"So are these supposed to be birds or something?" he asks Alexa.

"These are Lollipop Man's helpers called 'Swooshers,'" Alexa says, pulling her eyes from Lollipop Man. "They're going to help carry Don Juan up the hill because Don Juan is having trouble reaching Lollipop Man."

"And why's that?"

"He's sick, well, more like broken."

"Broken, huh? Broken how?"

Alexa innocently shrugs her shoulders.

"So let me get this straight," Key says directly to Alexa, "we're talking 'bout the same Don Juan from the movie your Paw-Paw be working on?"

Alexa nods her head.

"*The Effigy: The Curse of Don Juan*." Her round face lights up. She chirps, "You've seen it yet?"

"Me, you know I don't do horror movies," Key says closely, glancing at the living room TV where a Breaking News story flashes across the screen.

"Why not?" asks Alexa.

On the TV, a shaky overhead shot from a helicopter is filming protests on the streets of Los Angeles. Violent riots are forming among the streets outside businesses and shopping malls. Protestors using rocks and Molotov cocktails to vandalize parked cars and property. Abandoned police cruisers are being set ablaze. Along a strip mall, a mob of looters are shattering shop windows with bricks and street signs, storming through barricades, tearing through fencing and metal gates, and breaking into small family owned businesses. Major retail stores completely gutted of merchandise. In a busy intersection, swarms of mobs are pulling drivers out of vehicles and beating them senseless. One of the victims—a truck driver—is beaten to death and left to die on the streets. While the man dies, two protestors cover the man's face and body with black spray paint.

Staring at the violent images, Key finally answers the six-year-old's question: "Reality is filled with enough horror as it is."

Key faces Alexa, who, in return, follows his eyes toward the TV; however, Key pulls Alexa's attention back to the conversation at hand. "Besides," he says directly to Alexa, as those images on the TV intensify and become more graphic in nature, "aren't you too young to be watching horror movies like *The Effigy*?"

"I don't watch them," she says. "I'm not allowed to. Plus, they're too scary for me."

"Yeah," Key says, laughing. *"And* your momma would kill your Paw-Paw if she found out he was sneaking you on set without her permission."

"How come you never talk to Paw-Paw?"

"I talk to him."

Alexa immediately detects the lie and displays her disapproval on her face.

"Can you keep a secret?" Key says, guilty.

Alexa nods again, this time more vigorously.

"Between you and me," he says, "your Paw-Paw and I don't exactly see eye-to-eye, meaning we're not as close as, say, the way me and your momma are."

"Are you saying you don't like Paw-Paw?"

"It's not like I don't like him. It's just we often have a difference of opinion. There's nothing wrong with having differences; in fact, it's those differences that make us closer."

"That means you should be closer to Paw-Paw, right?"

"Sure," he says, backtracking. "It's just, at times, your Paw-Paw has a way of saying things that would get most people in trouble."

"Trouble how?"

"Trouble like something bad happening to him," Key says more coldly. "But we wouldn't want that, would we?"

With exaggeration, Alexa shakes her head and indicates a clear "No!"

Key's comment finally settles, causing Alexa to stop drawing. She hangs her head.

"You know, when Ralph's not playing The Wolf, he's not that scary."

"I'm sure he isn't," Key says. "There's a reason why they call it acting. It's all make-believe."

"I know," Alexa returns.

"From what I heard, he and Paw-Paw are pretty close."

"Well, Ralph's always cracking jokes and Paw-Paw gets a real kick out of his jokes," Alexa says briskly as if she's trying to say it all in one breath. "There was this one time I was doing my homework in the trailer while Paw-Paw was putting on Ralph's mask—which took like, hours, because Paw-Paw had to mold Ralph's face before he could paint the mask—and Ralph cracked this joke about Imani's butt. Paw-Paw was laughing so hard that he started to cry and I asked him why he was crying and he said he wasn't and that not all people cry when they're sad."

"Yeah. That's true," Key says, amazed by the girl's energy. "Your momma told me how much you like movies. That's must be cool, right? Spending time hanging around actors and all kinds of celebrities?"

"Well, I don't look at Ralph as a celebrity. To me, he's no different than you or Paw-Paw."

Leaning over the table, Key nods at the drawing.

"So, he put that in your head, huh?"

"Well, no."

"Then, who did?"

"Jacob says I have a wild imagination."

"Who's Jacob?"

"He works with Paw-Paw. He's a set designer."

"Well, Jacob is spot-on about your imagination."

"I know," Alexa says and returns to her drawing.

In the corner of his eye, Key sees yet another more graphic scene on TV. A liquor store on the street corner—but not just any liquor store, he looks closer and realizes it's Terrell's store—is burning while protestors gather in front of the store and bask in the fiery blaze. Palls of black smoke pour into the sky and, at times, block out the overhead shot from the helicopter hovering above. Terrell, an older man whom Key had gotten to know over the past couple of years, is standing outside, trying to push protestors away while his business burns down to the ground.

But there's nothing Terrell can do to stop the fire.

"RAT RACE"
(PRESENT DAY)

ON one side of the alley, you have "Stat," whose attire consists of a brown leather vest worn over a tight white Tee with a Snakebreath logo, black jeans that, similar to his shirt, appear two sizes too tight, a pair of checkered Vans that match the red logo on his shirt. Red, being a common theme sprinkled throughout Stat's getup, is the color of a band to hold his dreads in a bun. His accessories include twenty-four wrist bracelets that his daughter, Deja, made for him. Each bracelet, according to Deja, represents each year of her poppa's existence, each one varying from rubberbands to multi-colored beads, pearls, or faux jewels to twine, including nylon and hemp.

On the other side, Key, who, more or less, given his capitalist-like nature and willingness to devour any and *all* competition, self-branded himself the nickname "M16," a cross between a less punkish Eel-Baby and a more vitriolic MoVega, minus the villainous bleached blonde bowl-cut wig and Youngblood Priest sideburns. Contrary to Stat, Key's attire is consistent to what you'd see in a rap video from the mid to late Nineties: each article of clothing oversized, including a New York Knicks basketball jersey numbered 00 with the sales tag uncut and hanging from the bottom seam, as well as Nautica blue jeans which he wears sagging well below his waist. Like the baggy jersey, the jeans appear untouched and unaltered, the long size sticker, XL, still attached to the back of the pant leg. The Yankees hat with the flat, stiff bill was cocked to the side in an angle. His footwear: a pair of wheat-colored Timberland boots, unspoiled and unlaced, despite scattered rain showers. His accessories: an 18k gold plated chain, as well as an off-brand gold watch that he bought half of what you'd normally pay at a retail store from a hustler on the street.

Hugging the edge of the sidewalk while taking cover from a passing shower, Key and Stat are chilling against the side of two adjacent buildings, one being a law firm,

Willhouse and Maylay, while the other, a rundown apartment complex, which is in the middle of a renovation project, albeit temporarily on hold due to the weather.

To their right, a bunch of news reporters, as well as protesters gather and conform along the blocked off street in front of the New York City Court House.

As droplets of rain splash on the back of his shoulders, Stat slightly hunches over with both hands in his pockets. Key remains in a fixed position, "posted up," his lower half shaped like a reverse letter four with one foot pressed against brick, the other one planted on the slick asphalt. Key's interest is directed more at pedestrians walking along the sidewalk instead of those forming crowds.

With the thought weighing heavy on his mind, Key points out the passerbys to his eager prodigy, Stat.

"Take a good look them," Key says to Stat, as he flicks his head in a nod at the pedestrians shielding themselves with umbrellas. "What do you see?"

"Well," Stat says, sighs, and pays closer attention to the passerbys, "Besides the small worlds that keep 'em occupied, either it be the hot-blooded text from a fling that expires in two weeks, maybe three, depending how imaginative she can be, or the misleading headlines that bait her in for clicks in order to profit from her gullible character or NSFW photos from that fine-ass pawg who is everything his average wife ain't or the group email of a plotted coup, using all sorts of code words to throw off whistleblowers who are anything but righteous in their pursuits, or a rigged game that helps ease anxiety of a stressed-out homey from being in public, besides all of that, shit," Stat shrugs, "I see opportunity."

"What else?" Key says with a blank expression.

"What else?" Stat repeats, his mind wrapping in thought. Then says thoughtfully, "*Pasts.*" Stat focuses on one particular woman who's scrolling through the texts on her phone while trying to stay dry underneath the black umbrella. "They all have pasts, whether or not they like to admit it. Everybody's either running to or from something. *The past or the future.* How else can you get where you need to be? Then, there are those who prefer to walk, and I guess that's a'ight by me. Just get out of my way, you feel me?" Stat chuckles but squelches the laughter after receiving another icy stare from Key. "But then," Stat says, more seriously, "you got those who ain't even moving at all, who just sitting as if they waiting for something awful to happen."

"And once they remove their eyes from the self-serving worlds that bind them to their masters, what do you see then?"

"Hard to see through so many layers without making contact, but I guess I'd see people who just want purpose."

"You guess?"

"People want a purpose, Key," Stat says, more confidently. "No doubt."

"You want purpose, right?"

Stat shrugs.

"Of course," he says shortly. "Why not?"

Key says, "You said earlier that you felt as if there was something 'missing' from your life, but you didn't know what exactly."

Once more, Stat shrugs.

"Yeah," he says. "That's right. The blur. But that's the trade off, yeah?"

"It can be," Key says. "Every gift has a curse, and every curse has a gift."

"Lately, it's felt more like a curse," Stat says. "Just a curse."

"Well, of course, we got an election coming up soon, Stat. Emotions are particularly amped up around this time of year. There are some who choose to capitalize on those emotions while others simply ignore them."

Stat says from the corner of his mouth, *"Man,* it's hard to ignore this shit."

"Let me ask you something personal, Stat, if you don't mind."

"Shoot."

"How do you feel about your family?" Key ask, then adds: "And try to push past the blur, if you can."

"Family?" Stat says, as if the repeating of the word opens up more space for brain chatter. "There ain't a blur there when I think of my family. My whole life I felt like I never had one. My dad was never there. He spent most of his life in and out of prison. Briefly worked as a loader before he bit the bitter end of a bullet. My moms did the best she could raising me and my sisters. But, eventually, when I was twelve years old, it had gotten so hard on her that she decided she was done with us. She dropped us off at my grandparents' crib and was gone for good from my life. By the time my grandparents passed, I dropped out of high school. They left the house to me and my sisters, but, eventually, they let the house go to shit by turning it into a hotel for broke-ass, wannabe gangstas who took full advantage over both my sisters. Like a bunch of vultures with bottomless appetites, always lingering around, picking up the scraps. As hard as I tried to put down my foot, act like man of the house—no matter what I did—I was still that younger brother who didn't even know how to change a light bulb. It don't take a gift to realize when one ain't wanted. I was done with it. With *all* of it. So, yeah, family, for me, that shit don't exist. Never has."

More thoughtfully, Key asks, "You ever hear about the cat Andre St. Croix, who was locked up for murder a while back?"

Stat half-frowns.

"Name sounds familiar."

"Changed his name to Drenelle."

"Drenelle, right," Stat says, the frown moving into a grin. "The she-male."

"Just a *she* now," Key says, as he keeps a tight hold over his blood.

"Right," Stat says, more dismissively. "Whatever."

"Before Drenelle's transition, she spent years alone, trying to figure out who he was. Like yourself."

"You comparing me to some prissy, eye-collectin' ass clown who can't even figure out his own sex?"

"So, you *have* heard the stories about the eyes?" asks Key.

"Now that you mention it," he says, more heated, "*yeah*. Who hasn't? If you trying to make a point or something, why don't you just give me a Cliff Note Version."

"Well, my point is, Stat: When Drenelle looked at herself in the mirror, she didn't like the person looking back at her. The body she was in, it wasn't her on the inside, you feel me?"

On the verge of saying "No," Stat hesitates.

"In a way," Key says before Stat can give him an answer, "she felt as though it didn't belong to her. So she rejected that person, *that body*, then started to alter it to the way she looked on the inside. Before the transition, Drenelle lived in fear for most of her young adult life, always wondering when his mother, Shakira, or any of her extended family members, would figure her out—if they hadn't already but just kept it secret, like the same way she was keeping how she really felt secret from those who surrounded her. After she hit puberty and her 'male' body started to change, she got hooked up with a crew of older people—mentors, you could say—in charge of running this small theatre on the ass-end of town called *Common Theme* Theatre. They were once misfits, like her, lone wolves who were trying to break the mold and most importantly, fit in before they created their own thing. Once she joined Common Crew, she started seeing and *feeling* things differently, like she had this image of herself deep inside her the whole time, locked away, protected, and then once she put herself with the right people, all of these feelings started flooding out of her. Everything *clicked*. The transition was a long process, but it was one she was willing to take. One day, she had reached the end of the road and had gone as far as the Common Theme would take her. She decided to leave the Crew, went off and did her own thing. She went 'mainstream,' if you will. Leaving Common Crew would eventually be

Drenelle's greatest mistake; however, it later would set forth a Series of Unfortunate Events that would lead us to the inevitable Now. After Drenelle started up her own brand and became a success in her own right," Key carefully thinks of his next word of choice, "an '*event*' happened, one that nobody could explain—even if they tried. She was no longer Drenelle, even though she looked and acted like Drenelle. She changed into something else, something she had absolutely no control over, something beyond visceral, deadly, something that only thrived in the dark. And the world saw her for what she became and it came running for her with torches and pitchforks; now, she's back in that prison, the same one she was in when she was a boy trying to figure out who the hell he was. Only this time, it's a prison with bars and four walls."

Stat tilts his head to the side and narrows his left eye.

"Key," he says, thinking hard, "why you telling me this?"

Staying unperturbed at his post, Key directly calls out Stat and the talent that he has been given. "It's yours and yours only to bear," he says. "If you lose control over it, the world will change you into something you're not. You must recognize your talent for what it is, as well as the power it possesses. If not, you will wind up like Drenelle St. Croix. The street is an unforgiving place, and it's too crowded for talented people like yourself. You have a purpose. We *all* do. You may not be sure of what that is right now. But if you let me, I can show you."

Across the street, the crowd starts to buzz with rage.

Commotion builds higher, forcing the two to pay attention.

A security team exits first from the courthouse, which causes the angry mob, as well as a swarm of news reporters and cameramen to rush to the barricades that have been set up by the NYPD.

Surrounding himself with an entourage, disgraced journalist, Miles Straum, is next to exit from the courthouse. He walks down the front steps of the courthouse while one member of his security detail shields his face with a jacket. The other members circle Miles and protect him from the ensuing chaos before him.

"What goes around comes around," Key says to Stat. "It doesn't matter who you are and what you look like. If you're against them, they will do everything in their power to destroy you—"

"—He didn't do It," Stat says, referring to the Big "It."

Key glances at Stat through the corner of his eye.

"They don't care whether or not he killed that young girl," he says. "They've already chosen their man. But it doesn't matter anymore, does it?"

Key and Stat watch the growing crowd surround Miles, as one of his bodyguards blocks a projectile from hitting Miles with his shoulder.

Underneath his blank stare, Key clenches his teeth and tries to hold back his anger from the sight alone of the scoundrel who tried to steal, copy, and profit off his "world" by peddling it off as an animated TV show, which, ultimately, would, as he put it mildly in a podcast, "Make Miles Great" again.

"One thing's for sure," Key says mindfully while watching the news reporters bombard Miles, "you're either on the top or on the bottom. If you're on top, those on the bottom will do anything to erode the foundations that made you reach the top. They'll try to tear you down by delegitimizing you and eventually, breaking you. Miles Straum was *never* on top, even though throughout his career he thought he was. He created a lie to the world, and the world bought it. But it didn't stop the world from wanting more. The world enjoys watching people like Miles Straum squirm. Even after Miles was exposed for what he was, which was a sham, *they*," he nods at "they," the news reporters who, according to Miles post-controversy, constantly "feed and sicken" the world with the disease of misinformation and extreme bias, "still give him coverage and will continue to do so until there's nothing left of him but bones. Their goal is to make you feel less threatening because they believe that anybody who's on top will always be the threat when, ironically, it's the top that they strive for. Then," Key says while carrying a dark light in his eyes, "you have those who are on top but nobody has the slightest clue they're on top." He looks Stat directly in his eyes and asks, "You're not scared of heights, are you?"

AFTER suggesting hailing a taxi opposed to riding the subway from Manhattan to Brooklyn, Stat agrees to take the subway. Plus, Key says it'll be quicker, which is fine by Stat, especially with the circus in town.

By the time they reach the subway, the rain eases down to a drizzle. Part of the sun peeks through the dark clouds and is destined to create a rainbow over the steamy skyline of Manhattan.

"Back in the late Sixties, early Seventies, when I worked briefly at a loading dock in Newbay," Key says while stepping onto the train with Stat, "the honkies I used to work for called me Midnight."

"Honkies?"

"You know, it's a term used for white people," Key says. "Forgot. Way before your time."

"So, the Sixties, huh? How da fuck old is you?"

"I told you 'I'm ancient.'"

Key takes a seat next to the door.

While chuckling to himself, Stat sits down next to him

"For realz," Stat says, smirking. "Fuckin' vamp over here."

"Listen, Stat, it doesn't matter how old am I. Sure. I may look like your age. Check this out here. Lesson Number 1: *See with your ears.*"

"See with my ears? How da hell am I suppose to see with my ears?"

"Exactly. How you supposed to see with your ears? It's physically impossible, right?"

Stat shrugs.

"Guess so."

"How do you see with your eyes?"

"Is this a trick question?"

"Just answer the question," Key says.

"*Focus*," Stat mentions. He confirms his answer by saying more clearly, "By focusing."

"Now close your eyes and apply that focusing part to your ears. What do you hear?"

"For realz?"

"Yes."

"A'ight."

Stat closes his eyes and listens closely to his intimate surroundings, from the back and forth chatter of two overzealous guys breaking down each track of a latest Eel-Baby and The Cuts album to the rustling of a finger-heavy hand reaching into a bag of potato chips followed by the crunching of the same person chomping down on a mouthful of potato chips to the digital chirping of a sudden notification on someone's smartphone to the rapid clicking of someone texting to the booming "ha" of laughter to the raspy whisperings of a trip-hop jam scolding from a pair of headphones to the crinkling of someone flipping a page in a magazine to the shuffling of a bookbag to the phlegm-logged sniffle of a running nose.

Stat cracks open his eyes and says to Key, "Life."

Key appears amused by Stat's answer.

"You know what I hear?"

"What?"

"Noise."

"Maybe so," Stat says, "but there life behind that noise. Don't you agree?"

Key doesn't answer Stat's question. Yet, he remains quiet and amused.

Stat nods at Key.

"So, Key," Stat says, his tone sharper, "why those honkies you work with call you Midnight? Hold up. Lemme guess. Your dark complexion?"

"You'd think being black certainly had something to do with why they called me Midnight—" Key says, "—I mean we talking 'bout the Sixties here. The way I see it, though: People looking for an excuse can easily find one. Your skin tone, your color, whatever it may be: Of all the excuses out there, it's the easiest ones to find. But, *for real*," Key says, emphasizing the very words Stat is known to use, only without a common letter that normally indicated sleep, "whether they like to admit it or not, most people are considered visual-creatures, meaning they rely on visuals: appearances, colors, shapes, and sizes. To these certain people, it's much easier to understand something, for instance, a person, they can see with their own eyes. However," Key says, pausing, "the color of my skin had nothing to do with the reason why they called me Midnight, even though most liked to think it did."

"Then why did they?"

"I always worked late in the night, mostly till midnight, even well past midnight, hence the name Midnight. The guy working the next shift was the one who actually came up with the name. After a while, it sort of stuck."

"Busy bee, huh?"

"I didn't mind working late," Key says casually. "I get all my best ideas late at night. You see it gave me a sense of comfort knowing that, while people were sleeping, I was blueprinting worlds inside my head."

"I can't go a day without sleep," Stat says, easing farther into the seat. "If I don't get at least eight hours in me, I'm one cranky bitch-ass nigga the next day."

"People, like yourself, Stat," Key says, "sleep is like fuel for your talent."

"Yeah," Stat says. "If you want to look at it like that. Sure."

They ride in silence for a while until Key comes up with an idea—a "test," if you will, to pass the time.

Key searches the train and spots a lonely woman sitting just a few seats away. Her hair is held in a ponytail by a black scrunchie. Her attire, which consists of a black, thigh-high skirt, as well as a silk buttoned down blouse underneath a metallic-colored lapel, long sleeve blazer that stretches past her thighs, is professional and business-like, yet it accommodates the warm weather. Both of her sleeves are rolled up to her forearms. The only piece of the woman's outfit that seems out of place is a black silk scarf worn loosely around her neck. In one hand, she's holding a worn paperback in front of her and using her thumb to keep the pages spread open while, in the other, she's massaging a tiny object. Her head is planted in the book; however, most of her interest appears to be solely directed at that object in her other hand.

"A'ight, *Thermostat*. "Let's see your magic," Key says, nodding at the sister without a mister. "How about the bookworm over there?"

"What about her?" asks Stat.

"You tell me," Key says. "Go on," he urges. "Do what you do."

Stat accepts Key's challenge, which, for Stat, isn't much of a challenge at all. Based on the slack expression, the woman is distressed; however, broken-hearted may be a more accurate description. Stat guesses, no, corrects himself, tells Key that she's somewhere between the age of thirty-three and thirty-five, even though the woman looks much younger, say, early twenties. The woman takes, not good care, but great care of her body, works out four times a week, alternate days from free weights to cardio, eats foods that don't have two or four legs, never indulges, uses facial creams and moisturizers to combat wrinkles and blemishes.

With his male gaze sharpening, Stat closely studies the woman, starting with her gestures and moving toward each one of her possessions. The woman's story unfolds right before his eyes.

"She's upset, obviously," he says right off bat. His eyes narrow. "She's not one to hide her emotions, even though she considers to lean on a more introverted side. She prefers to find comfort in a cat. A white long-haired that sheds a lot."

"You can tell she has a cat just by looking at her?"

"She has cat hairs on the bottom of her pant leg," Stat says. "She has one of those sticky roller thingamajigs.

Considering she was in a rush today, she missed a few hairs on the bottom of her pan leg."

"You can see the cat hair on her pants?" Key says in doubt. Then, raises his brows in astonishment. "Not bad," he says.

"Well, it's there if you look hard enough; however, a cat can't give her solace on a day like today. The objects in her hands will, first starting with the book in her left hand." The **Braggadocio** font on the spine, as well as the front cover makes it trickier to read from where he's sitting. Stat leans forward to get a closer look at the book. "*New Harlem. . .*" he reads, leaning more without making himself seem too suspicious. "*New Harlem At Sunrise*, I think."

Key says, "It's a story that follows a young couple whose love is put to the test after the girlfriend and protagonist, Raven, learns about her boyfriend's dark past."

"So you've read it?"

"A few times, yes."

"Whatever, man."

Key replies with a question of his own for Stat, "When you've been known to work till midnight, what else you suppose to do with your free time?"

"I ain't judging." Stat says jokingly, "You don't strike me as a brother who reads romance novels."

"It may sound like a romance novel," Key says, his tone shifting darker, "but it's not."

"Then, what is it?"

"It's a horror story."

"Okay," Stat says, more interested in the book.

"Regardless of the contents of the book, from the worn condition of the cover and those faded pages, the book has been touched by many hands. The dog-ears on the corner of the pages are significant as well. Same goes for the writing along the pages and the highlighted paragraphs, *key* excerpts. The person who gave her the book did so with guidance and good intentions."

"How do you know it was given to her?" asks Key.

Stat notices the top half of the eReader tablet protruding from floral patterned purse.

"Normally, she reads her books on her tablet," he says. "The person could've shared the book with her through the tablet or bought the ebook version as a gift. This person is old school, though. This person is not her father but, more or less, an important figure in her life who had given the book to her before he passed to let her know that everybody has a past, even the person who looks back at you in the mirror, which brings me to the item in her other hand. It's a special pendant." Being the keen observer he is, he points out the jagged yet smooth volcanic glass-like rock held inside an interwoven swirling silver pendant attached to the collar necklace made out of a black leather cord. With the underside of her thumb, the lonely woman pets the pendant as if she's releasing energy trapped inside it. Each stroke radiates throughout Stat's body. "From what I can sense, it's sentimental, *not to her*," Stat emphasizes, as he shoots a glance at Key, "but to the person who gave it to her. Like the book, the *contents* inside the pendant carry a tremendous weight. They're irreplaceable, priceless; and based on how carefully she holds it in her hand, it belonged to a very special woman, one who was adored by many." Again, Stat finds himself glancing over at Key as though Key chose that particular woman for a reason. "However," Stat says, redirecting his attention back at the woman, "the thing is she's not entirely sad. She's actually relieved."

"Relieved?" Key says. "Relieved from what?"

Stat studies her closely, gestures and mannerisms, even the way she looks up at the passengers seated in front of her when she turns a page.

"Ever since she was in her early twenties, she lost her trust in guys. She went through a spell of bad relationships that ended up in disaster. Over time, she became more cynical. She lost confidence in herself. Relationships got shorter and shorter until any love life at all was reduced to a casual weekend hookup. It all started when she was around seventeen. She was in love—or at least, thought she was in love. Ever since that moment she first felt love, she spent years searching for that feeling again but nobody lived up to him and the way she felt for him. He was much older and meant everything to her. One day, she caught him cheating on her with one of her friends and she never forgave him for it. What he had done to her hung over their relationship up until the very end; planted doubts inside her head about *all* guys, especially one whom she thought she loved." Stat moves his eyes back to that pendant in particular. The stroking stops. She reads more aggressively. "Eventually," Stat says, "the relationship ran its course. Now, years later, she finds herself in love again. She's sad that, of all the women out there to choose from, he chose her to give her that special pendant because she knows that in the end the relationship will, like the previous ones, run its course. She enjoys her freedom, yet she enjoys his company even more. He's good to her. He never raises his voice at her. He treats her right. He's strong, too, and makes her want to be better in everything she do. He's nothing like the man who she once looked to as a father, the one who both her grandparents talked about with such hostility; in fact, it was her grandfather who had given her that book. However, she *feels* like her grandparents, especially her grandfather, whom she adored growing up, might've gotten this father figure all wrong, and a distant part of her feels like he was a good man, despite all the stories she heard about him over the years and just that feeling alone reminds her of the special person who gave her the pendant and that feeling alone, it brings her great ease. But that's not the only reason why she's so relieved. Throughout all her struggles, she finally found someone who she could struggle with."

Key digests Stat's rundown of the woman.

"You got all that just from looking at her?" Key asks.

"Yeah," Stat says and shrugs. "It just comes to me like a feeling. But it's not just any feeling. It's *her* feelings."

As though on cue, the train slows down while approaching their stop.

The two stand up as soon as the train comes to a stop.
The doors slide open.

Key taps Stat on the arm.

"What do you know?" he says and nods at the woman, who slips the crinkled paperback back into her purse, and readies to exit the train. "It's her stop too."

✿

"WHO those cats I saw you hanging out with the other day?" Key asks Stat, as the two exit from the subway tunnel.

"The skinny fool is named Deadwave," Stat says. "The loudmouth is this cat from Queens named 'Stream. The big fellow is Big Magma. The sketchy muthafucka is N17."

"N17?" Key repeats. "You shitting me?"

"Shit you not, Key."

"Well I dunno know who that fool thinks he is," Key says, his tone rather bitter, "but if he doesn't change his name, I'm going to have to make him change it myself. Make sure you pass along that message for me next time you see N17."

As they make their way to the sidewalk, he grabs the Coffin Nail tucked over his ear, as well as a lighter from his pocket. He lights the cigarette as soon as they approach the bagel shop, Sal's. Key looks toward the mini-van with the Virginia license plates parked along the side of the street. He hones in on the hooded passenger sitting in the back seat of the minivan.

The door next to Sal's bagels swings open.

Key drags from the cigarette and blows out a cloud of smoke as soon as Jack steps outside the building.

In the smoky cloud, a pair of dark slits for eyes takes shape, then two nostrils to form a nose, then a gaping mouth, wicked like a V, extending well-past the two eyes. The wavy, demonic face materializes and lingers in front of Jack's face before it funnels into his nose and mouth, causing him to cough.

164

With his hand firmly pressed against the inner pocket of his jacket, Jack uses his other hand to wave away the cloud of cigarette smoke.

As he walks past, Jack gives Key a look of detest on his face; however, from his rushed manner and the valuable possession that he holds inside his jacket pocket, he appears in absolutely no mood to confront Key or his friend. Not only that, based on a recent confrontation that he witnessed between two hot-blooded New Yorkers who were about to swap bullets on this very street a few moments ago, Jack realizes that breathing in someone else's secondhand smoke isn't at all worth dying over. He doesn't know whether or not Key is packing any heat, but he has a pretty good idea.

Or, does he?

As Jack proceeds toward the minivan, he slows down to a near-amble. Eventually, he stops in his tracks. His face slackens, as he rotates around toward Key and stares at him before walking away. He passes the minivan, causing Star, that hooded passenger, to slide open the door. She extends her head outward and calls out to Jack; however, Jack ignores Star and keeps walking by.

Key and Stat wait at the edge of the alleyway. As before, Stat observes other pedestrians before him and takes mental notes of each and every one of them as if he's readying himself for another one of Key's off-the-cuff tests.

Keeping to himself, Key carefully watches Jack and tracks his every move.

Once more, Star calls out to Jack.

"Where are you going?" she asks.

As before, Jack doesn't respond; in fact, Jack acts as if he doesn't even know Star, as he walks toward a construction site.

🐾

TWO construction workers, first, Peter, forty-six years old, a husband and father of two children, Liam and Mateo, and second, Paul, twenty-seven, a proud parent of a chocolate brown Labrador named after one of his all-time favorite video games called *Goliathon*, dig into both their lunches on a scaffold along the thirty-seventh story of a partially constructed high-rise, which, except for buildings like the Empire State Building, Peter calls "*Second best seat in the City.*"

Peter takes a bite of a classic Reuben sandwich from Louie's Deli and Shakes and says from the other side of his mouth, "This country's going straight down da tubes. You know that, right?"

"Oh yeah?" Paul replies, peeling the rest of his orange. He says with a mock-innocence, "What tubes?"

"You know, the fuckin' tubes."

"Haven't heard that one before."

"Quit being such a smartass, will ya?"

Peter wipes the juices from the warm corn beef and sauerkraut dripping down the side of his chin with a napkin.

"I never understand that expression and why so many people from *your* generation use it all the freakin' time," Paul says and breaks off a wedge from the orange. "I mean, where these tubes go? Huh, Pete? Underneath the streets? In the sewers? These are important questions you should be askin' yourself."

"How the hell am I supposed to know, Parrot?"

"Then, why you say it, Peter Peter Reuben Eater?"

"Hey, it's an expression, knucklehead," Peter says, voice loud, face even redder.

"Well, you and your generation might wanna think about updating your expressions because, frankly, Pete, they don't make any sense."

"Yeah, yeah, yeah," Peter says, trailing off. He takes yet another bite of the Reuben and waves off Paul and his comments. "Mr. Wise Guy here," he says upfront, "I tell you what: It's all of this commie bullshit that you hear about lately on the Fake News Network."

"Settle down, McCarthy," Paul says to Peter, as if he's unofficially taking a neutral stance.

"What the hell you know about McCarthy?" Peter asks Paul. "You were still swimming around your daddy's balls."

Paul shrugs.

"The Internet."

"Get outta here," Peter says, waving off Paul. "Just another way for you kids to get brainwashed by your YouTubes and Twitters. You can't fuckin' escape it, all of the nonsense out there, especially with the election coming up. It's everywhere you turn the gaddamn channel."

"Sure," Paul says, as Peter's passion starts to wear off on him, "the headlines, the anchors reading the headlines, the rage-reporting with an *obvious* slant against Rhodes— Not like I'm a fan of his but come on! Doesn't take some 'wise guy' to figure out the media's bias toward him—all of that is probably tweaked, some of it, sure, as fake as your wife's tits."

Peter puts down his sandwich and points at Paul.

"Hey! Watch it, Parrot—"

"—But you agree. The images ain't fake."

Peter fired back, "How you know Washington and her goon squad don't have a director out there, directing people to act a certain way for the camera? It's all staged. You know that, right? Washington's practically got the media wrapped around that claw of hers. They did that same exact shit in Vietnam, reporters directing soldiers to burn down villages, all to fit their narrative. Besides, they can manipulate images on that Photo-Thingy. . . "

"Photoshop?"

"That's the one."

"I guess, anything's fair game these days," Paul says, losing confidence in his stance.

"Now, what? You think 'Avanti Washington' is gonna swoop down here and save the day? It doesn't take a miner to dig up her past." Peter takes another bite, laughs. "The woman should run under the fuckin' Halloween Party."

Paul shakes his head from the insult, as if he wants to laugh but doesn't want to contribute or further invoke Peter's prejudices.

"Get this," Peter says, slapping Paul on the arm, "she could appoint all of her goons to her Cabinet. The Wolfman as her Secretary of Defense. The Mummy as Secretary of the Treasury. Frankenstein as Secretary of Energy—"

"—Dracula as Secretary of Transportation?" Paul joined in.

Peter bursts out laughing, Paul not so much.

"What a world we live in," Peter says to himself. Then more directly to Paul, "This ain't the first time this county has gone through a rough patch. You should know, Computer Boy. What people don't realize is that this country was founded on rough patches and it's up to us folks to help smooth them out."

"Gee," Paul says sarcastically, "that's something, Pete. You should make it one of your 'Quotes of the Day.'"

"Get outta here," Peter says bitterly. "Wake up and smell the manure, Parrot. We've gotten soft, and if you let all of these little snowflakes, who want us to live in a gaddamn utopia, continue to run around these streets and destroy the property of hardworkin' folks, we won't have a country anymore. I tell ya just the thought of that piece of shit torching Bucky's Place really chaps my ass. That spoiled rotten fuck. Inbreeds like him telling me what I can or can't say. Like you can't say 'this' or you can't do 'that' cuz you might offend somebody. Last time I checked the First Amendment of the United States Constitution still exists. *And*," he says, his voice growing louder, "by the way, who in the hell are these little shitheads to judge with their purity tests and moral fuckin' authority and all their mommy and daddy issues when these shit-for-brains can't even hold a gaddamn job? You stop one of these morons on the street and they don't have a fuckin' clue what they're talkin' about. You ask 'em to explain what communism is and then grab yourself some fuckin' popcorn."

"Man," Paul says, casual yet, at the same time, entertained by Peter's passion, "these kids are really getting to you, huh? You were young once, weren't you?"

"Yeah," Peter says, "I was young. I did the whole peace, love, and war bullspit until I realized that holding each other's hand and singing Kumba-fuckin'-ya around a campfire ain't gonna pay the gaddamn bills. Hey, you know what these people remind me of?"

Paul shrugs and says while chewing his orange, "You got me."

"A bunch of two-year-olds throwing temper tantrums whenever things don't go their way," Peter says. "Maybe they should start calling their little organization 'The Terrible Twos.' See how far that takes 'em?"

"If you go so far left, you end up all the way on the other side. A full circle, you know?"

"Right," Peter mumbles. "The circle of fuckin' life. It don't take a gaddamn genius to see what they're doing to our country. Think about it, will ya? They're literally becoming the very thing they stand against. First, they want you to conform and build their mob of drones who can't even hold a thought, let alone think for their gaddamn selves. If you don't obey, then they destroy you. Look at what they did over in Europe after World War I. Who's to say they won't do it here?"

"You talkin' about Cancel Culture, aren't you?"

"Fuckin' Cancel Culture," Peter repeats in agreement.

"Last time I checked, though," Paul says, "these so-called socialists ain't killing other people."

"You mean, commies?"

"What did I say?"

"You said 'socialists.'"

"I thought we were talking about socialism."

"Hey, Cheech, how much weed did you smoke last night?"

"What?" Paul says sourly. "You my father now?"

"Listen, Parrot," Peter says. "I don't know what in the hell you smoking, but to say these little shitheads ain't a threat to our democracy then you, my friend, as the kids say these days, are 'out of touch.'"

"Me? Out of touch?" Paul says quietly. "A'ight, McCarthy."

"You serious? What about that one guy who got gunned down during a protest the other day? The guy was minding his own fuckin' business!"

"I mean, sure, Pete, some people are gonna get hurt, even die, when you got a whole bunch of people boiling over with emotion and protesting a whole bunch of different stuff, but you agree, the world is in a better place than it was sixty-some years ago. Pete, I mean, come on. We live in a country where you can say whatever you want without having to worry about waking up in the middle of the night with a black bag thrown over her head and being rushed outta your house into an unmarked van."

"They've already started canceling the movies we watch," Peter says, staying firm in his stance. "Even the *books* we read. Wait till they start burning books."

"Wait a sec," Paul says seriously. "You know how to read?"

"Speaking of comedians, you and your kind are next on the chopping block. Imagine that, will ya? A world where we can't even laugh at ourselves."

"You're one to talk."

"Hey, Parrot," Peter says, the passion holding tightly in his voice. "I ain't no saint, you neither. But I ain't gonna live in no world where I can't even laugh at a joke. I mean, you know that's how it all starts, right? They start changing around things, what we see, what we read, then eventually, they start erasing things. *Peter Peter Pumpkin Eater?*" Peter says, letting out a cross between a hiccup and a sigh. His eyes light up in a eureka-like moment. "Bet you didn't know this, but that nursery rhyme wasn't originally about Peter learning 'how to read' or spell or loving his wife very well. Peter was a murdering son of a bitch before they soften him up. Peter, the Peter I read about before they changed him, he killed his whore of a wife after he caught her sleeping around with other guys, then hid her corpse in a pumpkin. Huh? There's even another version where he threw his wife down a chimney. But still, you get my point."

"What's that?" Paul says, the passion bubbling up. "You rather read the version of Peter being a murderer to some poor kid who's about to go nite-nite? Talk about giving a kid nightmares. That kid's gonna be so messed up in the head that every time he looks at his old man, he's gonna be thinking: 'So, when's Dada going throw my mommy down a chimney?'"

Peter removes the white hardhat for a moment to comb back his sweaty hair. He places the hardhat back on his head, but this time wears it more loosely.

"My point is, Parrot," Peter says and pulls out a fruit smoothie from a brown bag, "you can't just go around changing things for the sake of changing things in order to cater to what's fashionably acceptable. Okay. Sure," he says, less confrontationally. "You can make things better. I'm all for making things better, but a nursery rhyme, give the fuck outta here. If these know-it-alls don't like it, then they can make up their own fuckin' nursery rhyme. But, no, that'd be too difficult to create something. For these fuck-holes, it's much easier to destroy."

"Man, Pete, you're on a roll today."

Paul places the rest of the corkscrew-shaped orange peel back in the Tupperware and closes the lid.

With his appetite ruined from the latest rant, Peter picks up the fruit smoothie and struggles to open the cap.

"Eating healthier today, are we?"

"At least I'm not the one eating fruit and nuts for lunch, you fuckin' rabbit."

"Sounds like you got ya animals mixed up."

"Why don't you eat some real food?" Paul says. "Look at you. You're nothing but skin and bones."

"Why?" Peter snaps back. "So, I can to make your ass feel better about your weight? Not my fault that you're so damn insecure about your 'weight problem' that you have to tell other people to eat more so they can look as pathetic as you."

"Whatever," Paul says dismissively. "Can't take a man away from his meat."

"You're disgusting, you know that?"

"Hey, I'm only doing this for the wife. It helps balance out the corn beef."

"That's not how it works, you know?"

"Well, it does for me."

"Sure."

"The wife's trying to get me on this special diet. Ever since my blood work came back last week, she's been up my ass about me taking better care of myself. My cholesterol was through the roof. The bad kind, not the good."

"I didn't know there was such thing as good cholesterol."

"Well, look it up on your *Internet* toy," Peter says sarcastically.

"Maybe you should throw your wife down a chimney, huh?"

"Not my Sally," he says softly. "Don't know where I'd be without her."

Once more, he uses more arm strength to twist open the cap. The cap doesn't budge at all.

"Who the fuck they expect to open these things— Superman?" Peter nods at the adjustable wrench on Paul's tool belt. "I got an idea," he says, holding out his hand. "Here. Hand me your wrench."

"And get your greasy fingers all over my shit? Hell no?"

"Come on," Peter pleads. "I left my tools with José."

"That ain't my problem."

"Are you gonna hand me the fuckin' wrench or what?"

"Fine," Paul says and pulls out the wrench from the holster. Right before he hands it to Peter, he playfully recoils, causing Peter to grab air.

"Quit jerkin' off, will ya? You tryin' to kill someone?"

Peter makes it much easier for Paul to hand over the wrench by casually wiping the grease off his palms and fingers with a napkin.

Eventually, Paul hands the wrench to Peter, who uses it to open up the fruit smoothie.

Once he twists open the cap, Peter hands the wrench back to Paul.

"There," he says. "Was that so fuckin' hard?"

"You can be pushy, you know that?"

"Yeah, yeah, yeah." Peter waves off the comment. "So, how's your lunch so far, Rabbit?"

"You know what you need, Pete?"

"What's that?"

". . ."

Fed up with Peter's insults, Paul rotates his hips around until he can see the empty holster along the tool belt. As he insets part of the wrench into the holster, the wrench suddenly slips from his hand!

In a desperate attempt, Paul reaches out his hand, trying to grab the wrench before it falls below. He comes up empty. The wrench hits the side of the scaffold and pinballs around the metal beams before plummeting thirty-seven stories to the ground.

As both Peter and Paul lean over, they both fall witness to what appears to be an accident. On the sidewalk below, a man's laying face first on the ground and a red puddle of what looks like blood forming below his head.

A couple of construction workers, one of who is responsible for keeping pedestrians from the work site, gather around the motionless man.

With his long face slackened and pale-white from the shock, Paul watches a hooded woman hurry over to the lifeless, unresponsive man. She kneels over his body, reaches inside his inner jacket pocket, removes an item— maybe a wallet— and then darts away.

BELOW, a couple of construction workers rush to Jack, who remains still, lifeless.

Other construction workers are screaming and pointing at Star, who is fleeing from the scene.

In her hand, she's holding a small pouch, *not* a wallet.

FROM above, Paul watches Star run into an alleyway where she escapes through a manhole.

Peter sits up from the overturned bucket and steps closer to Paul, who is still ghost white. Growing even more concerned by what had just happened, he asks Paul, "Did that girl just take that guy's wallet?"

KEY and Stat observe a growing crowd, consisted of mostly construction workers and passerbys, circling around Jack's body.

Some of those pedestrians, giddy and gluttonous, all brandishing their phones and anticipating a "viral-worthy" moment in which they're about to capture, rush past Key and Stat.

In a studious manner, Stat carefully watches the people passing by him. His eyes light up with deep thought, as he identifies the very lifeless source that compels each one and them.

"Amazing how things come together in the Eleventh Hour," Key says to Stat, but more so himself.

"What you mean, Key?" asks Stat.

Key continues to watch the crowd, which gets larger by the second. Among the crowd, each spectator is clinging to their phones, either capturing Jack's final moments of life or filming themselves capturing those moments with their own selfie-like shot followed with commentary. Only one person, a young man in his early twenties, shoulders his way through the crowd, rips off his shirt, and tries to stop the massive hemorrhaging. But his attempts appear to be too late. In one last attempt to save Jack, the young man cries out for someone to call "9-1-1!" But all he receives in return are the lens-side of over a dozens smartphones beating down at him, as if he has unwillingly found himself in a horror movie that he so desperately wants to end, and God willing, never see the light of day.

Stat nods at the crowd and asks Key, "What the hell's going on over there?"

Key doesn't respond. Yet, he remains still, observant.

Stat steps next to Key for a closer look.

"Key," he says, "you okay?"

Once more, Key doesn't answer. He watches the people and the smartphone that controls them, as if, in a way, it has become a part of their very fabric, not an extension but, more or less, a replacement, a master to his or her slave.

"Yo, Key," Stat says, leaning into Key's range of vision, "you good?"

Key turns his head toward Stat.

"Couldn't be any better," he says distantly.

He's already *seen* enough.

As Star climbs down the ladder and enters the sewer system, she takes a moment to find her bearings by scanning both directions of the tunnels, all of which appear to trail off into darkness. She wonders which way will lead her back to what she scathingly calls that "other world." However, Star doesn't put too much decision into which path; yet, she simply follows the strongest stench.

The stench leads her to an intersection of tunnels.

Four dark tunnels wait before her, each one dark and smelly, the air thick and soupy.

Unable to detect the strongest since the stench is everywhere, Star pulls out the small pouch from the hoody pocket. She removes the black crystal from the pouch and holds it in her hand. She breaks down and cries.

While sobbing, a shadow darts along the tunnel wall.

The water splashes behind her, seizing her attention.

Immediately, Star stops crying and remains vigilant.

"Who's there?" asks Star, as she looks down each tunnel.

She stops at one tunnel in particular. In the middle of the tunnel stands an old and raggedy dressed figure, which Star first assumes is a homeless man.

"Hello."

A strange voice rises from the darkness.

"You too, huh?"

The stranger's bony shoulders bob up and down, up and down from what is supposed to be a laugh but comes off like a fiendish snicker, which sounds like a soaked rag being wrung.

Underneath a wall of shadows, the movement reveals an inverted corkscrew-shaped mouth layered with sharp, jagged teeth.

Star immediately recognizes that mouth for she had spent days, even weeks, during her transformation trying to make sense of the mouth while staring, picking, and dissecting it in the mirror.

"Who would've thought?" the gravelly, hissing voice says.

"Who are you?"

"An old friend," the voice says.

To Star, the voice has a certain *click* to it as if there's a certain name attached to it; in fact, she recognizes it, that click, that voice—at least, pieces of his voice.

"Myko?" she says suddenly. "Is that you?"

"I'm afraid Myko's dead," the voice says, as the raggedy-dressed man steps closer into the ray of dim, steam-covered light. "The Myko you once knew. All that remains of him are the memories we share."

"Who are you?" asks Star.

"The real question you should be asking: Who are we?"

"I know who I am," Star says, louder and more ticked off while rejecting the very thing that she has become.

The must, as well as the mugginess, wears on her.

"Who the fuck are you and what do you want?" Star asks, lowering her right gray hand along her waist. Each elongated finger slowly stretches downward and hangs by her side like unwinding spools of rope, revealing these tiny faces similar to her very own face on each fingertip.

"Easy there," he says and points at Star's hand-weapon. "You sure you know how to use that thing?"

"I don't have fucking time for this," Star seethed. "Who are you?"

"I'm Harry," he says.

"What'd you do with Myko?"

Harry holds out his hands.

"*He who wearsss the Crown shall rule the Town.*"

"What the hell does that even mean?"

"Myko was weak, unworthy of the Crown," Harry says. "I can say the same about you, that is before you *crossed* over, but everybody knows that vamp poison turns you into something you're not."

"You don't have the slightest clue of who I am," Star rebukes.

"Maybe not entirely, but I do know: What doesn't kill woman only makes her stronger. Most of us wouldn't dare brave this world, let alone try to take back the life we once had."

Losing her patience, she asks the parasitic creature formerly known as Myko, "Why are you following me?"

"You haven't changed one bit, Star Walker," Harry says, stepping closer into the light, "well," he corrects teasingly, "despite your new. . . *look*. When are you ever going to learn that the world doesn't revolve around you? Funny, though, us bumping into each other in the bowels which binds us from this world. . . " Harry points at the streets, his beady gray eyes faintly glowing from the streaks of light pouring through a rusty grate along a busy sidewalk above, ". . . to the next. Perhaps it's a sign from the *Catsss*."

Fearful of her safety, Star carefully takes a step back.

"Ever since our last candidate, who couldn't handle the pressure of wearing the Crown," Harry says to a more timid Star, "we've been searching for the One to rightfully wear the Crown and represent our cause."

"Your cause?"

Approaching Star, Harry says, "A New Age of Disinformation is upon us and it's gaining momentum." Between the raggedy and ratty raised collars of his coat, Harry reveals part of his ill-colored face, like Star's, wrinkled and inhuman. "For decades, the world has become more sterilized. Now, it has reached an era where it must be ridden of its cleanliness and artificiality. The chemicals, disinfectants, sanitizers, all of it must come to an end once and for all." He steps closer to Star, revealing more parts of his face in the dim light. "The Dirty One who *wearsss the Crown* will bring back order and balance to the natural world. Those who oppose us will be baptized in the Righteous Filth in which they loathe."

"Yeah," Star says slowly. "Good luck with that. Now, if you would excuse me. . . "

Tempting to deviate from her planned route, which is straight through Harry, Star turns toward the tunnel on her right, which appears safe.

Left at a crossroads, Star's choice becomes clearer to her as she hears a series of laughter, higher in pitch and witch-like, coming from the end of the tunnel directly behind her.

Underneath the chorus of haunting sounds, she picks up at least a dozen footsteps splashing through the sludgy water and heading directly her way. The footsteps grow louder and louder to the point where they demand Star's full attention.

Those clownish and witch-like giggles resonant throughout the maze of sewers, creating a siren-effect. She rotates around and finally acknowledges the disturbance. There, at a distance, she witnesses beams of flashlights cutting through the darkness of the tunnel.

"The *Catsss* have spoken," Harry says grandly. "You are the chosen One."

"Cut the shit," Star says, growing more panicked. "What's going on here?"

"From the smell in the air, I detect Cutas."

"Cutas?"

"Part of the CROCUTA Clan. And hungry too, I may say."

"You mean, as in. . ."

Star can barely muster the words from her mouth as if, by speaking them, she will be hexed by one of their spells.

"Yes," Harry says. "*That* CROCUTA Clan."

"I've heard rumors about them."

"And more than likely, they're all true," Harry says, his tone remaining calm. "What your friend, Myko, would call 'fiercer than his ex mother-in-law.' An elite group of heavily-armed mercenaries with only one objective. Sure, they may not sound like much, but these group of gals, when in numbers, are a force to be reckoned with. I can smell at least eight of them, maybe more."

"And what's their objective, these Cutas?"

"Seek and devour, of course."

"Great," Star says, as the sharp laughing sound grows louder and louder. "So can you help me or not?"

"I can hold them off, but you must leave now before it's too late."

Star starts making her way to the tunnel on the right.

"This way," Harry says, pointing toward the other tunnel on the left. "If you follow this tunnel toward the end, you can take drainage pipe and wind up in California in just a few minutes. I know," he says before she has a chance to respond, "not so bad, huh? These tunnels can come in handy."

"I'm not trying to get back to California," Star says. "I'm trying to get back to the other world."

"*That world*, huh? Why didn't you say so?" As though he's in no rush at all considering the possible danger quickly approaching, he steps aside and points at the tunnel directly behind him. "Take this tunnel here to the first intersection," he directs. "Once you reach the inter-section, take a right and count twenty steps, no more, no less, until you find a crack on the right side of the wall. It's going to be a tight fit," he looks over Star's slender body, "but you'll fit. We *alwaysss* fits."

"I'm not like you," Star says with indignation.

"Don't be ashamed of what you've become, Star Walker."

Star hears yet another sound, much deeper yet, at the same time, much higher in pitch than the laughing hyenas.

"What's that sound?"

"Just a few friends of mine," Harry says calmly.

To Star's right, she witnesses a growing wave of what looks like thick brown floodwater charging through the tunnel. She peers closer and realizes that it's not a wave but a wall of scurrying rats, each and every one of them moving directly at Star whether it be rolling or toppling over one another, nonetheless, a mad dash to the present danger.

Suddenly, Star hears gunfire coming from the other end of the tunnel, forcing her to stay low.

Bullets buzz over her head and strike the walls around her.

Once she spots the shooter—or multiple shooters—she's left stunned by what she's actually seeing with her own eyes.

In a highly trained, tactical stealth-like manner, the clan of half-woman half-hyena mercs storm through the tunnels. Each one is dressed in dark tactical clothing, bulletproofs vests, heavily armed, assault rifles drawn and aimed directly at Star. Their shoulders are much wider, their posture slightly more hunched over.

In a quick glimpse, Star acknowledges their facial appearance, which appears more animal than woman: their wide eyes are black and sinister, their coarse skin spotted with brownish spots and birthmark-like patterns, their hairdo worn in Mohawk-fashion. The flashlights bring out their manes, creating a disturbing silhouette. The only feature of their face that appears the most human is the mouth and nose region. Instead of a snout, their nose is smaller and slightly darker in color.

Each one is quite vocal too, with their giggles and growls.

Right before Star takes off, she leaves with a snapshot of one image in particular in her mind: a heavily-armed mercenary gawking at her, eyes black, sweat like slime dripping down the sides of her face. Of all the Cutas—eight of them, as Harry indicated—based on the unique patterns along her skin, she appears different than the other Cutas. She has dark stripes, *not* spots.

While the highly dangerous clan closes in, the wall of rats barrels past Harry and acts like a shield against the barrage of gunfire.

Among the chaos unfolding behind her, the Cutas still remain the most vocal by whooping and whining or grunting and groaning; however, the one sound that stands out the most is the giggling.

Star barely manages to escape without getting struck. Harry stands back as if he has an unspoken bond with the rats—in a way, he's like a maestro conducting his great symphony, his rats being his orchestra hitting each note, whether it be an aggressive attack on one mercenary or a sudden formation of a barricade to prevent bullets from striking him. A mischief of at least a hundred rats swarms several mercenaries, nibbling at their paw-like hands and pulling the rifles from their grips and smothering them.

As Harry "holds off" the mercenaries with his backup of rats, Star manages to barely escape from the chaos.

She makes it to the first intersection where she is given three pathways. She does as Harry said and takes a right. She counts out each and every footstep until she reaches the number twenty. There, she locates a crack in the wall. She kneels down and peeks through the narrow opening. "It's tight," as Harry said; however, Star understands that she has no other way out of here.

As Star's about to kneel down, a shadow appears in the corner o her eye. The dim light becomes dimmer.

With the tension building, she hears that familiar laugh next to her. She turns her head upward and finds one of those mercenaries, the one with stripes, bearing down on her.

The mercenary uses the butt of the assault rifle to strike Star in the forehead.

Dazed by the blow, Star is forced to the ground. She struggles to gain control over the mercenary's weapon; however, the hyena-looking woman is stronger and much more aggressive. For her, she doesn't need her clan. She is a hunter, not a scavenger; however, what the mercenary doesn't realize is that Star has a weapon of her own.

As the mercenary overpowers Star for the assault rifle, Star rears back her fist and using all the strength in her body, punches the mercenary directly in her gapping, drooling mouth right before the mercenary open fires. Star's hand—better yet, most of her arm—rams down the mercenary's throat, causing her to choke.

Squealing and, at the same time, laughing, the mercenary pulls the trigger but wildly misses her target. A string of gunfire runs across the tunnel ceiling above in an oscillated sprinkler-like motion.

With her snake-like fingers crawling deeper down the mercenary's throat, the mercenary drops to one knee. Hundreds of those pervasive snake worms are visible underneath the mercenary's skin, slithering around her brain, strangling vital organs, clotting certain vessels.

Once the mercenary flops over dead, Star retracts her hand from the mercenary's throat. Her hand and forearm covered with salvia and chunks of vomit.

"Yuck," Star says, wiping her hand along the hoody.

She directs her attention back to the narrow opening in the wall.

Now, where were we?

STAT glances down at a manhole in the parking lot and can *feel* the tension rising from below.

Key nods at Stat and tells him to wait a minute while he handles some business inside the dilapidated, decaying structure tagged with graffiti and gang signs, which was once a pump house before it was abandoned in the early 1960's. Over the years, kids have branded the building "Stickman," due to the shape of massive steel beams constructed along the rusty pipes that crisscross the interior walls. If you stand at a certain angle, the beams look just like a stickman.

While Stat waits outside, Key enters the pump house. The floors caked with mounds of dust and leftover bits of coal and old gutted out cars, which was said to be the remnants of a chop shop that was once in operation years after Stickman's House was abandoned.

As Key stands before the Stickman, five of the surviving Cutas of the CROCUTA Clan emerge from the shadows.

"Where's the rest of the group?" asks Key.

Heloisa steps forward and assumes her role as the alpha of the Clan. Among the Cutas, Heloisa's injuries are minimal. She has a couple of cuts and bruises on her face and arms, unlike the other four Cutas whose injuries vary from torn, nibbled off flesh to severed fingers, even arms, to deep, war-like wounds. Each one limping or clutching their injuries.

"We were outnumbered, sir," Heloisa reports. "She knew we were following her."

"You tellin' me she was responsible for the way you look?"

"She wasn't alone," Heloisa says, struggling to look Key in the eyes. "She had help."

Key surveys the other four Cutas behind Heloisa.

"Where's Taytu?"

Knowing how close Key was to Taytu, Eshe, who is considered the mouthy one of the Clan, answers timidly,

"She didn't make it. It was the girl. She is responsible for Taytu's death."

"The girl is responsible," Key says, as a heavily concealed anger floods over him. "Right."

Key asks for Heloisa's assault rifle. Willingly, she hands it over. Key looks over the weapon.

"Did I ever tell you how I earned the name, M16?" asks Key.

Heloisa responds with a shake of her head.

"The year was 1984," Key says, "just two years before I rescued Taytu from those savage witch lords in Addis Ababa. Peak of summer," he says, as he paces around Heloisa. "The heat has a way of bringing out the best in people—and the worst. One hot afternoon, these two cats wearing whiteface stormed into a small Mom and Pop shop on the street corner and robbed them blind. They took all the money from the cash registers. Both armed. Both desperate. The two didn't stop with the registers, though. You see the Pop in 'Mom and Pop' goes by the name, Clint. Clint keeps his life savings inside a safe in the back of the store. The obvious question is 'So how'd these cats know about a safe to begin with?'" Key asks but doesn't expect Heloisa to answer. "Well, one of the cats happens to be Clint's nephew, Bobo. I couldn't recognize Bobo's face because of the white paint on his face; but anybody who knew Bobo, knew that nervous tick he made in the corner of his face. He lived on my street, but I never spoke to him. I didn't particularly care much for Bobo's gang and their so-called 'mission.' Two days later, police busted them based on an anonymous tip they received. So, initially, I was the first person on their radar. Me, and of course, Uncle Clinton. I didn't give a shit about the crimes those two fools committed. But I knew they had already made up their minds. First, it was Mom and Pop who caught a bullet—the thing about the bullet is that the bullet has a way of bringing out the truth in any man. Turns out Uncle Clinton would do about anything to save his own skin, even if it meant making up some bullshit about the snitch who he made me out to be. On the next night after they came for Mom and Pop, Bobo's boys waited till I left work and followed me back home. Before I had a chance to turn to the car creeping up behind me, it was already done. They turned my ass into Swiss cheese. Bullets bounced around my insides like pinballs. Over the years I've been hit countless times before. I mean, after all, how many battles have we fought?"

"Too many," Heloisa responds, her head lowered in a dog-like shame.

"Never knew that I'd be named after the very thing that almost destroyed me. After awhile, the name sort of grew on me."

Key walks up to Eshe, who's clutching her side, and without hesitation, aims the M16 assault rifle at Eshe's lower half and pulls the trigger. Holding the rifle with only one hand, the recoil causes Key's arm to swing upward, bullets plugging Eshe's body from her lower abdomen and up.

After Key finishes off Eshe, he hands the rifle back to Heloisa. He turns his sinister gaze toward the others, Makda, Jazarah, and finally, Nuru, who is missing part of her arm.

"Find her and bring her to me," Key says to Heloisa and then emphasizes, "I want her *alive*. You understand?"

"Yes, sir," Heloisa says and as she's about to exit Stickman's House, glances at Eshe's dead body with a sense of melancholy in her black eyes.

"THE CURIOUS CASE OF BIFF CRALEY"

"YOU guys ever seen that one movie where he played a bank robber?" asks one of the head surgeons, Doctor Harcourt, who makes another deep incision through a second layer of tissue along the side of the patient's lower left abdominal area.

"*Stolen Heart*?" one of the nurses says.

Doctor Harcourt pauses mid-slice, looks up through the oversized spectacles.

Unsure of the name, he asks, "Was that the name of it?"

"Pretty sure," the nurse says in a monotone voice.

"I swear I thought it was something else, like, I dunno, forget it—" Doctor Harcourt says from the corner of his mouth, shakes off the thought, and proceeds to cut, "—move the light two inches to the right, will you?"

Another nurse moves the overhead light, as directed, two inches to the right, revealing what looks like an ear protruding from the bloody cavity.

"Thank you kindly, Teresha," Doctor Harcourt says and continues to cut until the full head of a man is revealed underneath all that flesh and bone. With a tube, the nurse, Teresha, cleans and sucks out the blood from the cavity, revealing more the side of a face, Biff's face. "Anyway, Karen and I didn't have anything going on last Saturday night so we decided to do a little dinner and a movie. We hadn't done one in quite some time, especially with the kids trying out these new virtual classes. I remember our last dinner and a movie Karen cooked while I picked out the movie, which was one of those shoot-'em up movies—*Maneater*. Seen it?"

The nurse's cheeks lift underneath the mask. "Nia forced me to watch it last week. It was. . . " she shrugs her left shoulder, ". . . meh."

"Just meh?" The nurse doesn't respond to Doctor Harcourt. "Who doesn't like watching a strong female protagonist take the law into her own hands?"

"Apparently, Teresha doesn't."

"I'm more of a rom-com type of gal."

"Well, anyway. . . " Doctor Harcourt says and hands off the bloody scalpel to the nurse while he adjusts a massive retractor system over the patient's morbidly obese body, ". . . this time I was in charge of the cooking while Karen picked out the movie."

"What'd you make?" asks one nurse from behind.

"Filet mignons sautéed in butter, two baked Russet potatoes, and then, a side of asparagus topped with Parmesan cheese, all local, of course. For dessert, Karen and I shared a slice of cheesecake dusted with flakes of white chocolate and drizzled with a raspberry sauce, which was to die for. I tell you it was the highlight of the night."

"Stop it, Richard," the nurse says, "you're making me hungry."

Doctor Harcourt inserted the retractor along the sides of the opening.

"So, I take it you didn't care much for *Stolen Heart*?"

"To tell the truth," he says, "no. Not really." He looks down at the covered patient on the operation table. "Sorry to break the news to you, Biff, buddy, but you should stick to the old Westerns."

"Really?" Teresha says. "I actually thought his acting improved when he left spaghetti Westerns."

"You sound just like Karen," the doctor says and maneuvers the bloody head from the opening in the patient's body. "If I didn't know any better, I'd say Karen has a crush on Biff here."

"Fun fact," one of the other nurses says from the darkness of the room, "you know Biff's not even his real name. It's his stage name."

"Huh? I didn't know that."

"Want to know his real name?"

"Absolutely—"

"—Sparrow Watcher."

"Sparrow, huh?"

Doctor Harcourt laughs following a string of nurse laughter. He jokes, "I can see why he changed his name to a manly name like," he quotes with the flicker of his brow, "'Biff Craley.'"

"Another fun fact: Craley is the name of the town he was born in."

"Well, *I did not know that*," Doctor Harcourt says teasingly in his worst attempt at a Johnny Caron impersonation. "Okay," he finds a grip around the sides of the head, "I think our new friend here is ready to enter the world."

Another nurse steps into the dark operation room and says from the doorway, "Narcissus has arrived, Doctor Harcourt."

"Great," he says, struggling to wiggle free the head, "tell him I'm in the middle of an extraction and I'll be with him shortly."

"Yes, sir," the nurse says, exiting the room.

As Doctor Harcourt pulls the body from the vessel, two other nurses step in and give him a hand.

"On the count of three, I'm going to ease the specimen down on the other table," he says, gently removing the so-called "specimen."

The team eases the bloody naked body onto a smaller table while the pulse of the other body, the obese one covered in a greenish blue sheet, begins to fade.

"Okay," Doctor Harcourt says to the nurse. "Finish him."

The nurse injects the "finish-all" drug into the IV, causing an immediate flatline.

The doctor snaps the face of a newly born Biff.

The newest version of Biff slowly cracks open his eyes.

Doctor Harcourt removes the surgical mask from his face and says kindly to him, "Welcome back."

❧

AFTER scrubbing down, Doctor Harcourt meets Narcissus in a waiting room outside the operation room.

"Narcissus," he says professionally and shakes Narcissus's hand.

"Richard," Narcissus says.

"How's Mickey?"

"Busy."

"I bet," Doctor Harcourt says.

"How are the elephants doing?"

"As a matter of fact," the doctor says, "they couldn't be better."

"And the vaccine," Narcissus says. "How's it coming along?"

188

"Well, we've just finished the first test on the rats and already started the next trial," Doctor Harcourt says. "We won't know much until results come back. But so far, knock on wood. . . " he says and searches for a piece of wood to knock on, finds a coffee table, *knocks* on it, ". . . everything's going according to plan."

"Key will be pleased to know."

"So, what's Mickey up to these days? Still trying to take over the world?"

"He's preparing a trip to Heaven where he's going to wrap up some last minute business. Tie up loose ends."

Carrying a small portable ice cooler, the nurse enters the waiting room.

"The package, sir," she says and hands the cooler to Doctor Harcourt, who, in return, thanks the nurse, Melissa, and hands the cooler to Narcissus.

Narcissus opens the cooler and grabs the bag of two recently severed eyeballs sitting on a couple of ice packs.

"I assume these are the right ones."

"As Mickey requested."

Narcissus closes the cooler.

Doctor Harcourt holds out his hand.

"While you're here, would you like to take a quick tour of the complex? I'd like to show you around the housing units. We have a new—"

"—Can't," Narcissus interrupts. "Gotta long drive ahead of me."

Even though Doctor Harcourt realizes Narcissus can't see his expression, yet he only senses it mainly with his ears and nose, which are rumored to be stronger than both a bloodhound and wax moth combined—in fact, rumor has it that these two senses are so strong they're able to sense the dead—he smiles anyway and in a friendly manner, gives Narcissus a gentle touch on the shoulder. Finally, the doctor says to Narcissus, "Some other time, then."

DRIVING in a white unmarked van along a narrow two-lane road, Teresha makes her way through the pitch-black desert until she finally reaches the hazy, unnatural lights radiating from the Red Rocks along the outskirts of Sedona, Arizona.

Passing through mountainscapes, she drives down a rugged valley that opens up to even more desert. The source of light comes from the main headquarters of Neuvak Corporation, the entire property covering roughly seven thousand acres.

Once she reaches the massive state-of-the-art complex, she stops at the first security post where she's greeted by a security guard named Elliot.

"Back again, are we?" says Elliot.

"I forgot a couple of my belongings."

"If you want, I can have one of the guys bring them to you."

"That won't be necessary," she says. "I promise I'll be in and out."

Instead of using the implant, Teresha swipes her key-card along the scanner.

Once Elliot authorizes Teresha to enter, he nods at yet another security guard who is camped inside the station. The guard hits a red button, which opens up the heavy steel gate.

"Have a good night, Ms. Dolby," Elliot says, nodding goodbye.

Upon entry, Teresha arrives at yet another security post where another security guard opens another much smaller gate without any question. Teresha drives through the town-like complex with numerous buildings until she reaches a parallelogram-shaped building numbered "36." She parks the van behind the building where yet another security guard, younger and scrawnier looking, named Bautista, exits from the backdoor.

"About time," he says, surveying the back lot in paranoia.

Teresha exits from the van and opens the backdoor while Bautista disappears inside for a moment and reappears with a bagged body tied to a wheeled stretcher.

Trying not to tear or rip the bag by hitting the sides of the doorway, Bautista struggles to wheel the corpse to the back of the white van and with Teresha's assistance, slides it off the stretcher and places it inside with a loud grunt.

Teresha unzips the bag and peeks inside. Among the pile of flesh stuffed inside the bag, she locates Biff Craley's head. She immediately notices that both of the eyes are missing.

"What happened here?" asks Teresha, nodding at the hollowed out eye sockets.

"The hell if I know," Bautista says. "I did my part. Now, it's time for you to live up to your end of the deal."

"Very well," Teresha says, zipping up the bag.

She closes the doors behind her.

Nodding to the front of the van, she first removes and loosens the tucked shirt from the waistband, then unbuttons the top button of the shirt.

"Let's make this quick," she says, walking toward the driver's side.

Teresha opens the door and steps inside.

Licking his lips, Bautista follows suit and walks to the passenger side.

AFTER Teresha drives off with Biff's corpse, Bautista casually makes his way into Building "36" and stops at the men's restroom to take a piss before heading back to the surveillance room. Once finished, he stops by the sink to, not only wash his hands, but also wash other areas of his body. Using a paper towel, he vigorously washes his genitals, making sure to scrub away every inch of Teresha.

Afterwards, he returns to the surveillance room.

While skimming the monitors, another security guard, Harrison, glances over his shoulder at Bautista, who, strangely, develops a cough after returning from the restroom.

"Nice work, *Don Juan*?" Harrison asks, kicks up both legs, crosses them, and rests the backside of his heels against the edge of the table. "You finally get that bug outta your system?"

"Shut up," Bautista says, fighting off the sudden cough.

"Hey," Harrison says, "I know how long you've being trying to hit that. I'm surprised you're not doing flips right now."

"Whatever," Bautista says, powering through the words. "Least," cough, "I can," cough, "get," cough, "some action, unlike you," cough, "miserable prick."

"I got ninety-nine problems and hooking up with a co-worker ain't one."

Bautista coughs more, his face reddening, veins in his forehead swelling.

"You okay over there, Don Juan?" asks Harrison.

Annoyed by Harrison, Bautista waves off the security guard.

"Good," he says, gaining control over the cough.

NARCISSUS parks the car in front of Forest City Penitentiary, a maximum-security prison located in North Ridge, California.

He pulls out the small case tucked away in a breast pocket and carefully removes the contact lens with his index finger. He tilts back his head and with his other hand, pries open his left eye and inserts the first contact lens. Following the same method, Narcissus inserts the other contact lens into the other eye. Once the contacts are in, he blinks both of his brown eyes, as if, by doing so, he's straightening the lens. The last thing he'd want to do is walk in there with one eye looking one way and another eye looking the other way, like a walleye, and having the guards guessing, even asking unnecessary questions.

Adjusting to the contacts, he reaches over the center console, grabs the cooler from the passenger seat, and cracks it open, revealing that bag of eyeballs resting on several ice packs.

STROLLING along Cell-Block 6, a prison guard named Ray stops at one particular cell and slips a pack of *Gypsy Wides* through the food slot.

Ray leans down next to the opening and says, "It looks like you got yourself a secret admirer, Pretty Boy."

Sitting behind a desk along the cell wall, Drenelle, who's sketching an outfit with a shrapnel of graphite, glances over the purple-framed reading glasses at that wider than usual cigarette pack lying on the floor.

"You know I don't smoke," she says sassily at Ray.

"Sure," Ray says shortly, closes the slot, and walks away.

Drenelle drops the graphite along the messy desk, which is covered in various sketches of outfits and new clothing designs, and runs her hands over her shaved head.

With a sigh, Drenelle slides the chair out from under the desk, stands up from the seat, walks over to the door, and picks up the pack of cigarettes. Immediately, she notices two slight bulges along the surface of the pack, as well as the weight, which seems inconsistent. She takes the pack back to her desk and while bracing herself, cracks it open. On the underside of the lid are a couple of streaks of dark blood. Carefully, she pulls out the two eyeballs from inside the cigarette pack and sets them along the edge of the desk.

FIGHTING against strong gusts of wind created by the rotary blades, Ruby stands firmly at a safe distance as the helicopter descends onto the helipad, which sits on top of one of the tallest buildings in Downtown Los Angeles.

After the helicopter sticks the landing, Key, who's sporting a white suit, exits from the cabin and meets up Ruby.

"Any word from Narcissus?" Key asks over the sound of the helicopter behind him.

Holding the hair from her face, Ruby leans in closer and says, "I'm sorry."

"Narcissus," Key says, louder. "Any word?"

"Not yet, sir," Ruby says, as she escorts Key to the seventy-third floor where, along the side of the entranceway, those letters of the logo "U.S. BANK," which were once displayed on the crown of the tower, remain stacked against the wall.

"Something's not right," Key says, passing the famous logo. "He should've called by now."

Another item catches his eye.

Perched next to the logo are two large cardboard boxes, which have recently been delivered to the building formerly known as U.S. Bank Tower.

Key cracks open both boxes, first starting with one box. He digs through the popcorn padding until he reaches the massive letter "M," which will replace the former logo on the crown of the tower. He checks the other box and discovers the other letter, "W," buried underneath all that Styrofoam popcorn.

"I was meaning to tell you," Ruby says, walking ahead, "the new logo came in."

"Looks nice," Key says, leans down, and runs his hand along the giant letter "W."

"Also," Ruby says, recalling the recent phone call with the copyright holders of the movie franchise, *The Effigy*, as she makes her way to the bar. "We also secured the rights to *The Effigy*."

"Good," Key says plainly and leaves the sign. He walks into the penthouse-like room overlooking Downtown Los Angeles while Ruby waits by the bar and does some last second primping, as well as adjusting her black blazer and matching skirt.

Her phone rings. She checks the number.

"Speak of the devil," she says.

"Is it him?" asks Key, as he removes the white well-tailored sports coat and tosses it on the back of a sofa.

"Unknown number," she says. "Must be."

"Answer it."

Ruby does.

Turns out Ruby is right.

"Narcissus," she says, walks over to Key, and hands him the phone.

"Give me good news, Narcissus."

"She'll do it," Narcissus says. "It took a little convincing, but she's in."

"How was she?"

"Well, she's making the best of her time. She mainly focuses on her work. It keeps her sane. Every now and then, the guards give her a hard time. She won't have to worry about them anymore. Other than that, I believe she's ready."

"Good," Key says. "Well done, Narcissus. I'll see you soon."

Key hangs up and hands the phone back to Ruby.

"So, it's on?" Ruby says, her voice dragging out like a question.

"It's on," Key says and walks to the window overlooking the downtown. "I would like you to be there, Ruby."

"Sure," she says plainly.

As Key gazes at the city before, he says to Ruby, "I bet you didn't get views like this when you were prancing around New York."

"I can't say I did."

An awkward silence forms between the two.

Ruby does what she does best and kills the silence with questions.

"So, how was your business trip?" asks Ruby.

"Terrible as always," Key says with disdain. "Never seen so many repulsive creatures throughout my entire

THE TRAGEDY OF THE FIVE FISTFULS

existence. Those gluttonous fools call themselves the High Order, yet there's absolutely nothing 'high' about them. If they were so goddamn enlightened, they would possess the intuition to see what's coming their way." More disgusted by the recent business trip to Heaven, he shakes his head. "Not like anything I have to say to those gassy blowhards would make any difference. Their days are numbered," he trails off and moves his attention toward the exterior structure of the building. "You know what they used to call this building?"

"No, sir," Ruby says.

"The Library Tower."

"Why'd they call it that?"

"Never thought you ask." Key turns his deep study from the structure to the fading sun along the hazy horizon. "Before this property was leased back in 2003 to U.S. Bancorp, whose parent company happens to be U.S. Bank, the tower was originally constructed following the two fires at the nearby library in 1986 as part of a one billion dollar Los Angeles Central Library redevelopment area. The City of Los Angeles ended up selling air rights to the project's developers to pay for the reconstruction of the library, hence naming the tower the Library Tower."

"I learn something new from you everyday," Ruby says, standing anxiously next to the bar.

"I know sometimes you feel like you might've made a mistake leaving your cozy job working at that failing magazine to work for someone whom you know very little about," Key says, facing Ruby. "Not to come off as. . . " Key pauses, searching for the right word, ". . . What's the word? Right. *Pretentious.* I assure you, Ruby, that what I'm doing here will change the world forever."

Ruby's cheeks fill with red. She shakes her head.

"You don't have to stress importance of what you're doing, Mickey. Otherwise, I would've never accepted the job."

"Right," Key says, grinning. "Of course."

Key walks closer to Ruby, who, in return, becomes more fidgety by his presence.

"But *still*, you have doubts, as you should. You must realize that you have a role here, Ruby. And it's not just assisting me. You play an intricate part in shaping how the story plays out."

"Yes," Ruby says, finding the strength within to display confidence. "And I want to thank you for the opportunity."

"It's normal to feel uneasy, Ruby," Key says, standing before Ruby. "After all, it's not everyday you get to work for a god."

Despite the unusually "big" magic trick he pulled the other day with making a real-life dragon appear slumped over directly the iconic *Hollywood* sign situated on Mount Lee in the Hollywood Hills of the Santa Monica Mountains, she nearly loses it from what she perceives as his male ego. Sure, he's good at getting inside people's heads. But an actual god is stretching it, Ruby tells herself.

Maintaining her best straight face, Ruby says sharply, "Right."

Her eyes trail downward, head following, which causes a rogue bang of hair to loosen from the ponytail and fall alongside her face.

Key uses his fingers to curl the bang of hair around her ear, securing the hair in place.

"Thanks," she says, as she remains unflustered by Key's closeness.

"Say," Key says, drifting off in mild reflection, "did I ever tell you the story behind the High Five?"

"No, sir," Ruby says, shaking her head. "You didn't."

"Except for the name, which, as I speak, is still a work-in-progress—"

"—Yes," Ruby interrupts, "well, according to the latest update on the roster, they came up with a new name for the show."

"Really?"

"Want to hear it?"

"Absolutely."

"The. . . " Ruby stops for a moment to compose herself.

"The?"

"The Fuck-It-All Five, sir."

A thick, tense silence forms between the two.

Surprisingly, Key laughs, his booming laughter cutting through the silence.

"The Fuck-It-All Five," he repeats, trailing off with laughter and disbelief. "I like the name. I do. *But* I'm afraid they're going to have to come up with something else."

More relieved by Key's amusement in the new name, Ruby says in good spirits, "You should've heard the other two names the girls were work-shopping before they landed on Fuck-It-All Five."

"I'm listening."

"Five Spice was the first one," Ruby lists, pauses, and thinks about the second one.

Unimpressed, Key makes a face.

"And what was the other one?" Ruby asks herself; however, she doesn't have to think too hard about the name. "Right," she says. "Fist Fuck Five."

"Blunt yet, strangely, catchy," Key says with a grin on his face, "maybe too on the nose, though. Those girls know we can't use the word *fuck* on cable TV. I know, right? We can televise a werewolf snake tearing apart a pig, yet we can't even use the word *fuck*. It's too bad we couldn't cut a deal with HBO. But, then again, not everybody has HBO."

"That's what I told them, sir."

"Don't worry. I'll handle it. Now, where was I?" He stops Ruby before she has a chance to answer, "Right." His face lights up as he repeats the name, "The Fuck-It-All Five!"

"THE ACT"
(THE WITCHING HOURS)

PAST the firelight, a tall, lanky silhouette appears along the dark, reddish horizon, following the dribbling sound of jagged pebbles rolling down the mountainside.

"I told you so," a voice says from the darkness outside the fire.

A cloaked figure returns to a circular platform right below the steep summit of Dark Mountain where the other four members of the group formerly known as the "High Five" gather around a small fire inside a rock pit.

All five of them are dressed in matching costumes: a frayed, oversized cardinal red cloak that stretches to the ground. The hoods help keep their faces lost in the shadows. Except for those trademark personalities (which haven't changed one bit!), it's hard to distinguish who is who based on the similarities in their appearance; however, one of the members of the group, who was once known in another life as Rhonda Abbott—or as her "kids" referred to her as simply "Ms. Abbott"— stands slightly hunched over.

"Told you she'd say 'I told you so,'" Carmen says to Rhonda.

Fay approaches the fire pit and takes her position next to Star, who has stayed relatively quiet ever since her return from the Big Apple.

"They want us to change the name," Fay says boringly.

Carmen says in an uproar, "You're kidding me?"

Fay sighs.

"I shit you not."

"After we spent what felt like years trying to come up with the perfect name."

"FYI, Carmen," Rhonda says, "two years, to be precise. It took us two years to come up with that name."

"Two years?" Fay says questionably. "You mean two months."

"No," Rhonda says, more steadily. "Two years."

"How you know? Have you been crossing over without telling us?"

"Fay, I know it's difficult to get used to, but you must come to terms with the change in time—"

With a stern, almost dark, composure, Mandy says over Rhonda, "—So back to the drawing board."

"We're cutting it kind of close, don't you think? I'd say we go with our second choice."

"What? Five-O?"

"No," Fay says. "Five Spice."

"Seriously?"

"What's wrong with Five Spice?"

"It's super lame. That's what. Can you imagine having to explain what the five spices are in an interview? You didn't think we could name ourselves Five Spice without identifying ourselves as five different spices, did you?"

"Well, it's more collective, you know, like a blend of spices—"

"—More like tribal. We are still individuals, aren't we?"

"I got dibs on Cayenne Pepper," Fay says abruptly. Then tosses in a joke on the side, "Cuz you know I'm come with a little kick. "

"Is Cayenne Pepper even considered a spice? It's grounded from dried chili peppers."

"I know it's grounded from dried chili peppers. But thanks for informing me, Ms. Abbott." Fay mocks Rhonda using a whiny voice, "I'm so sorry for not being a good girl and not raising my hand. Please! Oh please don't punish me!"

"How about ginger?" Mandy says to Fay. "You do come off as somewhat—you know—*gingery*."

Fay looks around the circle.

"Is she calling me what I think she is?"

"Face it, Fay. You have turned into a klutz every since, you know. . . "

"Don't even go there, Carmen."

"Oh! I went there."

"Watch it, Carmen. I'm warning you—"

"—Would you two chill the fuck out," Star says over the two, the sudden interruption bringing about a wave of silence and stares.

"What's up with you, Dark Star?" asks Carmen.

"Obviously, nobody is satisfied with Five Spice. That's why it was our second choice. So, let's just come up with another name. It can't be that hard."

"I'm totally fine with that," Mandy says.

"So, what? I can't be Cayenne Pepper."

"You can still be Cayenne Pepper, Fay," Star says, lifting Fay's crushed spirits, "but we're not using the name Five Spice. Period."

"So, Fuck-It-All is too offensive. So, what then?"

"Ruby said that it wasn't exactly offensive. She just said we couldn't use the word *fuck*."

"Can anybody remember any of the other names we had?" asks Mandy.

"Well," Fay lists, "there was Five Hole, Five Fingers, Top Five—which was, personally, my favorite. Five Below—"

"—Five Below has a ring to it, don't you think?"

"Yeah, I get the whole double entendre. Five Below actually means the five of us below the ground. But face it. Most people are going to associate that name with temperature. So what? Are we going to show up on stage wearing fur coats, toboggans, and snow boots?"

"And have PETA come up with their own campaign in order to cancel us because we're wearing fur? No thank you."

"Any publicity, good or bad, is the best publicity."

"We can always wear faux fur—"

"—That's not the point. Five Below goes to the Slush Pile."

"Not the Slush Pile," Fay whines.

"Bye-bye Five Below."

"I wish we still had High Five. High Five was us. That was our thang, was it not?"

"The name's already been taken, Fay."

"We should sue that nerdy piece of shit for taking our name."

"Technically, he used it before us—well, publicly that is."

"Yeah, but we've been using that name for years."

"I know we have—and yes, High Five was who we were until somebody else used it—but if we use it on the show, then it'll look like we stole it."

"I heard a saying once," Fay says, thinking, "not sure where I heard it, but it went something like this: 'A good artist borrows. A great artist steals.' Or something like that."

"I think it was a good artist replicates, not borrows."

"You sure?"

"I'm pretty sure."

"I got it!" Carmen blurts out. "How about Five Stars?"

"I like it," Rhonda says, nodding. "Or, how about Five Star Review?"

"Five Star Review," Star repeats. "I don't know about that."

"What? Come on! Five-Star Review. Get it? When you review a meal or a book or movie or whatever, you rate it from one star to five stars. There are five of us. Five stars. Get it?"

"Yeah," Star says, her voice drawn out. "We get it. But, Carmen, just think about what doors we're opening with that name. Critics are going to use the name as their own pun."

"Star's right," Fay says. "If we have a bad showing, then we're basically giving people the opportunity to ridicule the name or use it toward their advantage."

"People—critics especially—are always going to take advantage of a name or idea in whatever they're reviewing."

"Five-Star Review is a little *too* confident, don't you think?"

"Fine," Carmen says. "You're the creative one here, Fay. Let's hear it."

"How about we drop the adjectives, cut all the bullshit, and just simply name ourselves The Five?"

"Lame!" Rhonda says after Fay. "Not only lame, but also *super*-lame."

"Really," Carmen says. "Come on, Fay. You disappoint me. The Five? The Five-What? The Five Parasite-Looking Bitches Whose Sole Act Involves French-Kissing Some Poor Schmuck. . . " Carmen rotates around and points to the "poor schmuck," who happens to be a frail naked man lying on the ground with his right ankle chained to an oblong-shaped boulder and a gag tied to his mouth, ". . . Who, Eventually, Will Turn Into Some Parasite-Looking Bitch? Or, should we be a little more concise?"

"How about The Scaly Five?" Mandy suggests while peeling a piece of dead gray skin from the side of her cheek.

"Being a giant snake worm has its advantages like smelling things from miles away or being able to squeeze into tight places. It reminds me of the time I was a girl crawling my way through tight spaces, like under the bed or inside a closet or inside this cubbyhole underneath the staircase. It was probably the one cool thing about being a kid, crawling into places that most adults couldn't."

"Well, now you can, Fay?"

"Yeah," Mandy says over Carmen, "but its disadvantages do outweigh its advantages, like dry, scaly skin."

Mandy flicks away the piece of skin.

"Does your skin ever get dry and scaly?" Fay asks Star.

"Yes," she says. "At times. Why wouldn't it?"

"Well, you know, black don't crack."

"If I may, let me ask you a question, Fay."

"Be my guest."

"Do I look black to you?"

Fay looks around at the others until, finally, she rests her beady black eyes on Star.

"No, but you were—"

"—I was, but not anymore. *Clearly*." Star composes herself. "It looks like I'm no different than you now, Fay, only a little less two-dimensional and a little less racist."

"Damn," Many utters. "She said the r-word."

"Ouchhh," Carmen hisses, as if she's slowly rubbing in the diss like salt to an open wound.

"Does that offend you, Fay? That we're now the same color? You, no longer 'white' and me, no longer 'black.'

203

Or, hold up. Didn't you describe yourself as 'light orange,' was it?"

"Oatmeal-brown, to be exact."

"Right," Star says sarcastically. "Oatmeal-brown. How did I forget?"

The other three, Carmen, Rhonda, and Mandy, burst out laughing at both Star and Fay picking at each other's former skin tone.

"Are you through, Star?" asks Fay.

"How would you describe this tone?" asks Star, as she holds up her hand.

"Looks like gray to me," Carmen says before Fay can answer.

"Well, technically, it's cerulean frost."

"Cerulean frost? Get outta here!"

"I dunno, Fay," Mandy says, studying yet another dried flake of skin between her flat, wrinkled fingertips. "Looks more like manatee gray."

This time, all five, including Fay, laugh.

"But seriously, guys—

"—Where we go again."

"What?"

"You offended the pronoun police."

"You know we're not allowed to use the word *guys* anymore."

"Says who?"

"Says, you know, them."

"Them who, Fay?"

"Now, what's wrong with the word *guys*?" asks Rhonda, as Fay thinks more about who these mysterious "them" are. "I've been using 'guys' for years. None of my students had a problem with it back then. So, what gives?"

"It's sexist."

"Sexist? How is it sexist when the plural word 'guys' refers to either male or female? What are they going to complain about next: the word *human*? Does the 'man' part in human offend them? Or, how about *mankind*?"

"Well, Rhonda, take a good look in the mirror," Mandy says grimly. "I don't think this argument involves us?"

"Whatever," Rhonda mutters. "Let's just start referring to ourselves as letters in the alphabet in order to identify our sexual orientation."

"Pop quiz, Rhon-Rhon," Fay says, "but you're, like, I dunno, two generations late to the party."

Rhonda shoots a glance at Fay and says with a patronizing tone, "No offense, darling. But this is how it all starts. People get offended by words we use, even if it's as innocent and trivial as the word '*guys*,' which inevitably leads to those who we vote into power to ban certain words; then, those who use these certain words will be severely punished. What's even worse is when they 'soften' the words for our ever-so precious children, who need to be coddled and told that everything is going to be okay. They've been doing this shit for years; and then, when banning words isn't good enough, because nothing ever is, what do you know? They start eradicating speech altogether—"

"—Are you through, Rhonda?"

"You haven't changed one bit, *Ms.* Abbott," Fay says, emphasizing the "Ms." in Ms. Abbott. "As one of those letters you were referring to, I take great offense toward your blatant insensitivity—"

"—First of all, Rhonda is clearly upset and doesn't mean what she's saying," Carmen says over Fay and aims those menacing black eyes at Rhonda. "And secondly, when's the last time you looked underneath your cloak?"

"You're right, but still," Fay says sadly, "words do hurt. Not all the time, but sometimes."

"Sorry, Fay," Rhonda says, more sincerely.

With her head lowered in the long shadows of the hood, Fay struggles to look at Rhonda.

"As I was saying before you two interrupted me," Carmen says, as she rotates around and points to the gagged man chained to the boulder, "we have our debut coming up. We have *no* name. No only that, not a single one of us has mastered, you know, 'that,' whatever you want to call it."

The rest of the group waits in an awkward and rather uncomfortable silence.

Finally, Mandy is first to speak.

"Star has," she says bluntly.

Star chimes in, "Star has what?"

"You know. . . "

"No," Star says over Mandy, "I don't know, Mandy. You're going to have to be more specific."

"I thought you knew how to *do* 'that.'"

Star doesn't reply, not at first. Instead, she contemplates her next response.

"Is Mandy telling the truth, Star?" asks Carmen.

"Of course, I'm telling the truth. I've seen her do *that*."

"Oh yeah," Star retorts. "When?"

Mandy says to the others, "I followed her into Leatherwood. She was doing 'that' to some bar fly—*literally!*—a six-foot tall walking-talking horse fly dressed in a trench coat. She followed the fly from the zombie bar and grabbed him in the alleyway."

"How'd you know it was a male?" asks Rhonda.

"What?"

"You said 'him.'"

"Him, her, it," Mandy rants, "whatever it was Star did the thing on the fly and it worked. Not too long after Star walked out of the alley, I saw that fly crawling behind her. Its coat was frayed and tattered. Part of its wing was missing. It was no longer a fly."

To say that Star isn't relieved by Mandy's statement is an understatement.

"Mandy's right," Star says, holding her head downward. "I know how to do it."

"You do?"

"Yeah," she says. "I do."

"Why didn't you tell us?"

"I wanted you guys to figure it out on your own."

"You said 'guys.'"

"I did, Fay," Star says, reserved in manner. "Just because we might look different on the outside doesn't mean we're not the same person underneath."

"Well," Carmen says, growing excited, "are you going to show us or what?"

"Okay," Star says finally. "Just one of you. Afterwards, the rest of you have to learn how to do 'the act' on your own." Star turns to Fay, who's still wounded from Rhonda's previous remarks. "What do you say, Fay?"

"I dunno," she says. "Can't we like spin a bottle or something?"

"Come on," Star says with encouragement. "It'll be fun."

"Fun?" Indicating disgust, Fay's round mouth curls inward in an hourglass-like shape. "Seriously? What's so fun about regurgitating your insides into another *man*?"

"You might enjoy it."

"What's to enjoy?"

Star nudges Fay.

"It's like learning how to ride a bicycle."

"I dunno, Star."

"Quit being such a drag."

"I'm not being a drag."

"Yes," Star says. "You are—"

"—All right!" Fay seethes. "I'll do it."

Together, Star and Fay tend to the man lying in a fetal position on the ground. She kneels down and removes the gag from his mouth.

"Please," he begs, "whatever it is that you're about to do, don't do it—"

"—Sorry, pal," Star says. "It's nothing personal. You drew the short end of the straw."

"Technically, Star, the 'drawing the short end of the straw' is irrelevant, considering the usage of straws are banned throughout most of the country."

Star glares at Fay.

The man cries out, "Please!"

With Fay gripping next to her, Star places the gag back in his mouth when, at times, she'd like to place the gag in Fay's mouth.

"Why are people always so whiny before the shit hits the fan?" Star whispers to herself.

"They don't want to get covered in shit," Fay says simply with a shrug.

"Also," Carmen says, as she and the others gather around Star and Fay, "who in their right mind want to clean a room afterwards. Can you imagine trying to remove shit from the wall, let alone the carpet? More than likely, you'd probably have to repaint the wall and if you couldn't remove the stains with carpet cleaner, more than likely, you'd have to replace the entire carpet. I can remember whenever Charlie went number two it was like prepping for surgery. I'd deck myself out in PPE equipment. I'm talking facemask, goggles, gloves; then, afterwards, I'd burn everything in an empty oil drum in the backyard, as if I was burning evidence."

Both wearing a look of concern on their faces, Star and Fay look over their shoulders at Carmen.

"Thanks for the visual trip there, Carmen San Diego."

"What?" Carmen says, shrugging. "My memory's coming back."

"Is that a good or a bad thing?" Fay says to Star.

"Okay," Star says straightforwardly and reels in Fay's attention back to what appears to be nothing more than their guinea pig. "It's not like swapping spit with another person. That's too easy, right?"

"Well, to be honest, I can't even remember the last time I kissed a man."

"Don't worry," Star says. "It's not like that. Take your hand, for example."

Star holds up her hand, Fay mimics.

"Got it," she says. "Now what?"

"The concept is precisely the same," Star says to Fay. "Once you're able to do it with your hand, then you can do it with your mouth or any part of your body for that matter."

"What do you mean 'any' part?" asks Fay.

"I mean *any* part."

"So, for instance, if I wanted to do it with, say, my nipple, I could?"

Fay's face twitches.

"Don't," Star says before Fay bursts out laughing.

"Got it," Fay says, collecting herself. "Any part."

"I know. It sounds insane, right?"

"Yeah."

"Once you unlock the potential of what you're capable of, the options are endless, Fay."

"Tell me more, Professor Walker," Fay says jubilantly.

Star raises her hand again.

"The hand," she says.

"Why not start with my elbow?" Fay asks, as she bends her elbow inward as if she's striking the air. "I feel more comfortable using my elbow—"

"—*The hand*," Star says over Fay.

Fay listens.

Following suit, Fay holds up her hand.

"M'kay," she says.

"First off," Star says clearly, "you have to forget about everything you once were. Believe it or not, you can do things with this new body that your old body wasn't capable of doing; however, you must understand that the way of doing the most basic things is not much different from the way your old body once operated. I mean, how long does it take a baby to walk?"

"A year, maybe more."

"So, think of this as walking."

"Easy for you to say."

"Once you've mastered it, Fay," Star says, honing in on the hand before her, "it will come natural to you."

"I'm confused, Star."

"Let me show you," she says, her hand slightly trembling.

All of a sudden, a tiny slit along each one of her fingertips opens up, releasing several snake worms from the openings. The snake worms squirm and wiggle freely in the air. With her other hand, Star pulls one of the snake worms from her hand and holds it in the air. Once exposed to the elements, the snake worm slithers down her palm and into another pore-like opening along her forearm.

"How'd you do that?" asks Fay.

"I like to think of it as—how do I make it simple for you understand? I think of it as peeing when you don't have to pee."

"Peeing?"

"Yes," Star says, narrowing her eyes as if she's bracing for a verbal assault of harsh criticism. "That's right," she says with a burdensome sigh. "Peeing."

"How would I know what it's like to pee when I don't have to pee? Whenever I had to pee—that is, in my other body—I just went. I never like forced myself to pee. That would be absurd."

"I never really thought about it like that," Carmen says to Rhonda.

"Yeah but Fay. . . " Star says, stumbling around her words as she tries to clarify herself, ". . . have you ever felt like you were being pressured to pee like when someone was waiting for you outside a bathroom stall or maybe a time when you were outside, maybe camping, and there were no bathrooms in sight, except for, of course, nature, and you were around other people, maybe some guys, as in the male kind, and you didn't really have to pee, but you were about to do something really fun or whatever, and you knew that this was the only time you could pop a squat so you did and you somewhat forced yourself to pee."

Fay thinks over Star's comments.

"No," she says blankly.

All of a sudden, a snake worm slithers out of what used to be Fay's middle finger.

"Whoa!" Carmen shouts out. "How'd you do that?"

Fay shrugs and says, "I was just thinking how much I'd for this moment to be over with."

"Well," Star says, "that's just like peeing, am I right? We all just want it to be over with. I mean, who looks forward to peeing?"

"Bet you can't do it again, Fay," Rhonda says from behind.

On command, Fay concentrated on her hand. More snake worms slither from the tips of her fingers.

"Wow!" Fay says. "Now, I know what it feels like to be a man shooting his load."

"Fay! Gross!"

"What?"

"You're ready," Star says, as she removes the gag from the man's mouth and holds his arms behind his back. "Now, I want you to do the same thing with your hand, but this time use your tongue."

"I'm not going to kill him, am I?"

"No," Star teases, "but he's gonna wake up wondering why the hell he looks like Some Parasite-Looking Bitch."

Except for Fay, who remains more nervous from the upcoming performance, the remark draws a couple of laughs from the group.

As Fay anxiously prepares to stick her snake worm-riddled tongue down the man's throat, Carmen sets the mood by singing the song "Let Me Kiss You" from Morrissey's album, *You are the Quarry.*

"Eat your heart out, Morrissey," Mandy says, impressed by Carmen's voice.

Fay kneels down to the man's level.

The man struggles with Star; however, he's too weak to overpower her.

As Fay leans in closer, the man turns his head to the right and holds it firmly in place with his chin pressed against his shoulder as though by doing so he's trying to shield his mouth from Fay's. Star wraps part of the chain around the man's wrist and uses her hands to keep the man's head steady.

"Go on, Fay," Star says, maneuvering both of her arms into a headlock. The man wildly swings around his arms, landing several blows and slaps to the side of Star's head, which forces her to tighten her grip. Eventually, the man's arms lose velocity. He's too pooped to fight. Even when Star forces him to open his mouth by pinching his nose he barely has enough pneuma to resist and uprise.

With a sinister grin growing on one side of her wrinkly face, Mandy whispers to both Rhonda, "He actually believes that's air he's breathing."

Intrigued by what happens next, Carmen stops singing.

The moment the man opens his mouth gasping for what he perceives to be a breath Fay realigns her mouth with his and leans in for a kiss. She uses that same tactic she used earlier, that "think of waterfalls" and "get it over with" type purge, which, considering the circumstances, works even better this time around, especially with all those beady black eyes pounding down on her.

Fay sticks her tongue into the man's mouth, causing his eyes to balloon outward in a state of sheer panic. The panic ripples throughout his face in a domino effect, spreading from his eyes to his brows, which rise into the trench-like lines of his forehead. Fay's tongue presses against his. Her tongue suddenly multiples, doubling at first, then tripling, quadrupling. In similar fashion as his eyes, both of his cheeks balloon outward as dozens of those vicious snake worms slither and fill into his mouth.

Before he can clamp down on her tongue, Fay suddenly pulls her head away in the nick of time. Star moves her hand from his nose to his mouth and covers it completely, not giving him any chances to spit out what Fay had given him.

The snake worms slither down his throat and enter his body, allowing Star to remove her hand.

As the man starts convulsing on the ground, both Star and Fay back away and give him space while the snake worms, in essence, work their so-called "magic."

"How long does the transformation take?" Carmen asks Star.

"It varies," Star says. "Considering his current fragile state, I'd say not long; however, it takes much longer in our world."

Star ignores the tongue-slip and hopes that none of the girls call her out on it.

"Could affect the timing of our act."

"I don't think Mic*key* would want to cut to a commercial," Rhonda says. "I mean, wouldn't that ruin the whole trick?"

"It won't take that long," Star says, confident. "If we can keep the act within our allotted time, then it should be fine."

"We can totally toss out the whole introduction then."

"If we have to, then we will," Star says. "Besides, you really think the viewers care about who we are. All they want to see is what we can do."

The group doesn't have to wait long at all.

Gradually, the man's skin texture becomes rougher, the tone much paler. His once white eyes start to rot away, turning black and gooey.

"I got it," Fay says over the man's whimpers. "The Tongue Twister."

The other members of the group don't respond to the name.

"Not the name of the group but the name of the trick," Fay says. "Let's call it 'The Tongue Twister.'"

"Hey, not bad," Rhonda says. "I kind of like it."

While the name of their trick is debated, the transformation process suddenly intensifies, causing the man to scream out in bloody horror.

"I'm okay with the name," Mandy says calmly over the man's screams.

"What'd you say?"

"I said 'I'm okay' with the name," Mandy says louder.

"Sure," Star says in final agreement. "Tongue Twister it is."

Rhonda turns to Fay and says, "At least we can agree on one thing."

Repulsed by the man's reaction to the snake worms, Mandy points at the man squirming around on the ground and asks, "Does he have to be so fucking loud?"

"I say we put him out of his misery," Fay says.

"Thank Cats," Mandy says and grabs the Blade of Axlar from the top of a flat rock. She walks over to the man, kneels down, and puts an end to his suffering by slitting his throat.

"Wait!" Star hollers out, as Mandy runs the blade across the man's throat.

The man's screams come to a gurgling silence.

Mandy rids the dead body by rolling it from the platform. The body tumbles down the side of the mountain, the bolts of the lightning flickering in the distant dark clouds. Mandy glares at Star and says, "Circle of life."

"Hold up," Carmen says more thoughtfully, as she directs her attention back to Star. *Too late.* "You said 'our' world? What'd you mean by that?"

Star's too shocked by what she had just witnessed to digest Carmen's comment.

Mandy says before she can answer, "Star didn't tell you, did she?" Any relief Star has about Mandy and whether or not she knows about what she was doing—or better yet, planning—back in "our world" dissolves. "She's been making secret trips back to our world with second-rate crossers."

"Have not," Star says, her response strategic despite the shock to her body.

Mandy comes back at Star and says, "Have to, you skank."

"Okay," Star says hysterically, "since we're doing this right now, Lady *Justice*, who'd do about anything to catch a lift even if meant cutting deals with filthy dredgers, you want to tell them about what you were doing back in our world?"

"I don't know what you're talking about," Mandy asks innocently.

"Don't give me that bullshit!"

"I seriously don't know where she's getting her information—"

"—Jack told me you've been paying him visits."

"Jack said that?"

"Yes," Star says. "Jack did."

"Why are you talking to Jack, Star?"

"I wanted to see how he was doing," she says, as the internal wounds left behind by the recent events start to open. "That's all." She contemplates whether or not she should tell Mandy about Jack's fate and how Mickey was the one responsible for him receiving a swift visit from the Eventide. She nearly breaks down in front of the group. She collects both her thoughts and composure. "I know you don't want to hear this right now," she says, gaining more confidence, "but he's not doing good." She makes sure not to slip her tongue again by speaking of Jack in the present tense, *not past*, since past tense would raise one too many red flags. "He blames himself for what he did to you."

"Good!" Mandy cries out.

"Jack loved you, Mandy, *not* me. I was just a... a toy to him."

"Aw! You need a tissue, Star?" Mandy asks with scorn. "No," she answers for Star. "Good! 'Cuz you're not getting one! You ruined our relationship!"

"I didn't ruin your relationship, Mandy," Star says. "Jack needed someone to talk to, and let's face it, you weren't there."

"You're a heartless bitch," Mandy says, struggling to look at Star.

Speak for yourself.

"Sure," Star says, as she pushes aside the insult, which, she knows, is more of a reflection of Mandy herself than the recipient of her verbal lashings. "I can take it," Star says, but she really can't. "Now, you want to explain to everyone why you've been going back to our world to haunt Jack?"

"Seriously, Mandy," Carmen says, disappointed.

"Like you have any room to talk, Dust Buster," Mandy fires back at Carmen. "I know about you and your addiction to dust. You've been cutting it with Lazarus light to sneak away on your own little private vacays." She looks at the others in disbelief. "You all actually believed her when she said she was making trips to Leatherwood—"

"—That's total BS, Mandy."

"You know it's true."

"This isn't about Carmen, Mandy," Star says over Mandy.

"I don't have to explain myself to you, *Skank*."

"You know, Mandy, I heard those dredgers carry a plethora of diseases," Star says with a concealed, deep-seated anger. Her beady black eyes flick downward at her waistside. "I wondered where that strange smell was coming from. Now, I know."

"You're an evil bitch—"

"—Right back at you, Sweetheart."

"Enough," Fay shouts over Mandy. "Would you two stop fighting? It's getting old, you know?"

Even though Mandy still wears that same lopsided expression on her face, the one where she looks as if she's hiding important information from the group, she has said what she needed to say and will gladly wait for her turn to speak again.

"Real talk," Star says, ready to unburden herself, "I ran into Myko."

"Myko?"

Right, Mandy wanted to say. *Your partner in crime.*

"I've been looking for him for a while now," Star says, diverting the conversation from the real reason as to why she went back to our world. "I just wanted to tell him how sorry I was for dragging him into all of this mess."

"So, what's Ol' Myko been up to these days?"

"Well, let's just say he's made a lot of new friends." Star pauses and contemplates whether or not she should tell the group about her plans. "Fuck it," she says to herself. "I'm not coming with you all to the show."

"What?" Fay says. "Why not?"

"Last time I checked the Fuck-It-All Five requires all five members."

"We still haven't come up with other names."

"You will," Star says. "It will have the word five in it. I found someone who can replace me."

"What?"

"Who?"

216

"She lives in Leatherwood."

"Why are you telling us now, Star?"

"I was going to tell you sooner, but I had to be sure that you all know how to perform the trick without me."

"Star, we're not going to do this without you."

"Well, you're going to have to," Star says. "I would love to join all four of you, including you, Mandy—"

"—Gee," Mandy says darkly. "Thanks."

"But I have some personal business to attend to."

"Personal business?" Fay says, more heated. "Where is all this coming from, Star? You can't just back out at the last second—"

"—But I am, Fay."

"What is it that you're not telling us, Star?" asks Rhonda.

"You know something, don't you?"

"Let me ask you something, Fay: Do you remember anything about how you got here?"

"Of course," she says, turning to the spiral set of stairs right below the summit. "I took the stairs."

"No, Fay," Star clarifies, "here. How did you wind up here, in this world?"

Fay stumbles with her response, forcing Star to look at the confusion on the other members' faces.

"None of you know," she says.

"Know what, Star?"

"Warrick didn't save you."

"Of course he did," Carmen says in defense.

"Why exactly are you sticking up for him, Carmen, especially what he did to you?"

"But he saved my life. We wouldn't be here if it wasn't for Mickey. . . "

"He didn't save you, Carmen, like he said or whatever he planted inside your head," Star says.

"You're saying he's lying to us?"

"He killed you," Star says candidly and looks around at the other three members. "He killed *all* of you."

"Mickey didn't kill me," Fay says. "Some distracted little piece of fucking shit who was yapping on his phone while driving killed me."

"I'm sorry, Fay, but some distracted little piece of fucking shit who was yapping on his phone while driving did hit you, but he didn't kill you."

"What are you talking about?"

"Think about it, Fay," Star says convincingly. "You were fed a lie by a very deranged individual who doesn't have your best interest at heart."

"But I was. . . " Fay trails off, her head wheels spinning those final moments before she crossed the great divide.

She specifically remembered that day as if it was yesterday. She was driving home from picking up lunch at an Indian restaurant called Tandoori Takeout. Her go-to dish whenever she was feeling down was the famous red curry chicken, which, as most customers described, was better than sex. She had just pulled out of the parking lot and was making a right turn onto the highway when the song "One of Us" by Joan Osborne came on satellite radio. Fay used to own the album, Relish, when she was younger; however, like most of her CDs, she lost it during the move after college. Now, it was mp3s that sounded like hammered shit or random jams from 90's Craze on satellite radio or the small collection of expensive vinyl, which, when played, was like listening to liquid gold slowly ooze from the speakers. Halfway through singing the song—in fact, it was right after the lyric "God is good"—Fay was droning the words "Yeah, Yeah," when she caught a large dark object in the corner of her eye. Before she even had a chance to turn to see what the object was crossing the intersection, this large dark object, a forest green Rav-4, plowed directly into the side of her Prius, T-boning her. Her Prius violently spun like a coin. The back half of the car was crushed like a soda can. All four windows, as well as the back windshield, shattered. Pebbles of glass in her hair, her eyes, her mouth, and scattered all over the seats, the floors, as well as the street outside. As the driver, who was texting when he sped through the red light, lay unconscious with the side of her bloody face pressed against the air bag inside his totaled Rav-4, Fay managed to crawl her way out of all that chewed-up metal. Fay collapsed onto the glass-covered street. A smelly, hooded homeless man leaned over her dying body and inserted a snake worm into Fay's mouth. He placed his gloved hand over Fay's mouth. He didn't have to worry about plugging her nose for it was broken and shifted to the side like a page that had been dog-eared. Fay struggled a bit, but she was fading too fast to make any attempt at prying his hand from her face.

"Someone was there with me," Fay says softly, "in the end."

"It was him, Fay," Star says. "It was Warrick."

As she falls deeper into the memory, she recalls the sound of a man *whistling*, which triggers an image of a homeless man skipping away from the wreckage as he twirls his raggedy rainbow umbrella and whistles the song "One of Us."

"I dunno," Fay says. "Maybe. Everything was so blurry."

Star nods at Rhonda.

"Same goes for you, Rhonda."

"What? No way."

"Yes way."

"It was an accident," Rhonda claims.

"Are you sure?"

Mentally grasping at the fuzzy images beyond the ball of snake worms swirling inside her head, Rhonda finds herself traveling to that one particular day, her Death Day. Like Fay, Rhonda easily accesses that day she crossed over; however, as she delves farther, her memories become clearer in detail than Fay's.

According to Rhonda's recollection, she just returned home from her teaching at Red Valley High School. She was behind in grading and had promised her "kids" that she'd have those grades for their quizzes finished by tomorrow, which only added more stress to what was, in Rhonda's case, a beautiful day. On top of that, she was exhausted from spending the previous days off not as eleventh grade English teacher, Ms. Abbott, but "Ron," the fearless weekend warrior who could drink any man underneath the table. The aftermath of two days of heavy drinking left her with a three-day hangover that was best remedied with uninterrupted sleep and a strict liquid diet consisting of Gatorade and chicken noodle soup. She was tempted to call out sick, both days, Monday and Tuesday, but she was saving her sick days for a getaway to Belize. She dropped her belongings on the kitchen table, removed a handful of quizzes from her first and second period, poured herself a tall glass of Zinfandel, locally grown and bottled, and went straight to the bathroom where she stripped down to her undies and turned on the hot water and prepared to take a nice warm bath to help melt away the frustrations of the day. Despite their misdirection, she loved her students, her "kids," as she called them, but something was in the air that day and they were extra-wild. She ended up having to throw a couple of them out of class for misbehaving. One of them called her a "Lonely-Ass Bitch Who Had A Dick Stuck So Far Up Her Ass That She Needed A Shrink To Pull It Out" as he was being escorted from the classroom. The student's comment had eaten away at Rhonda like a tick for the remainder of the period and well through the school day. As water filled the tub, she decided to skip the bath. She turned off the water, threw on her jammies, which was an old No-Cal shirt and a pair of loose, holey sweats, and took her pity party outside. With a glass half full of Zinfandel in one hand and quizzes in the other, she hung out on the hammock, which was secured to two cypresses in the backyard. The temperature was more than ideal, low seventies, low humidity, a nice—and rewarding—break from the heat wave last week that left her longing for cooler fall weather. As she kicked back on the hammock, sipping wine and grading quizzes with a red pen, she was struck by a hit of euphoria. After working her way through yet another glass of wine and knocking out the first period quizzes in no time, she suddenly became flushed, then lightheaded. She set the glass of wine on the ground and did so heavily, causing the glass to topple over. The trees above her started to spin, branches and leaves multiplying and becoming one intertwined mess. In the chaos, she witnessed a dark, shadowy face materialize among the rays of sunlight pouring through the openings of the treetops. As the world shrunk all around her, she fell from the hammock, trying to stand to her feet. Even a simple task

220

such as standing felt impossible. She crawled toward the bottle of Zinfandel, pulled off the cork, and smelled the inside of the bottle. She couldn't detect anything out of the ordinary. She inspected the cork next. Next to the jagged hole where she inserted the corkscrew, she saw what she perceived to be a much smaller, finer hole. Immediately, she realized that the wine had been tainted. Before she could reach for her phone, the world tightened. She struggled to catch her breath. She fell to her back where she witnessed a creature moving toward her feet, leaving behind a serpentine-pattern track in the grass. She couldn't even move. She felt paralyzed, even when the snake worm started to slither up her leg.

"Rhonda?"

Rhonda searches for the words but can't find any.

"I think Star might be onto to something here," Carmen says, remembering. "The day before I wound here," she pinches each side of her red cloak, extending it outward as if she's displaying a dress, "looking like a monster straight out of a Creature Feature, I was at home preparing a lovely dinner for Maxime. It was our seventh year anniversary. I picked up some steaks from the butcher at the grocery store. While I was cooking, I heard a story on the news about a famous actor, Biff Craley, who had been reported missing for two years. After two years of searching for Biff, his wife, Ivanna, decided to end the search and finally, lay her husband to rest. I smelled. . . smoke coming from the kitchen. The steaks, I remembered. I checked on the steaks and nearly overcooked them. I know how much Max liked his steak rare in the middle, so I wasn't looking forward to breaking the news to Max. When Max returned home from work, I noticed that he was acting incredibly odd. It had nothing to do with the overcooked steak. It had nothing to do with me. When I looked into his eyes, I saw someone— *something*—else. The man standing before me wasn't the man I married."

Carmen remembered Maxime walking straight through the front door, dropping his bags in the foyer, and not saying a word to her when she asked about the "important thing" that he had earlier that day. He had spent the night before in his office, making last-minute tweaks to his "big" presentation. All Carmen received in return was a foreign stare coming from an entity that had stolen the body of her husband.

"It happened so fast," Carmen says, skimming through the images of violence inside her head. "Before I could make a run for it, he was already on top of me."

Maxime hit Carmen over the head with her old violin that she had displayed in the dining room. Bloody and dazed, she floundered on the hardwood floor.

"The man who killed me wasn't my Maxime," Carmen says without a doubt.

With the violin string, Maxime strangles Carmen from behind until she's blue in the face.

Somewhere among the violence, Carmen saw herself stepping out of her own dead body and witnessing a strange man casually strolling from the dining room. The power flickered throughout the house. The man turned down the switch on a dimmer. The lights *not only* darkened, but the man's skin also *darkened*, as if he was dimming the tone of his skin. He removed several features, including a nose as well as a cheek and brow that appeared glued onto his face and dropped them on the floor. Next, he removed the contact lenses from both his eyes. Finally, the stranger looked toward the staircase where a young boy stood clinging to the banister. He glanced at the terrified boy, then rotated around, and faced Carmen. Before she could recognize of the stranger's face, the lights suddenly went out.

"I can't believe you're actually believing her," Mandy says, pointing at Star. "You all know she went nuts, right? She was admitted to Stillwater."

"After everything that happened to you," Star says in return, not at all rattled by Mandy's comments, "you're still going to take that monster's side." Star turns to the others. "None of you know how she crossed over, do you?"

The other members shake their heads.

"She's never told us—"

"—Don't force her, Star. She'll tell us when she's ready."

"Now's a perfect time," Star says over Rhonda, who, despite her favoritism, tends to sticks up for Mandy whenever situations get heated between her and Star. "Why don't you tell them what happened to you, Mandy?"

"What happened to me is irrelevant," Mandy says coldly.

Star retorts, "Irrelevant, huh? You're in denial, Mandy."

Mandy waves off Star and her comment.

Star seethes, "You think getting gangbanged by a bunch of fuckin' vamps is irrelevant?"

Stunned by the accusation, Fay says more seriously, "Is that true, Mandy?"

"No," Mandy says hesitantly. "Of course it's not true. Who are you going to believe? Me? Or, some full-on nutcase who did a swan dive from thirteen stories off Stillwater *Mental Institution* because she was one-hundred convinced that one of the orderlies slipped snake worms in her body and she was going to cut them out if they didn't take her seriously?"

"But that part sounds pretty accurate, Mandy," Carmen says over the silence. "I mean, take a look at us."

"After they took their turns on her," Star says, as Mandy's black eyes start to water, "they tossed her body in the lake as if she was trash. Warrick was behind it all. That monster orchestrated the whole thing. And what makes it worse is Rhodes used Mandy's story for his own political gain. Mandy became nothing more than a pawn in a chess match for power."

"I don't get it," Rhonda says soberly, "why us? If what you say is true, Star, then what does Mickey want with us? What makes us so special?"

"It's not like Warrick just drew our names out of a hat," she says. "Who the hell knows? Maybe he did. What I know for sure is that he chose us because he knows he can manipulate us by sending us to Dark

Mountain to. . . " she points at the spot where the man once laid,". . . to master some ridiculous act for his ridiculous TV show."

"How do you know all of this?" asks Carmen.

"Yeah, Star," Mandy says, the anger coming through her voice, "how do you know all of this?"

"I know his type," she says.

From the reaction of the other three members, Star realizes her response isn't adequate enough to put the topic to bed.

Lastly, she turns to Mandy, witnesses that sinister look on her face—in fact, the same exact one she gave her the moment she found out about Star and Jack—and right then and there, she realizes that Mandy knows the reasons as to why Star went back to our world.

A hunched-over silhouette appears behind Mandy.

Star experiences what she can only describe as a sinking feeling.

Another silhouette appears behind Rhonda, then Carmen, then, finally, Fay.

A series of clownish high-pitch giggles pierce through the darkness.

Startled, the other members turn to the sounds, except for one member in particular: Mandy.

She doesn't even flinch.

Instead, she stares directly at Star, as if she's burning a hole right through her, condemning her.

"*And what type is that*?" Mandy finally speaks.

Star has no reply.

"What the hell is going on here?" asks Carmen, as Nuru, one of the members of the CROCUTA Clan, holds a Beretta Cheetah against the backside of her head while, at the same time, nurses her other ghost hand.

Jazarah appears behind Rhonda, Makda behind Fay, Jazarah aiming an M16 while Makda aiming a Colt AR-15.

Lastly, Heloisa walks around Mandy and makes her presence known behind Star, who, in return, holds up her hands in surrender.

"Don't do this, Mandy," Star says directly at Mandy.

Heloisa giggles at Mandy.

"You're not allowed to speak to me anymore, Star," Mandy says. "You gave up that privilege as soon as you betrayed us."

"I wasn't going to betray you, Mandy," Star says.

Heloisa glances down at the back of Star's cloak and notices the large snake worm slithering up the side of her back.

"Don't even think about it," Heloisa says, as she sticks the barrel of the assault rifle along the back of Star's neck.

The snake worm recedes back into Star's body.

"You win, Mandy," Star says, surrendering.

"What the fuck is going on, Mandy?" asks Fay, her voice shaking.

"They're here for Star," she says. "That's it."

"Why?"

"She stole a valuable object that doesn't belong to her."

"What object?"

"Doesn't matter, Fay," Star says.

"All right, Ms. Walker," Heloisa says, tapping Star with the barrel of the assault rifle, "you're coming with us."

As Heloisa holds the assault rifle on Star, Nuru handcuffs Star and escorts her from the platform.

The rest of the CROCUTA Clan slowly eases away in the darkness.

Star walks past Mandy. She stops walking and says to her, "Whatever happens to me, just remember: Death is the only thing we'll *ever* have in common."

"Enough chit-chat," Heloisa says, tugging on Star's arm.

As the Clan walks Star down a flight of stairs made from stone, a well-known crosser, who goes by the name Saggelstache, appears along the side of the mountain, ready to accompany Star and the Clan back to our world.

"Where are they taking her, Mandy?" asks Rhonda.

Mandy doesn't answer.

"Mandy?"

"I'm afraid it's out of our hands," she says finally. "Star made her decision."

"That's fucked up, Mandy, and you know that," Carmen says, raging. "You could've told us. We could've *all* talked it over. Instead, you'd rather throw her to the wolves?"

"Hyenas," Fay corrects.

"Whatever!"

"Mandy, you can't do this—"

"—It's already done, Carmen," Mandy says and glances over her shoulder at Star, who shares one final stare down with Mandy before she's walked back down Dark Mountain.

THE two heavily-armed Cutas, Heloisa and Nuru, escort Star into Chop Soy while the remaining members of the CROCUTA Clan wait outside.

All of the lights are off inside the restaurant. The only sources of light come from the amber-colored floodlights outside. Beams of light pour in through windows and cast monstrous-looking shadows along the walls and floors. Among the shadows, Star witnesses a dark figure sitting at the end of a table near the back of the restaurant. His dark face is momentarily brought out by the orangish glow of a cigarette. A cloud of smoke rises from his face. Heloisa guides Star to the mysterious man while Nuru stands guard at the front door.

Once Star reaches the table, she recognizes Key's face.

He takes yet another drag of the Coffin Nail.

As he blows the smoke from his mouth, a wicked-looking face appears in the cloud of smoke. The face gracefully moves toward Star's face. Immediately, she waves the smoke from the face and says, "Sorry but that little magic trick of yours won't work on me."

Key points at a chair at the other end of the table.

"Thank you, Heloisa," Key says. "I'll take care of her from here."

Heloisa leaves Key and both she and Nuru exit Chop Soy while Star timidly takes a seat at the table. Her eyes move away from Key and trail downward to a juice glass that has been turned upside down on the tabletop. She can't make out the creature for it remains lost in the shadows—possibly a spider, she assumes—however, whatever the creature is, it appears trapped inside the glass.

"What's the special occasion?" Star asks, as she draws her attention back to Key's white suit.

"What? This?" He grabs his white sports coat and says casually, "I just got back from crashing a dead man's party."

Completely flustered by Key's comment, Star surveys the dining room. As her eyes adjust to the darkness, she maps out an exit strategy. She knows that she can rule out the front entrance. More than likely, the Cutas are hanging outside, waiting to pick her off if she should make a run for it. The only exit is the one in the kitchen; but, of course, Key is sitting directly in the path of the kitchen.

Discreetly, she redirects her attention back to Key, who's staring at her.

"Did I say something?" asks Star.

"No," he says. "It's just, you remind me of her—I mean, the you before your five-star makeover."

"Let me guess," Star says, studying Key. "She broke your little ole heart."

"Not exactly," he says, pausing. "She was taken from me."

"Sorry to hear," Star says and for a moment, feels saddened by Key's heartbreak. She turns inward and acknowledges her own heartbreak. The sadness dissolves and all that's left is anger. "What does this have to do with me?"

"Nothing."

"Right," Star says, the emotion building inside me. She feels almost depleted by the feeling. "Nothing."

"Her name was Nevaeh," Key says, as he drags from the cigarette. "She was struck in the head by a stray bullet during the infamous 1992 Los Angeles Riots. While she lay dying on the sidewalk, rioters were walking all around her. Half of them didn't even know she was dying until a couple of hours later when her girlfriend stumbled across her body. By then, Nevaeh was already dead." Key takes another drag from the cigarette, savors it, then blows out the smoke, a sad-looking face appears in the cloud of smoke. "The next night after her death I hunted down the man who shot her. I brought Neveah's girlfriend Jada along with me because, in a way, she was also responsible for Nevaeh's death by leaving her behind when she should've been looking after her. What I did to them would result in me being branded in a name that still lingers over the streets of LA?"

"Let me guess," Star says cynically, "you shot them with a *M16*."

"No," he says, glaring at Star. "That would be too easy. After that night, the word spread on the street. People were whispering the name 'M80' with a quiver in their voice. Now, granted, M16 sounds much cooler than M80—my opinion."

"Am I getting my numbers mixed up here?"

"Not the gun, Star."

"I give up," she says. "Why were people calling you M80?"

"Like I said," Key says, "I found the man who shot Nevaeh. I tied both him and Jada to a chair. I placed a M80, the firework—" *That M80* "—inside Jada's mouth and Nevaeh's shooter's mouths, lit the M80s, and duct taped their mouths closed. Nevaeh's shooter received a special touch. I decided to duct tape both his hands to his mouth." With a cigarette still in hand, Key animatedly demonstrates with his hands placed flat against the sides of his gaping mouth in an "uh-oh" type of expression. "The explosion didn't kill both of them—not at first. Jada later died in the hospital. Which wasn't part of the plan; but every now and then, when you're trying to get your point across, sometimes the point triggers another point. Nonetheless, Nevaeh's shooter survived, which was *the point*. Killing him would be too easy. I wanted him to wake up every single day and be reminded of what he did whenever he looked at himself in the mirror."

"You know I've witnessed this scene play out a million times in my head and even if I try doing something differently, each scenario ends the same."

"The power of the crystal has its limits," Key says, "especially to those who are *limited*; although if the crystal should wind up in the hands, its power can be endless."

"You can't change the course of the future," Star says, as if she's accepting her fate. "Everything that's going to happen will happen. It's inevitable."

"Curious, Dark Star," he says sarcastically. "Why do you care so much about this place?"

"I care because. . . " Star says without thinking, ". . . it's still home to me."

"Right," he says softly and cracks a smile.

"After listening to your little story, I can tell it was once your home too."

The smile melts from Key's face as he takes a puff of his cigarette. He lifts up the glass just enough to blow smoke underneath the glass with that small creature trapped inside. Once the glass fills up with smoke, Key closes the glass and leans back in his chair. He says vacantly to Star, "Looks like it's time for you to face The Inevitable."

Star carefully watches the smoky glass, as well as the small creature squirming around inside.

All of a sudden, the glass shifts a couple of inches along the table.

Despite having already witnessed the same exact scenario play out by gazing into the future with the black crystal, Star accepts her fate and waits for the great beast to tear her to shreds. The creature grows in size, causing the glass to crack. The tiny fracture zigzags up the glass in the shape of a lightning bolt.

As more cracks spread, the creature continues to grow until it can no longer fit inside the glass.

Eventually, the entire glass shatters all over the table.

The small creature isn't so small anymore. It grows into the size of a fist and from there, it continues to grow and grow.

From a fist to the size of a basketball, the creature's tentacles stretch outward and crawl over the edge of the table. The creature ends up becoming so large and heavy that its weight causes one of the legs of the table to snap in half, resulting in the table to collapse. The chair overturns. Star falls backward, as foreseen. The blob-like creature, now as wide as a walrus, wraps one of its many slimy tentacles around Star's ankle. Star tries to kick away the tentacle, as foreseen; however, her attempts at breaking free are pointless.

Star searches for a weapon—anything! She finds a shard of glass on the floor and stabs the side of the creature's body as it makes its way up her leg. The creature's hide is so thick and leathery that the glass breaks in her hand as soon as it makes contact. The glass cuts the inside of her palm.

In one last desperate attempt, she tries to crawl away. Again, her attempts are pointless. Once the creature sits on the lower half of her body, she can't move at all. Hoping to scare it away, she punches and elbows at it. Each blow has little to no effect on the creature. Star lands a blow directly in its spiraled shaped maw.

The pain bolts up her arm and radiates throughout her entire body.

As she pulls away her arm, she realizes that her arm is gone.

The creature had completely bit it off!

Screaming and bleeding for help, Star continues to strike the creature, but this time using her other arm. The creature's tentacle strikes back. The tentacle enters Star's mouth and slithers down her throat, causing her to choke.

Key stands from the chair and walks up to Star as her eyes start to roll in the back of her head.

His face—that face—is the last thing she witnesses before she blacks out.

In the flash of blackness, Star springs upward in a burst of life!

She opens her eyes and before her sits Key at the other end of the table. That creature, which was once choking her, is back to its normal size and resting comfortably in Key's palm.

"For a moment, I thought I lost you there," says Key.

Out of breath, Star takes a moment to find her bearings.

"What. . . " she says, catching her breath, ". . . what the hell just happened?"

"What just happened is that you just died," Key says. "In your head, that is." He pets the small creature in his hand. "Something, ain't it?"

"What did you do to me?" asks Star, as she surveys the dark dining room.

"Not me," he says and showcases the creature for Star, "That was lil' Genette here. She takes up after her old man, only her telepathic abilities are much greater than his. My opinion."

"But how?"

"How what?"

"How was it able to get inside my head?"

"What part of telepathic don't you understand?" Key asks but doesn't expect Star to answer. "Forget it," he waves off Star and stands up from the seat. "You see, Star, like lil' Genette here, I can do whatever the hell I want." Approaching Star, he asks, "You know why?"

Again, Star doesn't answer and even so, he doesn't give her any opportunity to answer.

Key stands next to Star, leans in closer, and whispers in her ear, "This is *My* Fuckin' *World*. That's why."

As Key stands back upright, he holds out his other hand.

Confused, Star looks up at Key and doesn't know what he wants from her—at least, not until she feels the black crystal climbing up her throat. Star gags and tries to prevent herself from vomiting. Maybe it has something to do with that lil' creature in Key's hand. Maybe it's Key's presence alone. Or, perhaps the cigarette smoke that he's been blowing in the air. Whatever the case may be, Star feels extremely nauseous. The gag turns into a cough. The cough then turns into a violent hawk. She vomits up the black crystal into Key's palm. He wiggles the phlegm-soaked black crystal in the air before he dries it off inside a napkin.

"Good girl," he says, as Star recovers from the exhausting purge.

"Can't believe you actually swallowed the damn thing," Key says, looking over the black crystal.

Key holds it in his hand and closes his eyes as he embraces its power.

He opens his eyes, glances over the black crystal in surprise, and says, "Huh? So, that's what's going to happen." He shrugs. "We'll see about that."

Without wasting anymore time, he closes his hand until it forms a fist. After he crushes the black crystal in his hand, there's nothing left of it but black pepper-like dust. He blows away the black dust onto the floor and wipes his hand on another napkin.

"Are you going to kill me or not?" asks Star, as she hangs her head.

"Kill you?" Key repeats. "Why would I kill one of the 'Stars' of my show?" He pauses, waiting for Star to laugh at the comment. "Get it," he says. "Stars of my show. Cuz your name is Star." He waves off a poor attempt at comical relief. "Never mind." He nods to the front door where Heloisa and Nuru are waiting for Star. "Let's get you back to your friends. Shall we?" Key holds out his arm and shows Star to the exit. "By the way," he says, as Star hesitantly stands to her feet, "you *guys* ever come up with a group name yet?"

"AN OLD FOE"

EXCEPT for the California license plate, not Arizona, the same exact van that Teresha was driving pulls into the parking lot of a small dive bar called, of all names, Dive. Like the name of the bar, everything about the bar is simple and straight to the point, nothing too fancy. The building itself, shaped like a soggy, worn down shoebox, is painted off-white. Displayed on the front windows are pink and green glowy signs that read several "Domestic" beer brands. Wrapped around the structure is a sidewalk littered with smothered cigarette butts as well as earthquake-like cracks where weeds sprout through the concrete.

The driver—a woman—turns off the ignition of the van and places what appears to be an ancient-looking wooden case inside the glove compartment before she steps outside. She is dressed "comfortably," red plaid sweat pants and a navy blue hoody jacket with the word *pink* written in PRINCETOWN font. Definitely not Teresha; however, the woman has the same weight, same height, and a similar profile as Teresha, and can probably pass as a distant cousin or sibling. Even one of her eyes, her left eye, is the same color green; however, her other eye, her right one, is the color brown.

The young woman, called Polly, which rhymed with her favorite Saturday night drug, and would often get dirt from the boys, who'd ask her if she wanted a "cracker," walks around the back of the van. She opens the back doors, revealing the body bag holding Biff Craley's corpse lying over a fresh bed of ice, as well as one other addition being a black heavy-duty garbage bag stuffed to the brim. The bag, too, is surrounded by ice cubes; however, a couple of ice cubes are starting to melt, causing sludgy water to leak onto the parking lot. Polly rips open the last bag of ice that she bought at the convenient store and pours the ice cubes over Biff's corpse. One at a time, Polly closes the doors and heads toward the front of Dive.

The interior of Dive, like the exterior, is very Plain Jane. They pretty much have one of everything, a billiards table, a dartboard, a TV, even one of those machines where one could play nudy games. Polly counts only five people inside, a couple sitting in a booth, two men hanging out at the bar, one of the men wearing dark shades, then, finally, the burly bartender, who's having a conversation about the Dodgers with the one shade-less hombre at the bar. Polly has her eyes on the man with the dark shades, Narcissus, who's sipping from a glass of aged whiskey while listening to the Local News at the other end of the bar.

The bartender gives Polly a subtle yet tentative nod of hello. Polly nods back at the bartender and makes her way to the far end of the bar where she approaches Narcissus. She passes the couple at the booth. The two are sharing a nacho platter and are so engrossed in each other's company that a violent riot could be raging outside, straight up the making of fire and brimstone, and neither one of them would give what any riot or rioters so urgently crave.

Polly finally arrives at the other end of the bar.

"You mind?" she asks, as she points to the bar stool next to Narcissus.

Speaking of attention, Narcissus doesn't even acknowledge the young "comfortably-dressed" woman standing next to him, doesn't need to; instead, he takes a whiff of the air, as if his nose is doing the looking for him. He can't tell whether it's the rot or just a bad laundry day. Either way, he shrugs it off.

With his senses slightly dull from the liquor, he says, "Be my guest."

Polly slides out the bar stool and takes a seat next to Narcissus.

Chewing on the toothpick, the bartender walks up to Polly.

"What will it be, miss?" he asks, throwing the damp rag over his shoulder in all its stereotypical glory.

"I'll have a beer," she says.

The bartender, who not only looks, but also acts as if he was pulled directly from a movie set, grabs her a domestic beer from the cooler, cracks open the bottle by pounding the serrated lip of the cap along the edge of the countertop—here, bottle openers are for amateurs—and slides it in front of Polly.

"Two-fifty," he says, as the foamy head of the beer slowly oozes from the top and slides down the neck of the bottle.

Polly plays a game of pocket-pool in her pocket before she pulls out a crinkled five-dollar bill. She hands the bartender the money and tells him to keep the change.

"Thank ya, ma'am," the bartender says, springs open the cash register, places the five inside, removes two dollars and fifty cents from the cash register and then places the leftover change inside a weaved basket labeled, "Tips," the messy writing on the label sharing the qualities of a third-grader.

He walks back over and asks "Stevie Wonder" if he'd like another double.

Narcissus says, "Sure thing, Father."

"That's strange," Polly says, as the bartender pours Narcissus another whiskey. "You two don't look related."

"We're not," Narcissus says loosely.

Polly still wears that scribbled-on confusion on her face.

Narcissus makes it clear for her.

"When Father Dawson isn't plying his patrons with alcohol," he slurs, as he downs the last sip of whiskey, "you can find his ass down at Saint Patrick's reading scripture to his congregation."

"By the way, Narcissus," the bartender, Father Dawson, says, as he brings the glass of Pillars aged whiskey to Narcissus, "what's it gonna take for *me* to get *you* to join *my* flock?"

"You couldn't pay me enough to listen to you ramble on for hours."

Father Dawson laughs as he sets the Pillars in front of Narcissus.

"One day," he says, grinning.

"We'll see about that," Narcissus says.

"We will see, won't we?" Father Dawson says mysteriously as he makes his way to the other end of the bar where he reignites a controversial topic about the star left fielder simply known as "Mando," who is currently leading the league in most hit home-runs. The scrappy patron believes the rumors are true and that the big slugger might be on "the juice"—hence why, in the past year, his physical appearance has significantly altered: he put on at least thirty pounds of lean muscle; his head has gotten slightly bigger, whereas his balls have shrunken down to a couple of *Raisinets*—Not like the patron was "looking" or anything and even so, he'd never say so—not to mention, Mando's temper has been reduced to a three year old throwing fits on the field. In the past year alone, Mando has gone through an average of three bats a day—you don't want to see what the man does to one after he strikes out. According to the patron, these are the top three indicators (thirty pounds of muscle, big head and small, shrinking balls—which he pairs together—and the uptick of temper tantrums) that the man is clearly juicing.

Narcissus removes the shades from his face and rubs the backside of his eyelids.

"Long day?" asks Polly.

"I've had longer—" he says.

He nearly stops midway through his sentence as he picks up a more pungent smell in the air.

On the Local News, a sudden news report flashes over the TV. Polly draws her eyes to the screen. The TV shows a camera crew from Local News positioned outside a rundown convenient store next to a gas station called Gas and Go, which sits along the border of Arizona and California. A heavy police presence is seen in most—if not, all of the shots. One of the shots includes a pair of detectives lingering near a white tent, which has been used to shield the human remains behind Gas and Go.

A reporter appears on the TV. Next to him stands a clerk named Emmanuel Pierre. The reporter asks Emmanuel about the suspect—or "person of interest." Emmanuel states that he saw her walking away with the bathroom key and that he stopped her right before she was about to drive off. He went on a rant about the key and how it had stayed in the store for the twenty-one years that he had worked at Gas and Go, "always returned," Emmanuel emphasized for the reporter. When he approached the woman, she was searching around the floor of the vehicle and he thought maybe she had dropped a key, not his key, but the car key, between the seats and somehow, it had gotten lost underneath the floor mats and stuck in that tight space next to the seat. He knocked on the window and when she looked up at him, she was squinting one of her eyes. The clerk made sure to demonstrate to those late-night viewers out there who were watching Local News what a squint of an eye looked like. His thinking was that maybe she had something caught in her eye, like an eyelash or piece of debris or dirt—the winds have been known to kick around dust from the desert. Nonetheless, the woman reached in her pocket and handed him the key and said that she was sorry, that she "forgot." What struck Emmanuel as "odd" was that she arrived in a "blue sedan," came inside for the bathroom key, used the restroom out back, left the restroom, walked through the parking lot, got inside her vehicle, although *not* a blue sedan, as he witnessed her driving when she pulled up to Gas and Go, but a "white van"— that is where he stopped her and was given back his priceless key attached to the round head of a gear shift— then drove away into the night.

When pressed about why he didn't stop her, knowing that this "person of interest" was leaving his store in a different vehicle, Emmanuel shrugs and says to the reporter, "It didn't occur to me at the time."

"You're getting sloppy," Narcissus says to Polly, as a weather report flashes across the screen.

"Did you know a rat is no different than a human when it comes to peer pressure?" asks Polly.

"No," Narcissus says quietly. "I did not. . . "

He takes another sip of the Pillars, this time a gulp.

Looking forward at the vibrant shelf of liquor, Polly says, "The desire to feel accepted among its peers is so great among the rat community that one single rat would literally eat shit if it was in the company of other rats who were eating shit. If that's not conformity, then I don't know what is. The urge to feel accepted can be man's greatest strength and weakness." She faces Narcissus and says directly, "I'd say it's no different than gaining control over another man's free will."

"Free will, yeah, sure," Narcissus says, inwardly laughing at Polly's remark. "People don't have a choice when they hang around you. I'd say you do a pretty good job at deciding who lives and who dies. Free will," Narcissus says, taking yet another gulp, "free will gets thrown out the window."

"How's Melanthius holding up?" asks Polly.

Narcissus responds, "I haven't heard anyone use that name in quite some time, and believe me, I've been around the block for a minute."

"Your boss is interfering with my business," she says and leans dangerously close to Narcissus.

"Don't even try it," Narcissus says with a scowl, as he turns and faces Polly. "I'm immune to fleas like you."

"I know," she says, still leaning in close to Narcissus. "You are indeed a rare specimen, Narcissus. Forged by the hands of a god, only to be later exiled by his own creator. Enlighten me, Narcissus: What's the world look like through those eyes of yours?"

Narcissus thinks carefully about his next response.

With a smirk, Polly waits patiently.

"*Dark*," he says glumly. "It looks dark."

Polly leans back and takes a sip of beer. She glances around the bar, first at the couple, who are both oblivious to their surroundings, and then Father Dawson and the other patron, who are arguing about Mando's cup size.

As Narcissus slides on his pair of shades and faces forward, Polly removes a knife from her sleeve, the same one that she had stolen from the table while those two lovebirds were stuffing their mouths with pulled pork nachos and strumming their heart strings with the melody of sweet murmurings.

In the blink of an eye, she makes one swift jab across Narcissus's neck, precisely nicking his carotid artery, which is one of the major blood vessels that supply blood to the brain. She drops the knife handle-side down into the slit of Narcissus's coat pocket, grabs his other arm, and settles the crook of his elbow along the side of his face while the gash starts to squirt blood. Finally, once Polly positions Narcissus's upper body against the bar, she holds him in place as he bleeds out in a matter of minutes. Narcissus doesn't struggle. He doesn't even call out for help. Yet, he accepts his fate.

As Narcissus loses consciousness, Polly takes another sip of beer and leaves the bar. She nods goodbye to Father Dawson, who wishes Polly a good night.

He wraps up his conversation with the patron and checks on Narcissus, who, from Father Dawson's perspective, appears to be taking a nap against the bar.

Amused, Father Dawson says teasingly, "Calling it a night already. Are we, Mr. Wonder?"

It's not until Father Dawson stands in front of Narcissus and witnesses a puddle of blood forming on the bar that he realizes the severity of the situation.

By the time he races out of the bar, Polly has already driven away in a white van.

❧

DETECTIVE Prentiss digs through the trash strewn all over the ground while Detective Moriarty still remains in a state of disbelief from the sight of the Jane Doe.

"What kind of individual would do such a thing to a person?" asks Moriarty, as she closely examines for any entry wounds along the bloody corpse.

"Could be the cartel," suggests Prentiss, as he holds up a used condom on the tip of his pen. "They've been known to make an example of their victims. . ." the detective trails off and flings away the condom. "Yuck," he says, making a face.

"What example is that, Mike? We're looking at a young woman, probably in her twenties. Not one single mark on her body. This was done by a professional, possibly someone who knows his or her way around the blade."

"Hey," one coroner says from behind, "it could be like one of those creatures from that one movie. Skins its victims, hangs them from trees. You know which one I'm talking about—"

"—Cut the crap already, will ya?" Moriarty says, as she stands up and glares at the coroner, who's taking a break from photographing the crime scene.

The coroner holds up his hands and backs away from the detective.

Detective Prentiss joins his partner at the other end of the tent where both of them gaze out into the heavy rainstorm.

"We have a young woman who's been skinned alive, body possibly dumped here," Prentiss says, as if thinking out loud is his way of gathering a motive. "Car without plates. Owner of the car, a woman named Polly Krakauer, a college student, bags in the backseat suggest she's driving back to her parent's house in New Mexico. Possibly freaks out after coming across the corpse. Speeds away in another vehicle—"

"—Which doesn't make any sense at all."

"She could've been driving away for another reason," says Moriarty.

"Your gut?"

"My gut's in knots, Mike," Moriarty says bluntly, as she draws her eyes to a surveillance camera on the corner of the gas station.

THE dark entity stands in front of a furnace and burns the flesh of what used to be Polly Krakauer when, from a distance, an old, dusty payphone rings underneath a pile of rubble.

The entity leaves the fire and answers the call.

The payphone isn't even hooked up to a line; yet, the phone appears as if it hasn't been used in over three decades. And yet, somehow, the phone manages to still work.

The entity holds the phone to its shadowy slender face.

On the other line is a crumbly voice, which sounds like broken-up static.

The Void speaks, and the entity known as "Black Death" listens.

"NUTS AND BOLTS"

TWO prison guards escort the now former prisoner, Drenelle St. Croix aka the artist formerly known as the one and only Poochy Queen, who's rocking a tangerine orange Adidas tracksuit and "faux" rabbit fur boots with an emphasis on the *faux* in order to put that loyal fan base of hers, or her "lil Poochies," from trolling the Internet—one faction of her tribe tearing her to shreds and calling for her cancellation while the other defending her choice in attire until their fingers fall off—from the front gates of Forest City Penitentiary.

Both local and national news networks from around the country are gathered outside. A cloud of smoke lingers in the air like a thin blanket of fog.

With their microphones and digital tape recorders ready, starry-eyed reporters anxiously await Drenelle's release. The cameras are running. "We're live at Forest City Penitentiary!" Of course, it wouldn't be Poochy without its fair share of controversy.

As the guards release Drenelle into the sweaty arms of a private bodyguard of Samoan decent named Mahi, who escorts the former inmate of Forest City Penitentiary toward a black town car parked along the curb, an aggressive "pissed off" reporter manages to stick a recorder into Drenelle's face and shout out a question over the hoopla, *"How does it feel to be a free woman?"*

Drenelle stops in her tracks, causing the crowd noise to ease down a bit. She eyes the reporter up and down while she puckers her lips in the most exaggerated way. She suddenly lets out a high pitch *paa-kaw*, which sounds like a screech of a bird. More exaggeratedly, Drenelle rolls her eyes at the reporter, who, any other day of the week, she'd call out as your typical soy boy who read too many *Hardy Boys* books growing up in a privileged household where you could pee with the toilet seat down without being punished.

Mahi makes a hole through the crowd as he walks Drenelle to the town car.

The back window of the car is cracked about two inches and a cloud of what smells like to Drenelle as cigarette smoke is pouring out.

As Drenelle approaches the car, he peers through the bodies surrounding him and spots two men, who, from outside the car, appear to be Arendt and Zwicker, two high profile lawyers, or "celebrity lawyers," sitting in the backseat.

Mahi carefully pushes aside a couple of reporters from the car without breaking one of their limbs, even though breaking one of their limbs seems like a more suitable option, and opens the back door for Drenelle.

Becoming more and more agitated—but making damn well sure not to show it—by the growing hysteria from the mob, Drenelle steps into the vehicle without much thought. Before her are seated Key and Stat, not those two lawyers, Arendt and Zwicker, as she first observed from outside the car.

"I assume I should be thanking you two for getting me out," Drenelle says, cautiously studying the two strangers.

"You assumed right, Drenelle," Key says while Stat remains silent. "I had to pull a lot of strings to get you out, Drenelle, but you don't have to worry anymore. It's done. Based on 'new' evidence, you are no longer part of the system."

Mahi is next to enter the town car. He takes a seat in the passenger seat while the driver pulls away from Forest City.

"Well," Drenelle says as she does what she always does in situations that she can't explain and "runs" with the story, "what should I call you two?"

"This is my colleague, Stat," Key says, introducing Stat to Drenelle.

Stat doesn't say much at all; instead, he gives Drenelle a nod of, more or less, acknowledgment.

"Stat?" Making a frown, Drenelle shrugs and says sassily to Stat as both of her loose, flappy hands do most of the talking, "Okay. So what? I take it you're like *Robin* and he's your *Batman*. After all, you do look like a side-kick. No offense, Boo."

"Not exactly," Key says patiently before Stat has a chance to respond to that "sidekick" claim.

"So," Drenelle says, crossing one leg over the other, "what'd they call you?"

Drenelle waits for a response from the man who calls himself "Key," but it's nothing close to what she ever expected.

🐾

AT the base of Dark Mountain Star is greeted by Fay while Heloisa and the rest of CROCUTA Clan wait till Star is safe and secure within her group before leaving.

Star and Fay join the group.

Each one of the members embraces Star and welcomes her back to the group, except for Mandy, who, as of now, feels as if she's become a "fifth wheel."

REACHING the halfway mark of the tour through Neuvak Corporation & Pharmaceuticals, Doctor Harcourt walks American investor Rakesh Sorbet, philanthropist and CEO of Sherman Faulkner, to a secured door in front of a massive corridor.

The doctor places the underside of his wrist against a sensor next to the door. The red light remains red.

Doctor Harcourt gives Rakesh a crooked smile and says, "We've been having some issues with the implants." He reaches in his pocket. "No need to worry," he pulls out a card and shows the card to Rakesh. "Fail safe," he says and places the card against the sensor.

The door lights up green, opens.

Doctor Harcourt guides Rakesh toward one of the latest attractions.

"The housing units," he says, reaching a narrow hallway that stretches as far as the human eye can see. "Each one of our units is specifically furnished based on a subject's interest."

The doctor shows Rakesh the first unit where, inside, one of these "subjects" is sitting in a recliner chair and watching TV inside an average, homey, cozy living room.

"Each housing unit, which is roughly the size of a one-bedroom apartment, comes with a kitchen, a bathroom, one bedroom, and as you can see here, a living quarters."

The two occasionally stop and look through a monitor outside the unit, which displays the subject inside.

Rakesh points out the weight of each subject.

"Are they normally this, you know. . . "

"Fat?"

Rakesh nods, glancing inside the housing unit once more to observe the thousand pound man lying on the bed, hooked up to an IV.

"Yes," Doctor Harcourt says and finds himself backtracking, "well, not at the beginning stages. Thanks to your generous contribution, Mr. Sorbet, we found a way to speed up the process of growth from four to now two years through a new procedure known as 'dripping.' During the first trial runs, we would set up a location for our subjects outside the compounds, but after a while we realized how extremely difficult it was going to be to safely monitor the subjects without drawing any *unwanted* attention. Not only that, we soon learned that administering the Quidaquin through a drip feed increases the growth, opposed to the capsule form. So," he points at the housing units and showcases them as if they're works of art inside a gallery, "we decided it was best manageable to create these special housing units behind Neuvak." Doctor Harcourt goes on to say that eventually, he and his crew would like to expedite the process with such sufficiency and speediness that, once they *obtain* the subject—which Rakesh knows is just another word for kidnap—it will seem like a "quick swap."

The doctor says directly, "Nobody will ever know they went missing."

"Do the subjects ever interact with other subjects?" asks Rakesh.

"No," the doctor says. "Each subject is separated from other subjects—"

"—And how's that any different than a prison?"

"Well," the doctor says, not missing a beat, "we have a team of highly trained caretakers from all around the globe. Each one of our first-rate caretakers is specifically tasked to forge an unbreakable bond with our subjects in order to give the subjects a sense of belonging, as well as companionship." He turns his eyes back to a section of housing units before him. "This particular wing right here houses subjects who are at the final stages of their transition—or as we like to call around here, their 'awakening.'" He cracks a smile, leans in closer to Rakesh, and utters from the corner of his mouth, "Hence why they look like beached whales."

Rakesh doesn't find much amusement from the doctor's joke; in fact, he can barely bring himself to react to the comment.

"Anyway," the doctor says, continuing the tour, "we've already started Phase Two of the expansion of the housing units, which are scheduled to be complete by late fall."

Finally, the tour stops at one particular section, which Doctor Harcourt calls the "recovery room." Behind the glass window, Biff Craley is being instructed to recite from a script that has been given to him. On the table lays a folder named "PROJECT SLEEPING ELEPHANT."

"So," Rakesh says, stating the obvious, "how exactly are you going to explain Mr. Craley's disappearance to the public? If the press ever found out—"

"—The press isn't going to find out," the doctor says, more seriously. "And, as far as I see, the press will *never* find out. Our team of writers is now working on a story regarding Mr. Craley's disappearance. Next time you stop by, I would like to introduce them to you. Let's just say they're quite an imaginative bunch. Having said that, I have faith that they'll come up with something truly inspiring."

Both Doctor Harcourt and Rakesh pay closer attention to the commands Biff is given by one of Neuvak's staff members.

"And now, without further ado, it is my honor—"

"No, no, no," the frustrated script supervisor says, "he wants an emphasis on punctuation. Not 'And now,'" she says sluggishly, "'without further do.' Instead, it should to be 'And now!'" she cries out, her voice more booming, "'without further ado, it is my honor to introduce the talented, the haunting Five Fistfuls!'"

Rakesh turns to Doctor Harcourt and asks, "Five Fistfuls?"

"It's a group that's going to be part of the big Telethon next Saturday night," he says. "Originally, they called themselves Fuck-It-All Five, but they ended up changing the name because they're not allowed to use the word *fuck* on TV. So, the girls changed their name to 'Fistful Five.' Grammatically, the word *fistful* is considered a noun so they thought it would be in poor taste to use a noun before a number so one of the girls, Rhonda, suggested that they just switch the two words around—"

"—You know what. . ." Rakesh says over the doctor and returns his focus to Biff inside the glassed-in room, ". . . forget I asked."

The script supervisor places the script aside on the table and tells Biff to recall the movie, *The Runaway*. She explains that, in the movie, Biff played a confused young man who, after the death of his father, ran away and completely shut off society. She wants Biff to channel the character, Spud, particularly, the one scene where Spud got upset at his mother and yelled at her in his best imitation of his father, who was a car salesman; and using his father's game show-like personality, Spud vociferated his fears of turning into his father after years and years of loathing him.

"Remember that one line," the script supervisor says to Biff, "*I have one helluva a Beamer. She's quite the screamer. . .*"

"*Come on down,*" Biff recites the line with the script supervisor, both their voices punctuating each word, "*give her a spin,*" his voice gets louder, his manner more animate, "*Fully loaded with AC, radio, and adjustable seating. . .*" he rambles on and on about the features of the automobile until, eventually, Biff stands from the seat to read those lines from the script, "*And now, without further ado, it is my honor to introduce the talented, the haunting Five Fistfuls!*"

"That's it, my man," the script supervisor says, more than pleased by the performance. "Now, you got it!"

"I can't believe it," Rakesh says in awe. "The man actually sounds and looks just like Biff Craley. The resemblance. . . it's uncanny."

"Amazing, huh?" Doctor Harcourt says. "But don't be mistaken, Mr. Sorbet. The subject is still Biff Craley, only now he's *our* Biff Craley."

ALL morning long movie fans from across the world were posting about late actor and activist, Ralph Hood, or as he was best known among the horror community as playing the iconic role of Don Juan—"The Wolf"—in the controversial franchise, *The Effigy*.

Below, the posts all over social media read as followed:

Craig's Corner @CraigFarley A true horror icon. RIP.

Ringer Slade @StuntmanSlade Ralph was a mentor, a brother, and most importantly, a friend. Throughout the ups and downs, the blood, sweat, and tears we shared on and off set, Ralph was the one constant in my life. He was the kind of man who'd give a stranger the shirt off his back. A master at his craft. What an honor to have worked with such a magnificent individual. Godspeed, Hoody.

Kurt Harvard @HarvardBaggage A great talent who was taking away to soon

Sam Smiley @SmileyInkandSupplies I had the opportunity to work with Ralph on the '78 Effigy. My agent was fortunate enough to land me the part as Sheriff Striker. It was my third gig as an actor, first in major role. I was extremely nervous at the time—terrified, to be honest. Ralph gave me some advice that stayed with me throughout the rest of my acting career: 'Enjoy the ride, brother.' And what a ride it was.

Edwy Bromwich @GlasgowAudio Fun fact: That crunching sound you hear when Don Juan and his army of Juanites snap their victim's bones is made from breaking dried pasta with a touch of reverb. Good times. Going to miss you dearly, #RalphHood.

Shade Givens "Actor" @ShadeGivens They don't make em like Ralph anymore

The other James Dean @JamesDean87 Was so looking forward to Sergio Beneventi's reboot. Never has a franchise been so relevant than it is right now with the Mob/Cancel Culture. Will not be the same without the Master of Slashers himself. Much love, Ralph.

The OG Scream Queen ({*o*}) @TheOGScreamQueen We need you now more than ever, Don Juan. Please tell me this is a publicity stunt created by the studio

Jamie Le Pierre @StarsdaleAcademy Luv u, Hoody. Eternally. #TheFinalEffigy

Felipe Jovanovich @FelipeDirects The original Effigy was the reason why I ditched my job as an engineer to pursue a career in the film industry. No regrets.

The Effigy marches in 2020 @TheEffigyMovie OFFICAL STATEMENT from Screengasm: From the time we first met Ralph to the brief time we spent together while filming the reboot of what was promised to be a new, more inclusive chapter in *The Effigy* franchise, it became clear to us that Ralph was not only an actor who played one of the most iconic slashers to ever grace the silver screen

The Effigy marches in 2020 @TheEffigyMovie but also a 'visionary' who provided us with a blueprint for future stories to come. Through these trying times, the story of Don Juan will hopefully reunite us once again.

S. Howard @Showard86 (Video Ralph Hood in 1994 Interview with Trey Syjek): "It's not about the money or fame—those are extra bonuses on the side and can be, at times, distractions. It's about the journey—for me, always has been—and the people you met along that journey."

Derail Rhodes or Die @PopGoesTheWeasel FUUUUUUUUU-UCK!!!!!!!!!!

Sharon Bell @TheSharonBell Words cannot explain or put into context how I feel right now. The amazing Ralph Hood was, by far, one of the greatest humans I have had the privilege to meet. Regardless of the character he played on screen, he was gentleman and warm spirit off screen.

Kenneth Smith @KSmithJournalist Around 5AM, activist Ralph Hood's body was discovered on 15th Street by a resident who lived nearby. Hood was pronounced dead at the scene. Police suspect foul play was involved. Link: MW2c/Newslink/article/7239.hp

A Soul Called Mischief ✈➔🌐 @BizzyBee74 So sad to hear the news about the legendary Ralph Hood. You will be dearly missed. Thanks for the scares, my friend.

Tom Cheers @Tom-Tom RIP #ralfhood #donwuan #theeffige #thecurseofdonwuan

Cameroon Diaz @CamCam Thought 2020 was gonna be the best year eva #Nope

Kat Industries @KittyPrideCEO I didn't care much for the sequels or the spin offs. The original Effigy still remains a time classic.

The Crescent Moon @DonJuanFanPage Legends never die. Rest in Power, Mr. Hood.

Deez Nutz @ThereCanOnlyBeOneDeez @DonJuanFanPage You mean Rest in Peece

> **The Crescent Moon @DonJuanFanPage** Peace? **@ThereCanOnlyBeOneDeez**

> **Mateo Ramirez @MateoRamirez95** Let the dude sleep for God's sake

Courtney Preston @CourtneyPrestonUK Worst year ever! First, the great Biff Craley is taken from us. Now, Rafael Hood! It's official. I'm canceling 2019!

> **Don Juan Fanatic ✎ @JillSteinmen** Me reflecting on 2019 (Gigi from the TV show *4 Reelz* "shaking her head in disappointment"-meme)

Double Dipper @LionelHeart Me looking forward to 2020 (Gigi from the TV show *4 Reelz* "frolicking on a sidewalk with Cheshire grin on her face"-meme)

Go Green @TheGreenInitiative Today, all of us here at The Green Initiative are mourning the loss of one of our own, José Rafael Hood. The world will not be the same without Rafael. He is simply irreplaceable. Our thoughts and prayers are with his family.

Hermano Santiago @TheHermanoShowOfficial Least the man went out in style

> **Nicholas Wye @NicholasWye98** Life replicates art and art replicates life

> **Jacob Loame @JL01** That's fucked up **@TheHermanoShowOfficial**

Frank Littlefield @ProducerLittlefield I am deeply saddened to hear about Ralph Hood this morning. In the thirty-six years of working in the film industry—can't believe it's been that long!—Ralph stood out the most and in my mind, will be known, not as the man he was on screen, but the remarkable man he was when the cameras weren't rolling.

Tadpole @MadTad1776 "Give me your soul. Your flesh belongs to me." — The Wolf

> **M. Wells @TheHornyToad** Best. Line. Ever.

Not A Spambot @Dude'sDude #StinkyTheatre

Rebbie Cosley @DownWithRC u hav no ♥ @HermanoShowOfficial

Your Favorite Actor ® @TheRealKarlBrooks It was a pleasure to have woked with Ralf on **@TheEffigyMovie**. For me, one of best experiences as a actor.

Lazy Larry @LLPodcast The Effigy Part Two gave me nightmares for three months.

"Marge and in Charge!" @MargaretCharger I met Ralph Hood at Horror-Con back in '98 where he was guest at Crowd Favorite panel. He was such a sweetheart.

Victoria DeLuca @TNSFXMakeup Despite what the critics say, the last two remakes, The Effigy Rises and The Effigy Burns, are perhaps the most underrated films since the original '84 Effigy. Bob Camp doesn't get enough credit. #RalphHood #TheEffigyRises #TheEffigyBurns

Goth Girls XXX @SiennaSinn The rumor is true about Ralph. All twelve inches of it!

> **Brad Carmichael @BCarmichael** Is @SiennaSinn really saying what I think she's saying?

GamerSoldier @TVTRoverMuffin94 It's fair to say dat Don Juan was 1 of the main reason y so many ppl walked around likes zombies

> **Blue Collared Assassin @TimothyYhtomit** Hey @TVTRoverMuffin94 If he didn't, he wouldn't be good at his job, now would he?

> **GamerSoldier @TVTRoverMuffin94** I didn't ax @TimothyYhtomit 4 ur opinion.

> **Blue Collared Assassin @TimothyYhtomit** Dfuuck you @TVTRoverMuffin94

> **GamerSoldier @TVTRoverMuffin94** Learn how to spell

> **Blue Collared Assassin @TimothyYhtomit** *Fuck

Fig Newton Aficionado @SpaceLady That one scene in the original **@TheEffigyMovie** when actress **@SharonBell** wakes up in the middle of the night and turns on that lamp next to her bed and Don Juan's face is right there, staring down on her, nearly gave me a heart attack. No joke. I felt my heart hitting the back of my throat.

> **Movie Critic @ChuckWinfield** The Effigy is so overrated.

> > **EllenMcQueen @EllieM** Get outta here, you piece of shit!

> > **Marcey @Hellcat!!!** Go kill urself, **@ChuckWinfield**

> > **EllenMcQueen @EllieM** LOL!!!

> > **Zoey's World @ZoeyBrooks** What a troll

> > **Thomas Rake @RakeSale** Buy 6 Q-caps for only the price of 1! Do NOT miss out on this INCREDIBLE

once-in-a-lifetime deal! Sale ends tomorrow! Clink on
the link below for more information http://Qcapf0925aa~

Keeping it Real @DavidReal And of course, the mainstream media clowns said Hood's death was Y. Pestis-related. The "knife
(which Hood was stabbed with over twenty-seven times) was
laced with the plague," so, of course, it has to be true because the
media said it's true. All The Halloween Party cares about is the
death count. The more people who die the greater their chances
are at winning the upcoming election.

> **Vote 4 Washington** 🔁 @BlueDog What do you know?
> Another Yersinia-denier

Not A Spambot @Dude'sDude Don Juan, played by actor Ralph
Hood, was, inarguably, one of the greatest slashers of my genera-
tion FYI responsible for "literally" scaring the shit out of moviego-
ers—the myth goes that, during the very first screenings of The
Effigy, several people shitted themselves in the movie theatre.
Watch the documentary Inside The Effigy #StinkyTheatre #RIP
#TheWolf #KingRalph

THREAD

Gary Player @RealPlayer Series was RIP anyways all thx to Irvin
Landslide and his debauchery of the sequels. The man should be
locked up in jail for what he did to The Effigy. We're talking about
the same guy who wanted to turn Don Juan into a black guy.
Pt.1/3

↓

Gary Player @RealPlayer Not only were most of the characters
ill-used in the sequels, but also the whole backstory of Don Juan.
Irvin Landslide's "version" shouldn't have saw the light of day. Yet,
the only reason Hidden Forest released it was because of a bunch
of whiny brats on the Internet. Pt. 2/3

↓

Gary Player @RealPlayer Please. Do us all a favor. Enough
with the remakes Pt. 3/3

> **Shanty Jones @QueenShanty** Racist.

Erin Summers @EasyEWC Crazy I didn't even no who he was till
I bought his honey

Bobby Bodean @BoBodeanSays... Fo shizzle my nizzle. Dat shit is lit!

Tiffany Bell @BellTiffany @RealPlayer All u white asholes want black men in jail

> **"J" @JanineAnime @RealPlayer** Go back to European, white colonizer

> **DBF @Don'tBeFrontin' @RelPlaya** (Carolina from The Effigy "waving bye"-meme)

New Album Out Now @Taylor Swipe Not Ralph Hood I met him once during premiere of The Effigy Burns in Los Angeles was super cool RIP ☹☹☹

> **Boogeyman M.D. @TheDripCC** You garbage. Why don't you crawl back to your little clan, you Neo Nazis Scum. BTW you don't write your own music

THREAD

Go Tarheels @GregTerrance Sure. You may reads posts about actor Raphael Hood being a saint on and off the set and how he was a chivalrous man despite the sadistic, manipulative character he played on TV. When I ran into Mr. Hood at Charlotte Douglas, he was anything but the person being described through the #RalphHood trend.

↓

Go Tarheels @GregTerrance I wasn't sure it was him at first because he had a beard and was wearing a hat and sunglasses. Once I witnessed a couple of fans shake his hand and overheard one girl mentioning "Effigy," I knew the man sitting only three seats away from me in the terminal was, in fact, Raphael Hood.

↓

Go Tarheels @GregTerrance Having watched Mr. Hood's movies for years, I was immediately star struck. My hands became clammy. Without trying to come off as a super fan, I kindly asked him for an autograph on the back of my ticket. He completely ignored me. For a second, I thought that he didn't hear me. So, I asked him again. That's when he told me to "Fuck off."

↓

257

Go Tarheels @GregTerrance I haven't felt so humiliated in my life. Even till this day, I remember that one day as if it was yesterday.

I am MATT @MATTMAN Stranger danger

Martha Brinkley 📖☺ **@SupGurl99** Creeper **@GregTerrance**

I am MATT @MATTMAN Creepers gonna creep

Carly Dixon @Carlydixon You're a little angry man @Greg Terance

Hank Lively @HankyPankySpanky FAKE NEWS

Swiper 4 Life @PrincessJessica @TheDripCC Die already.

Go Tarheels @GregTerrance Says the one with an Eel Baby fan page **@SupGurl99**

Martha Brinkley 📖☺ **@SupGurl99** Your mother should've had that abortion

Monica Beckham @MooMooB Poor baby

Harry McDuggins @TVTSavageBeast_23 Burn in hell Greg

Drake Stole My Shit @DJCutlass Greg's life is canceled.

Porn Daddy NSFW @PornDaddy Russian Bot

GreyFoxx @GreyFoxx69 Maybe Ralph didn't want your dumb ass mouth-breathing all over him. #SuperSpreader #DeathBreath

James Warbird @WarbirdJames so says the one who eats dicks for a living **@GreyFoxx69**

GreyFoxx @GreyFoxx69 your just mad you don't have a dick, Buffalo Bill

James Warbird @WarbirdJames kiss my ass

GreyFoxx @GreyFoxx69 Right back at you, Sweet cheeks ✌

Movie Quotes @TheMQ Get your lotion ready **@WarbirdJames**

Zac Wilco @TradingSpaceInc. According to Data Check over two million people suffer from a deviated septum in this country. Don't hate on the science.

James Warbird @WarbirdJames Eat my dick @GreyFoxx69

Ms. Yagerbomb @YagerBombSquad You'll have to find it first ✐

Holler   @YoBoy4
🍆🍆🍆🍆🍆🍆🍆🍆🍆🍆🍆🍆🍆🍆🍆🍆🍆🍆
🍆🍆🍆🍆🍆🍆🍆🍆🍆🍆🍆🍆🍆🍆🍆🍆🍆🍆
🍆🍆🍆🍆🍆🍆🍆🍆🍆🍆🍆🍆🍆🍆🍆🍆🍆🍆
🍆🍆🍆🍆🍆🍆🍆🍆🍆🍆🍆🍆🍆🍆🍆🍆🍆🍆
🍆🍆🍆🍆🍆🍆🍆🍆🍆🍆🍆🍆🍆🍆🍆🍆🍆🍆
🍆🍆🍆🍆🍆🍆🍆🍆🍆🍆🍆🍆🍆🍆🍆🍆🍆🍆
🍆🍆🍆🍆🍆🍆🍆🍆🍆🍆🍆🍆🍆🍆🍆🍆🍆🍆
🍆🍆🍆🍆🍆🍆🍆🍆🍆🍆🍆🍆🍆🍆🍆🍆🍆🍆

Kelvin Pratt @BigKelv00 @YoBoy4 Is that a chili pepper or an eggplant?

Holler @YoBoy4 Pepper, nigga

James Warbird @WarbirdJames @YagerBombSquad is straight up fat shaming me

Oliver Kircher @JusticeForRayJay Racist @YoBoy4

Sebastian "Thunderglove" Clogs @FormerWarriorSC Im going to find out where you live @WarbirdJames and throw a 💣 through your window

Ms. Yagerbomb @YagerBombCrew Don't play the fat card with me, boy!

Eugene Basset @EBasset89 Warriors are trash

Sebastian "Thunderglove" Clogs @FormerWarriorSC 💣 @EBasset89

Eugene Basset @EBasset89 Cool bomb emoji, Yosemite Sam

You Know What They Say @boutBigFeet LOL

Sebastian "Thunderglove" Clogs @FormerWarriorSC STFU

Kelvin Pratt @BigKelv00 Haha thought it was an apple

Mustafa @MEGAMagic Apple Ripper!!!!!!!!!!

The Power of Kush @PurpleMushrooms 420

Robert Chow @SanFranChef Ain't 420 yet son

The Power of Kush @PurpleMushrooms 420 24/7

Sebastian "Thunderglove" Clogs @FormerWarriorSC Apple?

John Doe @HotTicketsUSA It looks more like a woman's head with her ponytail on fire

Dillon @DillPickle666 #ShatMyPants

And that was just a few of the million or so posts. 'Nuff said.

☾

INSIDE the morgue, Sheriff Dwayne Hershel of Musk-tucket County Sheriff's Department and head detective Christoph Mather stood with Ralph's girlfriend, Liana Bodums, as well as his sister, Raquel.

"You don't have to do this if you don't want to—" Sheriff Hershel suggested to Liana, who was holding a balled-up tissue in her hand.

"—No," Liana said over the sympathetic detective. "Let's get it over with."

The sheriff approached the coroner, Darrel Metz, who was standing next to the table where Ralph's body lay underneath a white sheet. Following a nonverbal command, he pulled back the top-half of the sheet, revealing the marred face of the sixty-two year old man, Ralph Hood, birth name, José Rafael Hood.

The tears streamed down Liana's face.

She could barely bring herself to look at Ralph.

Raquel, who had made the trip up from Tennessee, excused herself from the room as soon as she witnessed her brother lying on that cold table.

Liana decided to stay while the sheriff checked on Raquel in the hallway.

"Yes," Liana said finally, as she wiped the tears from her face. "That's him," she said to Detective Mather. "That's Ralph."

As Liana forced herself to examine Ralph's pale grayish face, she noticed the cuts along the sides of his face, lip, and chin, as well as the left cheekbone, which had been shattered like glass.

"Who would do this to him?" asked Liana.

Unable to give Liana an answer that would put her at ease, like "We're going to find the person responsible," or any response that would give Liana more clarity about Ralph's tragic demise, which, to a degree, was nothing more than a politician telling a voter exactly why he or she wanted to hear, Detective Mather remained quiet. He had been around enough grieving victims throughout his career to know when to shut up and let the griever get out what he or she needed to let out—even if it meant asking questions, which, ultimately, involved answers that ranged from concise to complicated.

"I don't understand," Liana continued. "So many people adored him."

"My son," the detective said finally, "he was a big fan of his; in fact," a smile crept up on the side of his face, "he wouldn't shut up about him."

Mather's son wasn't a fan; in fact, the man hardly spoke to his son.

But he knew that sometimes a white lie built the bridge to healing.

All teary-eyed, Liana faced the detective.

"How old is your son?" she asked.

The detective had to think for a moment.

"He just turned seventeen," he said. "He's sort of a horror buff. He's got the posters on his walls and everything."

Not *Effigy* posters but movie posters nonetheless.

Liana tried to smile off the remark but couldn't bring herself to react.

Making an attempt to bring more closure—and clarity—to the moment, Detective Mather asked her, "Did Ralph have any enemies, Ms. Bodums? Any come to mind?"

Liana thought, but only for a second, then shook her head.

"No," she said surely. "Not that I'm aware of. He was well-liked, maybe too well-liked, which is one of the reasons why he moved to Philip's Head."

"He have any, you know, stalkers?"

Liana made a noise with her mouth, which sounded as if she was blowing out a breath.

Curious of Ralph's injuries, Liana stepped closer to the table and pulled the sheet farther down his chest. She ran her finger along several deep lacerations from where he had been repeatedly stabbed by what the coroner believed to be a knife of some kind.

"Isn't everybody a stalker these days, with the social media and all—" Liana suddenly paused and put a brake on the remark before it turned into a rant. "All I know is that he didn't like the spotlight. Although, you'd never tell by looking at him." She was tempted to stroke Ralph's thin yet silky salt and pepper hair. She recoiled her hand into her chest, as though she was afraid to touch him. "No doubt," she said more mindfully. "Ralph had his share of demons. We all do."

ONE YEAR AGO
Philip's Head, Michigan

DRESSED in an altered beekeeper suit that Liana had made for him after he ripped several holes in the first one, Ralph placed an inner cover over one of the boxes in which his "babies" were occupying, set a double jar feeder that contained his famous recipe of a 2-to-1 sugar-to-water ratio—the sugar being white granulated— as well as a pinch of Vitamin C from a crushed tab to add a touch of acidity, or as his grandma used to call "sugar syrup" or simply "sugar water," which she used to pour over her famous crêpes—over the small circular hole, and surrounded it with an empty box. Lastly, he placed the outer cover over the box.

As he made his way to the second box, a voice cried out from a distance.

"Ralph!" the voice said from what sounded like the house. "Telephone!"

He ignored the voice, which he concluded was Liana's voice, as feeding his babies before Old Man Winter showed his teeth seemed far more important.

"Rafael!" Liana said once more, this time clearer.

Ralph had no other choice than to answer Liana; otherwise, she'd keep going on and on about the telephone call until she went hoarse or even lost her voice.

Frustrated, Ralph stopped what he was doing and left the apiary. On the edge of the back porch, Liana was standing with her arms crossed over her chest.

Immediately, he recognized that frustration on her face, which made his own frustration come off as mild, even fringe-worthy of playful.

The portable phone was dangling along the side of her waist.

As Ralph approached Liana, she uncrossed her arms and handed the phone to Ralph.

Ralph removed the mask from the suit and asked Liana, "Who is it?"

"It's Shawn," she mouthed.

"Who?"

"Shawn," she said with a loud whisper.

Ralph noticed Liana's thumb covering the speaker of the phone.

"Stackhouse?"

Liana was nodding her head before Ralph could finish speaking his name.

"Tell him," Ralph said, thinking, "tell him I'm busy."

"He said it's important."

"Leave a message—"

"—Just take the call," Liana said madly.

Ralph huffed and as he stepped forward to grab the phone from Liana's hand, he removed the gloves from his hands. Ralph exchanged the gloves for the phone and finally took the call.

While walking away from Liana, he said with a phony excitement, "Shawn, how you doing, man?"

"Are you sitting down, Ralph?" asked Shawn.

"Why?" he said, his voice drawn out.

"I got some great news."

Ralph stood in his tracks.

"What happened?"

He glanced over his shoulder at Liana, who was eavesdropping over the conversation. With her eyes widened, Liana held out both of her arms, as though she was motioning a similar question to Ralph.

In return, Ralph gave Liana a "just one minute" hand.

"Beneventi's on board."

"Sergio Beneventi?"

"Yes," Shawn said. "*The* Sergio Beneventi. He and Cesar from Screengasm had a meeting this morning. He's in. All the way in. He wants to reboot *The Effigy* franchise. 'A trilogy,' he said. However, he said he'd only do it if you were involved."

"Involved how? Are we talking cameo?"

"No," Shawn said more seriously. "They want you to put the mask back on."

Once more, Ralph glanced at Liana, who was waiting in anticipation.

He thought about Shawn's offer.

Only a couple seconds of pondering whether or not he should reprise his role as the iconic slasher, Don Juan, Ralph said finally, "I can't, Shawn."

"What?" Shawn said, his voice bursting over the phone. "You can't be serious? Beneventi wants to reboot *The Effigy* and you're going to turn it down?"

"You're not my agent anymore, Shawn—"

"—I know I'm not, Ralph, but this is a once-in-a-lifetime opportunity. We're talking about one of the most sought-after directors in Hollywood, the man who's responsible for *Death-R-Us*, *The Shallow Whisperings*. He's earned himself quite a reputation for taking old, tired franchises and turning them into pure gold. They call him 'Doctor Reboot' in the industry—"

"—I'm aware of his work, Shawn. He's good at what he does, and I'm sure he'll bring a new vision to the story. But Shawn," Ralph said clearly, "it's not my story. Not anymore. I have a life out here now. I told you this before and I'll tell you again: I'm done with the industry."

"But Ralph," Shawn pleaded, "the industry ain't done with you. Come on. I know that you know that this time it's different. Cesar's going to give Beneventi full-reign over the project. No suits involved, telling him what to do. Just an artist painting his masterpiece. Let him paint, Ralph."

He sighed and once more, looked at Liana, whose anticipation turned to deep concern.

"I'm sorry, Shawn, but I'm not interested," Ralph said and hung up.

He walked back to Liana and handed her the phone.

"I'm going to finish feeding the babies," Ralph said depressingly.

"Thought you were against that kind of stuff."

"I am," Ralph uttered. "Trust me. I am. But for some reason, the colony just doesn't look as strong as it did last year. Maybe it had something to do with having an earlier summer. Who knows?" He waved his hand in the air and said under his breath, "Climate change. . ."

"So," Liana said and prevented Ralph from tending to his so-called "babies," "what he'd want?"

Ralph stopped, turned around.

"What'd who want?"

"Who do you think?"

As he had been doing throughout the last few minutes in front of Liana, he let out something between a heavy sigh and huff or both.

"They want me to do another movie."

"Another one?"

"Yeah," he said. "A lead role, it sounds like."

"What about what you said last time?" asked Liana.

"I know," Ralph mumbled and hung his head for a moment.

"Well," she said, walking down the porch steps, "do you want to do it?"

"You know I'm done with that part of my life," he said, looking up at Liana. "Now, I got you." He glanced up at the trees above, then moved his eyes toward Liana, then hooked his finger around the belt loop along the waistband of her blue jeans and pulled her closer. "The birds and the bees," he said, as he kissed Liana on the lips.

"I'm starting to think you like your bees more than you do me," she said and rested her head against the side of Ralph's shoulder.

"You can't make love to a bee," Ralph teased.

The comment repelled Liana, causing her to playfully push Ralph a few feet. Even though Liana was twenty-three years younger than Ralph, at times she'd act half her age. Liana's playful spirit was one of the many traits she possessed that attracted Ralph.

"But," she said back, "I'm sure you would if you could."

"No," he said, reeling Liana back into his arms. "You know you're the only queen around here."

Liana handed Ralph's gloves back to him and leaned into his range of vision. "If you're going to be moping around here for the next few months I'd rather you reconsider the offer."

"I'm not moping."

"Maybe not yet," Liana said, grinning. "But I know you. You will be."

"I just wish they'd be done with it already," Ralph said with another sigh. "I mean, how many damn times do you need to kill off a character?"

Liana leaned away from Ralph.

She asked, "How can you even say that without reading the script?"

"Are you saying I should do it?" asked Ralph.

"All I'm saying is that you do what's best for you, Ralph. If it comes straight down to it, I can take over the biz while you're gone. Besides, I've watched you plenty enough to learn how to take care of your 'babies.' Plus, I got Renoir here to help out."

"Renoir's a damn idiot."

Liana laughed.

"Yeah," she said. "He is, isn't he? But he sure does come in handy."

"It's a full-time job, Ana."

"Not like I have anything else to do around here."

Ralph suddenly backtracked.

"What am I saying?" he asked himself. "No," he said. "I can't put that kind of stress on you."

"I don't mind."

"Well," he said over Liana, "I do."

Ralph slipped the gloves back on and kissed Liana on the forehead.

"Let 'em make their little movie without me," he said resentfully and walked back to the apiary. "The hell with 'em."

Ralph left Liana alone in the backyard and tended to his babies.

"Remember," she said, her voice growing louder as Ralph walked farther and farther away from her, "we have to leave in about an hour. . ."

Not losing a step in his pace, Ralph waved his hand in the air and indicated to Liana that he heard her loud and clear.

☾

THE older Ralph had gotten, the less fearful he was about a doctor's office; in fact, he looked at seeing a doctor as no different than taking your car into a shop to get an oil change or tire rotation, or in essence, basic maintenance, making sure the gears still worked. He was sixty-one years of age and pushing sixty-two, which meant he was getting closer and closer to the tendentious "65 and older" category, which very well meant, according to the growing stigmas surrounding the age group, his life was no longer important. His life *did not* matter anymore, and according to our "brave new world," the acceptance of his own mortality was nothing more than the price of taking up too much space and air. "He's past his prime," they'd say, "and has nothing to offer the world anymore." On the contrary, Ralph knew the best days were ahead of him, not behind him, and everything he did in the past was merely a childish game of dress-up. Which made the visit to the doctor's office completely unnerving.

When the nurse called out Liana's name and ushered her through that door as he sat uncomfortably in the waiting room, the man, who had spent his career scaring the living shit out of moviegoers, was utterly, unequivocally scared shitless.

☾

AFTER waiting for what felt like an hour inside the bland waiting room and spending most of his time imagining the worst case scenarios, Ralph decided to grab a magazine from the table next to him. He skimmed through the reading the doctor's office had to offer: a *Fitness Wonders*, *Northern Living*, *Sad Comics*, as well as a *Crazy Cooking* magazine.

Underneath the stack of magazines, he came across none other than the latest issue of LOCAL: the Retirement Edition.

On the front cover of the glossy mag was, as Ralph would say, "yours truly." At first, he wanted absolutely no part in the magazine; however, after some convincing from Liana and her explaining how the LOCAL magazine would not only help generate publicity—not like he needed it, though—but also possible revenue for the business. He glanced over the cover, which was a photograph taken outside the apiary. In the photo he's posing for the camera with one of his trademark bottles of Wolf Honey™ in his hand. The title above him reads: "Beeing Happy: How famous actor Ralph Hood found his calling outside the silver screen."

The door opened.

Never had Ralph welcomed such a sound.

His hopes were flattened as soon as another patient, not Liana, exited.

Ralph turned his attention back to the LOCAL magazine.

He drew his eyes upward from the cover and witnessed one of the townspeople sitting across from him. Once he looked her way, she moved both of her eyes away. Which wouldn't be the first time he had received such looks—after all, he was, in a way, a local celebrity even to those who hadn't watched any of his movies or followed his acting career.

As Ralph placed the magazine back on the table, the door opened yet again.

Ralph witnessed Liana standing at the doorway.

Immediately, Ralph knew it was bad from the look on Liana's face.

☾

AS Ralph sat with Liana and her gynecologist Doctor Date inside her office, they went over Liana's treatment options.

By the time Ralph left the office with Liana, he couldn't recall a single word the doctor said to him or on the contrary, a single word he said to the doctor. The entire conversation was a jumbled up mess crossed between fact and fantasy. All he could think about was losing Liana if she didn't receive the proper surgery and treatment.

They drove past a pharmacy where outside pumpkins and Halloween decorations, such as witches and skeletons, were positioned on top of bales of hay; however, the decorations didn't stop there. Each one of the lampposts lining the sidewalks was covered in your typical spider-web ornament made out of plastic. Other places, like various businesses such as a barbershop, numerous bars and pubs and even the front of the older houses scattered in and around the downtown area, had gone away from that cheap-looking spiderweb decorations one would find either online or at any major retail store and used nothing more than cotton—as well as an aerosol can of hairspray for added effect—to create gnarly black widow spider webs stretching along the window corners, porches, chandeliers, and ceiling fans. Ralph could've taken a left on Prince; however, it was clear that he was trying to avoid the small crowd of tourists and horror buffs hanging outside the themed-bar called "Possession," an establishment roughly based on Ralph's character, Don Juan, from the 1978 movie *The Effigy*.

Ralph, who had remained dead silent throughout the drive, finally opened his mouth to speak: "*I fucking hate this time of year.*"

"I know you do," Liana said quietly.

They continued down Main, passing a courthouse as well as a town hall, until they reached the end of the street where at the very center of a roundabout intersection stood a gigantic obelisk-shaped statue of a Philip's head screwdriver—which could be spotted from three towns over and was often referred to by the locals in an inebriated state of mind as their own "Wasshushton Mon'ment." According to *The Guinness Book of Records*, the statue was considered to be the "world's largest screwdriver" and was known to draw many tourists in search of oddball attractions and, of course, spirits. Like many storefronts in the downtown area, the surrounding base of that massive screwdriver was decorated with all-things Halloween: ghosts, goblins, you name it.

"*Welcome to the town of Philip's Head*," read the sign decorated with spider webs, "*Home of the largest Philip's Head Screwdriver.*"

Despite having driven through the downtown several times before the "infestation" of Halloween, Ralph still remained repulsed by the decorations. He half-circled the roundabout, hung a left on Lake Street and continued on Lake until he reached 4th Street, took a left on 4th, then wound up back on Prince. He stayed on Prince, which turned into Wacamaw Creek Street where he took a right on his neighborhood street, Doris Lane. Like the downtown, some of the houses on his street were deco-rated as well. Unlike the sight of the businesses and whatnot, he found a strange comfort while driving through the wooded neighborhood. He retreated farther inward and reflected on those innocent times when he used to go trick-or-treating with his neighborhood friends. He felt so small between the ages of, say, eight and twelve years old, not only in size but also in importance. All he cared about back then was the love he received from his tight circle of friends, his younger sister, Raquel, as well as both his parents. He didn't need any love from the world and that was okay by him. He specifically recalled that one neighborhood kid Doug Gayheart, who earned the nickname "Double D" for having boy- breasts. Truth be told, Double D Doug was only liked around the neigh-borhood for one thing and one thing only: he had a cam-era, a Yashica Super 8, which belonged to his father, whom some of the kids thought worked in a real-life Q Branch. Every now and then, Doug would "borrow" his father's Super 8 and show it off. Ralph and the other neighborhood kids would document their adventures—and misadventures—and afterwards, laugh, tease, and ridicule each other among their group while watching what they had recently filmed. At times, they'd make their own horror movie, reenact their most favorite movie monsters such as *Dracula*, *The Mummy*, or *Creature from the Black Lagoon* and show the penny budget films to their parents, which would almost always result in one of the parents, usually Ms. Read, to react with threats and neighborhood-wide protest as her suspicions came to fruition that her own flesh and blood was stealing her eye shadow and mascara for mummy makeup, as well as their own toilet paper for mummy wrap; however, Ralph, like most of the other kids in the neighborhood, including Edward "Ed" Read, hung out with Doug "Double D" Gayheart simply because he owned a camera. Now, everybody was a Doug.

☾

RALPH, who, except for expressing his grievances against a day widely celebrated by children, both young and old, hadn't spoken a word about the diagnosis from the time he left the doctor's office to the moment he stepped foot inside the cold house, was stopped by Liana before he retreated upstairs to his office.

"Please don't make what Doctor Date said put you in a bad mood for the rest of the day," Liana said to Ralph as he made his way up three steps. "Don't make this about yourself—"

Ralph pouted and said, "I'm not."

Liana continued, "All she's doing, Ralph, is stating the facts. I have to—we have to accept these facts and make a decision in order to proceed forward."

"We'll get a second opinion," Ralph said, towering over Liana.

"You don't trust her?"

Ralph stepped from the stairs until he was eye-level with Liana.

"I don't trust any of them, Liana—"

"—You don't trust the MRIs? How about the ultra-sounds? You don't trust them either?"

"I'm not saying that," Ralph argued. "All I'm saying is that we should keep an open mind."

"—Then, what's going to another doctor to get a second opinion have to do with anything?"

Ralph internally cringed from the tone of Liana's voice. He hated hearing her so upset.

"I was a fool for not having my mammogram sooner," Liana said, losing confidence. "I kept putting it off and off. I accept responsibility. It's my fault. My grandmother had the mutant gene as well and I thought it'd never happen to me, but you saw what happened to her when it was too late for her—"

"—Don't go there, Ana."

Ralph grabbed Liana by both her shoulders.

"I feel like an idiot. *What if*, deep inside, I wanted this to happen to. . . "

The words were becoming harder and harder to speak for Liana.

"You stop talking like that, you hear me?" Ralph asked yet, at the same time, demanded, as he held Liana in his arms. "We're going to get through this. We've been through so much. This is nothing. It's just a bump in the road—"

Ralph immediately regretted that poor usage of words before he could finish his thought.

All red and teary-eyed, Liana leaned away from Ralph. "Seriously?"

"Don't give me that," he said, backtracking the untimely remark. "You know what I mean, Liana."

"What if it spreads?" Liana said panicky. "I'll cut them off myself if I have to. I can't go out like this, Ralph. And Aunt Harley," she said, tracing the cancer in her family, "her last days before she died from liver cancer. She turned into a fucking skeleton—"

"—Stop, Liana," Ralph tried to calm down Liana.

"I remember watching how quick she went."

Stop.

"One day, she was walking around; and then the next, I couldn't even recognize her anymore."

Stop.

"*She looked like a skeleton,*" Liana cried, "like something had crawled inside her and eaten away her insides. I'll kill myself before I go out like that way—"

"—Stop it!" Ralph yelled over Liana. "Right now!"

"This is my body, Ralph, not yours!"

"Liana," Ralph said, softening his tone, "I'll support you in whatever you do. You know I will. . . "

Before Liana could state her case to Ralph, Ralph's daughter, Arely, who was oblivious to the argument in front of the staircase, walked past them and made her way into the kitchen. The ethereal drones of Eel-Baby pulsed through her wireless ear buds. Dripping wet with sweat from the recent jog around the neighborhood, she removed the buds from her ears and shot a glance over at Ralph.

"Arely," Ralph said fatherly as he looked over Arely's attire, which consisted of a power bra and skintight shorts, exposing the bottom part of her butt cheeks, "what I'd tell you about going out dressed like that? You might as well be wearing a bathing suit—"

In a discreet manner, Liana turned away from Arely and wiped away the tears from her eyes with the underside of her wrists.

"Ralph," she said, shielding herself behind Ralph, "she's twenty-seven years old. She can dress anyway she wants."

Ralph glared at Liana, who, in return, gave him an innocent shrug.

While Arely was preparing a protein smoothie, she grabbed the remote from the couch and switched on a 60-inch 4K smart TV mounted above the fireplace. She only flipped through a couple of channels before landing on, of all movies to be airing right now, *The Effigy*, as in the 1984 re-release version.

"What do you know?" Arely said sarcastically, as she made her way into the kitchen. "You're on TV, Dad."

In the scene, Don Juan was stalking a young woman through a dark, steamy alleyway.

"Turn it off, Arely," Ralph said, his temper flaring.

"Here it comes," Arely said, all child-like as Don Juan was about to break the young woman's back over a dumpster.

Ralph demanded over the actress's screams, "I said, 'Turn it off!'"

On the TV, Don Juan violently slammed the young woman over the dumpster, her body folding sixty-degrees the opposite direction.

Arely finally switched off the TV.

"Okay," she said, her voice trailing off. "Angry-much."

As Arely walked back into the kitchen and started adding nuts, like walnuts and almonds, yogurt, and vegetables, including carrots and kale, into the blender, she turned to Liana and said to her, "I almost forgot." She asked Liana, "How'd the doctor's visit go?"

☾

LATER that night after Ralph broke the news about Liana's diagnosis to Arely, he found the perfect moment to finally sit down and talk with Arely while Liana was upstairs finishing up her last episode of *Desperate Housewives of Newbay* before she started on her nightly Pilates in front of the TV. He grabbed himself a bowl of Dragon Puffs and while eating inside the kitchen, caught the pale glow of a TV flickering along the hallway walls.

Not bothered by letting the Dragon Puffs get soggy, he set the bowl of cereal on the granite countertop and made his way to the theatre room where, in a similar fashion as Liana, Arely was sitting in a lounge chair and watching a horror thriller series on the steaming service, Shh!

From the cracked doorway, Ralph, more or less, spied on Arely making one of her selfie-videos for her followers—or fans, Ralph couldn't tell the difference.

Not once did he pay much attention to the TV show. All he could gather was something about a killer who had the ability to move through walls, which, Ralph knew, wasn't at all original. But what was in a time where ideas were commonly recycled like plastic?

Curious, captivated, yet, at the same time, concerned by his daughter's ability to share her thoughts to that device, Ralph held his gaze on Arely, who was snuggled with her black cat named H.P., who, of all people, was named after the horror writer H.P. Lovecraft.

"What are you watching?" asked Ralph.

Arely stopped recording and lowered the phone from her face and barely acknowledged Ralph or his presence.

Ralph turned his attention back to the screen.

The killer was emerging from the wall of a girl's bedroom.

She delved back into her phone, texting to her thousands of followers on social media who were live-streaming the new TV series, *Five Walls*, spelled Walls, with a Roman numeral 5—or V—inside the W in *Walls*.

"Cool effects," Ralph pointed out.

The effects—or efx—were, like the Halloween decorations he saw earlier in the day, cheap-looking to Ralph. "Bunch of CGI garbage," Ralph would say with a hint of hostility; however, he knew it was his only way in.

Arely shrugged.

"They're a'ight," she said, turning to Ralph. "Kind of lame if you really want to know the truth."

"Super lame."

"You just said they were cool."

"I lied."

Finally, she put down the phone.

For Ralph, it seemed like his way in—more or less, his "cue."

"Say Arely," Ralph said over a throbbing synthesizer-heavy soundtrack, "can I have a word?"

"I'm trying to watch a show," Arely said, pointing at the screen.

"Just a second of your time," Ralph said louder. "Please. . ."

Annoyed, Arely paused the TV show during an explosion, which provided a bright orangish light inside the dark theatre room.

Ralph sat down next to Arely, who picked up her phone and started texting.

"Those people can wait, Arely," Ralph said patiently.

Arely rolled her eyes, closed the phone, and said directly, "How is she?"

"She says she's fine, but. . . " Ralph said, sitting back, ". . . I know she's not."

"Is she going to lose her hair?"

"If she decides on the chemotherapy, yes, it's a possibility."

"I was doing some research on the Internet. They have this device you wear over your head called a Keep-Cap. Supposedly, it freezes the hair follicles, which prevents from hair loss. It's worth a try—"

"—We'll look into it, Arely."

"If not, I know this one guy who makes all kinds of wigs," Arely suggested. "I can tell him about Liana's situation."

"What guy?"

"He's just a guy who follows me."

"About that," Ralph said, reaching the "reason" for the father-daughter chat, "the Internet stuff. I'm aware you have quite an audience," he corrected, "or 'followers' who appreciate your exercise videos—"

"—They're not just exercise videos, Dad," Arely stated. "I give tips and advice on how to live a healthy lifestyle."

"Well, whatever," Ralph said sternly. "I don't want you going on the Internet sharing Liana's diagnosis. This doesn't involve those people. This is strictly between us. Which means no videos, no texts, *no tweets*. Can you do that?"

"Dad," Arely said, sitting upright, "what's the big deal?"

"Big deal? It's none of their business, Arely. Period." He collected himself for a moment. "Listen," he said carefully, "I know how close you two are. I wish you had a woman like Liana when you were growing up, but you didn't. And that is on me, *not* you. She's more like a friend to you than a mother or a big sister—"

"—Sister? Come on, Dad," Arely said, making a face. "Gross. Liana has no labels. Liana is Liana."

"Yes," he agreed. "You're right, Arely. Liana is Liana. And if Liana wants to talk about her illness one day or share it, then she will tell you when she's ready. She has that choice. For now, I want you to give her the respect and dignity—"

"—Okay, geez," Arely said, shrinking in her seat. "I won't tell anybody."

As though on an innate reaction, Arely reached for her phone.

"Arely?"

"I won't, Dad," she said louder.

An awkward silence formed.

But not for long.

Ralph had a way—which Arely swears was like a superpower or mutation—of making uncomfortable moments less comfortable by changing the subject.

"I got a call from Shawn today," he said to Arely, who, strangely, perked up a little from the remark.

"You did?"

"Yeah."

"Man, when's the last time you talked to him?"

"Years."

"So, what's Itchy Pants up to?"

"He said," he said, pausing midway through his sentence to make sense of the name, *Itchy Pants*. "He said they want me to do another film."

Arely's eyes lit up in the glow of the screen.

"Really?"

"Yeah—"

"—That's great," she said exuberantly. "Well, you gonna do it?"

"Taking care of Liana right now is more important."

"Right," she said, her spirits dampening. "Sure. If you decide to do it, I can take care of her while you're gone."

"Let's not get ahead of ourselves," he said and stood up from the seat. "Let's be real here, Arely. That franchise died a long time ago. You know some things are best left in the grave."

"True." Arely shrugged. "But you're not dead."

"Enjoy the rest of your. . . " Ralph glanced at the bright still of the explosion on the screen, ". . .watch party or whatever. And remember," he said and turned his shoulder as he reached the doorway, "what I said about Liana."

Arely picked up the phone with one hand, while in the other, she was twisting the invisible key over the corner of her closed mouth.

☾

WHEN Ralph made it back to the bedroom, Liana was already dressed in her holey gray *Soulstain* Spring Tour 2006 T-shirt that was at least five times larger than her normal size, the worn shirt acting more like a short dress than an actual top.

Standing next to her side of the bed, Liana plumped up her pillow and pulled back the corner of the comforter like a dog-ear on the page of a book.

From the doorway, Ralph watched Liana prepping the bed as if she was ready to melt into the sheets—which was unusual because normally she didn't go to bed until around midnight after watching her round of late-night shows.

He checked the time on the nightstand.

It was only nine-thirty.

Stating the obvious, Ralph said with a question, "You going to bed?"

Liana gave him that "What the hell does it look like?" kind of expression and said annoyingly, "Yeah. I'm tired."

As Liana tucked herself in, Ralph went to the bathroom where he brushed his teeth, flossed, gargled, and lastly, used the head before he undressed and slipped into bed.

As Ralph tugged his share of covers, Liana stirred in bed.

Ralph noticed that Liana hadn't turned off her lamp, which, if she were tired, would've already been off. But it was still on. And Liana hadn't closed her eyes just yet. Instead, she lay on her side with her back facing Ralph.

"Listen, Ana," he said finally, as he propped up two pillows behind his upper back, "I was thinking more about Shawn's offer. If I accepted it, I would only been gone for a month or two, three the most. We're talking possibly a year from now. By then, the cancer will already be in remission—"

"—You don't know that," Liana said with her back still turned.

"Liana, it would definitely help us out finically."

"Is that what you think this is all about?" she asked with her voice more sour, as she rolled over on her other side. "Money?"

"No," Ralph said, "but it wouldn't hurt to have some on the side."

"You and I both know it's not about money, Ralph. Insurance will cover the expenses for the treatment."

"Yes," he said. "I know, but. . . "

"But things have changed, Ralph."

"I just. . . " Ralph said, thinking, ". . . I don't want to spend most of my time caught up in the business when I should be using my time to take care of you."

"What are you saying, Ralph?" asked Liana.

"Think about it, Liana: If I decide to take up Shawn's offer, there would be no comparison as to how much money I would make in just a few months than I'd make producing honey."

"What about the business?"

"I could sell it," Ralph said unsurely.

"No," Liana said. "We're not going to rearrange our lives over this disease."

"Well, we have to do what's best for you. . . "

"Let's be honest, Ralph," Liana said, sitting up on her elbow. "You didn't go into the honey business because of the money. Right?"

Ralph had no response for Liana.

"If worst comes to worst, there are many ways that we can get money without having to give up our dreams. They have GoFundYourself and other fundraising-type sites now. You're a well-known figure. Once word gets out—"

"—It's for lazy people who aren't willing enough to put in the hard work."

"I'm just saying, Ralph, there are ways."

"Well, that's not how I was raised." He rolled over on his side until he was face-to-face with Liana. He held her by the hand and asked her, "Have you told Alonzo or Rocky yet?"

Liana shook her head no.

"Not yet," she said. "I haven't worked up the courage."

"You will when you're ready."

"I don't even know where Zo's living these days," she said, moving her other hand toward her chest. "Last time I talked to him he was in Alaska, I believe. It was that time he called to wish me happy birthday. "

"That long, huh? Maybe we can all get together for Thanksgiving."

"And Rocky," Liana said, "I talked to her just a week ago. She's not going to take the news well."

"She could stay with us for a weekend or however long she wants to," Ralph suggests. "Her and Arely seemed to get along pretty well, didn't they?"

"Yeah," Liana said shortly, as she started rubbing the side of her breast. "The thing I can't wrap my head around is the fact that nobody in my family had breast cancer, except for my grandmother."

"These things sort of skip genes, don't they?"

"Maybe," Liana said quietly. "I worry about Zo and Rocky, though. Vigo's family had all sorts of ailments. You could spin a wheel of ailments and chances are one of Vigo's family members had whatever the needle landed on. I wonder if it has to do with breastfeeding them when I was younger. I read in this article that breast-feeding increases a woman's risk for breast cancer. It all has to do with the hormones you lose or something—"

"—Save your energy," Ralph said over Liana. "You can drive yourself crazy trying to play the detective here."

"It could be from the environment."

"Yes," Ralph said, as he ran his thumb across the side of her face. "It could. But it could be from anything, Li-ana." He scooted closer to Liana. "I'm going to be here for you every step of the way. Together, we're going to get through this. We *always* do, don't we?"

Liana kissed Ralph.

Ralph kissed her back.

Together, they fell asleep in each other's arms.

☾

RALPH dreamt that he was wandering through down-town Philip's Head.

He didn't exactly remember how he had found his way into the dream—who did?—but the first thing that caught his mind was the sign that read "Main Street" along the empty intersection.

The streets were eerily deserted, not a soul in sight, yet, somehow, among the quietness, he could hear the low buzz of life inside each and every building that lined the street. Even the air still had an early morning thick-ness to it that stuck to his skin. He felt as if he was the only person left on earth yet, strangely, other life had raged on well beyond these building walls.

As he continued along Main Street, he passed a bak-ery, Aunt Ruthy's, which, like the streets, remained quiet and from the exterior, closed; however, unlike the streets, it wasn't empty. The two hunched over silhouettes of what appeared to be human—or at least, what Ralph knew to be post-human—paced back and forth in the dark kitchen, not making any sounds, just pacing. The air was thicker, heavier. He walked faster down the sidewalk, searching for potential exits, if the moment should arise. In the corner of his eye, he fell witness to a large horde, which consisted of at least a thousand or so of these post-human entities standing in the middle of the alleyway next to the bakery. Ralph stopped and studied the horde, each figure among them breathing heavily from their gaping mouths. Each one of them had their eyes closed, as though they were in some kind of "sleep mode."

Trying not to awake these "things," Ralph cautiously stepped forward on the sidewalk. His foot missed the pavement and landed in a puddle along the edge of the alley. The splashing noise caused several horde members to open their eyes, creating a domino-like effect. It was at that moment when their eyes bolted open Ralph realized these things weren't people at all; in fact, they were far from people. Their eyes were mad and blood red. Once they set their eyes on Ralph, each one of them started foaming from their mouths.

The mob of rabid creatures proceeded toward Ralph, causing Ralph to flee on foot.

The mob chased after him.

Like the air, his legs were extremely heavy, and he wasn't gaining much—or any—distance from the mob. No matter how fast he ran, the mob remained on his heels. He cut through a seedy alley and briefly lost the mob for a second until yet another larger one caught up with him on another street. He knew that if he could make it to 4th Street he could beat it in a foot race.

By the time he reached the Main Circle, the mob had cut off his route. Now, he had a mob in front of him and a mob behind him. He had nowhere to go except for the building on the sides. He checked the doors, but they were locked.

The mob closed in!

Ralph had no other choice than to fight.

He could only fight off a dozen or so before he was completely overrun. He stayed on his feet, shielding punches and throwing several of his own. When they clawed at him, he fought back even dirtier, like biting them or chewing off an ear or gauging out an eye or punching them directly in their windpipe, which was effective. When they used objects on him, like a street sign, brick, or chair, he beat one of them into submission and used its lifeless body as a battering ram.

Blindsided by a fist to his temple, Ralph staggered before falling toward the ground. He knew once they knocked him to the ground, it was over. He grabbed hold of one of the rabid creatures and tried to keep himself upright. Another blow sent him straight toward the ground where the mob repeatedly kicked him until he was barely conscious. One creature managed to rip off his arm. First, two other creatures fought over the limb. Then two creatures turned to four. Then an entire mob was fighting for scraps. They hoisted Ralph's lifeless body through a sea of frail bodies and carried him toward the world's largest screwdriver, sipping from the very blood that poured from his dismembered body.

Once Ralph reached the Main Circle, they tied a noose around Ralph's neck and hung him up on the massive screwdriver. He attempted to pull on the noose from his neck with his only hand, hoping to loosen it.

But it was done.

Ralph was done.

The mob relished in Ralph's torment and cheered in celebration.

As Ralph began to fade, a force suddenly pulled him out of the darkness!

Gasping for air, he sat upright on the bed.

The lights were off, even though he remembered falling asleep with the lights on. *Maybe Liana had turned off the lights.* He pushed past the thought and tried to make sense of the dream. Somewhere among the haziness of the disappearing dream, he recalled the town of Philip's Head, not Johnstown, the historic fictional city in *The Effigy*, where he was being hung up on the town's famous screwdriver, not the Don Juan statue, like the one from the movie.

As Liana was snoring next to him, Ralph rolled out of his bed, leaving behind a body shape of sweat along the sheets. He threw on a white T-shirt and made his way downstairs where Arely had left a couple of lights on in the living room.

Frustrated by Arely's ability not to turn off lights—*how hard is it*, he thought, *the switch not only goes two ways*—he walked into the living room to turn off the lights. He switched on the TV, the glow of the screen providing enough light in the room. He flipped through a few channels until winding up on NNN, which was airing a primetime special on the serial killer known as "The Snipper."

Ralph watched a couple of minutes on TV before turning it off.

As he was about to turn off the last light in the kitchen, he heard a *thud* followed by a giggling noise coming from the backyard.

The shotgun was upstairs, and he didn't have enough time to run upstairs and grab the shotgun. He grabbed the closest weapon he could find: a butcher's knife.

With knife in hand, he switched on the back porch light, as well as the floodlight on the corner of the house, and walked outside. Coyotes had been known to roam these woods; in fact, little H.P. had himself a run in with a couple of coyotes last year and managed to escape them by running up a tree.

Next, Ralph decided to check on the bees, who, as the name perceived itself, were sleeping like "babies."

Once he knew his babies were okay, Ralph walked back to the house where he came across a mask of the character, Don Juan, lying on the back porch. The mask appeared as if it was one of those cheap flimsy plastic masks one would find at any party store; however, it still carried similar characteristics of Don Juan, that being his face was a cross between man and beast, as if man was in the middle of a transformation until it was cut short, the face not fully developed, the features of its face disproportionate from the rest of its man, wolf-like, freakish.

Cautiously, he picked up the mask.

From the woods, he heard more noises, this time a more distinct giggle.

"Goddamn kids," Ralph uttered and walked back inside.

He tossed the mask in the kitchen trashcan.

He stopped halfway down the hallway and looked around the living room and felt a presence with him as if he was still being watched. He could sense the bees in that tacky honeybee wallpaper moving and buzzing around at a blinding speed. An eye revealed itself behind the slowly unpeeling wallpaper. He shook away the image from his head. It was all in his head, Ralph realized, nothing more than his body telling him that he needed some shuteye.

Not only that, in the very-back-of-the-mind way, he was formulating a useful excuse for his contempt for the wallpaper. Clearly, he wasn't the one in charge of the interior designs throughout the house. That was Liana's territory. If he had it any other way, he'd paint the room the color red.

Ralph shrugged off the night terror.

As he was about to head back upstairs, he came across a spider walking along the kitchen floor. Normally, he'd pick it up and set it free outside, especially if he were in the company of Liana or Arely, who were both animal lovers, regardless of shape and size. Liana was asleep, and he assumed Arely was asleep as well.

With his slipper, Ralph stepped on the spider, picked up its squashed remains with a paper towel, flushed it down the toilet, then turned off the downstairs lights and walked back upstairs and went to bed.

☾

THE next morning while going through the tedious process of winterizing the apiary for the upcoming months ahead which forecasters predicted to be a colder winter than last year, Ralph became lightheaded as he was placing the last mousetrap below the boxes. He leaned up against a post, took a deep breath, and thought about the three cups of coffee he drank this morning to make up for the lack of sleep last night. Normally, on a decent night when he caught at least four to five hours of shuteye, he'd be fine with two cups. Last night, from the time he dozed off to the time he woke up from a terrible nightmare, he only caught about an hour of sleep. He figured the lightheadedness would go away after he got some food in him. He closed his eyes for a minute and continued to breathe in through the nose and out through the mouth, which helped lessen the spin.

Once he was okay to walk around, he pushed aside any health concern, went back to work, and finished setting the rest of the pest guards.

As soon as he tended to his babies, he was struck by yet another dizzy spell. The high pitch *buzzing* sound reminded him of the recent nightmare where he was being torn apart in the street. Last night's nightmare, once as vivid as reality, had, like most nightmares, turned into a lost memory as the morning dragged on. The graphic images buried underneath the sight of waking up next to an already awake Liana. He looked into her eyes and all of the blood and gore had faded away, as if the violence itself was only a manifestation of an old demon resurfacing into his now insouciant country lifestyle. The *buzzing*, which was caused by the bees rapidly moving their wings, only intensified those horrific images reconnecting inside his mind. That *buzzing* turned into what he could only make out as incoherent noise, which gradually turned into the bloodthirsty screams of a red-eyed mob. Yet, somehow, among the hunger, the *buzzing* still remained.

☾

RALPH decided to take a break from work and check on Liana, who was sitting in the computer room and searching for alternative treatments on the slow Internet— Liana was all into holistics and would proactively prefer any natural remedy to rid the disease inside her—however, checking on Liana was only an excuse.

Liana put the computer to sleep and the first thing that came out of her mouth once she saw Ralph walking through the house with his shoes still on was "Take off your shoes! How many times do I have to tell you? You're tracking mud into the house."

Ralph abided by Liana's commands, walked back outside, and kicked off the muddy boots from his feet.

Liana acknowledged Ralph by touching him on the arm, as if her touch alone was a small gesture that she meant nothing by the outburst. In other words, it was her way of saying, "Sorry for snappin', Hoody. Still love you to death."

With last night's nightmare on his mind, Ralph didn't spend too much time nagging at Liana, even though, at times, he felt any comeback at her verbal assaults would end in the most epic failure.

As Liana made her way into the kitchen, Ralph walked past the living room, past the theatre room, past Arely's bedroom where she had EDM playing behind the closed door, and made it to his office at the end of the hallway.

The office, which was off limits, was dedicated to the fictional character, Don Juan, aka "The Wolf," from the movie franchise, *The Effigy*.

Inside, he had all sorts of *Effigy* memorabilia scattered throughout the office, including movie posters, Wolf masks and various Wolf Halloween costumes, as well as Don Juan toys, action figures, twelve-inch tall models, a golden machete award that read "Slasher of the Year," which Ralph received at the Music World Awards in 1989, as well as boxes full of copies of his autobiography *Unmasked*—not to mention, the one artifact that stood out the most: the original effigy created by late makeup artist and good friend, Bernard Knowles. The six-foot tall model was used throughout the first three movies, *The Effigy*, *The Effigy Part Two*, and *The Effigy: The Curse of*

Don Juan. He picked up the leathery effigy, which was attached to a metal rod to keep it upright. The model was designed to look as if a diabolical witch—whose dark origins would come to light in the third, most controversial movie—had stitched together the figure with various pieces of flesh.

As Ralph lost himself in the effigy, he heard a series of noises outside the office, first a couple of *knocks* on Arely's bedroom door, the squeaky door opening, EDM blaring, then lowering, then, lastly, the front door opening and closing.

From the office window, he peeked through the closed blinds and saw both Liana and Arely playing with Liana's chocolate Labrador, Duke, in the front yard. The two were laughing and acting as if they didn't have a single care in the world. The sight of both his partner, Liana, and his daughter, Arely, who knew very little about Ralph when she was a child and later in her late teens decided to forge such a lasting relationship with her once estranged father, had made his answers clearer than ever.

Not wasting anymore time, Ralph picked up the phone and called Shawn.

PRESENT

LIANA'S neighbor, Griff, who not only lived across the street, but also developed a mutual friendship with Ralph, Liana, and Arely throughout the eleven years of being neighbors, was kind enough to pick up both Liana and Arely from the Hotel 7 where they were currently staying and drive the two back to the house—or what was left of the house. As for the other two furry-leg members of the family, Duke and H.P. were currently staying at a boarding facility until Liana and Arely could find a temporary residence. Arely was still in a state of shock after learning about the tragic demise of her father. It never actually dawned on Liana that Ralph, to put it mildly, had quite the "passionate" fan base until Griff warned her about the crowds in front of the house. She wondered how it was possible for "them," the fans that Ralph often praised and at times, griped about, to know where they lived; but Griff, who was a couple of years younger than Liana, had sarcastically enlightened her about this relatively new phenomenon called "Internet." She didn't take his sarcasm well; however, he reassured Liana by telling her that he called Sheriff Hershel, who had sent a couple of his deputies to the location to maintain order, which, strangely, did *not* put Liana at ease, even though somewhere deep in a place inside her, she felt it should.

"Don't believe everything you hear about in the news," Griff, who was stark opposite in politics, would go on to say to Liana. "Police can be useful."

When Griff arrived at their neighborhood street, there were crowds, as Griff had warned Liana, but they weren't as large as they were earlier in the day. Two deputy cars were positioned next to the orange and white striped "ROAD CLOSED" barricades in the middle of the street. Maintaining order were several deputies of the Musktucket County Sheriff's Department. Parked not too far away on the side of the street were a couple of news vans, including MWN Channel 3.

The sight alone of the news team, a handful of news reporters, as well as the cameramen, camped on the street, ready to capture their arrival, caused the anger, which had been festering inside Liana every since her diagnosis last year, to boil over. *They don't even care about Ralph*, she thought, realizing that all these vulturous people wanted to do was film her and Arely's grief so it would fit whatever narrative they were going to run with on their broadcast. If anything, Liana felt as if she was nothing more than a prop. But, of all times, why now? Where was the decency? Or the compassion? Did these basic human qualities—and functions—that separated man from animal exist anymore? Her thoughts spiraled out of control and had gone from thinking about those good times she shared with Ralph to questioning the very existence of the news media and the root cause of their gluttony for attention. Was it nature or nurture? Were they not loved as a child? Did their parents not pay any attention to them? Or, was it something more perverse? Did they get off on filming someone else's pain and misery? At that moment, she was convinced that it wasn't sensationalized journalism. Not anymore. It was an underlying sickness spreading its dark roots throughout the climate of today's culture and the only remedy was to remove it, weed it out, before it consumed society, if it hadn't already.

Several fans in the crowd were holding up colorful signs for "Ralph Hood," a "warm" "kindred spirit" who was the "light" of the horror community. Liana did her best to ignore the local news crew who were hanging outside the crowd; a reporter was interviewing fans and spectators. She wished for them not to point the cameras her way, but she knew it was only inevitable.

As soon as Griff pulled up to the barricade, the crowd turned toward the approaching vehicle.

Most of the fans in the crowd brandished their phones and started filming.

Liana shielded the side of her face from the phones.

The reporter snubbed an *Effigy*-dressed fanatic who was answering the sassy reporter's question and stating the twenty-three reasons as to why he drove across three state lines to pay his respects to Ralph Hood.

The deputy, who was stationed at the barricades, walked to the driver's side of the vehicle, leaned down, and saw Liana sitting in the passenger seat, as well as Arely in the backseat.

As the crowd started to get riled up, Griff cautiously rolled down the window for the deputy.

"Hey, Griff," the deputy said, leaning over the window. He gave Liana a nod and a closed, sympathetic smile. "Liana," he said first, then acknowledged Arely in the backseat. "Arely. My deepest condolences to the both of you. Ralph was a great man who'll be deeply missed."

"Thank you, Ja'mel," Liana said, leaning over the center console. "I appreciate that—"

She noticed Ja'mel's eye flicking toward the crowd.

Before Liana had a chance to figure out what the commotion was about, she suddenly flinched from the sound of a *thud* against the car.

In the corner of her eye, Liana witnessed that same impudent reporter and his cameraman outside the car. The reporter, who earlier had been coping an attitude with the deputy, was knocking on the passenger side window

"Can I ask you a couple of questions about Mr. Hood?" asked the persistent reporter.

Terrorized by the reporter's audacity to even question her within forty-eight hours of her partner's death, the red-hot anger rose in Liana's face. She wanted to yank that microphone from his hand and stick it where the sun didn't shine.

"Hey!" the deputy, Ja'mel, shouted at the reporter. "Back! Now!"

While the deputy was handling the reporter, he motioned to the other deputy, who, in return, opened the barricade for Griff.

Griff drove through the opening and finally, after evading the so-called news reporters, arrived at the house. Except for burnt rubble, there was nothing left of what one would consider a house. Griff parked the car in front of the driveway, which was marked off with caution tape. He stepped out first, helped Liana from the passenger side, while Arely was the last to exit the car.

As Liana and Arely combed the scene, Griff, out of respect, remained at the edge of the front yard and gave the two their much-needed space.

Stopping in front of the black ruins, Arely, who had barely spoken a word all day, said to Liana, "He relapsed after your diagnosis."

"Yeah," Liana said over a pause. "I had a feeling he did."

"But he got better," Arely said in defense. "I helped him to clean."

"He never wanted to do the role. In a way, I think he felt that I was pressuring him to do it."

"Don't blame yourself, Liana."

"Maybe I should," Liana said morosely, as she tried to take it all in.

There was nothing left.

Her entire life and everything that she and Ralph had worked for, gone.

Even though the possessions were replaceable—some, at least—in a way, she felt as if nothing was replaceable. Each part of the house had a memory attached to it, its own signature of senses, and now, the memories smelled like char.

Arely went straight to her bedroom, which was flattened by the fire. Among the standing rubble, she found her iMac, which, surprisingly, was still fully intact, burnt but intact. Mindful of the debris, she stepped around the burnt pile of wood and dug out a laptop, which, like the desktop computer, was burnt but still intact.

As for Liana, she aimlessly wandered through the ruins of the house. Of all the destroyed possessions, one caught her eye. She removed a board of wood from the rubble and pulled out the original effigy. To Liana's surprise, the movie prop was intact; in fact, it appeared as if was untouched by the fire, despite everything around it being charred and burnt to a crisp. She examined the surroundings more closely and tried to make sense as to how the prop was able to endure such an unforgiving fire. It was as though the effigy was placed there after the fire.

EIGHT MONTHS AGO
Los Angeles, California

As Ralph waited inside the waiting room of Screengasm Productions main offices where framed posters of their breakout movies such as *Blood Hunters*, *Elephant Head*, *The*

Counting, *SHIFTERS*, as well as the award-winning documentary, *Behind Freeze* were hung like trophies on the walls, Ralph started to question himself as to why, after spending the last thirteen years of his life convincing himself he was, in his own words, "done" with show business, he reunited with his former agent, Shawn. His palms sweated from the thought of thrusting himself back into the spotlight. For a moment, he contemplated walking out before they called his name. He even stood from the seat and made his way toward the exit.

The twenty-something secretary received a phone call, stopping Ralph in his tracks. She answered the call and talked timidly over the phone, mostly responding with several "Yes, sirs" before hanging up.

Clearing her throat, the secretary put on her best impersonation of what normal people called a smile and said freely to Ralph, "They're ready to see you, Mr. Hood."

Wiping the sweat from his palms along his blue jeans, Ralph faced the secretary before rerouting his course toward Cesar Mamar's office.

As soon as he reached the doors, one of the interns opened the door for Ralph and greeted him with another smile, which was about as artificial as an Instagram filter. The intern walked Ralph down a narrow hallway with more movie posters hanging on the walls and showed him to the massive office where two screenwriters, Cosmo Dennehy and John Yorke, eccentric director, Sergio Beneventi, who had flown in from Italy, as well as the producer, Frank Littlefield, and founder of Screengasm, Cesar Mamar, were seated at a conference room-style table. Each one in the room had his own copy of the final drafts of *The Effigy* reboot. The working title called "*Bitch's Brew*." On a side table laid an endless spread of pastries and coffee. A window wrapped around one side of the room in a half-circle and provided a postcard-like backdrop of the City of Angles. In the not-so distant background was the famous "Hollywood" sign situated on Mount Lee.

"Ralph in the flesh," Frank said first, as he stood from the seat to greet Ralph. "How you doing, old friend?"

"I'm good," Ralph said, reaching out to shake Frank's hand. Frank pulled it in for a hug, instead.

"How's Liana?" asked Frank.

"She has her good days and bad," Ralph said with a sigh. "She's almost finished with her treatment."

"Chemo?"

"Yes," he said. "That's right."

"I'm sure she'll be glad when it's all over."

"Last treatment nearly killed her," Ralph said, losing confidence, "but she's a fighter."

"The most important thing is that you make sure she has a support group."

"Arely and I have been taking shifts," Ralph said seriously and teased on the side. "Although it's fair to say that Liana was relieved to finally get me out of the house."

"Don't give up hope," Frank said, holding him by the arms. "My Jamie had a partial mastectomy, like Liana. Ralph, I can't tell you how many times Jamie just wanted to throw in the white towel. The doctors put her on a hormone therapy. Three years later, she was cancer-free. Knocked it right out."

"That's great, Frank," Ralph said.

"Hang in there, Ralph."

"Thanks," he said.

"Make sure to send her our love. We're all rooting for her."

"Will do," he said, searching for the right opportunity to change the subject. "So," he said over the silence, "how you doing?"

"I can't complain," Frank said, walking Ralph to the table where Cosmo and John stood from their seats. Cesar was last to stand. "How was your flight?"

"Little rough," Ralph said honestly. "But nothing I haven't experienced before."

"Shawn was telling me you're going to rent a car and make a pitstop in San Francisco?"

"Already did," Ralph said. "I actually just got back from San Francisco."

"Well, in that case, how was the drive?"

"Breathtaking as always," Ralph said. "Every now and then Liana and I used to fly out here, rent a car, and drive from Los Angeles to San Francisco on the Pacific Coast Highway. Taking the trip alone brought back a lot of fond memories."

"I bet it did," Frank said and introduced Ralph to Cosmo Dennehy and John Yorke, who chimed in. First, Cosmo: "Heard they're burning people in San Francisco." Then, John followed up: "You're talking about the man who was burned alive?"

"According to sources, he's in bad shape," Cosmo said. "Right now, he's at San Felisa."

"That's a shame—"

"—Well, it's not a surprise," Frank said. "It's a crazy world out there."

"Well, it's about to get a little more crazy," the director, Sergio Beneventi, was last to speak.

Ralph shook Sergio's hand.

Last but not least, Frank introduced Ralph to Cesar, who remained seated in his chair.

Ralph shook Cesar's hand.

"Did you read the script?" asked Cesar.

"I wouldn't be here, if I didn't."

"What did you think?"

Ralph paused.

"I loved it," he lied.

PRESENT
Guthrie, Tennessee

THE funeral was held at Francis Doyle Cemetery for family members and Ralph's closest friends, as well as actors and crewmembers he worked with throughout his twenty-eight years in the business—forty-one, forty-two, if you included his most recent role in the upcoming reboot of *The Effigy*, which was slanted for 2020 but cut short due to a series of "untimely" events.

Liana's brother, Larry, and his wife, Janelle, drove to Detroit where they took a flight from Detroit to Nashville and after landing, rented a car for the remainder of the trip. Her grown children, Rocky and Alonzo, flew in from different parts of the country and made the funeral, so did Ralph's first wife, former lingerie model, Bridget Bolshevik, who didn't hold anything back while sharing stories of her late husband's wild—often times—secret lifestyle. Lastly, all of Ralph's most loyal and hardcore fans showed up in droves outside the gates of the cemetery to pay their final respects to the beloved actor, even though not a single one of them were allowed inside. The local media was there as well to film and interview the teary-eyed fans, which, in producers' minds, made for A-quality television. Kiss goodbye the ole "If it bleeds it leads"-mantra most commonly used throughout the media circus. Nowadays, it was more like "If it rains it fucking pours."

Since Ralph wasn't at all fond of men of the cloth, Liana had one of Ralph's dearest and less "controversial" friends, Sam Smiley, who played the role of Sheriff Bob Striker in the first *Effigy*, speak the eulogy. He kept the eulogy short. He spoke about the ups and downs of filming *The Effigy*. He talked about the good times and the bad and how his friend, Ralph, was in a far better place.

After the funeral was over, Ralph was buried in the ground next to his father, James Oxford Hood, and his mother, Mary García Hood.

℃

THE reception that took place at Ralph's childhood home, which Ralph's mother had handed down to his sister, Raquel and her family, was only three miles away from Francis Doyle.

While Raquel was downstairs plying most of the guests with snacks and alcohol, Arely spent most of the reception in her father's childhood bedroom, which appeared partly frozen in time. Raquel had converted the old bed-room into what could easily pass as a shrine. She boxed up most of his childhood toys and stored them inside a packed closet, which was still full of clothes her brother wore right before he ran away from home at the age of sixteen. She filled up most of the room with memorabilia, including posters signed by her brother, Don Juan figu-rines, as well as framed photographs of Ralph posing with other famous celebrities that she had printed out from the Internet.

As Arely walked around the bedroom and glanced at the various framed pictures on the wall, the room started to get smaller and had gotten so small that she could no longer breathe.

☾

STEPPING out of the bedroom for a fresh breath of air, Arely was making her way downstairs to check on Liana in the kitchen when she bumped into her two annoying cousins: Herman, a six-foot five tall eleventh grader with skin that looked as if it was made out of alabaster, gamer name He-Man; and his shrimpy, super annoying sidekick, Gustavo—or Gus—who was a grade below Herman.

"If it isn't the Greek goddess herself," Gus said, stop-ping Arely from walking into the kitchen.

"What do you want, Gus?" asked Arely.

Gus rolled up his shirt and flexed his bicep in front of Arely.

"I was wondering if you had any advice on how I can improve the size of my biceps, you know, since you're a fitness expert and whatnot."

Gus tapped Herman on the arm and giggled at Arely.

"What do they call her again?" asked Herman.

"I believe it's Athena," Gus said. "The a's spelled with triangles."

"Just Athena?"

"I believe so."

Herman nodded at Arely.

"Why don't you have a last name?" asked Herman.

"It's a pseudonym, smart guy."

"Yeah," Herman said, densely, "but why don't you have a last name—"

"—I think she's going for the whole one name persona, like MoVega."

"That's pretentious."

"Get a last name."

"I know, right?" Gus turned his attention back to Arely. "So, what," he said, "you think you're better than us?"

"Are you serious?" said Arely, who couldn't believe that her knuckleheaded cousins were ridiculing her on the day she buried their Uncle Ralph, who, by the way, had little to no relationship with Herman or Gus. He, too, thought they were pampered, privileged little shits who sat in their rooms and played video games all day.

Arely walked between Gus and Herman and shouldered her way through the two.

"What'd I say?" Gus asked Herman with a guilty expression on his face.

Arely stormed outside onto the front porch and braced herself against a rickety railing that she was tempted to shake until it came loose. She felt a need to scream to the top of her lungs and redirect all of her frustration toward something inanimate, like the railing or a piece of wicker furniture or a glass side table. Following in her own footsteps and practicing the very same breathing techniques that she had taught Liana while she was going through waves of nausea during her chemotherapy treatment, she pulled out her phone from her back pocket and went through her Athena website, Athena spelled $\Delta \approx \Delta$. The two A's—or triangle's, as her dickwad of a cousin pointed out—stood for Arely's Aerobics.

Questioning herself and her life choices, Arely scrolled through her website, as well as each one of her social media sites, including her YouTube Channel, Instagram, Facebook, and Twitter.

In that moment, she wished that she was as strong as that woman in all those photos and videos, the one who inspired many of her followers to be better in anything they set their mind to in life. #StayStrong #Don'tGiveUp #BeBoss

Arely heard the sound of a strange woman clearing her throat from the other side of the front porch. She turned to her left where a woman, who sat as silent as a prop on the wicker sofa, was staring directly at Arely. She must've been a few years older than herself, Arely guessed. She was smoking a cigarette and during each drag, exuded a confidence that one couldn't buy or replicate. It wasn't until Arely took a second glance at the woman that she realized it was one of the same women whom she saw in one of the framed photos hanging on the wall in Ralph's bedroom. She supposed that maybe she was an actress or the daughter of a producer, nonetheless, someone of elite status.

"Hey," Arely said shortly, as she leaned up against the railing.

The woman, who called herself Alexa, replied with a "hey" of her own.

"I think I saw you at the funeral," Arely said, pocketing her phone. "Did you work with my father?"

"Briefly," Alexa said, smothering the cigarette butt along the back of the heel of her shoe.

Respectfully, she placed the cigarette butt inside the pack of Trendy Lights.

Curious, Arely approached Alexa. She recognized a familiar face in her face, one attached to youth and innocence.

"I worked with Ralph back in 2006 on *The Effigy Burns*," she said. "I helped with the set design—"

"—Wait a sec," Arely interrupted. "You're Bernard Knowles's granddaughter, correct?"

Alexa shyly lowered her head and then nodded.

"Correct."

"Your grandfather was a legend," Arely said, more up-beat. "I've heard stories about your father. Apparently, he and my father were extremely close."

She walked over to Alexa, who, in return, stood to her feet and shook Arely's hand and formally introduced herself to Arely.

"Alexa Knowles."

"Arely Hood," Arely said.

What do you know?

Both our names start with the letter A.

"Nice to finally meet you."

"Likewise," Arely said finally. "Too bad we didn't meet sooner."

"Well, funny how death brings people together."

Arely didn't care much for the remark; however, Alexa was right to a degree.

"Thanks for coming," she said.

She couldn't help but draw her eyes to the strange markings around Alexa's neck, which, to Arely, appeared like birthmarks underneath the black silky scarf. The skin was folded and twisted like a wrung towel.

"Your step mom was the one who actually invited me to stop by," said Alexa.

"You mean Liana?"

Alexa hesitated.

"Yes."

"She's not my step mom. She and my father never got married."

"Is that so?"

"After my father's second marriage, he told me that he'd never get married again."

"I see," Alexa said, forcing a smile on her face. "Well, I'm deeply sorry for your loss."

"Thanks," Arely replied. "And sorry to hear about your grandfather, as well. He was a true artist."

"Thanks," she said, waving off Arely's comment. "That was a long time ago. But I think about him everyday." Alexa reflected. "I remember when I was a girl I used to hang out on the sets. Practically grew up on a set. The producers didn't like it, though."

"I envy you in a way."

Alexa tilted her head to the side.

"Why's that?" asked Alexa.

"I wish I could've been there, too," Arely said depressingly, "to see what it was like to be on set."

"Believe it or not, it can be pretty boring at times. For a kid, it's like going to an amusement park without touching the rides."

"My mom wouldn't take me anywhere near a studio."

"Why not?"

"Let's just say she didn't care much for my father's work."

"Well, I guess, somebody has to do it. Right?"

"Yeah," Arely said, still thinking about her mother. "I didn't have much of a relationship with my father when I was a child. I hardly saw him because he was too busy traveling the world, making films. He'd literally go from one film to the next with no break at all. It wasn't until my mom got sick we started seeing each other more and more until, eventually, he took over the role as mom, dad," Arely struggled to get through the last word, which was *friend*.

"I'm so sorry to hear about that, Arely."

As Alexa had done before when Arely had shared condolences, Arely waved off the comment.

"She had what they told me was a mental breakdown. She couldn't take care of me anymore. I was fourteen when I moved in with my father. It's strange because, when I moved in with him, we immediately clicked. He gave up everything for me, including acting. We used to go to Fantasy World a lot. Believe it or not, he was like a 'big kid' who was always acting out, doing about anything to put a smile on my face." She drifted off for a moment, recalling one particular memory. "I remember one day I got violently sick. I'll never forget that day. He had a bunch of errands to run, but he dropped everything, all to nurse me back to health. He made me chicken noodle soup, and we spent most of the day watching cartoons. By the time night arrived," Arely shrugged, "I wasn't sick anymore."

Arely turned to the sound of the front screen door squeaking open.

Liana was poking her head outside the door and waving Arely close.

"What is it?" Arely asked.

"Can you give me a hand in the kitchen?" asked Liana.

"Yeah," she said. "Sure. Just give me a. . . "

She turned back around to say her goodbyes to Bernard's granddaughter, but Alexa was nowhere in sight.

SIX MONTHS AGO
Philip's Head, Michigan

COME April, a month known as one of the most unpredictable and at times, cruelest months for a beekeeper, Ralph spent the next couple of weeks leading into the warmer days of spring by doing basic maintenance such as repairing the hive, removing mouse guards, or replacing broken frames, and finally, the most important task of the season, which was a process called "marking the queen." He picked out a strong colony, one that possessed traits he needed to propagate such as mite and disease resistant and even gentleness, and with a yellow marker, placed a dot on the back of her thorax. Later, when the flowers bloomed and his babies were ready to forage, the queen would ultimately go on to be confined to a separate box where she would mate and lay her eggs in the available empty cells.

With the upcoming movie role for *The Effigy* reboot on his mind, Ralph decided to hire a couple of extra workers to help out around the apiary. Most of the work was basic maintenance for the time being, but, eventually, down the road, he planned on stepping aside to let one of his apprentices take over the biz.

While Ralph's newly hired workers, who had recently graduated from college and shared a particular interest in beekeeping, were cleaning the apiary, Ralph left his future beekeepers alone and checked on Liana.

On the way to the house, Ralph ran into Arely, who was currently filming an exercise video, one of her infamous "Omega (Ω) Sesh"-es, which took place on the last workout day of a week. Setup on the porch was all of her gear, including a yoga mat, dumbbells, all ranging from ten to twenty-five pounds, bands, and a workout bench. Perched in front of Arely was a tripod supporting a camera.

While Arely was doing what Ralph considered a provocative exercise involving hip thrusts, he immediately noticed his daughter's attire: black shorts so tight that looked painted on and a sports bra that could've pass as lingerie. Sure, as Liana had pointed out to Ralph numerous times, she was a grown woman who was exploring her body and in that exploration, finding strength and confidence; however, the father in Ralph, and most importantly, the man in Ralph, couldn't help but come forth and stat the obvious.

"Arely," Ralph said, as he stepped onto the porch, "dear, can you please wear something *less* revealing. You might as well be making a porno."

Arely stopped filming and stood with her arms planted on her hips.

"Excuse me," she said aggressively, "FYI, I'm providing an invaluable service for my frans."

"For your what?"

"My frans."

Ralph was still confused by the word *frans*.

"Friends and fans," Arely said but received nothing in return from her father. "Get it?" She waved off the comment. "Never mind."

"How about wearing those sweat pants I bought you?" suggested Ralph.

"What? You mean those parachute pants?"

"Or, how about the spandex?"

She furrowed her brow and said brazenly, "No thanks. The Eighties trend is so last year."

As Ralph made his way inside, he said indirectly, "All I'm saying: you're gonna attract the wrong crowd dressing the way you are, if that's what you want."

"This is coming from the same person who murders people on TV."

Ralph stopped at the door and faced Arely.

"I'm playing a fictional character, Arely," he said, his eyes narrowing. "Sure. I might draw some interesting folks, but it comes with the territory."

Fully aware of what her father used to do for a living, she pointed at the camera and asked, "Did you ever stop to think that maybe *I'm* also playing a fictional character?"

Ralph paused.

"You mean—"

"—Yeah," Arely said, nodding her head to Ralph's un-asked question. "Believe it or not, at the end of the day," Arely pointed at her father and then herself, "we are products. So why not look good while selling the product?"

"Are you sure that's not all you're selling?" Ralph said darkly.

He immediately regretted saying the comment as soon as it left his lips.

"And what is that supposed to mean?" Arely asked, shifting her weight to one side of her body.

Ralph raised his hands.

"I'm an ally, Arely, not an enemy," he said, opening the door.

"I'm really looking forward to the new film," Arely said before Ralph walked inside.

"Is that so?" said Ralph.

"I read that they just cast Olivia Hill to play Donna Juan as the 'strong female lead.'"

"Wrong."

"It's on the Internet," she said, furrowing her brow.

"Exactly," he said teasingly. "FYI, she backed out."

"Seriously. Who's gonna play the part. . . "

"You know I'm not allowed to discuss the film," Ralph said. "It goes against my contract."

"It doesn't bother you, though," Arely said, "that a woman is possibly going to be taking your place as the next Don Juan?"

"How would you know?" asked Ralph.

Arely shrugged.

"Let's just say I have a hunch."

Ralph grinned.

"Well," he said, "good luck with that."

He closed the door behind him and searched the house for Liana. He finally found her in the upstairs rec room lying on a futon next to the window.

"What'r you reading?" asked Ralph, as he checked on Liana.

Liana showed the front cover of the hardback *Still Intact: The Heartbreaking Journey One Woman Of Color Took In Order to Win Back The Soul Of America*, written by Governor Avanti Washington, one of the potential candidates who was rumored to be throwing in her hat for the 2020 presidential bid.

"Any good?" asked Ralph.

"I'm only a few chapters in," Liana said, "but so far, it's pretty amazing. The woman has been through a lot."

"Well, if she decides to enter the race," he said flatly, "she's gonna have a lot of ground to cover. Her opponent's favorability just skyrocketed in the polls."

"When have the polls ever been right?" asked Liana.

"With the exception of the last election—"

"—Did you come up here to talk about politics?" Liana asked, her tone more hostile in nature.

"Sorry," he said. "I was just checking in. Is there anything I can get you?"

"No," Liana said, feeling bad. "But thanks for asking."

Ralph kneeled, ran his hand over the top of Liana's bald head, and kissed her on the forehead. How he missed running his hands through her hair. However, it occurred to Ralph that Liana sort of "liked" her new do.

After all, to Liana, it was rather convenient not having to primp and prep everyday.

"Enjoy the rest of your book, okay?"

Liana, who returned to her book, stopped Ralph as he was leaving the room.

"Actually," she said from behind, "there is one thing. We're out of eggs."

"Eggs," he said. "Got it. Anything else?"

"We're running low on milk and bread."

"I tell you what," Ralph said and grabbed a yellow sticky note and a pen from a nearby desk. "Why don't you make a list?"

☾

WITH a grocery list in hand, Ralph stormed to his truck, opened the door, and then slammed it behind him.

Frustrated by the very idea of having to coddle Liana, he threw the list on the passenger seat and shook his head in apparent disgust. He started the ignition and didn't even bother to allow the truck to warm up. Instead, he put the gear in drive (D) and did so with extra muscle.

And sped away.

☾

PUSHING a packed shopping cart full of groceries inside the family-owned grocery store called Food Run, Ralph bumped into a familiar woman, who he realized after trying to put a name to the face, went by the name Kristy (?).

"Katherine," he'd later remember after taking a whiff of that coconut-scented lotion that she always wore.

The six foot tall brunette was a friend of Liana's—or at least, an acquaintance of Liana's. Every now and then, as in around four to five times a year, Liana and "Katherine" would go out to grab lunch in town and catch a flick afterwards. Liana being asked to go to the movies wasn't at all a hard sell, considering her tastes ranged from sleazy, lowbrow horror to mainstream rom coms to art house films, meaning she'd basically watch anything that involved images that followed a basic plot. Katherine's older brother—Ralph couldn't exactly remember the dude's name either—knew Liana's brother, Larry, who lived in Lansing. They both attended the University of Michigan located in Ann Arbor; and from what he was told, were once "close." It was Larry who introduced Katherine to Larry's sister after Katherine struggled to make any connections in Philip's Head.

After identifying the woman by her trademark smell, he did his best to detour from the checkout line; however, the two had already made eye contact.

"Hey, stranger," Katherine said next to Ralph, who, in return, turned away at the last second.

Mentally kicking himself, Ralph finally acknowledged Katherine.

"Hi there," he said cordially and searched for her name, "Katherine, right?"

"Boy," she said lightheartedly, "hanging around those bees all day have done quite a number on you."

Ralph didn't exactly understand the purpose of the comment. He thought it was cold in nature, despite Katherine's two-dimensional glow.

"How's Liana?" asked Katherine.

"She's doing good," said Ralph. "In fact, she's finishing her treatment."

"That's good news," Katherine said ecstatically. "I was meaning to stop by to see her. Last time we talked she was having a hard time."

In no mood to talk about Liana's condition, Ralph's eyes wandered from the conversation and fell onto the contents inside Katherine's basket.

Katherine followed Ralph's eyes and held up the basket full of clear wire and boxes of different colored beads.

"A hobby of mine," she said bashfully.

"I see."

"Can you do me a favor and pass along a message for me?" Before he had a chance to respond, Katherine said,

"Tell Liana to give me a call, would you? I've been meaning to call, but I didn't want to disturb her."

"Will do," Ralph said, making an attempt to end the conversation. "I'm sure she'll enjoy hearing your voice."

"By the way," Katherine said with a wide grin on her face, "I heard you were going to do another *Effigy*. When I told Les, he couldn't believe it. He can't get enough of your movies."

Except for Liana and Arely, he didn't tell anyone about the upcoming project. Immediately, he wondered where she had heard about it.

"Where did you hear that I was making another film?" asked Ralph, curious about what Katherine had to say.

"The Internet, of course," she said weirdly. "It's all over social media."

Again, Ralph backtracked and put together the clues as to how anybody outside of production would know about the film, let alone details of the film, which brought to mind Arely's comment about the lead role of the upcoming film. She, too, had obviously gotten her information from the Internet. Actress Olivia Hill's name had been floating around among tight circles. *Maybe* the information was *leaked. Who the hell knows?* Cesar and company throwing out names in order to get a reaction from the fans. Like throwing chum into an ocean and waiting to see if the sharks take the bite. Regardless, he was left more skeptical about the film, especially with the "Internet" being so involved in the moviemaking process. At the height of Ralph's career, the Internet hardly existed; and in a way, except for launch parties, interviews, and special themed events, the lack of public attention had given him liberty, not knowing that somehow, somewhere, someone was secretly filming him with a smartphone behind his back—or, in this case, releasing tight-lipped details about the movie for public consumption.

"Anyway, it was good to see you," Katherine said, snapping Ralph from his trance.

"Yeah," he uttered. "You too."

"And good luck with the new movie." She grinned again. "It's gotta be nice making the big bucks, huh?"

"It's not about the money," Ralph said, as he mistakenly reeled her back into another conversation.

"Right," she said flippantly. "Don't be so modest, Ralph. Sure Hollywood's going to be paying you millions."

"It's just money," he said more seriously, as if he had to put Katherine in her place. "What you won't find on your Internet is that I was only paid a thousand bucks to make the first *Effigy*."

"A thousand bucks?" Katherine laughed and waved off Ralph's remark. "Get outta here!"

"Serious."

"Really?"

"Sure," he said. "Later, I made more money. But I was young at the time. I didn't invest it well. In other words, I blew it all. That's life, right? You live by your mistakes and you learn from your mistakes."

"Absolutely."

Other shoppers walked past Ralph, forcing him to end the conversation.

"Well," he said, changing his tone. "Nice seeing you."

Kill 'em with kindness, his mother, Mary, used to say.

Feeling even more doubtful about the upcoming *Effigy* reboot, Ralph parted ways with Katherine. At that point in time, he wanted to hide and never show his face in public ever again.

PRESENT

CHRISTOPH Mather, the head detective on the Ralph Hood Case, and his partner, Detective Ludlow, drove back to the crime scene between 15th and Hamlet Street. The surrounding area was mostly the projects filled with low-income housing and a park that had turned into a hobo hangout. The north side of Hamlet Street— which the locals called NoHam—a district of old rundown businesses and warehouses, once ruined and forgotten, was gentrified into trendy establishments such as upscale diners, hot yoga studios, craft breweries, and lofts for young middle-class professionals.

On the south side of Hamlet Street, most of the business establishments, unlike the ones on the north side, were left to rot and decay and become a breeding ground for sickness while others remained clinging onto survival. The only activity, most of it being nocturnal, within a three-block radius came from a nail salon; two convenient stores, one called Snopes, the other, PrimeCo; and then, finally, a nightclub, The Liquid Lounge, unseen from the street for its rather "low-key" entrance and tucked away in a shabby-looking alleyway behind what assumed to be an abandoned hotel. According to the several eyewitnesses whom detectives had interviewed, Ralph Hood was seen at the club on the night of his death. Surprisingly, each statement by eyewitnesses came close to matching one another, if not, came close to sharing a common storyline: Ralph was hanging out at the bar, had a couple of beers, was, as most eyewitnesses put it, "keeping to himself." One of the witnesses claimed he appeared "shook up," as if he was "hiding from someone." Another eyewitness claimed that Ralph was "strung out" and coming off a binge.

Detective Mather parked the car near the spot where a nearby neighbor, who was walking with her son to a bus stop, came across the dead body on 15th Street and worked his way backward.

Scanning the sidewalk, the detective combed the crime scene while his young partner, Detective Ludlow, followed close behind.

Mather came across a broken piece of glass from what appeared to be a headlight in the middle of the street.

"What'd you got?" asked Ludlow.

"Glass," Mather said. "You remember seeing any photos of broken glass?"

"Not that I can recall."

Mather put aside the glass and combed the crime scene. He stopped and took a moment to survey the old rundown neighborhood.

"A man gets violently attacked," he said, "surely neighbors must've heard at least a scream or some kind of commotion."

"Real talk, Mather," Ludlow said, approaching his partner, "even if they did, most people who live in these parts of town aren't going to be forthright with the cops, if you feel me. It's just a fact of reality."

The detectives turned right from 15th onto Hamlet and made their way down Hamlet until they reached The Liquid Lounge on 17th.

"If Hood did have a security detail with him, as his agent said," said Ludlow, "why in the hell would they abandon him?"

"We don't know that yet, Giraud," Mather said. "As far as we know, they're still suspects. But I suppose," Mather said and stopped at a stop sign to survey the street, "that would be the first question we'd ask if we could find them."

"Hood doesn't strike me as the type—least, not anymore." The detective rattled off, "But who knows with these people who work in entertainment?"

Mather turned his shoulder to his partner.

"And what type is that?"

"You know, the shameful type."

"What do you mean, Giraud?"

"Normally, with these celebrity-types, when they relapse they do so out in the open for everybody to see. Deliberately get it captured on TMZ, you know, the whole 'Look at me. My struggles are more important than yours.' It's their way of building sympathy and bringing more attention to whatever issues they're dealing with and most importantly, promoting whatever project they're working on."

"Any publicity is good publicity, huh?" Mather mumbled, as if he was filling in the blanks. He said louder, "Everybody knows that little ploy."

"More attention means more money."

"You're thinking he came here because he didn't want anybody to see him?"

Detective Ludlow pointed at the "low-key" entrance in the alleyway.

"Small shithole bar where he could hardly be recognized," he said. "Sure."

"But people did recognize him, Giraud. So what are you getting at? Besides, how does that theory of yours factor into the possibility that Hood could've been involved in burning down his own house?"

"Let's just say the fire was coincidental."

"Coincidental? Hood was the only person at home during the time of the fire."

"How'd you know?" asked Ludlow. "How do you know he didn't go straight to Pinkie's house?"

"We don't know for sure Hood was at Forte's house on the night of his murder—"

"—But Ralph's sunglasses at his house proves that he was, at some point, at Pinkie's. We both know he has a history with Pinkie, even Liana said so herself. What if whoever killed Hood found his address on his driver's license, then went back to Hood's place in search of more money, took what they could, then burned down the house to cover up any evidence they left behind?"

"Now that's a possibility," Mather said, more skeptical.

"One thing's for sure," Ludlow said, gazing around the rough area, "if I were Hood, I wouldn't be caught dead in a place like this—that is unless I was looking for trouble."

"Did you ever stop to think that maybe he was looking for trouble?"

Ludlow thought about his partner's question and carried around the answer on the walk to the sketchy alleyway across the street.

"In Hood's autobiography *Unmasked*," he said finally, "he shamelessly talks about his drug use. The guy hit rock bottom after his father got sick. Unable to cope with his father's illness, he ran away from home at the age of sixteen. Got hooked up with the wrong crowd. Got in-

volved in drugs—hard stuff from A to Z. Made Keith
Richards look like a recreational drug user. By the time
Hood turned eighteen, he was waking up to a fifth of Jack
Daniels and three lines of blow. The guy was on track to
die by the age of twenty-one. A couple of years later, after he joined the Devil's Fist biker gang, he got into a
fight with a rival of the gang, was stabbed over twenty-
seven times, resulting in losing one of his kidneys, as well
as part of his liver."

"Twenty-seven times, huh? You making that number
up?"

"No," he said. "Why?"

"Well, according to Metz, Hood was stabbed twenty-
seven times."

Ludlow drifted into thought.

"Huh?"

"Yeah," Mather said. "Huh? So, you were saying. . . "

"Right," Ludlow said, shaking away the thought.
"Anyway, after Hood was hospitalized, he had no other
choice than to turn his life around, otherwise he'd find
himself in an early grave. Then, one day, out of the blue,
he ran into director John Verhaeghe while he was eating
lunch. Verhaeghe liked Hood's look. Eight months later,
Hood was playing one of the most iconic movie roles in
the history of horror. After *The Effigy* was re-released
sometime in the early Eighties, Ralph Hood became a
household name. Man got rich. Blew all his money on
drugs and booze and expensive toys, went broke, made
some bad investments like most celebrities who weren't
careful with their money."

"If I didn't know any better, I'd say you sound like a
fan," said Mather, as he searched the alleyway for any
evidence he might've missed last time during their inves-
tigation.

"Not a fan per se," Ludlow said and shrugged. "More
of a critic."

"Liana thought that he was acting withdrawn and
might've been using again after she was diagnosed with

breast cancer. If so," the detective said, heading toward Hamlet Street, "then it fits his pattern."

"Which is?" Ludlow asked from behind.

Mather stopped before reaching the sidewalk and said over his shoulder, "He has a hard time coping with reality whenever things get tough."

Uninterested in what his partner had to say in return, Mather walked back to the crime scene.

Ludlow, eventually, tagged along.

☾

ON the way back from The Liquid Lounge, the two detectives approached the dilapidated one-story house once owned by Demoris Forte, also known as "Pinkie," whose body was discovered by his girlfriend, Stephanie Lear, the morning after the late actor had been beaten and left for dead in the middle of the street.

As with Hood's case, the two detectives were still waiting for the toxicology reports; however, in regards to Demoris Forte, based on the condition in which his body was found, the cause of death appeared to be from an apparent drug overdose. The drug of choice: heroin. Six needles jammed in both his forearms, three for each arm. Rubberbands hanging from the crooks of his elbows. He was practically crying China white.

Before making their way to Pinkie's place, they stopped at the corner of 15th and Hamlet and tried to playback the scene in their heads.

"Let's just say Hood was at Forte's house," Mather suggested, pointed down the street at Pinkie's house. "He started his party of shame at Forte's," he turned around, pointing at the direction of The Liquid Lounge, "after he smoothes out the edges, he grabs himself a couple of drinks at The Liquid Lounge." He faced forward, once more pointing at Forte's house. "He doesn't like the scene at the club. So, he winds up back at Forte's; however," he pointed at the location in the middle of the street where Ralph was found dead, "he doesn't make it that far."

"Someone must've noticed him at Liquid Lounge," Ludlow said. "Followed Hood back to Forte's. Robbed him before he could reach the house."

"Maybe," Mather said, as he finally embraced the idea. "But I'm guessing it would have to take more than one person. Ralph isn't exactly a small guy."

They continued walking down 15th Street, this time using the sidewalk unlike the first time when they walked against traffic—or lack thereof.

Before reaching Pinkie's, Mather couldn't help but notice a string of purplish beads along the side of the curb. He stopped, kneeled down, and picked up one of the beads.

After inspecting the bead, he found more of them father down the street.

"You remember seeing anything in the photos with beads in them?"

"Investigators already comb this entire area."

"Maybe they missed something."

"Say," Mather said, drifting off, "you remember those beads Hood's daughter was wearing?"

"The wristbands?"

"Yeah," he said. "Them."

"So what?"

Mather followed the beads to a storm drain along the curb. He found more of those purplish beads wedged in a crack in the grate.

"When's the last time it rained?" asked Mather.

Ludlow thought carefully about his partner's question.

"Two days ago," he said.

Mather walked back up the street while, at the same time, carefully inspecting the curb. Right before he reached Hamlet Street, he found a bead, as well as a piece of translucent wire next to the slightly tilted stop sign. He drew his eyes to the stop sign, specifically the dark, brownish smudge of what appeared to be old blood along the edge of a screw holding the sign together. He leaned forward and with a pen, removed several strands of hair wrapped around the washer.

"Didn't Metz say Hood had a strange hexagonal-like mark on the top of his head, possibly where he was struck by a ring of some kind?"

"I thought he said it was an old cut reopened."

Detective Mather backtracked and spent a moment diving into Metz's professional analysis.

Not only based on the evidence that he had gathered so far at the crime scene, but also the autopsy report where Metz described the injuries sustained to Ralph's body, which were, based on the coroner's thorough examination, considered "defensive wounds," except for the fractured cervical vertebrae, as well as the "subdural hematoma," which was what Metz determined as the cause of death, the details surrounding Hood's death had the hallmarks of a crime of passion.

After placing the hairs inside a napkin, Mather drew his attention upward at the house on the corner of the street. He immediately spotted the doorbell next to the front doorway. He crossed the street and walked toward the front lawn of the house. There, before the front porch of the house, Mather recognized the doorbell next to the front door.

"I'd be damned," he said with amazement.

€

WITH the homeowner's permission, Detective Ludlow made a copy of the BellCam™ video and took it back to the police station where he and Mather further inspected the footage.

Sitting inside the dark video room, Ludlow rewound the footage back to the initial conflict.

In the video, which was taken at 2:07 AM, a man stumbled onto the sidewalk. The only source of light came from a streetlight, which helped cast enough light onto the sidewalk to make out the shape—and soon-to-be shapes. Ludlow identified the first man as Ralph Hood based on his shape but was unsure due to the extremely poor quality of the doorbell surveillance footage. The faces of the three other men who crept up behind the first man—or Ralph (?)—were blurry as well. One of the three men was first to start the fight. Soon after he swung at Ralph (?), the two others joined in. Ralph (?) managed to hold his ground after his head was slammed into the stop sign.

"Could be where he broke his neck," Ludlow said, pointing at the screen.

The third attacker brandished what appeared to be a "knife," as Ludlow had pointed out, and started to stab Ralph in the side with it.

Ralph shielded each stab mostly with his arms and hands.

The detectives continued to watch a dazed and more discombobulated Ralph (?) stagger to his feet and run away while the three other men were catching their breath.

Altogether, the initial confrontation, as well as the fight lasted roughly a minute and a half.

"No sign of Stanley Richard or Boxer Brown," Ludlow said. "Which means they either bounced or..."

"Or what?"

"Or they were never there to begin with."

"You check nearby surveillance cameras?"

"Yeah," Ludlow said, shuffling through footage.

"And?"

"Nothing."

It wasn't until Ludlow rewound the footage for what felt like the hundredth time that Mather picked out a sixth person.

Ludlow slowed down the footage once the three men chased after Ralph (?).

Leaning closer to the screen, Mather pointed at a pale-looking face hiding in the bushes behind the sidewalk.

"There," he said, bumping into Ludlow. "What is that?"

"Where?

"Right there," Mather said, pointing at the shapely face with pitch-black eyes. "See it?"

Ludlow leaned close to the screen as well.

"Yeah," he uttered, leaning in. "Swear it almost looks like someone wearing a mask."

Strangely, Mather was thinking the same exact thing.

FOUR MONTHS AGO
Wilmington, North Carolina

AS a way of building camaraderie before the production began on what was being widely discussed as a reboot, not a remake, for the new *Effigy*—or in other words, the "calm before the storm"—Sergio Beneventi invited cast and crew to dinner at one of Wilmington's most exclusive spots located in the heart of downtown called Port City Grille, a five-star restaurant which specialized in American kitchen cuisine. Those who attended the dinner consisted of the following: former *Doghouse* actress Felicia Ramirez, who was going to be playing Donna Juan, the daughter of Don Juan and Carolina Reyes—who moviegoers liked to call the "Final Girl"—Rose McGregor (*One Day To Live, Glory Hole, Savage Nation*), who was playing the part of Donna's friend, Glad, Anthony Wince (*Countie, Demon Child*) playing Glad's fiancé, Oswald—or "Ozzie"—Shwin Boswell (*Howie's World*) as Deputy Ruff, Dha-La Sadith (*The Misery Diaries, Welcome Home Ms. Jackson*) as necromancer La Guardia, Jack Willhouse (*Prune*) as Donna's love interest, Michael Morrow, Karl Brooks (*The Green Thumb Project*) as Tadpole, original cast member, Sam Smiley, who was returning to Johnstown as former lawman, Sheriff Bob Striker, and then, last but certainly not least, Ralph Hood, who was reprising the role as the iconic slasher from disaster, Don Juan, aka "The Wolf." Frank Littlefield, producer of the original *Effigy*, as well as the reboot, was also in attendance. Other crewmembers such as special efx, makeup, wardrobe, lightning, as well as the two assistant directors (ADs) showed up for the dinner.

Finally, Ralph's longtime pal and stuntman, Ringer Slade, was last to arrive at Port City Grille.

There, Ralph, who constantly kept in contact with Ringer but hadn't seen him since the last film *The Effigy Burns*, reunited with his stuntman.

The two shared a photo on the patio, which overlooked the Cape Fear River. Karl Brooks clicked away a series of photos for Ringer to choose from, but ultimately, went with the one where he was holding a locally brewed IPA in one hand while his other was wrapped around Ralph, who fought through the urge, but willingly spent the night sober.

Before Ringer posted the photo on his Instagram, he turned to Ralph and said with a grin stretched across his face, "Ready to break the Internet?"

Below the photo, the caption read:

The moon is full tonight! #We'reBack #TheEffigy #DonJuan

Within only two hours of posting the photo on Instagram—which would've been about four drinks later for Ringer—the post in itself received over two million likes and over five hundred thousand shares.

To say fans were excited about the reboot was an understatement.

⟨

AFTER dinner, which consisted of a spread of appetizers, including crab cake sliders, cabo fish tacos, and Ahí tuna with wasabi, alongside Brown Eyed Goose IPA, except for Ralph, who stuck with mostly water with lemon for dinner and a cup of chamomile for dessert, which was blackberry cobbler, Ringer was slightly inebriated once he and Ralph stepped outside the restaurant onto the sidewalk.

While waiting for the rest of the crew, Ralph drifted off as he heard the sound of footsteps coming from an alleyway. He lost himself in that *thudding* sound and in an attempt, forced himself to concentrate on the people around him. The sound brought him back to the alleyway where shadows stretched outward along the side of the building.

In the blaring sound, which became louder by the second, one crewmember, a AD named Glenn Courter, said next to Ralph, "Sounds like a storm's coming."

Confused, Ralph turned to Glenn.

"What storm?"

"That one," he said, who was pointing up at the cloudy night sky. "It sounds close too."

Ralph was startled by Ringer, who wrapped his arm around Ralph's shoulder.

"I can't believe Double Trouble is back in business," he said with a slight slur in his voice.

As claps of thunder trailed off in a distance, Ralph turned to the alley where those shadows disappeared.

"I know, right?"

"I tell you what, Hoody. The fans are going to lose their shit. I have a good feeling about this one."

As Ralph was mid-word into his response, he caught an old face in the corner of his eye. He turned toward a crowd of people where, among those faces, he saw her face, Alexa's face.

Ringer gave Ralph a light shake on the shoulder.

"What's a matter, old buddy?" asked Ringer.

"Nothing," Ralph uttered to Ringer.

He turned back to the crowd.

Alexa was gone.

Ringer laughed.

"Okay, Poopy Pants," Ringer teased, referring to Ralph's open-book sobriety and his tell-all story about how the journey back on the wagon came with its fair share of the runs. He nodded to the rest of the crew. "Come on. We're gonna hit up a dive bar not too far away from where we're staying."

"I think I'm done for the night."

"Come on, you pussy—"

"—I shouldn't."

"I'm sure they'll have tea."

He thought over Ringer's proposal and did so excruci-atingly, which allowed more room for Ringer to pause.

"Listen, Ralph," Ringer said, as he detected Ralph's transparent discomfort and struggle to stay sober, "you know I'm here for you and Liana. Hell! If I went through half the shit you two did, I probably wouldn't have the strength to be doing what you're doing." Ringer tight-ened his grip around Ralph's shoulder. "Tell you what, my friend," he said, looking over Ralph. "Why don't we go grab some coffee instead? Cool?"

Ralph hesitated.

"I could use a cup," he said, pinching the side of his temple. "I'm starting to get a headache from those IPAs."

Finally, Ralph pointed down the street.

"Lead the way, pussy," he said jokingly to Ringer.

PRESENT

THE morning after discovering footage that was captured on a doorbell cam, Detective Mather decided to take a detour on his way to the station and drive back to the site where Ralph was initially attacked on the street corner of 15th and Hamlet.

With that "image" on his mind throughout the entire night, even causing him to lose sleep, the detective didn't waste anytime inspecting the shrubbery behind Ralph where he saw a strange pale-looking face protruding from a roughly eight-foot tall *viburnum dentatum*—best known as a roughish arrowwood.

The once dark foliage of the arrowwood had already started to change into its fall colors, which were a yellow-red burgundy. Its dark blue berries, left behind from the previous month, were all dried up and scattered on the ground from what appeared to be a disturbance in the shrub. Several of the stems were broken in half, others lying on the ground, as well as their leaves.

He walked around the shrub until he found an opening; then with his tablet in hand, he pulled up the grainy still from the BellCam^{TM} video in his photos album. With his index finger and thumb extending outward along the screen, he zoomed in on the pale-looking face in the exact same shrub that he was standing behind.

"I'm way too old for this shit," Mather said bitterly.

Using the still as a reference, he kneeled down and crawled into the opening of the arrowwood. He reached the same exact spot where the person supposedly wearing a mask was watching the violent attack from the shrub. *Clearly*, from the flattened dirt, as well as trampled leaves, Mather noted, *someone had been sitting right here*. He carefully inspected the area until one detail stood out.

On the ground, Mather found several small mounds of grayish dust. In other areas, the dust peppered the ground. He pulled out a small baggie from his pocket and using a pair of tweezers, collected a sample of dust.

A pungent smell, as faint as it was, had also caught the detective's attention. To Mather, it smelled like something dead. A nearby animal perhaps. Or, worse, something had just died here last night and he missed the show. He searched for traces of blood along the ground but couldn't find any.

As he pocketed the dust, he leaned in closer to a leaf next to him and smelled it. The leaf reeked like death.

More disturbed by the awful smell, he crawled back out of the shrub. On the way out, he found an object in the corner of his eye, which gave him a slight startle. Immediately, a snake shedding its skin came to mind. He plucked the loose skin, which was hanging from one of the stems, studied it closely but didn't think too much about it. He placed aside the skin and eventually, crawled out the shrub with part of his dignity still intact.

As Mather stood to his feet, brushed the dirt off his jacket, and checked for any spiders along his neck and shoulders, the detective suddenly realized that he wasn't alone. He looked up at a young boy, who must've been no older than five or six years old. He was wearing a Don Juan mask over his face.

The boy raised his hand, which was in the shape of a gun. He bent his thumb forward in a spring-like motion as if the finger itself was the hammer of a gun after firing off a shot.

"Bang!" he shouted out underneath the mask. "You're dead!"

Playing along, Mather grabbed his chest where he suffered an apparent gunshot wound.

"You got me," Mather cried out, as he did his best impersonation of stumbling around.

The young boy pulled off his mask, the color of his face a stark difference of the color of the mask.

As he held the mask over his forehead, he giggled at Mather and his antics.

Before the detective could engage in small talk with the boy, the boy ran off.

Mather's pocket vibrated with a *buzzing* sound. He pulled out his phone and saw that his partner, Ludlow, was calling him.

He answered, "I'm on my way—"

"—You might want to hurry."

"Why?"

As soon as he spoke, he witnessed at least three black SUVs pull up alongside 15th Street. Men and women wearing FBI jackets stepped out of the cars and onto the sidewalk.

The phone slipped farther from Mather's face.

He already knew the answer to his question before Ludlow could utter a single word.

THREE MONTHS AGO
Wilmington, North Carolina

"ONLY two weeks into the shoot and look at me. . . " Fran said, grabbing a handful of hair, ". . . I'm already starting to lose my hair."

"Isn't it considered like a bad omen that, within the first two days of filming, lightning strikes and burns down the set?" asked one of Fran's assistant.

"It was a freak accident," another one said. "Doesn't mean anything."

"Easy for you to say. I believe things happen for a reason. Like for instance: The other day when I was driving into the studio, I passed a billboard with a man who looked just like Bo. Not even a minute later I get a call from, of all people—"

"—Let me take a stab: Jimmy Hoffa."

Fran rolled her eyes.

"All that matters is that nobody was hurt."

"Yeah," Fran said over the assistant. "Thank God."

"I'm tellin' you, Fran," another one of Fran's assistants, Marsha, said to Fran, "you need to give yoga a try. I was a train wreck before yoga. Now, after a quick session, the frustration melts right off me."

"Yoga? At my age? Child please."

Making a face, Fran waved off Marsha's suggestion.

"I'm not in the minority here when I say this—that is, if you're doing it right way—but it can be better than sex."

Fran burst out in booming laughter, so too did actress Rose McGregor, who was sitting in the chair in front of a large vanity with a mirror. She was already prepped for the face casting with a plastic lightweight dust sheet wrapped around her upper torso as if she was about to get a new do. According to Fran, it was going to get "messy." Hence, also, the painter's plastic covering the floor below.

"Well," she said, laughing, "that boy toy of yours ain't doing it right."

"Regardless of what you say, Fran," Marsha said bashfully, "Gin is an exceptional lover. Trust me. His tongue can, how do I say, *perform* certain tricks that I never thought the human tongue was capable of doing." The comment stirred up several catcalls throughout the trailer. "However," Marsha said over the commotion, "the yoga, I'm telling you, Fran, it rids all the impurities from your body and helps you reconnect with your *pneuma*. For me, it's been a lifesaver."

"Your what?"

"Your pneuma," Marsha said, flustered by Fran's lack of knowledge on one's pneuma. "Your spirit."

Fran moved her eyes upward and held them there in thought.

"No thanks," she said with a shrug.

Which prompted more laughter from Fran's other two assistants, Dunkin and Bastian, who were diligently working on the full body prosthesis of a pale, putrid, rail thin swamp-like creature with its ill-colored skin covered in ulcers. The veteran actor behind the creature makeup was the legendary Leif Nilsen; throughout his lengthy career, his rather "thin" physique, as well as his ability to contort his body was used for many roles, all of which being creatures and monsters.

"You don't know what you're missing, Fran. . . "

Ignoring Marsha, Fran redirected her attention toward "the talent" and whispered, "Sorry about that."

Rose gave Fran a closed smile.

Before Fran could tend to Rose and her face, one of the PAs poked her head into the trailer and told Fran that Ned, Ralph's stand-in, told her that Monica, one of the actors who was playing a gypsy, was having trouble with her wig.

Fran rolled her eyes in annoyance. Her expression alone shooed away the PA from the trailer.

"Never ends with these people," she said and turned to Rose. "Nervous?"

With a nod, Rose said politely, "A little. Yes."

"Is this your first time face casting?"

Rose nodded again.

"Well," Fran said, "you're in for a treat. As I'm sure you've been told, it can be very intimidating at first. But don't worry. I will be talking to you every step of the way." She sorted through her art supplies, makeup and whatnot, along the disorganized worktable until she located a head cap. "Here we go," Fran said and faced Rose, "I always tell my clients to communicate to me through hand signals that way I know you're okay."

From another chair where the two assistants were individually inserting each strand of coarse spines into the back as well as neck of the gnarly-looking creature, Dunkin said to the others, "I once heard that Bernard used to play loud music to help drown out the actor's panic."

"I can't speak about that," Fran said, grinning, "but I will say, the man was a mad scientist. Outside work, he was a softy. He reminded me of a Doctor Jekyll and Mr. Hyde. I learned more about the industry having worked under Bernard for four hears than some artists learn after spending their entire lives in the industry. Sure," she said laidback, "most geniuses are tyrannical by design. But don't get me wrong. The man knew how to have fun."

"I would give my left nut to have worked with him," Bastian said.

"I'm sure you would—"

"—Please excuse those degenerates," Fran said to Rose, "let's get to work."

As Fran combed back any lose strands around her ears and tightened the hair into a fixed ponytail, she and Rose talked over the reason for the face cast.

The scene went as followed: *Rose's upbeat character, Glad, is experiencing a nightmarish hallucination inside her apartment complex after she gets into an argument with her friend, Donna, who, over the course of a topsy-turvy friendship, has developed strong feelings for Glad, ones that extend well beyond the boundaries of that 'just friends' category. The argument is centered on Glad and her unhealthy obsession with herself and how Glad's about to get married to her fiancé, Ozzie, for all the wrong reasons. Deep down inside, Glad is afraid to 'come out of the closet' because, having been raised in a devoutly religious family, she is petrified of the ramifications and fears that her family might disown her for her sexuality. Glad, too, has feelings for Donna. As Donna gets inside Glad's head, Glad starts to question her own reality while she walks down an empty, red-baked hallway. She comes across an empty apartment. The door is opened. She walks inside and finds a woman with her back turned. The woman turns around, revealing Glad. In a state of shock, Glad touched the imitation's face. The face starts to peel and break apart, revealing Donna's face underneath.*

"Purdy wild stuff," Fran said, as she placed the head cap over Rose's head.

"It's funny because, in a way, I can relate to Glad," Rose said. "When I was filming *Glory Hole*, I was petrified about what my mother would think of all the sex scenes. For the longest time, I tried to act as if the movie never happened. I'd do about anything to avoid talking about it. When she asked for a copy, I sent her an edited version. But, of course, being the curious cat she is, she got her hands on the theatrical cut."

"How did she react?" asked Fran.

"She was actually more cool with it than I pictured in my head. Maybe, in a way, I misjudged her. We're actually much more closer now than we were before the film came out. I mean, after all, it's just a movie."

"As long as you're happy with what you're doing and making a living out of it, honestly, a parent has no place to criticize but rather only encourage."

"I'd like to think so too," Rose said shyly while Fran paced around the trailer, grabbing everything she needed to make a cast of Rose's face.

As the opportunity presented itself, Bastian asked Rose, "So, let me ask you: What's it like working with Mr. Anthony Wince so far?"

"He's amazing actually," Rose said modestly. "Very sweet."

"I'd like to get my hands around him," Marsha said over Bastian. "Also, in case you haven't noticed, the man is hung like a horse."

"And I thought he was stuffing his pants with a sock or something—"

"Nope," Marsha said, emphasizing her letter p in *nope*. The remark spurred a forced laugh from Rose, who, despite attending one of the best, most elite acting schools in the nation, couldn't act away her discomfort. "Trust me," Marsha continued. "It's the real thing."

"And how would you know?" asked Dunkin.

"The other day, when he was talking with Sergio, he wasn't wearing any underwear. I don't think he knew anyone was looking, but the thing was just hanging out, catching a breeze, as if he had a baby's arm protruding from his shorts."

As Marsha and the others talked more about Anthony Wince's size, Fran returned with the bag of alginate powder.

Using a Q-tip, she gently applied a layer of Vaseline on Rose's eyebrows, as well as eyelashes; however, she was careful not to apply too much Vaseline, otherwise she wouldn't get the desired impression from the alginate.

"Make sure that, when I apply the molding, you remain as still as possible," Fran said closely. "If you need to speak, then just raise your hand. Right hand is a yes. Left hand no. Got it?"

Being the quick learner she was, Rose raised her right hand.

"Atta girl," Fran said and applied a pair of gloves. Most makeup artists didn't mind getting their hands dirty; in fact, most of the job consisted of sticking their hands into all sorts of gooey substances. Which, in a way, was kind of like cooking. Fran verbally stated to Rose that the reason for the protective gloves was primarily due to her dry, cracked hands: the side effects of having constantly washed one's hands while on set.

Set to apply the molding, Fran opened the bag of alginate and poured it into a tub.

Next, she added water.

Considering the alginate had a five-minute curing time, she poured the water into the tub; and with her gloved hands, she began to stir vigorously, adding more water if necessary, until she had a nice consistency. She smoothed out the lumps, as one would do while mixing cake batter. The water thickened the alginate, going from pinkish-purple to a white color.

Furrowing her brow in suspicion, Fran paused midway through stirring. The gesture had caught Rose's eye; however, before she could voice her concern, Fran continued to stir and stir.

"Eyes," Fran said, prompting Rose to close her eyes.

Since she was on the clock and didn't have anytime to waste before the white molding started to harden, she was super quick to apply. She grabbed a handful of molding and began applying around the nostrils area first, pushing the molding off the holes. Next, she covered Rose's nose and again, made sure both her nostrils were clear and provided her with enough opening for Rose to breath, considering Rose's mouth was soon going to be covered with molding.

After the nose, Fran worked on Rose's forehead, dumping handfuls of molding onto her face. She spread, then formed, then smoothed out the molding onto the sides of Rose's face, then worked her way toward Rose's eyes, spreading and pressing in order to form a perfect impression.

Once the alginate-water mixture had completely covered the actor's face, as well as chin and neck area, Fran covered the face with the wet plastered bandages, first making sure to wring out any excess moisture. She started placing each one of the pre-cut bandages on Rose's nose, then sides of the face, at times, doubling, even tripling the layers of bandages.

By the time Fran worked on Rose's forehead, Rose made a disturbing gesture that caught Fran by surprise.

"Can you breath?" asked Fran.

Rose, who was waving her right hand, straightened her right hand, indicating a yes.

"Do you want me to stop?" asked Fran.

Rose replied by raising her left hand.

Before Fran could continue, Rose attempted to touch the side of her face with her left hand.

"Do you have an itch?" asked Fran.

Rose replied by raising her right hand, indicating another yes.

"We're almost finished," asked Fran.

As Fran applied more plaster bandages, Rose raised both of her hands in the air. One of her hands hit Fran's, causing her to drop the plaster bandage.

In a frantic gesture, she began waving around both of her hands in the air, as if her face was on fire.

Underneath the molding, Rose, who was unable to speak, was making closed-mouth noises, which sounded like squeals and cries of panic.

"Okay, okay," Fran said, instructing Rose to lean her head forehead.

As Fran helped Rose remove the cast, her eyes lit up with horror.

Rose's skin was red and bubbling.

Immediately, Fran went for the glass of water and poured water over Rose's face, which was a mistake. The water only intensified the burning.

Other assistants rushed to Rose's hand.

One of the assistants, Bastian, who often and proudly described his youth as a "series of strange experiments," the kind of kid who'd set things on fire or blow things up for curiosity's sake, knew exactly what Rose was experiencing as soon as he witnessed the flesh falling from her face.

℃

AFTER Rose was rushed to the hospital with chemical burns, Fran was called into a meeting with the producers who, afraid of any fallout or backlash, had no other decision than to split ties with Fran and her team, even though the alginate had clearly been tampered with.

Pressed for time, Frank Littlefield continued production and hired a new visual efx team to fill in for Fran and others. Meanwhile, the writers ended up writing in a new draft, which freed up more room for Felicia's character, Donna, who "killed off" Rose's character, Glad, focusing more on a love interest with Michael Morrow, who was played by actor Jack Willhouse of the horror series *Prune*. The accident with Rose completely changed the story, since the character Glad played a vital role in Donna Juan's transformation into a killer. But like they say in the biz, "The show must go on."

And it did.

☾

THAT night, after catching a red-eye from ILM to LAX with a layover in Atlanta, Fran made it back to her apartment located in Burbank. The whole time during the flight, as well as an awkward UBER ride to her place, Fran had made the ugly mistake of going on social media (Twitter, Facebook, etc.) to read up on the latest comments, mostly exaggerations, like Rose's face rumored to have been burned off to the bone (#SkullFace), and straight up hate speech against what, according to all of the minions of Internet Land, that "devil," Francesca von Cappelen, and what she did to their darling, Rose McGregor, and how Fran should be put out of her misery via firing squad. She thought it was amazing what these soulless brats could say about another person, a human being, behind the safety of their keypads and keyboards, especially one whom they didn't know, let alone spoken to before.

When Fran finally reached her floor and pulled out the key to her apartment, she wanted to lock herself inside and never come out; in fact, as of now, Fran was finished with the world and its inhabitants. If she ever stepped foot into the public eye, she knew she would be shunned or even attacked, physically, verbally, even spiritually. Her career in Hollywood, as far as she knew it, was already over. She would never be hired by any production company ever again. The irony was what disturbed Fran the most. The thought alone caused her stomach to knot. She had spent most of her adult career creating award-winning makeup and special effects for creatures and monsters that were ultimately feared, vilified, mocked, scorned, humiliated, even laughed at, in the fictional worlds that they inhabited. Now, she felt no different than one of her very own creations.

Feeling depressed, Fran was about to insert the key into the apartment door when, all of sudden, she heard a noise coming from the other end of the hallway. With her eyes snapping toward the noise, she witnessed a dark, short and stout-looking figure which she presumed to be a man, carefully slide-stepping behind the wall where the other hallway intersected with her hallway. He was wearing a blank, expressionless mask over his face.

Creeped out by the man's sly—or possibly, deliberate—maneuver, she fumbled the keys in her hand, only adding pressure to her own suspense.

As though Fran was caught in a self-manifested horror flick, she dropped the keys.

Feeling the man's presence bearing down on her—or, at least, in her mind—Fran picked up the keys, grabbed the apartment key, slid it into the lock, and unlocked the door. She didn't have time to survey her surroundings. She knew that once she turned, it was all over. She swung open the door and jetted inside.

As Fran was about to close the door behind, she felt an object obstructing the doorway.

She yanked on the door, but the door bounced back open.

When her eyes trailed downward, Fran witnessed what appeared to be a black boot wedged against the doorway.

PRESENT

MUDDY didn't realize what day it was until he came across the familiar face of a twenty-five year woman named "Lola" while drunkenly swiping away on the app, Fling. Surely, he thought, it wasn't her. He hadn't thought about her in years; in fact, he can't even remember the last time her face popped up in his mind. Yet, as his eyes fell upon her face, he questioned the authenticity of the photo. Perhaps it was a scammer or a bot, a dark hooded figure, slumped behind a Matrix-like computer screen, who had hacked a look-alike's phone, even stolen a phone, and was now using a fake account to bait and reel in poor saps like himself.

Muddy gave his thumb rest from swiping left, leaving behind the word *NOPE* singed in his retina. He tapped on the phone's screen and shuffled through more dolled-up photos of the so-called "Lola" gal. She would've been thirty-eight as of today and going on thirty-nine.

As he tapped more aggressively through photos, he realized the woman was Blair. Of all days to come across the photos, on Blair's Death Day.

In the photos, the woman Lola—or what Muddy swore to be an ex-girlfriend, Blair—was bleached blonde, which was a stark contrast to how she wore her hair when she first met Muddy seven years ago at a hole-in-the-wall called Slur Slow Bar and Billiards. She was thirty-one years old at the time, brunette, bosomy, all natural, and what he perceived, despite his alcohol-induced gaze, as "vulnerable."

With his eyes bloodshot, Muddy closed Fling and sprung out of the recliner chair and stumbled into the kitchen for yet another brewski. He only had two left from a 12-pack and was in no condition to be making a beer run. He finished his last brewski, crushed the can, tossed it in the trash, and cracked open another one.

As he took a couple of gulps, the beer ran down the sides of his mouth, down his chin, and dribbled all over the white tank top—or what the kids used to call a "wife beater."

Catching his breath, Muddy slurred, "It can't be."

He walked back into the living room, picked up his phone, and reopened the app and clicked on the "flame" icon where he found yet another photo of another woman, this time much older, on his "Hot Picks."

At first, he couldn't believe his eyes.

The name of the sixty-five year old woman was different; however, the face, profile, as well as the gallery of photos, was the same.

"Mom?" said Muddy, lowering the phone in horror.

As soon as he realized the photos were, in fact, of his mother, Paula, not this so-called "Dina" woman, he dropped the phone as if the phone itself was infected with a contagious disease. He wanted to puke right then and there.

"What the fuck, man!" Muddy shouted out.

Over the sound of his pounding heart, Muddy heard what sounded like a *thud* coming from upstairs. He didn't know whether or not it was the throbbing in his head and ears. Either way, he stood in silence until he heard yet another *thud*.

"Hello?" Muddy said, waiting for a response.

As the blood ran from his once flushed face, he inched closer to the staircase where he heard yet another sound coming from his bedroom.

He rushed back into the living room, grabbed an aluminum baseball bat from the closet, and crept upstairs.

As he reached the landing, he heard a tune playing inside his bedroom.

Once Muddy heard the sound, his heart started to pound.

"It can't be. . . "

He nudged open the cracked door and inched into the bedroom and there, on his bed, laid a pink jewelry box. It wasn't just any jewelry. It was Blair's jewelry box. The box was open, and inside, the ballerina figurine was swirling round and round. Muddy walked up to the jewelry box. The ballerina's arms were broken; her legs covered in cracks. The mirror shattered.

An image suddenly came to Muddy, one that he buried under hard booze and brewskis: *Towering above on Pictured Bluff stood Muddy. Below him was Blair lying on the rocky shore of Lake Superior. Her contorted, bloody body was posed like a chalked sketch of a dead man at a crime scene. Both her arms and legs bent in opposite directions. The right side of her face was caved in from landing face first on a jagged rock, revealing part of her shattered skull.*

The ballerina came to a halt, as the song stopped playing.

Over the pounding silence, Muddy heard yet another sound: a piercing *creak* of the bedroom door opening or closing behind him. He couldn't tell which for, when he finally turned his shoulder, he only caught the tail end of the door coming to a rest. He dropped the jewelry box on the bed and followed the sound of footsteps trailing down the stairs, which, after reaching the landing, he had mistaken for the sound of his own heart beating like a piston against the walls of his chest.

Muddy ran his fingers over his worn eyes, as if, by doing so, he would wake up from whatever walking nightmare he was experiencing.

As he removed his hands from his face, he heard another *creak*, this time directly behind him.

Muddy spun around, only to find a bloody, disfigured-looking Blair standing behind him. Her skin was grayish-blue underneath her dark, wet hair.

She opened her mouth to speak.

Strings of watered down blood, crushed teeth, and lake creatures poured from the sides of her mouth.

"*What goes around comes around,*" Blair said through her watery voice.

Muddy gasped.

Blair grinned.

Before Muddy could react for he was left in a state of utter shock, Blair suddenly shoved Muddy toward the staircase behind him. He stumbled over his own ankles and toppled over on his back, violently rolling down the staircase. In the fall, he hit the side of his head along the stairs, as well as the wall and railing.

Eventually, he came to rest at the bottom of the stairs lying in a position that seemed, strangely yet comically, ironic.

☾

UNAWARE of Muddy's tragic demise, Detective Mather and his partner, Detective Ludlow, were still hung up on the details of Fran's death.

"LAPD brought in some special investigator who ruled her death as a homicide, even though her death was meant to look like a suicide," Detective Ludlow said, sitting anxiously in the passenger seat.

"You just can't stop thinking about it, can you?" said Mather, driving.

"It's just, I dunno, freaky," he said, turning his eyes toward the passing countryside. "That's all. I mean. . . "

"Whatever it was that happened down there, Giraud, it doesn't concern us."

Ludlow could no longer bite down on his silence for the notion alone of whoever murdered Hood being possibly involved in what happened "down there," as in beyond state lines, if not, connected to a series of tragic events that occurred on set during the production of *The Effigy* reboot seemed, if anything, widely absurd and one destined to become a Shh! docu-series.

"Say Francesca von Cappelen was part of some plot to sabotage the production," Ludlow said. "Maybe the person behind it all was trying to make it look as though Castor Lykaios was the killer. You know, a red herring."

"You mean the stand-in who the Feds questioned?" asked Mather.

"The man definitely had the credentials," Ludlow said. "He was arrested six years ago for assault. Judge went easy on him, though. Two years later, he had to pay a hefty fine for vandalism. A year after that, disorderly conduct. Then, a year after that, he was arrested for DUI. You see the trend?"

"Doesn't make him a killer, though," Mather suggested.

"Well, regardless, his downward spiral all started back in 2006, while filming *The Effigy Burns*, when Lykaios was let go for breaking his contract. A couple of years prior to the shoot, Lykaios wrote a controversial book—a sort of exposé—on the film industry under pseudonym, Evan Foster. In the book, he talks about his relationship with Ralph Hood. According to Lykaios, they were 'more than friends.' Many speculate that the two were, you know. . ."

Ludlow didn't even have to explain himself.

"Wasn't Hood married to his second wife at the time? The fitness guru—"

"—Calypso?"

"Yeah," he said. "Her."

"Separated," Ludlow clarified. "Long story short: She was a basket case."

"Fuckin' Hollywood," Mather uttered as if the word alone *Hollywood* needed no further explanation.

"I know, right?"

"That's what happens when you live in your own bubble."

"According to the tabloids, Lykaios lived vicariously through Hood and was completely obsessed with him."

"So this is what you've reduced yourself to. Huh, Giraud? Tabloids?"

Ludlow ignored his partner and finished his thought.

"Lykaios also called out several of the crewmembers for their shenanigans on set. The book ended up receiving a lot of pushback for mostly being exaggerated and simply fictitious. Word got out about the book. Some crewmembers, whom Lykaios threw under the bus, including the same ones who got violently sick during the recent production, caught Lykaios on film saying some pretty nasty things about other cast and crewmembers, racist, sexist comments. Basically, any word ending in -ist. Eventually, production, as well as studio execs, found out Lykaios and his bigotry. They banned him from set. If that wasn't enough, after a public outcry, they continued to smear his name until they ran him out of town. Those who were brave enough to come out about Lykaios got better jobs, some became producers, others directors, assistant directors; nonetheless, they moved their way up the ladder."

"Yeah," Mather said gloomily. "That seems to be the trend, doesn't it?"

"Not to mention the actor—or should I'd say *former* actor now turned backwoods recluse whose career has been reduced to ashes—Moiré Taughly, who was fired from the new movie after being caught on camera spewing all kinds of homophobic slurs during the shoot."

"That's the one who played in *The Effigy Rises*, right?"

"You've been doing your homework, I see."

"Had some free time on my hands."

"There was speculation that Taughly was involved in Cayson Nally's murder, considering, you guessed it, the two had a previous relationship. If case you were wondering, that's the extra who Feds thought was planted inside the cast in order to disrupt the production," Ludlow said before Mather could inquire further. "A few days later after *The Effigy* was postponed, his roommate, who was spending a couple of months with his family in Colorado, found Nally inside his duplex with a softball bat jammed down his throat. Apparently, he had been dead for weeks. Get this," Ludlow said in a more upbeat tone, "the bat recovered from the crime scene happened to be the same one used on the movie. Investigators found actor Anthony Wince's fingerprints all over the bat, as well as another set of prints they couldn't identify. Apparently, in the movie, our boy, Wince, shares a scene with Hood where he beats Don Juan to a bloody pulp. Wince denies any involvement in Nally's murder."

"Did Lykaios have any beef with Wince?" asked Mather.

"Not that I'm anywhere of."

"Interesting," Mather said, his mind running like a machine. "I'm just gonna throw this out there, but do the Feds know where Wince was the night of Hood's murder?"

"He was still in Wilmington." Ludlow shrugged off the thought, another one came to him: "Did you know, according to Whatsnext, the original *Effigy* movie hit an all-time record in streaming over the weekend? Blu-ray sales went through the roof. Several movie theatres around the country are even playing the original movies. Why is it that, often times, celebrities, especially ones who have been out of the spotlight, become more famous after they die?"

"This country has what most people are afraid to admit as a 'nostalgia problem,'" Mather said cynically.

"Tell me about it," Ludlow said, not missing a beat. "By the rate Hollywood keeps pumping out reboots, it'll reach the point where they're making a reboot of the reboot they just released a month ago."

Following suit, Mather asked, "By the way, what is a stand-in anyway?"

"I think the title speaks for itself," Ludlow said, amazed by Mather's ignorance of the industry—and most of the case. "They stand in place for certain actors while production sets up for an upcoming shot. Get it," Ludlow emphasized, "*stand*-in."

"But it's not the same as a double, right?"

"No," Ludlow said, backtracking. "I think they're the same."

"Can a person even make a living as a stand-in?"

"Sure," Ludlow said. "If you have the right connections, I guess."

"But I take this Lykaios fellow lost all the connections he had in Hollywood when he showed his ass."

"Ever since, the man has held a grudge against anybody who played any part in the making of *The Effigy* franchise."

"Even Hood?"

"After all, he was Hood's stand-in since the original movie."

"How did these two meet, Hood and Lykaios?" asked Mather.

"Lykaios had a sister who knew a friend who had a brother who knew Ralph. I guess that's how it works, right?"

"And what? You would know?"

"What? You really think it's about talent? Of course not."

Surprisingly, Detective Mather found himself thinking about the makeup artist, Francesca von Cappelen.

"Enlighten me, Giraud: What do you think about Ms. Cappelen?" asked Detective Mather. "Based on everything you know, do you think she killed herself?"

Ludlow drifted into thought.

"The fake suicide note," he said, referring to the suicide note, which was left on a nightstand next to the untidy bed where Francesca's corpse lay sprawled on the floor with a plastic grocery bag tied around her face. The bright "red flag" in the note being the handwriting and how it didn't match Francesca's, in particular, the capital letter "A" used in the word *Apologies*, which, except for the rest of the note, was not written in cursive. "It seems way too deliberate for sure," Ludlow said. "And incredibly amateur. Also Francesca had absolutely no motives to hurt Rose McGregor."

"How you know?" asked Mather.

"Hey," Ludlow said over Mather. "You wanted my opinion."

Mather lifted his hands from the steering wheel as if he was holding them up in surrender.

"We're talking about covering a person's face in sodium hydroxide," Ludlow said. "Whoever tampered with the alginate, not only did he or she want to seriously hurt McGregor, but—"

"—I'm leaning to the 'she' part," Mather said under his breath. "Angry ex-girlfriend, who knows?"

"—*He* or *she* also wanted to destroy Rose McGregor's career. Clearly, Francesca was setup. I mean, shit, it could've been Lykaios."

"If he wasn't in Wilmington at the time of production, according to his alibi, then he must've had someone working with him on the inside."

Over the heavy silence, Ludlow felt it was best to throw in one last remark.

With a grin on his face, he turned to Mather and said, "You know what the name Lykaios means in Greek?"

"Got me," said Mather.

"Wolf," Ludlow said. "It means 'wolf.'"

After recklessly going against Hershel's orders and spending the better part of the morning checking out the various quarry sites—so far, five of them in and around Philip's Head area—the two detectives finally arrived at their last stop on the list: Gray Bend Quarry, or as a couple of witnesses from The Liquid Lounge called "The Pit," which was a few miles outside Philip's Head in a small, nearly nonexistent town called Thumb Point.

Mather parked the car in front of the trailer where inside the manager of the quarry, Cornelius Sizemore, sat at a desk.

Before explaining the reasons for their unannounced visit—as soon as they mentioned Hood's name, Sizemore, knew exactly why they were here—the detectives showed Sizemore their badges and asked for a moment of his time.

Sizemore, being quite familiar with Hood's work but not frivolous enough to call himself a fan or "fran," was glad to help in anyway he could.

Ludlow showed the manager a grainy-looking still, which was taken from the doorbell cam, and asked if the people, in particular, the two most visible people, the third one being a dark and shadowy figure, inside the still looked like any employees he had working at the quarry.

Sizemore narrowed his eyes and peered closer.

"Take your time, if you have to," said Mather.

"Yes or no?"

Sizemore adjusted his orange-rimmed glasses, which were starting to fog up, and said, "Yeah. I mean. Maybe."

After the brief visit, Sizemore walked the two detectives into The Pit where an excavator was loading limestone into the back of a dump truck.

Sizemore waved at the driver, Weston Cloverfield, to stop what he was doing and step outside for a chat.

The other driver, who went by the name Yak, leaned his body out of the window while holding up his hand.

"What's the problem?" asked Yak, visibly frustrated.

Sizemore gave Yak the "Hold your horses, sweetheart" finger.

Weston switched off the excavator and stepped out.

"What is it, Corny?" Weston asked, as he approached his manager.

Behind him stood the two detectives, who were carefully trying to match the figure in the still to Weston. The nose, which was long and narrow, as well as his somewhat slouched posture, clearly matched one of the three men in the still. All of his features, however, were quickly overlooked by the man's arm. What really caught their eyes was that navy blue cast on his right wrist.

As soon as they introduced themselves to Weston, Mather didn't waste anytime asking Weston about the injury.

"Got it from playing football," he said. "Some asshole blindsided—"

Before Weston could finish a sentence, a gunshot suddenly blared out behind them!

The bullet grazed the side of Mather's arm, only catching part of his sleeve.

At first reaction, all four of the men ducked.

The fifth one, the dump truck driver, Yak, opened the driver's side door and cautiously peeked his head outside while both Mather and Ludlow drew their weapons. Mather grabbed Sizemore while Ludlow grabbed Weston; and together, they rushed the two men behind the excavator where they took cover from more gunfire.

As bullets kicked up tiny clouds of powdery limestone dust all around them, Ludlow peeked over the edge of the excavator and spotted the whitish figure who was crouched behind a red pickup truck, which was parked along a ridge above them. The shooter had the advantage with the higher vantage point, making the two detectives look like target practice.

Once the figure stood up to fire a shot, he revealed himself to Ludlow, whose eyes were better than Mather's, as a possible "second" person in the still.

Mather could only think of one option, which was, really, the only option.

"I'll hold 'em off while you get these two men outta here." A bullet bounced off the excavator, making a sharp *cha-ching* noise, which forced the detective to lower his head. "Once you get 'em to safety. . . " Mather glanced up at a hill behind the shooter, as gunfire continued to rain down, ". . . you make it to the hill up there and take him out once you find a shot. I'll keep him distracted."

Ludlow remained frozen, almost paralyzed.

"Giraud," Mather said, ducking. "Go! Now!"

After coming to his senses, Ludlow acknowledged his partner's orders with a nod of the head.

While Detective Mather returned fire at the shooter above, his partner as well as the two other men, Sizemore and Weston, sprinted toward the dump truck. The driver, Yak, stepped aside for Sizemore and Weston, who both slipped inside the truck via the driver's side. Yak was next to get inside. He closed the door and Ludlow stood on the step alongside the truck and ordered Yak to drive away.

Once everyone was safely inside, excluding Ludlow, who was hanging on the side of the door, one hand holding a gun while the other one holding onto the side view mirror, Yak sped off.

To Mather's surprise, the shooter got into the pickup truck and chased after Ludlow.

Mather holstered his weapon and took off after the two trucks.

During the chase, the shooter fired a couple of shots down at the dump truck, specifically at its rear tires.

The shooter finally caught up with Ludlow and company and cut them off at the entranceway of the quarry. He stepped outside and took aim at Yak, who had no other choice than to slam on the brakes. Weston reached across the driver and without Ludlow knowing, grabbed the gun from his hand.

With two guns now pointed at Ludlow, who stepped off the truck and held up his hands in surrender, Weston squeezed his way out, pushing Yak from the truck in the process.

"What the fuck you doing, West?" said Yak. "Don't be fucking stupid!"

His hand was trembling as he aimed the gun sideways at Ludlow, like all the wannabe gangstas do in the movies. It was clear to the detective this was a man who had never held a gun in his entire life, let alone shot one.

"West—"

"—Shut the fuck up, Yak!"

"Good boy, West," the shooter said coolly, as he squared both his shoulders at Ludlow and prepared himself to shoot the detective. "I can take care of it from here. . ."

As the shooter was about to pull the trigger, a gunshot blared out!

The gunshot came from neither the shooter's gun nor Ludlow's.

Weston flinched from the gunfire, causing him to lower the gun.

Behind them stood Mather, who turned his aim toward Weston.

"Drop it!" Mather shouted, as the shooter, who had a dime-sized bullet hole in his forehead, dropped to the ground.

Mather shouted out his final commands.

The steady-handed detective told himself that, if the punk didn't drop the gun on his third command, then he was going to put a bullet in his other head.

Weston's hand trembled even more.

Mather readied himself to put one right in the little pecker of his.

The boy was soon going to be pissing out of a catheter for the rest of his miserable life.

As Mather was about to call out his third and final command, Weston finally dropped the gun and surrendered.

Mather first walked up to the shooter. He didn't bother kicking the gun away from his reach. The man was already dead.

Next, he walked past Ludlow and shot him a glare, which, to Ludlow, came off more as a look of utter disappointment opposed to, you know, "Hey, kid, glad you're not dead."

While Ludlow retrieved his gun, his partner didn't waste anytime handcuffing Weston.

One dead.

One alive.

For Mather, he'd take those numbers any day of the week.

TWO MONTHS AGO
Wilmington, North Carolina

THE scene that was scheduled for filming involved thirty extras, including twenty-two prisoners and eight prison guards, as well as two actors, Moiré Taughly who was reprising his role as "Dial," a violent sociopath who played one of the street thugs in *The Effigy Rises*. Even though Moiré had one line in the movie, if you blinked, you'd miss his part; however, filmmakers wanted to give Moiré a cameo in the reboot where he was going to play convicted murderer who butchered a husband and his wife inside their home. The second actor was none other than the legend himself, Ralph Hood, who was reprising his role as iconic character, Don Juan. In this particular scene, which occurred at the opening of the film, Dial was not only starting to experience weird hallucinations of a strange man (Don Juan), but also his physical appearance, mainly skeletal structure and hands, were changing into the stranger (Don Juan).

The scene involved Dial bumping into a fellow inmate, which resulted in him spilling a cup of water over the gray floor. Tempted to start a quibble with the inmate, who seemed unapologetic for the "accidental" bump, his eyes trailed down toward the floor where he witnessed another reflection staring back at him. Soon, Dial realized that the reflection was not his own, yet it was one of a far more violent, manipulative body swapper known as Don Juan staring up at him.

The chatter was circulating around the set.

Everyone, including a couple of extras who had been following the details of the production, carried a look about them. One that you'd see at a funeral.

One of the prisoner extras, Cayson—"Cay," for short—was keen to point out the common demeanor among the cast and crewmembers.

He leaned in closer to another extra, Jobe, who was playing a prison guard, and whispered in his ear, "Dude, what's up with the vibe?"

"Think people are still torn up about Ringer," he said.

"Ringer? Who's that?"

"Ringer Slade," Jobe said, looking at Cay as if he was from another planet. "He's one of the stuntmen for Hood. You didn't hear about what happened?"

First to arrive on set was actor, Moiré Taughly, or as he was being called by his character name "Dial."

Distracted by the sight of the actor, Cay's demeanor went from slightly anxious to embarrassed. His cheeks clouded up with red. He was constantly shooting a glance at the former pop singer turned actor, who, in return, was taking turns sharing glances with Cay.

"A couple of days ago," he said, reeling in Cay's attention, "he got seriously injured while he performing a stunt that involved a house explosion. They were actually going to cancel today's shoot, but Hood was the one who insisted not to. I'm surprised you didn't hear about it. . . "

"Yeah, well," Cay said, glancing once more at Moiré, "I've been out of the loop these past couple of days. Looking for a new place and all. I need a change in environment."

"I feel for you, brutha," Jobe said. "The beach will do that to you."

Another extra chimed in, "So any word on Ringer's condition?"

"Not that I've heard."

"I heard he suffered third degrees over half his body."

Another one: "Someone was saying that one of the crewmembers deliberately screwed with his harness."

"I wonder how Hood's doing, especially with him being so close to Slade."

Jobe nodded toward the far end of the prison set.

"I dunno," he said. "Why don't you ask him yourself?"

As soon as the other extras turned their eyes toward Ralph, who, normally as of this time last year, would've been harvesting honey, entered the prison set and made his way to his own personalized actor's chair. Except for one or two extras who hadn't seen any of *The Effigy* films and were only here for money or the notion of being in a movie, everybody else immediately turned into a bunch of giddy fans. The star-struck extras—grown men that is— struggled to contain their child-like excitement as they whispered to each other in short, shallow breaths about the iconic figure. Ralph's presence alone was, as best as the extras could put it, a divine experience.

One said girlishly, "He looks much shorter in real life."

"Camera adds a couple of inches," another replied.

Next to enter the set was makeup artist, Jonathan-Michel Landig, who ended up replacing Fran.

Robin "Rob" Mesuda, one of the assistant directors, or best known on set as the "AD," approached the group of extras, who were dressed up as prisoners and prison guards. Some of the prisoners were given special "fake tattoos" while others came to the set with their own, albeit modified. The tattoos included fictional gang signs, menacing-looking snakes or dragons, crucifixes, a black teardrop under the eye, barbwire around the bicep, spider webs along the elbows, cartoonish hearts with the word *Mom* inscribed inside them, to name a few.

Speaking as fast as his mouth would let him, Rob gave a quick summary of the scene while the lighting guy was giving him an update via walkie-talkie.

With very little time to waste before the director Sergio showed up on set, he showed each extra where they were going to be sitting in their jail cells as well as standing outside their jail cells, what they were going to be doing around the recreational area; he even mimed a couple of poses, gestures, and movements for the extras in order paint a better picture of the image who they were going to portray. Some extras were going to be acting harder than a porn star on Viagra, a swollen chest, grim mien, narrow eyes, head high, chin even higher; some of them prowling the halls, looking for a fight, either mouthing words or biting their lip or snarling or even blowing kisses—the "Sisters" from *Shawshank Redemption* was one of the best explanations he could give the background actors—while others were going to be sitting as cool as silk at their designated tables, playing cards or crabs, talking shit, or better yet, since they were required and reminded to act as quiet as a mouse on the set—"Remember," Rob specified, "don't slide and skid, walk with soft feet"—they were going to be, in other words, "mouthing shit."

Then there were other extras who were going to be acting defensive, almost timid, surveying their surroundings, eyes wide, faces longer.

As for the prison guards, most of their acting would remain consistent: standing firm and tall like statues in their designated positions and keeping a close eye on the prisoners.

Finally, Rob specifically called out Cay, who was going to be sitting next to Moiré, the main star of the scene. The idea of sitting next to Moiré made Cay, a self-proclaimed straight man who was extremely proud to share in a bragging sort of way how many women he had screwed in the past month, more anxious; however, it didn't take long for Jobe, as well as many of the other extras to realize that Cay and Moiré had "history" based on their constant back and forth locking of the eyes. Cay would glance over at Moiré, who, in return, would move his eyes away from Cay at the very last second and vice versa.

As the extras took their positions on set, Jonathan-Michel Landig was prepping the final touches to Don Juan's makeup, which was best described as what a man's face would look like during his final and most brutal transition from human to werewolf, and yet, before his transition was complete, he decided to revert back to his human form but, somehow, he had forgotten what his own face looked like, and it was slightly "off." The eyes, still as sharp and pale blue as a wolf, uneven. The nose, more wolf than human. The grayish skin wrinkled, the texture coarse.

Not too far away, Cay was hesitant to take a sit next to Moiré, who struggled to acknowledge Cay.

For an extra, one of the main rules on set was not to disturb or even approach the "talent" for that matter.

And for Cay, never had a rule become so hard not to break.

Rob prepared the extras for the upcoming shot by demonstrating for the extras in the background how they should walk. It sounded incredibly silly, but Rob basically wanted the extras to walk back and forth while the two actors were exchanging their lines. "Remember," he reminded them, "don't look at the camera."

Across from Moiré sat Dial's friend, the character "Regs," short for Reggie, who was played by Grammy award-winning rapper, Bully from the rap-rock band Bully and The Mob.

As soon as Sergio arrived on set, he walked straight to the table where Moiré and Regs were sitting. Next to the two actors were Cay, of course, and two other extras, one of them being equally as anxious as Cay.

As Sergio explained the current state of Moiré's character and how, for these past couple of days, the thought of Don Juan had been driving him into a state of paranoia. "Dial doesn't know who Don Juan is—at least, not at first—however," the director said in his thick Italian accent, "the more he starts visualizing his face, the more he starts to feel a sense of urgency, like he really wants to know what's happening and in a way, the thought alone intrigues him."

"I take it this is the first time I'm coming to Regs with information regarding The Stranger."

"Yes," Sergio said, turning to Bully. "You're like," he demonstrated a shrug for Bully, "so what?" Then, pointed at Moiré. "You're going crazy. Everybody goes crazy in here, right? Got it?"

Bully nodded and gave Sergio a thumbs up.

"Got it, man," he said calmly.

"Okay," Sergio said, turning to the rest of the crew, which was already set up for the upcoming shot.

Lastly, Sergio made his way across the prison set toward Ralph, who was already standing in position next to a couple of prison guards where, previously, his stand-in Ned was standing. He talked to him for a little while and after receiving a few head nods from Ralph, was ready to begin the scene.

Sergio walked back to camera 1.

The camera assistant stepped in front of the camera with a clapperboard, then stated the name of the scene, as well as the "take," which obviously was "Take 1," then clapped the stick shut.

Rob, the AD, shouted out, "Quiet on set."

Then, another AD, "Rolling!"

Echoes of "Rolling, Rolling" ping-ponged throughout the set.

Next followed the shout, "Background!"

The tension was heavy in the air.

Cay's heart beat faster and faster the closer they began to filming.

Then, finally, Sergio, "Action!"

Cay played his part as a hard-ass prisoner sitting with his shoulders slouched, displaying an exaggerated curled lip, mouthing the first topic of discussion which came to mind, which was the *Ten Commandments*, to extra, Jobe, who was sitting across the table and mouthing questions about "Who do you think was hotter in last night's beauty pageant? Miss Argentina or Miss Sweden?"

Bully, who was playing the character, Regs, was the first to speak his lines to Dial: "You actin' quieter than you usual self, homie. What's on your mind?"

"Couldn't sleep last night," Moiré's character, Dial, said back to Regs.

Regs leaned back in his chair.

"Welcome to the club, man," he said. "Ever since I've been here, my ass has been sleeping with one eye open."

"Which eye is that?" asked Dial, teasing.

Regs waved off Dial's remarks.

"I actually came up with an idea for a movie last night," Regs said. "You see it's about this. . . "

On cue, Dial grabbed the bridge of his nose as he held his head downward.

"You good, man?" asked Regs.

Dial lifted his head upward and as he was about to look Regs in the eyes, he saw Don Juan standing on the other side of the recreational room.

"Dial? Say, man. What's your deal?"

"I need to grab some water," Dial said and stood up from his seat.

As Dial was about to stand up from his seat, he glanced over at Cay, who was sitting next to him. Cay glanced over at Dial and gave him a wink, which, clearly, was not in the script nor was it any part of Cay's role, which was to act tough and mouth stuff.

Dial's foot got caught underneath the leg of the chair, causing him to stumble forward and nearly trip onto the table.

"Shit!" he seethed. "My bad. . . "

Sergio chimed in, "It's okay. Start over with 'I need to grab some water,' but say with a smack of the gums, like. . . " Sergio smacked his gums while giving a little head shake, ". . . 'I need to grab some water.' And make sure not to trip."

The comment helped loosen up the rest of the cast, provoking laughter from Bully.

Moiré sat back down and got back into character.

"Action," Sergio said, watching the scene with great intensity.

Dial smacked his gums and gave a slight shake of the head.

"I need to grab some water," he said and as he was about to stand from the chair, he glanced at Cay once more. Who, this time, was flirtatiously flicking his brow at Moiré.

Once more, Dial messed up while standing.

"Fuck!" he said in frustration.

"Cut!" Sergio shouted out and tended to Moiré. "Something wrong with your shoes?"

"No," Moiré said. "There's nothing wrong with my shoes." He stood to his feet, naturally this time, and pointed down at the extra sitting next to him. "The problem is with this piece of shit right here. Who the fuck cast him? Was it you, Rob?" Moiré asked, directing his attention toward the AD. "You know who this little shithead is, yet it was you who cast him. Wasn't it? Is this your idea of getting back at me? If it is, you should be ashamed of yourself. . . "

At first, most of the people on set thought Moiré was just getting into character; but then, his rage turned directly toward Cay.

"And you. . . " said Moiré, ". . . what the fuck are you doing here?"

"What are you talking about?" Cay asked, blushing more.

"You know exactly what I'm talking about, you little shit!"

With a strange smirk on his face, Cay looked around the set.

"Hey, it was just a one night stand, man?" Cay said in return. "If I knew you were going to get all obsessed over it, I would've never fooled around with you to begin with."

"Fooled around?" Moiré smacked his gums, for real this time, and acted as if he didn't know what Cay was talking about, even though, despite being a highly trained actor who attended an acting school in New York City and spent several years performing plays on Broadway, his face had "guilty" written all over it. "I don't know what you're talking about." He turned to Tonya, the production assistant, or PA. "Tonya, would you get this fool outta here?"

Tonya remained frozen in shock from the blowup.

"I mean," Cay said with a sinister grin on his face, "I don't know about you, but I had a good time."

"I said, '*Get this faggot outta here!*'"

Everybody on set froze from the sound of the f-word.

Faces slack and left in a state of utter shock.

Despite the whole "no phones on the set" rule, several cast and crewmembers secretly brandished their phones, including Jobe, who was only feet away. Using the edge of the table to conceal the phone, he filmed Moiré's meltdown.

As far as the People of the Internet were concerned, you couldn't have asked for a more perfect shot.

PRESENT

WESTON sat alone for what felt like hours inside the interrogation room until the two detectives, Ludlow and Mather, who had a lengthy conversation with the two FBI agents and Sheriff Dwayne Hershel in the other room directly behind the mirror, were allowed a shot at getting a confession from Weston.

Detective Mather stepped inside first; Detective Ludlow entered next and was first to greet Weston with a cup of coffee.

Weston reached out with both his wrists handcuffed, grabbed the cup with his hands, and took a sip of coffee.

"It's cold," he whined.

"Yeah," Mather said and sat down across from Weston. "Sorry about that."

Weston placed the cup back on the table and slid it away from him.

Ludlow stepped closer to the table and handed Mather the iPad. Mather then clicked on the video and played it for Weston.

"Can you confirm that this you in the video?" asked Mather, as he showed a doorbell cam video of three figures—or men—beating the living shit out of who they believe to be Ralph Hood. One of the men appeared to be stabbing the suspect.

After watching the video, he looked at Mather and recognized that vindictive expression hidden underneath his old face. Weston knew people like Mather. He worked with a couple of them at the quarry. Men who saw the world in black and white. Yet, they completely ignored that little gray area in life. Weston turned to a younger, more trustworthy face.

"Should I get a lawyer?" Weston asked Ludlow, who returned with a shrug.

"I dunno, Weston," he said, chilling in the corner of the room. "Why should you need a lawyer? I mean, if that's not you in the video. . . "

Weston turned to Mather, who was waiting for a response. Then he turned to Ludlow, who was also waiting.

Feeling the pressure of the spotlight bearing down on him, Weston said, "It's not me."

"It's not?"

"Yeah," he said more confidently. "You heard me."

"So," Mather said, pinching his fingers outward along the screen to zoom in on the man who was standing next to the stop sign, "you're saying this isn't you?"

Mather showed the close-up shot to Weston, who, in return, shot a glance at the iPad.

"Yeah," he said shortly. "That's what I said, didn't I?"

Mather looked at the screen and sighed.

With amusement, he glanced at the iPad, comparing the two profiles.

"We must have a double," he said.

"I guess," Weston said, crossing his arms. "I know all kinds of people who have look-alikes, yet they're not blood related. Just because some guy in a video looks like me doesn't mean it is me."

"Right," Mather said, leaning back in his chair. "Well," he said more upbeat, "we have identified the other two men in the video." Technically, Mather hadn't, but he went along with it anyway. After years sleuthing around, he had his tricks. "The first one, you see here," he said, showing Weston the shadowy figure looming behind who Mather assumed to be Weston, "that's your boy, Kowalski. You may know him as J.J. You're probably wondering to yourself: How did we figure that out? Well," he zoomed in closer on the dark blot-like scorpion on the man's neck, "the tattoos match. And, according to eyewitnesses, as well as the owner of Liquid Lounge, J.J. was seen at the bar the night of Ralph Hood's murder."

Weston shrugged.

"I. . . I wouldn't know anything about that—"

"—The other fellow in the video is a lowlife named Marland V. Zappa. His friends call him 'Muddy.' Your friends with him, right?"

Again, Weston shrugged.

"I barely know him," he said.

"You're not friends?"

Weston shook his head.

"No," he said. "I'm not."

"Right," Mather said, as he carefully inspected Weston's soon-to-be reaction. "Then, you're probably not aware that his body was found the other day."

"What?" said Weston, uncrossing his arms. "What you talking about?"

"A couple of hours ago, a UPS driver came across your boy, Muddy, when he was delivering a package to his doorstep."

"Bullshit."

"The driver peeked inside the front door window and saw your boy lying lifelessly on the floor. He knocked several times on the door, but he wasn't responding. At first, he thought maybe the person inside had a long night and was passed out. He noticed part of the broken banister. So, immediately, the driver called the police. Apparently, Muddy tripped and fell down the stairs."

"Or pushed," Ludlow suggested, as he stepped forward. He nodded at Weston, "You didn't kill Marland, did you?"

"What?" he said, losing his cool. "No!"

Based on Weston's mannerisms, he was clearly distressed by the news.

"I thought you barely knew him."

"I don't," he said, more flustered. "I mean, I do barely know him."

"You look upset," Mather pointed out. "What's on your mind? You can tell us, Weston."

Weston hung his head and struggled to look the detectives in the eyes.

Mather even counted down the man's breakdown in his head.

5, 4, 3, 2. . .

"We didn't kill him," he said, his eyes tearing up.

"Are you saying you didn't kill Ralph Hood?"

Sniffling, Weston wiped his nose with the backside of his hands.

"We beat him up," he said, "but we didn't kill him."

"How do you know you didn't kill him?"

"Cuz I just know," Weston said. "By the time we walked off, we was sitting on the sidewalk, wiping the blood from his face. We didn't kill him."

Mather pulled out an evidence bag holding a butterfly knife.

"Investigators discovered this inside J.J.'s truck," he said, placing the bag on the table. "Didn't take 'em long. It was sitting right there in the glove compartment. Chances are it was the same knife that was used on Hood. You can save us the trouble right here, right now, by telling us the truth, Weston."

Weston barely looked at the knife.

Based on his reaction, Weston had already seen it before—Hell! Perhaps he had even handled it before.

"Why'd you beat him up?" asked Ludlow.

"It was fucking J.J.'s idea," he said. "He recognized him from the TV. Honestly I don't know he wanted to do it cuz, I dunno, it sounded like fun. That's just who he was. . ."

"So," Mather said, sliding his iPad back in front of Weston, "can you confirm that this is you in the video."

He showed the still of the man standing next to the stop sign.

Eventually, Weston nodded.

"Is that a yes, Weston?" asked Ludlow.

Again, Weston nodded.

"We need you say it, Weston," said Ludlow.

"Yes," he said depressingly. "It's me in the video."

Mather got cocky and swung for the fences when he could've just settled for a single up the middle.

He opened the folder and showed two photos, one of Stanley Richard and the other, Boxer Brown.

"Have you ever seen these two men before?" asked Mather.

ONE MONTH AGO
Wilmington, North Carolina

FOR the past couple of weeks, all walks of life, including people, as well as their furry four legged friends—Yes, there were several scenes with "real life" animals, not, as Ralph would put it mildly, that "CGI garbage"—who had any involvement in the making of *The Effigy* reboot were ninety-nine point nine, nine, nine percent convinced that the production was, in fact, cursed. Believe it or not, the most obvious signs that things were not quite right actually came from the dog actors, who'd misbehave or disobey commands or bark for no apparent reason or hide their heads underneath their tails—talk about a total nightmare for any dog trainer.

If the lightning strike that caused the set to catch fire or the makeup malfunction with Rose McGregor, which resulted in the firing of Francesca von Cappelen, who was murdered inside her apartment, or the unfortunate incident which led to the banishment of Moiré Taughly wasn't enough evidence to persuade those, as in the point zero, zero one percenters, who were on the fence about so-called "cursed films," it had become certain that something incredibly weird was going on when Ralph arrived at the back lot behind Screengasm to shoot his last couple of scenes for the upcoming film.

Outside Stage 8 several police cruisers, three ambulances, two fire trucks, as well as pickup trucks and unmarked vans were lined up next to an open hanger.

At first, Ralph thought it was for an upcoming scene. Perhaps a last minute rewrite that he wasn't aware of. Ever since Rose's character was written off, the possibility of a rewrite didn't seem so farfetched.

As Ralph's assistant, Connie, pulled up to Stage 8, Ralph soon realized that the chaos was real, *not* staged. A couple of police officers were talking to a man, dressed in plain clothes, tats all over his arms, black hat turned backwards.

The man was a caterer, Ralph realized after closer inspection. His name was Scotch, "like the drink," he'd say, "not the tape." Scotch owned a catering service called "Party Fowl." Scotch had catered for the cast and crew several times before and was considered "reliable" when it came to feeding armies of filmmakers with very short notice.

Based on Scotch's mannerisms while talking to the cops, he was torn up by recent events. He was childishly shrugging his shoulders a lot, as well as burying his head into both of his palms.

Connie parked next to the line of vehicles.

While Connie waited in the car, Ralph stepped outside and waved down one of the production assistants. He asked the PA what was going on. Before the PA could answer, Ralph witnessed Rob being wheeled out of the hanger on a gurney. His face was pale white. His shirt was covered in blood and vomit. He witnessed other members of the production team being wheeled out, including a young lady who worked in wardrobe, as well as one of the lighting guys. Each one looked as if they were at death's door.

As Ralph stood in shock, he watched one of the first vans drive away with a couple of sick crewmembers.

The van drove past him.

What caught his eye was the driver.

He knew her face.

Most importantly, he knew her story.

His heart sank into the bottom of his gut from the sight of the empty expression on her face.

And at that very moment, he realized that he was next on her list.

☾

ACCORDING to doctors, the crewmembers experienced probably one of the worst cases of food poisoning that they had ever seen before. Apparently, the red curry chicken was infested with toxioplexuses—or best known as "snake worms." Rob had to undergo surgery to remove part of his intestine, which left him with a colostomy bag. Many crewmembers were sick with dysentery, severe vomiting, as well as dehydration. Tragically, one of the crewmembers, a screenplay supervisor named Geraldo, died from complications. Most of the crewmembers would be out for the duration of the shoot, which, by the way, was looking grimmer by the hour.

THE next day, after an entire day of rumors and speculation, Sergio Beneventi released a statement, first address-
ing the many pitfalls of the production and how it had
been a disaster from the very get-go, and second, in his
most deepest sincerity, announcing his departure from
the project.

Following the statement, which caught many off
guard, producers rushed to find a new director to replace
Sergio Beneventi.

They wound up going with Ellery Nitesprig, whose
name had been floating around to direct an *Effigy* movie
for the past few years; however, at the very last minute, in
fact, the morning of an urgent meeting with the producers after flying from London, England, to Los Angeles,
Ellery caught a case of cold feet and withdrew her name
from the project. Her reasons were that she experienced
one of the most horrific, most vivid nightmares the night
before inside her Los Angeles hotel, which she'd later describe in a memoir as a three hundred pound incubus sitting on her chest in what she could only conclude as the
phenomenon known as "sleep paralysis."

For better or worse, Ellery's replacement was veteran
director, Howard Goldspeed, well known for directing
under a tight budget. He was also known as sort of a drill
sergeant-type of a director, this sort of rare auteur in the
film industry, who often times got under actors' skin with
his peddle-to-the-metal style of filmmaking.

On the way to the set, Howard was involved in a
deadly car wreck that ended up taking his life, as well as
the two passengers in the car.

The only survivor was the driver.

Those who had tenaciously worked on the project
knew Howard's car wreck wasn't an accident. It was far
from an accident.

AFTER the tragic demise of Howard Goldspeed, as well as the many whose lives were destroyed before him, the producers finally decided to make a decision. Instead of ending the production, the producers thought it was best to put a "temporary halt" on the current production, which would allow the cast and crewmembers to take a much-needed break in order for those in charge to reassess the situation.

Everybody involved in the project could see the end coming.

For most, they thought the decision was like delaying the inevitable.

PRESENT
Lakefront, Michigan

MATHER and Ludlow arrived at a small town few miles outside Philip's Head.

Having been mostly quiet throughout most of the drive, Mather finally broke the silence with Ludlow after Ludlow accused his partner as "cheap" because he preferred fast food.

"I watched one of those movies late last night," he said.

With disdain, Ludlow sipped from his "cheap" watered down coffee.

"Which one?"

"Number four."

"You must be talking about *The Repentance of Don Juan.*"

"That's the one," he said.

"So, what you'd think?" asked Ludlow.

"Kind of slow, if you want to know the truth. I turned it off about thirty minutes into it. Couldn't get into it."

"You get through the interrogation scene with his first victim?"

"You mean the woman who had her *uterus* removed?"

"Yeah," Ludlow said.

"Part of it."

"Man," Ludlow said more excitedly. "You missed the best part."

Mather was still stuck on one part of the story.

"Help me try to understand this," he said, thinking about that one scene in the movie. "So, if this Don Juan character is spreading his so-called 'demon seed' to all these women in order to create an entire population of baby Don Juans, right, why the hell does he remove certain women's uteruses?"

"He only removes the uteruses of those women whom he considers unworthy of bearing his seed," Ludlow said in a know-it-all way. "If you continue to watch the story, he also goes after men too."

"So, what? Lemme guess. He cuts off their balls?"

"More or less," Ludlow said, smirking.

"Then, how is he able to control people?"

"Through the bloodline," Ludlow said to Mather. "In the first one, the 'Final Girl,' Carolina tries to sever the bloodline, only to later realize that she'd have to destroy an entire population to do so. You have to remember Don Juan has been around for ages and throughout centuries, he's impregnated over thousands, even millions of women, using the disguise of other men. Have you seen the first *Effigy*?"

"Parts," Mather said.

Ludlow replied, "You have to watch the first one, otherwise you won't have a clue as to what's going on."

"Maybe that's why I was so confused."

"In the first *Effigy*, Don Juan's spirit lives inside an effigy that was created by an ancient sorceress known as 'La Guardia.' Many years later," Ludlow said with a fan-like enthusiasm, "his presence is accidentally brought back to life by recent protests and the unearthing of his legacy. All across the country, statues of Don Juan have been torn down or defaced. The movie starts out with a curator discovering the ancient effigy inside storage in the back of a museum. The curator accidentally rips part of the effigy, which, in return, releases his spirit which has been confined to the effigy for many decades. Don Juan ends up taking possession of another man, the boyfriend of the main character, Carolina Reyes."

"The possession part is what I don't get," Mather said over Ludlow. "If he's able to control people through his blood or whatever—"

"—The blood whisperer."

"Whatever." Mather reached back inside his thoughts. "Why does the mob rise up against him at the end?"

"Well," his partner said plainly, "it's simple: free-will. The act of not being controlled. Choosing your own fate."

Finally, after trying to make sense of *The Effigy*, they finally arrived at the townhouse where Liana and Arely were temporarily living.

Mather turned to Ludlow, who remained deep in thought.

"What is it?" asked Mather.

"Nothing."

Mather shook his head at Ludlow's coyness and shut off the ignition.

"I was thinking about our boy, Muddy," he said before Mather stepped out of the vehicle.

"What about him?"

"Did some more digging on him," he said to Mather, as he followed suit and stepped out of the car. "Did you know those who knew Muddy thought he was responsible for his girlfriend's death—"

"—She tripped and fell," Mather said, stopping midway through his answer. "We've been over this already."

"Yeah, but it can't be a coincidence."

"Well," he said, thinking more, "it could just be karma."

"Or," Ludlow said, wearing that same smirk on his face, "Don Juan isn't just a fictional character from a movie."

"I seriously think this man has gone straight to your head, Giraud."

"Most of Blair's friends and family members were certain that she didn't fall, yet she was pushed off the cliff. Nine times out of ten, you take a man with a violent history, sure enough the violence doesn't go away. Sure, there are some who find outlets for it. For others, the violence just festers inside them until an outside force tempts them into acting upon their deepest, darkest desires," Ludlow said, trailing off.

"You're losing it," Mather said, somewhat jokingly. "You know that?"

Ludlow snapped out of his daze and turned to his partner, "*What if* there was somebody out there who knew the truth about Zappa and his violent past and this certain somebody decided to get back at him?"

"If so," Mather said, as he leaned over the roof of the car, "that's not karma, Giraud."

"Then was it?"

"That's revenge, my friend," Mather said, closing the door behind him.

☾

MATHER could see a dark figure moving behind the peephole.

He stood guard from the sound of claws violently scratching behind the door.

After another round of knocking, the door finally cracked open.

Holding back Duke, a baggy-eyed Liana poked her head outside.

"Detective Mather," she said, cracking a groggy-looking smile.

"How you holding up, Ms. Bodums?" asked Mather.

"All right, I guess." She held the door farther open once she realized it was just the two detectives and not reporters. "Arely and I are just trying to settle in."

Duke, who had recognized the detective's scent from the other day, made an attempt to pounce on Mather with its tongue out, ready for licks and kisses.

"Easy, Duke," Liana said, restraining the Labrador by the collar.

"You remember my partner," Mather said, pointing at Ludlow, "Giraud Ludlow."

"Yes," Liana said quietly, holding out a free hand for the detective to shake. "Nice to see you again," he said, shaking Ludlow's hand. "Would you two like to come in?"

"Yes," Mather said, flashing his brow. "Please."

As the two detectives entered the house, Liana ordered them to take off their shoes. The detectives removed their shoes and placed them on the rug where two other pairs of shoes rested.

Liana asked the detectives if they would like a cup of coffee.

They kindly agreed.

As Mather made his way into the living room with a much calmer Duke, he couldn't help but noticed an empty bottle of Vodka in the trashcan.

Mather asked how Arely was doing; and at first, Liana was rather hesitant to respond to the question about Arely, who was currently upstairs in her bedroom.

"These past couple of weeks have been really hard on her," Liana said, preparing three cups of coffee along the edge of the kitchen.

Detective Mather cut straight to the chase and stated the reasons for his visit. Which, he figured, would be best for both Liana and Arely to hear.

Liana fetched Arely from upstairs.

Arely, who looked as though she had spent the entire night drinking, finally dragged herself downstairs and sat on the edge of the couch across from Detective Mather, who was sitting in the love chair, and Detective Ludlow, who was standing next to the fireplace.

Mather was well aware of Arely's hangover; however, Ludlow, on the other hand, thought maybe she had the flu.

Once Liana brought the coffee into the living room, Mather informed her and Arely about Ralph's murderers and how two of them were dead and one of them, a man named Weston Cloverfield, who worked at Gray Bend Quarry in the town of Thumb Point, was currently being held after having confessed to the beating of Ralph, which, according to investigators, ultimately led to his death.

Liana was first to break down.

Arely appeared more in a state of shock rather than upset.

Liana made her way over to Arely and embraced her; and together, they cried in each other's arms.

Even though Mather felt as though Liana and Arely could now find closure, a part of him—the seasoned part that is, the part where traits like cynicism and apathy commonly interwove between one another—knew it wasn't quite over (it never was) and that there was still a piece missing from the puzzle.

☾

AFTER trying to make sense as to why Weston Cloverfield and the two other men, J.J. Kowalski and Marland V. Zappa, murdered Ralph Hood on the same night he returned home from Wilmington, North Carolina, especially after going through all of the haunting details leading up to Hood's death, the two detectives said their goodbyes and told both Liana and Arely that they would be in touch.

As Mather was exiting the townhouse, he grabbed his shoes from the rug. He couldn't help but notice one shoe in particular, the pink Sketchers that belonged to Arely. One of the shoes was overturned. Mather figured he must've accidentally knocked it over on its side when he was placing his shoes on the rug. He looked closer at the pink Sketchers. On the bottom of the shoe was the old, faded sticker of an ANON mask stuck to the worn tread. He backtracked and combed through his thoughts until he realized where he had seen that face. *The doorbell video*, he thought. That *face* in the *bushes*. . .

LUDLOW was first to speak as he and his partner made their way back to the car, which was parked outside the townhouse.

"Arely seems to be taking her father's death pretty rough."

Mather didn't respond for he was too deep in thought.

Ludlow was quick to acknowledge his partner's pensive mien.

"What's up with you?" he asked, as he opened the passenger door.

"Say," Mather said, still thinking about that sticker, "where did Arely say she was at the night of Ralph's death?"

"She was staying in Lansing with Liana and her brother," Ludlow said foolishly. "Why do you ask?"

"Nothing."

For Mather, it wasn't nothing.

It was everything.

THE NIGHT OF
Wilmington, North Carolina

STOPPING himself from pulling out his hair, Ralph paced back and forth through the suite until making the decision to call Liana.

He sat on the edge of the bed, grabbed the phone from the nightstand, and as he was about to hit the green phone icon on the screen, he hesitated.

"What do I even say?" Ralph asked himself.

Honestly, he didn't know what to say.

He thought about how to even start the conversation.

The more he thought about calling Liana, the more his mind raced.

Without thinking, he hit the call button.

Liana answered after the second ring.

"I thought you were going to text me," she said.

"I wanted to hear your voice," Ralph said.

There was a pause on the other end of the line.

"Ralph," Liana said with concern, "what's going on? Arely just told me there was a rumor going around that they were going to pull the plug."

In a way, Ralph wasn't the only one who wished they had; however, the very thought of breaking contract and allowing Hollywood to have their way with him and basically, erase him, still weighed heavily not only on his mind, but also his entire body. Unable to hold down any food, he felt sick to the core. However, a part of him didn't care and wanted nothing to do with this place anymore.

After careful consideration, Ralph said, "They're going to put it on halt for a while until things settle down."

"That's terrible," Liana said, "but it's totally understandable, especially with everything that has happened. Have you talked to Shawn?"

"Yeah," he said. "Just got off the phone with him."

Once more, Ralph thought about telling Liana the truth, about his past, and the person whom he thought was responsible for all of this madness, even though *madness* sounded like a word used flippantly without having any grounds in reality. This was *beyond* madness, he knew.

"Listen, Liana," Ralph said before Liana could speak, "I want you and Arely to stay with Larry for a couple of days."

"Why?" asked Liana. "Is something wrong?"

Ralph paused, which left Liana even more concerned.

"Ralph, you're scaring me—"

"—Don't be," he said. "I'm being cautious. That's all."

"Well, I can give him a call tomorrow. You know how busy the man is—"

"—No," Ralph said over Liana. "I want you to leave tonight."

"Ralph, are we in danger?"

"I don't know," he said, trailing off. "Maybe."

"What are you going to do?"

"I'm going to hop on a flight as soon as I finish up here," he said, standing to his feet. "Meanwhile," he said, walking to the window, "I want you and Arely to get in the car and drive to your brother's. He'll understand."

"How about you?" asked Liana. "Will you have protection?"

"Yeah," Ralph said, as he peeked outside at the dark car parked on the curb. "As a precaution, Shawn set me up with these two bodyguards."

"Bodyguards?" Liana made a mouthy noise on the other end. "Serious?"

"Yeah," he said. "But don't worry about me. I'll be fine."

☾

ONCE Ralph got off the phone with Liana and finished packing, he headed downstairs where he bumped into one of the actors, Anthony Wince, who was playing Glad's fiancé, Ozzie, in the film.

"You heading out?" asked Anthony, who looked as if he had just gotten back from the pool.

"I'm afraid so," Ralph said dismally. "How about you? When you leaving?"

Anthony adjusted the damp beach towel around his neck.

"Tomorrow probably," he said. "It sucks 'cuz I was really starting to like this place. Now, it feels like we're all hanging in limbo."

"Well, you'll soon learn that most of the job consists of hanging around."

Grinning, Anthony flicked his head in a nod.

"You look like you can't wait to get outta here."

"I guess you can say that I'm taking advantage of the time off," Ralph said to Anthony, who followed with "I hear that."

Ralph glanced behind Anthony at the dark silhouette standing behind a tree along the street.

Displaying an even wider grin on his face, Anthony couldn't agree more with Ralph.

"Who hasn't, right?"

Ralph drew his attention back to Anthony first, then turned to the dark figure, who was no longer behind the tree.

"If you're going to stay in the business long enough like I have, Tony, you're going to learn that any chance you can spend time with your loved ones is a gift. You should already know this business isn't so forgiving to a steady man. If anything, it has a funny way of revealing the cracks in relationships."

"I don't plan on going 'steady' anytime soon, bro," Anthony said, laughing. "That's for sure. I swear this has probably been the craziest few months I've ever had on a job." Ralph's previous comment inspired an image in his head. "Say," he said, "have you seen Felicia?"

"Last time I saw her, she was with you."

"Right," he said, trailing off. "I checked her room, but she wasn't there. She must off doing something. You know Felicia. That one's a busy bee."

"Listen, Anthony, I got a flight to catch," Ralph said, making his way toward the exit.

"Well, damn," Anthony said, holding out his hand, "the way things are going this may be our last time seeing each other."

Ralph adjusted his luggage in his other hand and shook Anthony's hand.

"Take care of yourself."

"Good luck to you, Ralph," Anthony said and wished Ralph a safe trip home to Liana and his daughter.

Strangely, Ralph felt lifeless after chatting with Anthony, even though he reminded Ralph of himself. If anybody should know, it was Ralph who once shared that carpe diem "living in the moment" attitude.

As the night dragged on, a part of Ralph felt as though those "moments" were starting to catch up with him.

With his luggage in hand, Ralph left Morning Star Suites and made his way to the black town car parked along the side of 3rd Street.

Two heavyset bodyguards stepped out of the car and greeted Ralph.

They introduced themselves to Ralph: The first bodyguard went by the name "Boxer" Brown, but most people called him Box; the second one, the driver, was "Stanley" Richard. Boxer held the backdoor open for Ralph while Stanley helped him with his luggage by placing it in the trunk.

Once the car was packed and Ralph remained secured in the backseat behind Boxer, Stanley drove off.

Driving away, Ralph turned to the dark figure in the corner of his eye.

On the cracked sidewalk stood Alexa Knowles, who was staring down at him with an empty expression on her face. Her eyes even emptier, deeply hellish.

His heart fell into what felt like a void inside his stomach; and for a moment, his heart skipped a beat.

It was at that very moment when Ralph understood the severity of the current situation. Alexa wouldn't stop coming after him, yet even strangely, he knew she wasn't alone on the sidewalk. The amber streetlight cast an even greater and much darker shadow along the sidewalk. She had help from beyond the realm of reality, the kind that shielded her from accountability.

On the contrary, Ralph felt weak, vulnerable, exposed, regardless of being in the company of two chiseled men, who, more than likely, could bench-press twice his own body weight.

(

RALPH kept glancing over his shoulder at the car behind them while he was being driven from downtown to the airport.

"Is something wrong?" asked Stanley, as he shot his eyes at Ralph through the rear view mirror.

"No," he said. "I just want to get the hell outta here."

"We're almost there."

Once they reached Martin Luther King Junior Parkway, the drive from Morning Star to ILM airport was only a few minutes.

Once they arrived at ILM, Ralph and Boxer waited inside the airport while Stanley dropped off the rental car.

During the wait, Ralph became extremely paranoid despite his security detail. He swore he saw Alexa and another man entering the airport.

Turns out it wasn't her.

At least that was what Ralph thought.

Right now, he couldn't even trust his own eyes.

☾

AFTER making one stop in Charlotte, Ralph's plane landed around nine o'clock at GRR (Gerald R. Ford International Airport).

Even though Ralph had Boxer and Stanley watching over him, he didn't at all feel safe; in fact, during the entire flight from Charlotte to Grand Rapids, Ralph saw— or at least, he thought he saw—Alexa on the same airplane as him.

Walking through the terminal, Ralph thought he saw her in the glassy reflection of an airline sign.

Being so close to home now, he decided to confront her. He stormed toward Alexa, who was standing near the restrooms. He called out to her, "Hey!" As he was about to grab her by the arm, the woman looked up from her phone. She was not Alexa, but rather a woman who looked similar to Alexa. Ralph apologized for startling the young woman and followed the bodyguards from the terminal.

Upon arrival, the rental car was waiting for Ralph and his two bodyguards outside the airport.

Once Ralph was secured inside the car, Stanley, who was more worried about his client's behavior, which was becoming more erratic by the hour, drove off.

Ralph turned his shoulder and looked through the back window of the rental car and as before, saw yet another car following them.

☾

ONLY a couple of miles before they arrived in Philip's Head, Ralph lost the same car that had been following them from GRR; however, despite not seeing the car, it was clear that he couldn't go home. Alexa knew where he lived and more than likely, she eased back in order not to draw any attention.

With Alexa on his mind, Ralph told Stanley there was going to be a change in plans and instead of driving to the house, he told him to drop him off at a friend's place. That friend was Demoris Forte, or "Pinkie."

As soon as they pulled up to the rundown house, it became clear to Boxer and Stanley that their client had other intentions; however, it wasn't their place to question their client.

Ralph told Boxer and Stanley to wait inside the car while he visited with his so-called "friend."

Cautiously, he exited the car and walked across the desolate street to Pinkie's house. He knocked on the door, but received no answer from Pinkie. Losing his patience, Ralph banged on the door and followed by ringing the doorbell, which was broke. He resorted back to banging on the door.

Eventually, Pinkie answered the door with a pistol concealed behind his back.

"Don't you ever pound on my door again," Pinkie said resentfully. "Thought your ass was the fucking po-lice, man."

"Sorry," Ralph said and attempted to enter the house.

"What'chu doing, fool?" said Pinkie, holding out his hand.

"You holding?"

"What kind of question is that?" Pinkie furrowed his brow. "Of course, I'm holding. But you ain't coming in."

"I need just a hit, Pink," he said, looking around the street in paranoid.

"Lil' heads-up would've been nice. What in the hell makes you think I don't have plans tonight?"

"Come on, Pink," Ralph said, catching the glow of the TV in the living room. "I can hear Eric Cartman from *South Park* on your TV. You ain't got plans. And you don't have any company either."

"What makes you so sure, Don fucking Juan?"

Ralph glanced at Pinkie's attire, which wasn't much.

"'Cuz you're dressed in your fucking underwear and Steph's car ain't here."

Pinkie noticed the car parked on the street.

"You take a UBER or something?"

"They're just my chauffeur for the night. You gonna let me in or not?"

Arching himself upward on his tippy toes, Pinkie leaned over Ralph's shoulder for a closer look.

"You can't stay long, though," he said and waved Ralph aside.

☾

THE Glock was the only weapon Pinkie was packing.

After Ralph shot up, he took a hit of meth. Which was known on the street as a "screwball."

Sitting on the couch while embracing the hit, Pinkie showcased to Ralph one of his new weapons that he recently added to a vast gun collection: a M16 assault rifle with a M203 grenade launcher attachment.

"A'ight, Tony Montana," Ralph said with squinty red eyes, "why you need a gun like that? You plan on defending your home from the Colombian cartel?"

"Hey, man," he said. "You never know."

Ralph nodded at the TV.

"Can you flip it on something else?" asked Ralph.

Pinkie flipped through channels until he wound up on a previously recorded footage from Rhodes's visit to a car manufacturer in Michigan earlier that night. The headline: "Rhodes launches in new campaign for 2020." In the clip, Rhodes unveiled his slogan for his campaign, which was "Building a safer road forward."

Rhodes could only get out a couple of words from his divisive rhetoric before Ralph switched off the TV.

"Enough out of you, asshole," Pinkie mumbled to himself and turned it back to *South Park*.

"Put it back. . . " Ralph said, drifting off.

Ralph's head flopped back.

Pinkie laughed at Ralph's sudden highness, took a rip from a bong, sat back in his recliner, and watched yet another episode of *South Park* until eventually he dozed off.

As Ralph's head flopped back and forth, he felt a sudden pressure against his chest. His head snapped forward and there, sitting directly on top of him, was Alexa Knowles.

He must've been hallucinating her, he first suspected. *This isn't real*, he thought. *She isn't real.*

Then, he questioned whether or not the drugs were laced with hallucinogens.

Struggling to catch his breath, Alexa told him a tedious story about how she ended up with the scars around neck, which looked like deep wrinkles. She said that she got 'em when she was born—'86, as Ralph recalled. Same year an accident at a nuclear power station in Chernobyl resulted in a radioactive contamination, which left many causalities in its wake,

During her birth, her mother, Nevaeh's close friend, Shelly, who was unable to raise Alexa due to personal issues, underwent serious complications. The umbilical cord wrapped around Baby Alexa's neck, preventing her from breathing. According to doctors, Alexa's heart stopped beating for three minutes; but to her, those three minutes lasted for what felt like three hundred years. She spoke about a specific world, a dark one, where she was born. In this world, Alexa lived years as a baby who was raised by a massive serpent known as "Sheik." The great serpent protected her from all the dangers of this dark world. Eventually, after witnessing many battles between Sheik and the monsters that attempted to kill—or better yet, eat her—Alexa was thrust into yet another world, Ralph's world. An old soul thrown into the body of a baby girl,

As years went by and Alexa began to mature, images of that dark world randomly appeared in her mind; however, she couldn't make any sense of them even if she tried. It wasn't until a few years after her grandfather introduced her to the actor, who had gone from the man who wore a mask in a low budget horror movie to an A-list actor of one of the most popular movie franchises, that Alexa started to piece together the images and the world in which they originated.

While Alexa continued to explain the origin of the marks around her neck, he heard a *pounding* at the door.

The pounding intensified, drowning out Alexa's voice, as well as the sounds of *South Park* running in the background.

With his eyes swirling around the sockets, Ralph glanced at Pinkie, who was passed out in the recliner.

He tried to call out to Pinkie, but he couldn't find any air to speak.

☾

RALPH woke up gasping for air.

He didn't know whether or not he was still dreaming. All he knew was that Alexa was real. He could still hear her voice in his head.

Trying to shake off the high, he glanced over at Pinkie, who was lying motionless in the recliner. He got up from the couch and checked on Pinkie, whose arms had been stuck by six needles, Ralph counted.

Ralph tapped Pinkie on the shoulder. His skin was cold to the touch and left no impression. He searched for a pulse but couldn't find a single one. He immediately knew Pinkie was dead. He didn't know who was responsible, if it was, in fact, Alexa who stuck six needles into his arms. What Ralph did know was that Pinkie wouldn't have taken his own life, wasn't the type. The man shared stories with Ralph about building a castle on the lake and calling it "Fort Pink." Ralph thought about calling the police, but decided not to after realizing how suspicious Pinkie's death appeared. They'd pin his death on me, he thought.

Panicked, Ralph rushed toward the front door and ran outside. Halfway toward the parked car, he saw Stanley first, who wasn't moving. Then, Boxer, who was hunched over against the dashboard.

As he arrived at the car, he found Stanley and Boxer with gunshot wounds in their heads and chest. Two of the bullets penetrated the front windshield, leaving behind tiny holes with a spider web shape around it.

He opened the driver's side door and pulled Stanley's dead body from the car seat. He searched for a key inside the ignition but couldn't find any. He checked Stanley's pocket, but came up empty. He checked Boxer's pockets next. Nothing but only a pack of gum and a couple of coins.

Left with little to no option—the most obvious one being to call the cops but Ralph wasn't in his right state of mind—Ralph fled on foot. He stopped a couple of times to catch his breath. Eventually, after walking several blocks, he made it to The Liquid Lounge where it was fairly crowded with mostly locals.

He ordered a beer and hung out at the bar.

Keeping to himself while, at the same time, trying to keep a close eye on his surroundings, he nervously downed the beer and ordered another. The bartender struck small talk with Ralph, asking him how his night was going. Clearly, from his strung out appearance, Ralph was having quite a night. Ralph excused himself and used the restroom where he bumped into a wide-eyed guy with greasy, stringy shoulder-length hair who was doing lines of dirty-looking cocaine off one of the vanities. He asked

Ralph if he'd like a bump. Without thinking, he agreed and snorted up a couple of lines with a one-dollar bill. The guy narrowed his eyes and looked closer at Ralph and after a second study, recognized him.

"Hey, you're that guy from the TV commercial."

"I'm afraid you got the wrong guy," Ralph said, feeling the collar of his shirt where, before, his sunglasses were hanging.

"Nah, nah," the guy said, pointing at Ralph. "You're the fucker who sells the cars on TV."

In a way, he was somewhat relieved that the guy was completely out of his mind. He ignored the guy and searched for his sunglasses but couldn't find them anywhere. He suddenly remembered leaving the sunglasses on the coffee table at Pinkie's house. Ralph's thoughts started racing out of control again: *What if cops find my sunglasses at Pinkie's house? They'd trace my fingerprints on the lens back to me. If so, then they'd bring me in, stick me under the spotlight, and question why I left Pinkie for dead. Most importantly, they'd question me as to why, a clean man, would be hanging out at a junkie's house. Only guilty people run. . .*

Ralph left the restroom, the guy shouting out behind him.

As before, he ignored him, went back to the bar to pay his tab, and left before drawing too much attention.

Thinking that Pinkie's place was swarming with cops, Ralph walked as fast as his legs would take him down Hamlet Street until he reached 15ᵗʰ Street. From a distance, he could see Pinkie's. He didn't see any cruisers in the area.

Maybe they were camped out somewhere, waiting for Ralph to return.

Before his thoughts once more raced out of control, he stopped on the street corner to catch his breath. He heard footsteps behind him.

In the night darkness, Ralph witnessed the three drunken figures quickly approaching him.

In one of their hands, he recognized a sharp pocket-size-object glistening from the streetlight above.

Ralph recognized the blade as not a knife, but rather a sword.

And the darkly dressed man holding it was a fucking ninja.

PRESENT
Philip's Head, Michigan

SPREAD out along his coffee table were the two files on Marland V. Zappa and J.J. Kowalski. Each file was opened, the contents inside, including photographs taken at the crime scene of each one of the deceased, messily scattered everywhere.

Among the deathly images Mather spotted was the one image he had been searching for throughout the night. He picked up the photo and studied it closer. In the photo, which was taken at Muddy's house the day his body was discovered by a UPS driver, the "Guy Fawkes"-like face was engraved along a wooden post of the banister. Mather put aside the photo and searched through the photos, which were taken at the quarry the day Mather himself put a bullet straight through J.J. Kowalski's dome. Throughout his mad search, he couldn't find any connection.

Frustrated, he removed his tired eyes from the photos of the quarry and went into the kitchen to grab a drink. He needed something stiff. He reached into the top cabinet, grabbed himself a bottle of *El Valiente* blanco tequila. He grabbed a juice glass, poured himself two fingers worth, and downed the blanco tequila. He poured himself another glass and took the glass back into the living room.

He set the glass on the coffee table and continued to comb through photos. It was that moment when he reached for his drink that he saw the same face underneath the glass. The face appeared distorted and magnified in size from the shape of the glass. Inching closer to the table, he carefully lifted the glass from the photo.

There, Mather found the same face as the one on the leg of the banister post. In the photo, J.J.'s corpse lay in the middle of the dirt road. In the distance behind the corpse, the rock formation along The Pit was in the shape of a face. He compared the two photos, the one taken in Muddy's foyer, then the one he held in his hand.

Startled by his findings, Mather grabbed the phone and called Ludlow, who was half-asleep, and answered before the call went to voicemail.

As he had been known to do, Mather cut straight to the chase: "Liana said the last time she spoke with Hood he sounded scared over the phone. Like someone might've been following him."

"Give it a rest, Chris," said Ludlow, voice low and raspy. "We got the guys who killed Ralph. That's all that matters."

He laid out the two photos with the two matching faces before him.

"*What if* there's a connection between Muddy's death and Kowalski's death? Like, I don't know, someone else trying to clean up his or her tracks? *What if* the real killer is *still* out there, Giraud? You heard what Kowalski's roommate said, how Kowalski was talking all kinds of crazy a couple of days before the night he and his goons jumped Ralph, then, afterwards, he said he wasn't the same person. He acted like someone was following him, remember?"

"Yeah," Ludlow said, starting to wake up. "Us, Chris. We were right on his tail and he was getting spooked. No surprise there."

"People like J.J. Kowalski live in the heat—"

"—Listen, Chris," Ludlow said, losing patience, "if Hershel finds out you're still working the case, then he's gonna to have your ass planted behind a desk until your retirement, which, by the way, isn't far off—"

Another "what if" question came to mind.

As the phone started to slide from his shoulder, Mather adjusted his grip over the phone and said, "I'll talk to you later."

He hung up on Ludlow and grabbed the iPad from his bag. He pulled out the iPad, opened it by using his thumbprint, and searched through his recent videos.

Scrolling through videos, he finally came across the "Doorbell Cam" video. He played the video, fast-forwarding to the end. He reached the part in the video where the face appeared in the bushes behind the stop sign. He paused the video, grabbed the two other photos with faces, and held them up to the iPad.

Once he connected all the dots, he didn't even have to utter the word.

But he did anyway.

"*Bingo*," he said.

THE NIGHT OF
Philip's Head, Michigan

PROPPED up against the curb of the sidewalk, Ralph used the bottom corner of his shirt to wipe the blood from his face. The place where he touched along his face felt incredibly numb, despite the throbbing pain. He examined several of the cuts along his sides and forearms. Each one needed stitches for sure and except for the ones along his hands, several of stab wounds were deep enough to draw concern.

Beyond the ringing in his ears, the sounds of car keys jiggling caused him to turn his shoulder where he witnessed a dark figure walking from the trees, which lined one side of the street.

Finally, Alexa, who was wearing a black scarf around her neck, appeared in the hazy streetlight.

In her hand was a set of car keys. She was showcasing them like a prize.

"Too bad you don't have these," she said, flashing a sinister smile.

Ralph turned toward the direction where he last saw the car parked in front of Pinkie's house. The slightest motion of turning caused the pain to shoot through his body. He grabbed his side. Several of his ribs were broken, he knew. Even taking in small breaths hurt. The pain in his neck whenever he turned it was even greater. He felt as if he had a crick in his neck and whenever he turned his head, it felt as though the tip of a knife was twisting through crushed bone, causing hot pain to radiate up his neck. He was in a great deal of pain, despite the drugs in his system. Once they wore off, though, Ralph knew he was going to be in a world of hurt.

From a distance, he saw Pinkie's house, but no car.

"Hello, Alexa," he said depressingly.

Speaking hurt as well.

He helped ease the pain by looking forward.

The pain wasn't as bad as long as he didn't make any sudden movements.

He didn't even bother to acknowledge Alexa as she approached from behind.

"Looks like they did quite a number on you," she said, pointing out the injuries all over Ralph's body.

"So was it you who put them up to this?" asked Ralph, still grimacing.

"Well, not exactly," she said smartly. "I've recently made friends with a particular individual who has a special talent for *persuading* the weak-minded."

"Good for you," Ralph said. "So what? Now, you're here to finish me off? Is that it? Well, what you waiting for? Put me out of my misery, will you?"

Alexa stood behind Ralph, stopped a few feet away, and said to him, "I'll let the public decide what they're going to do with you? My guess is that they'll tear you apart once they find who the real monster is. Face it, Ralph: your side of the story isn't a popular one."

"Is that right?"

"How do you explain to people the reason behind raping a seventeen year old girl?"

"Get the hell out of here," Ralph seethed, as he grabbed his side. "You and I know that's bullshit—"

"A forty-six year old man forcibly steals the virginity of a seventeen year old girl without her consent," Alexa said over Ralph. "If that doesn't count as rape, I don't know what does anymore. You knew I was underage and you continued to have your way with me."

"You wanted it—"

"—I was seventeen, Ralph."

"Why didn't you go to the police sooner?" Ralph asked but didn't give Alexa time to answer. "You think people are going to believe you sixteen years later?"

"I was seventeen," Alexa repeated as if Ralph didn't hear her the first time.

In defense, Ralph returned, "So, this is what it's all about? Revenge? Why not come out, make up some exaggerated story about me, share it with the public, and tell them how the *evil* man broke your fragile heart? Also, don't leave out the part about how *obsessed* your were with me."

"When you're in love," Alexa said, "what's the difference?"

"It's been sixteen years and I see you still haven't moved on with your life. I have—"

"—Move on? How I am supposed to move on with my life when every Halloween I have to relive what you did to me? I can't even walk down the fucking street without seeing a Don Juan figure hanging in a storefront window? Did you know people are now putting up your decorations in September? September for Fuck's sake! That's two full months of having to relive this nightmare!"

"You did all this to ruin a movie you hadn't even seen yet?"

Ralph laughed, but the pain was so great that his laughter turned into groans.

"What's so goddamn funny?" asked Alexa with a flash of anger on her face.

"They were going to kill off Don Juan for good," Ralph said, amused. "Let's just say he would've gone out with. . . " he grimaced, ". . . with a bang."

"No," Alexa said. "They would've found a way to bring you back. They *always* do."

Over the silence, Ralph thought about the last couple of months and all of the planning that must've gone on in order to pull off such an elaborate scheme.

Fighting off the pain, he said, "I didn't force you to fall in love with me, Alexa."

Using the curb as support, he managed to stand to his feet.

As he clutched his injuries, mainly his side, he faced Alexa, who was holding a gun down by her waistside.

"Go ahead," he said, holding out his arms. "If you're gonna kill me, then do it already. But I'll tell you this: It's not going to change a damn thing."

Alexa held the gun to his head.

"Killing you would only complicate the story," Alexa said. "If I kill you tonight, then tomorrow the entire world will mourn you. Networks will be running *The Effigy* marathon in honor of your legacy. But once the world finds out that it was *you* who sabotaged the production, *you* who ruined the lives of so many people, *you* who ran away and hid without owning up to your mistakes, *you* who put a hex on the movie, they'll burn you at the stake. Any future productions will end in more tragedy. People will be so freaked out about making another *Effigy* that they won't touch it with a ten foot pole."

"How exactly are you going to convince people that it was me?"

"I'm not," Alexa said blankly and pointed the gun at his head. "You are."

"Like hell I am—

"—You're gonna confess to the world that you made it look like Lykaios was the one responsible when, in fact, it was *you* who wanted to bring down the franchise; and everything in between, the strange events, we'll just call it bad luck."

"You might as well shoot me now cuz I ain't confessing to a crime I didn't commit."

Alexa shrugged.

"It's the only way," she said. "Everything has been set in motion. You confess. You go to jail and spend the rest of your life behind bars. Whatever piece of property with your name on it will rot with you. Nobody will want anything to do with you ever again. Once the trial is over and you're exactly where you belong, I'll be able to finally live my life without having to see your goddamn face whenever I flip another fucking channel on TV. . . "

With the gun aimed at Ralph, Alexa stepped closer.

Clutching his side, Ralph backpedaled into the street.

Alexa took yet another step, forcing another step from Ralph.

"When you were getting high, you snapped and went on a killing spree," she said, her eyes honing in on Ralph's eyes. "First, you killed your junkie friend, but you didn't stop there. Next, you shot and killed your two body-guards. The three men tried to come to their rescue. Unfortunately, they were too late. They kicked your ass anyway. In the struggle, you dropped your gun while they were beating the shit out of you. You managed to find your gun, but they escaped on foot," she stepped even closer, "and then later that night, you found the three men. You shot them dead. Unable to cope with the horrendous crime that you had just committed, you called the cops and turned yourself in—"

"—Alexa," Ralph said, holding up his hands, "there has to be another way—"

A bright headlight shined along the side of Ralph's face.

Grimacing while turning his shoulder, he witnessed a car speeding directly at him.

The car suddenly swerved to the left.

Before Ralph had a chance to move out of the way, the right side of the car plowed into him, catapulting him over the roof of the car. He flipped and spun in the air, his body flopping around like a string-less puppet until he landed headfirst on the street, kissing concrete. His neck snapped in half, the forceful impact pulling him in and out of consciousness.

The car, which was a red 2000 Suzuki Swift, swerved back onto the road before sideswiping a car parked along the side of the road and continued to drive.

As though the driver had finally come to his or her senses, the car came to a stop a few houses down.

Concealed by the shadows outside an overhead street light, a man stepped out of the vehicle and remained close to the driver side. His shadowy face was slack and stupid. He struggled to stand straight for his body wobbled to and fro as if he was intoxicated. The man directed his bloodshot eyes toward the gun in Alexa's hand. The two shared a long stare down before, finally, the driver got back in his vehicle and sped away from the scene.

Alexa walked up to a bloody Ralph and stood over his crooked body.

Struggling to take in a breath, he looked up at Alexa, who was towering over his body and staring down at him with a strange wonder in her eyes.

Shortly after she kneeled down, he released a death gargle.

As the life exited his body, his eyes glazed over.

Alexa's face was the last face he ever saw before his world faded to black.

PRESENT
Lakefront, Michigan

MATHER spent the last six hours camped inside his car, which was parked outside Liana's townhouse. Most of the time was exhausted by waiting for the killer to arrive. He held up the Guy Fawkes-like mask called "Anon" in his hand and studied it carefully.

In the passenger seat sat several copies of the photographs of the face, which were taken at each crime scene. He even had a printout of the pale, grainy face, which was captured by the doorbell camera. If the clerk was right about the theories, Mather wondered to himself, then Arely was possibly next on the killer's list. He knew it couldn't have been a coincidence that Arely stepped on the sticker. If the theories were correct and the face was a mark—a "calling card," if you will—that the killer left behind at crime scenes, then there was no question that the killer had eyes on Arely.

SIX HOURS AGO
Fogg Bay, Michigan

AFTER making the short drive from Philip's Head, Detective Mather arrived at the closest party store in the area. Despite Halloween being days away, the store was fairly quiet. The clerk of the store, a man who went by the name Dex, a tatted up man with thick glasses and a *Game of Thrones*-inspired beard, greeted Mather in the "monster mask" aisle.

As Mather searched for the face from the photos on the wall of the most grotesque, monstrous faces, the store clerk asked the customer if he was looking for anything in particular. He didn't peg Mather as a father, but he asked anyway if he was looking for something spooky for the little one or, maybe, Dex suggested, something kinky for the wife—or hubby.

"Whatever turns you on," he said, leaving Mather more disgusted with Dex's depraved outlook.

Mather ran into these fetish types every now and then. He didn't try to spend anymore time than he needed to in the store figuring what turned the clerk on. He showed Dex the photo.

Dex immediately recognized the face.

"Yeah," he said. "We got that. So, you a hacker or something?"

"Excuse me," Mather said, following Dex down the aisle.

Dex waved off the comment.

Clearly, from Mather's tone, Dex knew Mather wasn't a "hacker."

"Forget I asked," he said, realizing the man following him was a cop.

He arrived at the end of the aisle, kneeled down, and grabbed the white blank faced mask from the bottom of the shelf.

"You're in luck," Dex said, handing Mather the mask. "Last one."

Mather looked over the mask and compared the mask to the face in the photo.

With his eyes narrowing in suspicion, Dex said, "Anon."

Mather furrowed his brow and looked up at the clerk.

"Anon," he said, concealing a grin behind his face. "You know, it's short for anonymous. You've never heard of Anon, have you?"

"Is that what the kids call it these days?" Mather asked, holding up the mask.

"It's not like the kind you're thinking of," the clerk said, making sure nobody was around to hear what he was about to say next. "Story goes: Anon isn't a man or a woman."

"Then, what is it?" asked Mather.

Dex said, "One legend says that it's part vampire, part sorcerer, has the ability to persuade its victims into carrying out sinister deeds by simply coming into contact with its victim. You know, mind control. Probably why so many hackers adopted the blank face look of Anon, rebranded it, and made it their own version. Other legends describe Anon as a giant frog with hallucinogenic secretions who wears the mask to cover up its true identity. In this legend, it's able to control its victims through its saliva, sweat, feces, or you know," his eyes flicked downward. "I know," he said before the detective had a chance to question the authenticity of the legend, "pretty wild stuff, huh? Other legends say Anon comes from another world and for the past hundred years, has been trying to find its way back home or whatever. Others say Anon is some second-rate witch. Rumor has it that it may be a relative of Ms. Necro—"

"Ms. Who?"

"Ms. Necro," he said. "The famous witch from Sinclair Leprieur." He eyed the bulge of what he assumed was a pistol on his hip. "I'm surprised you haven't heard of her, considering, you know, your profession."

"My profession?"

"You're a cop, right?"

"Does that bother you?" asked Mather, squaring up to Dex.

Clearly, *it would if you were up to no good.*

"No," he said innocently. "Not at all."

Mather eyed the mask in his hand.

"So how much is this is actually true?" he asked Dex.

"It's all bullshit," Dex said, leaning closer. "Stories you tell the kids to scare the living shit out of 'em."

Dex laughed, which forced Mather to make an utterance of what sounded like a laugh.

"There's even some theories that Anon is part of an underground covenant of these witch-like creatures whose services are broadcasted over the Internet in encrypted messages and secret code. I mean, how else you think Rhodes got elected into office?"

Mather was taken back by the comment.

"Why do you mean?" he asked.

"There's a conspiracy theory out there that Rhodes obtained Anon's services to get him elected. One respected newspaper ran a story on it last year. But," he said, showing Mather to the cash register, "who knows? Hard to tell what's real these days, you know, because of all fake news, right?

PRESENT
Lakefront, Michigan

MATHER waited and waited.

Once midnight rolled around the corner, the only activity outside the townhouse came from a black cat prowling the night streets in search of a snack.

Feeling discomfort of heartburn creeping up his esophagus from two cups of coffee that he drank earlier that night on an empty stomach, he asked himself the one question that he had been ignoring all night: *What if* the killer wasn't going to show up? *What if* the killer was never going to show up? Instead, planting that sticker on the bottom of Arely's shoe was a distraction to throw the detective off the killer's tail. All Mather had left were a bunch of "what ifs."

But he continued to wait anyway.

THE NIGHT OF
Philip's Head, Michigan

ALEXA left Ralph's body, walked back to the town car parked under a tree a block over, and made sure the trunk was all the way shut by giving it a push opposed to a slam.

She drove to Ralph's house.

Using Ralph's house key, Alexa entered the house. She piddled around the house, mostly looking over picture frames of Ralph's family, including Liana, her dog, Duke, and his daughter, Arely, and her sweet cat, H.P., which were hanging on walls, as well as scattered on tables and lined neatly on the fireplace mantle in the living room.

As Alexa walked down the hallway, she picked up one particular photograph of Ralph inside a workshop with makeup effects all around him. He was standing next to the man who had raised her after the age of six years old, her late grandfather, makeup artist, Bernard Knowles, who was best known throughout his career as the designer of the original mask for Ralph's iconic Don Juan character. In the photo, he and Ralph had their arms wrapped around each other's shoulders as they smiled from ear to ear. From the look on their faces, they looked as if they were having the time of their lives and creating memories that would last a lifetime.

With a whole range of emotions, mostly disgust, Alexa put the picture frame back on the table and made her way into Ralph's office. She looked over all of his work, including his starring role in *The Effigy* series. She pushed aside several torn boxes and dusty movie posters and came across the original effigy, which was used in the original film. She left the office, walked into the kitchen, and searched through the drawers until she found a grill lighter, as well as a can of lighter fluid. She went back to the office and didn't waste anytime dowsing all of Ralph's *Effigy* memorabilia with lighter fluid. She placed the torch to the effigy.

As the flames licked across the contents inside the office, including the effigy, movie posters, books, figurines, action figures, toys, and comic books, Alexa left the office and dowsed areas of the living room with lighter fluid, starting with the drapes and furniture. She first ran a flame underneath the dowsed drapes covering the living room windows and then worked her way through the rest of the living room. Eventually, the entire living room was engulfed in flames.

The fire spread to the bedrooms and the kitchen. Alexa exited from the house before the smoke could overtake her; and from the front yard, watched the house burn in the night darkness.

❦

WITH sounds of sirens screeching from a distance, Alexa drove through the night.

After an hour and a half drive to the northern part of the state, Alexa wound up at Black Bear Lake.

The same black Honda Accord that Alexa had stolen at GRR was parked on a cliff overlooking the rugged lake. In the driver's seat sat her accomplice, Winter Knott, who was wearing an Anon mask, as well as blue jeans and a grease-stained white NASCAR T-shirt underneath a faded jean jacket.

Alexa parked the Lincoln next to the other parked car.

Once she stepped out of the car, Winter exited the other.

"It's done," she said with a slight tremble in her voice.

Winter remained silent and stared at Alexa.

"If you don't believe me, Anon," she said, popping the trunk of the town car, "see for yourself."

She opened up the trunk and showed Winter the two recently deceased bodyguards, Stanley and Boxer, who were cramped inside, spooning each other.

"There," she said. "Happy?"

Winter grabbed the first body, Stanley, by the arms while Alexa grabbed the legs. They carried Stanley to the driver's side where they placed him behind the steering wheel. They did the same for Boxer and placed his body in the passenger seat. Once they two bodies were placed in their correct positions, Winter tied the seat belt tightly around the steering wheel, which prevented it from turning once the gear was switched to drive.

As the car remained in park, Winter grabbed a good-size rock that weighed at least ten pounds, heavy enough to set against the gas peddle.

Once the rock was in place and the car remained in idle-acceleration, Winter closed the doors and through the window, switched the gear from park to drive.

The town car sped off the cliff and plummeted into the lake below.

Standing along the edge of the cliff, Alexa and Winter watched the town car submerge into the water as the rear lights in the back of the car appeared like red devilish eyes slowly fading into darkness.

"Nice work," Alexa said to Winter, who, in return, plucked the index finger from his hand, which transformed into a scaly, reptilian-like hand.

The pinkish, gummy tissue and ligaments underneath the dark greenish scales stretched outward like rubberbands, then, once the human finger was completely removed from its hand, retreated back into a nub of what was once a claw.

Winter tossed the finger into the lake below.

Alexa drew her eyes to the scaly face underneath the Anon mask.

Creepily, Winter redirected its attention toward Alexa.

As Winter stared at Alexa with glossy dark eyes underneath the holes of that ghostly white mask, all she could think about was the ride home.

The silence, she knew, would be anything but comfortable.

☾

AS predicted, after riding through the early morning hours right before dawn in a car filled with uncomfortable silence, Alexa arrived back at GRR.

Before entering the airport, Winter pulled off to the side of the road, parked, and handed Alexa the ticket to EWR (Newark Liberty International Airport).

"*What if* they ask me questions?" asked Alexa, studying the ticket.

Winter held out its scaly hand.

"What?" said Alexa.

Again, Winter held out its scaly hand.

Eventually, Alexa figured out that Winter wanted her hand.

She held her hand.

With its smooth, cold hand, Winter grabbed Alexa's hand and removed the wristwatch from her wrist.

"What are you doing?" asked Alexa.

Winter wound back the time to nine o'clock last night.

"So, that's it?" asked Alexa, looking over the time on her watch. "And what about surveillance cameras? You gonna wave a magic wound over them?"

As though Winter was turned off by Alexa's remark, Winter faced forward.

"Sorry," she said with a heavy sigh. "Anyway," Alexa said, opening the passenger door, "thanks for all the help."

Alexa pulled out her smartphone and as she clicked on the app with the Anon mask icon called "ANON," Winter grabbed Alexa's hand before she hit the "Pay Now" button. With the tip of its claw, Winter tapped on Alexa's watch.

"Right," she said mistakenly, "I forgot. Wait till I'm inside the airport."

Winter released its hand.

Alexa pocketed the smartphone.

"Thanks again," she said and closed the door behind her.

☾

WITHOUT drawing any attention, in fact, it was as if she was a ghost as she glided to the airport and graciously made her way through the front check-in and into the terminal, Alexa tracked down her designated seat where a hazy mirage-like figure was seated. She sat down in the seat, the feeling along all of her extremities, fingers and toes, was similar to a pins and needles sensation.

Alexa pulled out her phone and waited until she was settled in before reopening the ANON app. She clicked the "Pay Now" button.

The app prompted a message, which allowed Alexa to rate her ANON. She decided to give Winter a "★★★★1/2" rating, adding to it's ninety-nine point nine approval rating. Considering the job didn't exactly go according to plan—maybe, for Winter, it did—she'd leave up to the witch-for-hire to figure out why she gave it a "1/2" star instead of a full one.

More showy icons popped up, displaying whether or not the Anon was either "Professional," "Methodical," "Fun and Enjoyable," or lastly, "Good Conversation." Clearly, Alexa could cross off the last trait. She decided to go with "Methodical." She clicked on the "Methodical" icon, prompting a message: "Thanks for your feedback!"

As Alexa closed the app, she fell into a sudden trance.

In the seat next to her, a man dressed in a business suit was staring at her with a strange look on his face.

"Are you okay, Alexa?" asked the man.

Alexa snapped from her trance.

"Excuse me," she said. "Do I know you?"

The man laughed.

"Funny," he said, as if he was in the middle of a conversation. "So, you were saying that you've never been to a Yankees game before."

"I was?"

"Are you okay?" asked the man, tilting his head in confusion.

"Yeah," she said, realizing that she had been talking to this man for an hour or so. Maybe longer.

Alexa couldn't quite tell pinpoint at exact time, if it was one hour or two, or even make the slightest sense as to how an app was able to wind back the last few hours of the night and make it appear (through surveillance cameras and travelers, including Mr. Green Eyes sitting next to her) as though she hadn't even stepped foot from the airport; yet, Alexa had been sitting in the terminal, "on layover," as she'd describe, waiting for the next flight to Newark, New Jersey. She'd later be questioned when Federal agents pursued each one of the passengers on the flight manifest and brought in the thirty-three year old— who happened to attend Ralph Hood's funeral—to inquire about her past relationship with Hood; and in return, she'd inform the agents that Mr. Hood was someone whom she knew as a young girl and that she wasn't aware of Mr. Hood's presence on the airplane, since she was riding coach and Mr. Hood was riding first class and their attention must've been occupied by their smartphones when she walked past him while entering the airplane. As she'd put it simply to the agents, it was a mere coincidence that she was on the same flight as Ralph Hood. In return, the agents would move onto the next passenger on their list.

"Say," the man said to a more clearheaded Alexa, "I got about an hour left till my next flight. Wanna grab a cup of coffee?"

Alexa looked over the nice businessman, shrugged, and said, "Sure. I can use some coffee right now."

PRESENT
Philip's Head, Michigan

STEVEN Gellhorn, who was the pastor and founder of One Up Church, parked the red 2000 Suzuki Swift in front of a squared building, which, from the outside, appeared more like a gymnasium than it did a traditional church.

Before entering the church, he checked the front side of the beat-up Suzuki, making sure there weren't any marks or noticeable dents next to the right headlight, which had been replaced, the bumper buffed out and repainted with the correct cherry red tone.

Steven's insecurity with his handy work soon turned to relief as he stepped back on the sidewalk and took a last glance at his Suzuki, in particularly, the area along the front end where he had plowed into a pedestrian.

Feeling more optimistic about the day, Steven made his way into the church. He ran into two volunteers, Amanda and Nicole, who were waiting for his arrival at the entranceway.

Amanda asked how Steven was doing and if he had recovered from the flu that kept him away from his flock for the past couple of weeks. Steven gave her a pleasant smile and said he was feeling much better. Amanda couldn't agree more. She said he looked different and "healthier." Which, in a way, he knew it was her way of saying that he looked cleaner, as in sober.

Nicole asked what the topic was going to be for tonight's sermon.

Without giving his answer much thought, Steven said, "Repentance."

THE MORNING OF
Burgaw, North Carolina

BLINDING sunrays cut through a dusty living room.

Hour by hour, the sunlight, which poured through the bare living room window and created a rectangular beam along the beige shag carpet, spread farther up the couch until it reached Nelson Sutherland's scruffy face.

With the warmth pressed against the side of his face, Nelson woke up feeling as if a weight had been lifted from his shoulders. Yet, he felt hungover without the whole puking routine that came along with it. Like, strangely, he had downed an entire bottle of Jim Beam the night before and yet, he didn't feel ill the next morning. Normally, these kinds of feelings, as heavy as they were, involved frequent trips to the bathroom where he'd purge everything he had inside his stomach.

Most of all, Nelson felt as if a piece of himself was missing from his body.

As he sat upright on the couch, he glanced down at the bandage wrap on his hand. His index finger was gone!

He cried out, "What the. . . "

The finger was, in fact, gone; and all he had left was a ghost of a finger.

Fully awake from the sight of his missing digit, Nelson balled his hand into a fist and thought maybe his finger was tucked underneath the wrap.

The finger wasn't there.

It was cut!

Surgically cut off, Nelson soon realized as he removed the bandage wrap and examined the clean cut just above the knuckle.

Despite Nelson's shocking discovery, he wasn't at all bummed out about the finger. He'd figure it was like finding a bruise on his arm or leg after he had gotten wasted the night before. He could spend hours trying to figure out how he had gotten the bruise or cut or whatever, but it was pointless to scrape through memories when he could've been doing more important things, like hitting up the Spit Bucket or going fishing with Hanky Pank or cleaning up the house, which was the one chore he had put off since Aricka left him eight years ago.

He put aside his worries and shuffled his way into the kitchen where he managed to hold down his black coffee, as well as two pieces of toast with grape jelly.

As he crammed the last bite of toast into his mouth, he couldn't help but try to remember what happened last night. Nelson—or Full Nelson, which was what all his buddies called him—wasn't a thinking man, definitely not the brainy type to sit pensively with his head rested against his hand while trying to debunk Einstein's general theory of relativity.

Most importantly, he wondered where in Sam Hill did that thing—his index finger—run off to. *Did it get up and walk away like that hand in Madam's Family?* Or, *was it Adam?* Nelson didn't remember how it was cut off either or who had bandaged it up. Did he go to the hospital? Was he hanging out with the ole Hanky Pank last night? If so, the Spank Man must've wrapped up the finger. But where in the hell did the finger go?

Nelson spent the morning asking himself these very questions.

Once he finished breakfast, he was more energized. He searched through the entire house for the finger: under the couch, underneath tables, inside sock drawers and whatnot. He went outside and checked his truck, but he couldn't find the finger anywhere nor could he find any blood inside or outside the house. *Surely*, Nelson thought, *there must've been plenty of blood.*

But no.

He couldn't find a single drop.

❨

LATER that same afternoon when Nelson's daughter, Joelle, who lived up in Jacksonville, came by the house to check on her old man, she walked on him digging through trash underneath the overturned couch.

After stating the obvious, Joelle noticed her old man's finger or lack thereof. Again, she stated the obvious: "Did you put it on ice?"

His daughter's question was soon followed by the obvious: "Well, I'd have to find it first. Now, wouldn't I?"

Joelle helped her old man and searched the entire house for the finger. They looked under every piece of furniture. Joelle even combed over the same places that Nelson had covered earlier that morning. Eventually, for Nelson, it had gotten to the point where Joelle's presence was making matters worse.

After a long search and coming up empty handed, the failure set in; however, it tasted a little less bitter with a glass of iced tea.

Joelle asked Nelson if she wanted to take him to the doctor.

Nelson declined with a "Maybe later."

Which was another version of "No."

She tried to put her old man at ease by telling him about her husband Dusky and how he knows amputees in the military who may have a prosthetic finger lying around somewhere.

Nelson wasn't at all interested in his daughter's sympathy.

He had a lot to do around the house; and what better way of getting rid of his daughter than with the "choirs" excuse. He told Joelle that he had to cut the grass. Which wasn't an excuse or even a lie by any stretch. He really did. The grass in the yard was getting so damn thick and tall that he'd probably have to take a weed whacker to it before using the lawnmower.

As Joelle said her goodbyes and left her old man to tend to his grass, Nelson walked his daughter outside.

Distant cars driving along the highway caught his eye.

A thought came to him—a memory perhaps?

"You still gotta wear a mask?" asked Nelson.

Joelle stopped in the driveway and said, "Masks? What masks?"

"You know," Nelson said, "to keep from spreadin' the darkness."

Joelle looked at her old man strangely.

"You're acting weird," she said. "Are you sure you're okay, Daddy?"

Nelson shook the thought from his head.

Must've been a dream or something, he thought.

He waved off his daughter's growing concern.

"Yeah," he said. "I'm fine."

☾

AS Nelson was trimming the weeds along the fence with a weed whacker, he shut off the engine and noticed a pink chalky powder underneath the fence.

Nelson placed his sweaty fingers in the powdery substance, got a little bit on the tip of his finger, and placed it to his nose. He recoiled from the fishy smell of the powder.

Baffled by the powder, he followed the trail of powder along the fence. After reaching the mailbox in the front of the house, he realized the trail of powder was circling his entire house. He took a step outside the pink circle and backpedaled onto the street.

As a car horn blared out behind Nelson, he remembered taking a flight to, of all places, Grand Rapids, Michigan.

"Well, I'll be," Nelson said, as a red truck drove around him and nearly came inches away from hitting him.

Those two Federal agents would later ask him: "*Business or pleasure?*"

"Pleasure," he'd say without batting an eyelash.

SIXTEEN YEARS AGO
Burbank, California

INSIDE Stage 3, each one of the crewmembers of the production team were preparing the set for the upcoming shot involving Ralph, who was reprising his role as iconic character Don Juan, aka "The Wolf," in the latest film, *The Effigy Rises*. It had been over five years since the latest production of the *Effigy* franchise, which was a television series called *The Offspring*. The series followed the TV movie, *Crowd Favorite*, as well as a spin-off in form of a mini-series called *Shadow DJ*, which, over the years, had gained a cult following. *The Offspring*, the last spin-off of *The Effigy* only survived one season and the owner of the copyrights, Rich Blumkin of Blumkin Pictures, to *The Effigy* seriously questioned selling the rights of the franchise after the latest attempts failed to live up to expectations. But, like always, a new director, possibly one with a critically acclaimed title under his or her belt, but certainly a "huge fan" of the franchise—in this particular case, Irvin Landslide—came along and decided to give a stab at the project.

The set was an art gallery. According to the script, the original loft from the first *Effigy* film had been sold to a curator after main protagonist, Carolina Reyes, defeated The Wolf, moved out of the loft, and pursued an acting career in New York City. The neighborhood, which, in the very first film, was located in a low-income area in New Orleans. Years later, the old, historic district had been gentrified.

The scene involved the iconic character, Don Juan, resurrecting through one of the pieces being displayed in the art gallery after a well-known artist, who was known for using trash for her various pieces of artwork, came across an artifact of the original effigy while she was dumpster diving. The artist incorporated the artifact into her collage-like painting, which happened to be one of the highlights of the gallery.

While the artist was describing the background of the piece of artwork, Don Juan's hand was going to suddenly emerge from the artwork and impale the artist. The scene was incredibly graphic with the usage of pints of fake blood that were going to be pumped through the chest prosthetic, which the actor was going to be wearing. As Don Juan's hand went directly through the artist's chest, the crowd would be sprayed with blood splatter.

Bernard Knowles, who worked on the previous films and was here on the set for, more or less, being a mentor, arrived on the set with his granddaughter, Alexa.

The makeup artist, Arlo Quinn, who was close friends with Bernard, in fact, one of Bernard's former apprentices, invited Bernard and his granddaughter to the set. A much younger Francesca von Cappelen, another one of Bernard's apprentices, was on the set helping out the special effects team as well.

Super-excited to show off the chest prosthetic to Bernard, he guided Bernard and Alexa into the art gallery set where the legend himself, The Ralph Hood, and his long-time stand-in, Castor Lykaios, were talking to each other outside the cameras. One of the wardrobe ladies stopped by to adjust Ralph's raggedy trench coat that the character Don Juan wore.

As the wardrobe lady left, Ralph pinched her butt and said, "Thanks."

The wardrobe lady playfully laughed off the butt grab and as she was walking away, winked at Ralph.

The action had clearly upset Castor, causing him to blush.

Ralph acknowledged his close friend, Bernard, who walked over with Arlo.

While Bernard reunited with Ralph, Alexa, who had become incredibly nervous from being in Ralph's presence, hung back for a while and decided to wander around the set while her grandfather was catching up on old times.

Castor excused himself from the conversation and stormed off the set.

As Alexa was admiring all of the detail that went into making the set, Castor forcibly bumped into her shoulder. He had hit Alexa so hard that one side of her body jerked backward. The impact nearly winded her.

"Excuse me," Alexa said, waiting for an apology from the stand-in.

Unapologetic, Castor eyed Alexa as if she had no business being on the set and stormed his way to the dressing rooms.

Never had she felt so unwanted based on what might or might not have been an accidental run-in or, worse, a deliberate act of intimidation.

Alexa wasn't so keen on the expression, *"What goes around comes around,"* for it required, in most cases, a willingness to believe in divine intervention.

As she watched Castor storm away, she told herself that she'd keep an open mind anyway.

What goes around comes around, huh?

We'll just see about that.

STANDING tall in his all black Mao suit, Key was beginning to lose his patience.

Behind Key sat his own personal "mood ring," Stat, who was slouched over a microphone on a desk tucked away in the darkest corner of the room.

In front of Key was a large one-way mirror, which was most commonly used for interrogation rooms.

In the other brighter, much larger room behind the one-way mirror were precisely ten chairs, each one placed next to one another in a perfect line. Ten volunteers of various ethnicities, as well as varying in weight, height, and size, sat like guinea pigs in each one of the ten chairs. In front of each one of these volunteers was a tray holding a smartphone.

Extremely cool in demeanor despite the screaming match of a million angry voices inside his head, Key embraced the sound of the door *opening* to his left.

"She's here," Ruby said, poking her head into the dark room.

"Thank you, Ruby," Key said with relief as his attention remained focused on the ten volunteers. "Let her in."

Only a few seconds after leaving the room, Ruby fully opened the door and revealed a team of doctors, who were gathered around in the hallway. She reentered with presidential candidate, Avanti Washington, as well as two secret service agents.

Avanti told the two agents to wait outside while she conducted her business.

Key glanced at Ruby, who, in return, was waiting for Key's permission.

"It's okay," he said calmly. "Leave us."

Following commands, Ruby escorted the two agents from the room.

In the corner of her eye, Avanti witnessed the volunteers.

"Don't worry," Key said to Avanti. "They can't see us."

Stat sat upright from Avanti's presence.

Acknowledging Stat, Avanti nodded her head with a "hello."

"This is my advisor, Stat," Key said, pointing at Stat.

"Nice to meet you, Ms. Washington," Stat said with a tremble in his voice.

"Yes," she said, her eyes keen on Stat. "Likewise." She walked up to Key, who greeted the candidate with a handshake. "If it isn't the Master of Macabre," she said, shaking Key's hand. "Hello, Mr. Warrick. It's a pleasure."

"Trust me," he said, maintaining his composure. "The pleasure is all mine."

"I have to say Mr. Sorbet was quite impressed with what you've managed to pull off," Avanti said, referring to the wealthy investor, Rakesh Sorbet, or better yet, Neuvak's knight in shining armor who, not only came to the pharmaceutical company's rescue after their stock was hit hard after the recent outbreak, but also one of Avanti's major contributors to her campaign.

"Well, it's fair to say an artist does his greatest work when faced with a deadline."

"If you can give me the votes to beat Rhodes, Mr. Warrick, then I'd say you created yourself one of the greatest tools money can buy. I'd go as far to call it a masterpiece."

"Oh," Key said confidently and at the same time, flattered by Avanti's comment, "I'll get you the voters you need to win the election. You just have to live up to your end of the deal."

"A deal's a deal," she said. "And as far as I see it, you're providing a service to this country."

"Well," Key said, cracking a smile, "like Bob Dylan said, 'The times are ah-changing.'"

"Indeed they are."

"Tell me, Governor," Key said, "if voters knew who you really were, do you think they would still vote for you?"

"People only criticize what they don't understand, right?" Avanti said. "Inherently, people are frightened of what they don't understand. For most of them, regardless of who they might think I am, they look at me as a threat to their perfect world."

"The age of decadence is coming to an end once and for all, Governor," Key said, turning his attention back to the volunteers. "It's an *awakening*. The people who occupy this world are finally realizing that they've been sold a lie."

"And isn't that what you're doing? You're essentially selling them immortality while promising them prosperity. Which we both know is a lie. . . "

"I'm giving them a way out from the madness."

"Funding your own death doesn't exactly strike me as way of the American Spirit, Mr. Warrick."

"If it makes you feel comfortable," Key said sarcastically, "the Great Merger will be, let's just say, more 'inclusive.'"

"You underestimate their kind," Avanti said to Key. "They're survivors. It's in their nature."

"Save the talking points, Governor."

"Well," Avanti said, holding out her hands, "let's see it then. . ."

With his arms held behind his back, Key turned his shoulder and nodded at Stat, who, through an intercom, instructed the ten volunteers to pick up the smartphones in front of them. Then, he told the first five volunteers to TEXT "7" at the number 32756377 while the other remaining five volunteers were told to dial the phone number "1-800-DARKNES, ext. 7."

"The signal is activated," Stat said, flipping a switch on a controller.

Somewhere in a dark corridor inside an unknown location hidden deep in the mountains, the lights on a wall of towering servers, which were covered in slimy roots, changed over from a beating purplish-blue to the color blood red.

As the volunteers texted, as well as called these specific numbers and eagerly placed the phone's receiver up to their ears, a piercing "bleep"-like sound blared out from the receiver, penetrating into their eardrums and deep into their brains.

All of a sudden, nine out of the ten callers and texters grabbed hold of their chests. Their hearts instantly stopped beating, resulting in some of the volunteers to fall forward over the trays while others to fall back in their chairs and collapse to the floor. The tenth volunteer—one of the five callers—wasn't clutching his chest, but rather standing up in a state of bewilderment. He staggered around and grabbed his head.

As the confusion turned to utter panic, the veiny red-faced volunteer cried out in bloody horror, "What the fuck is happening to me?"

As he screamed out, parts of his head bulged outward.

He suddenly darted toward the mirror on the wall and slammed the top of his forehead against the glass, partially shattering it.

Before the volunteer could ram his head into the mirror once more, his head exploded in the popping sound of a water balloon!

Blood splattered all over the mirror. Pieces of brain matter dripped down the glass.

The volunteer's body flopped to the ground.

A team of doctors and handlers entered the other room and carried out nine out of the ten volunteers on a gurney.

"Doesn't exactly count as a potential voter," Avanti said with a dark sense of humor.

"Well, it wouldn't be the first time a dead man's cast a ballot. Would it?"

"How about the others?" Avanti asked, referring to the other nine volunteers. "We need actual bodies to show up at the polls, not the Headless Horseman."

"As I'm sure Sorbet has already explained, each volunteer's pneuma will be injected with a special parasite by *our* folks on the Other Side. When the volunteer's pneuma returns to this world, his or her body will act as a host for the parasite. Within twenty-four hours, the growth will be removed from the body, which will be incinerated, and you, Governor Avanti Washington, will have yourself a voter. They'll be back at home before they were even missed."

"And what about the ones that won't make it?" asked Avanti, as she directed her attention back toward the headless corpse.

"Comes with the price of winning," Key said callously and watched the body handlers carry out one of the "temporarily dead" volunteers from the other room.

Avanti provoked the most obvious question: "And this so-called 'parasite,' it'll do whatever you tell it to do?"

Key nodded.

"If we wanted to, Ms. Washington," he said, "we can train it to roll over and play dead."

"CALLER BEWARE"
(THE DAY OF)

WITH Key's "*Midnight World!*" Telethon only hours away from airing "LIVE" on national television, Key was backstage going over the final design for the packaging of the "*Midnight World* Bundles" with controversial artist, Cleft Lip.

Key was dressed in a stiff yet showy oversized bright purple suit with shoulders pads twice the size of a football player. Lightning bolts in the shape of "Ms" and "Ws" were trimmed into the sides of his tight fade.

"Each donor will 'supposedly' receive a bundle containing various products," Cleft Lip listed, as he cracked open the MW box of goodies on the table, "Poisonous Flower perfume for the ladies," he said, pulling out all the MERCH, "or Dog Breath cologne for the fellas." Then, "trading cards, *Midnight World* T-shirts and shorts, vamp hoodies, and other swag. . ." he held up a black coffee mug with the political slogan "Vote 4 Washington or Die" written in bold red, white, and blue Arial font, as well as other swag, including "Vote" pins and buttons, the capital V shaped like the tooth of a vampire, ". . . books, including origin stories, as well as *The Chronicles of Krillish* and several Best-Selling paperbacks by the author Neil Reddy, a free one-year subscription to the *Midnight World* channel with *The Five-Minute History of Midnight World*, movies, posters and figurines signed by spin-celebrity Ericka Barnes, the replica scissors used by The Snipper, Mr. Moonlight glow-in-the-dark sunglasses, a 1,000 piece puzzle 'The Last Jam' featuring former professional wrestler Blaine Toussaint, a key chain with the good luck charm of a werewolf snake's claw, a Dr. Love stress-relieving plush toy, then," Cleft Lip stopped to catch his breath, as he pulled out one last item, the black matte-finished bottle with a skull and crossbones design embedded on the side, "finally, a bottle of Immortality."

With a look of surprise on his face, Key said straightforwardly, "Impressive."

"Thank you, Key," Cleft Lip said, all jittery. "It's a honor coming from you."

"Very nice work," Key said, lifting up the bottle of Immortality.

"Thank you," Cleft Lip, more relieved by Key's approval.

Key opened the bottle of Immortality.

The bottle was empty.

"It's a prop, of course," Cleft Lip said before Key could question the product. "They're all props."

Key picked up the book, *The Chronicles of Krillish*, and opened it.

The pages inside were blank white.

"You know, you almost had me convinced," Key said and nodded at a mound of *Midnight World* Bundles stacked on the pallet waiting to be transported to the display wheel behind the curtains. "How about the other boxes?"

"Props," Cleft Lip said and turned his focus back to the table. "This box here will be on display for the audience."

Cleft Lip waited in suspense for Key's *final* approval on his work.

Over a tense pause, he placed the book on the table and held out his hand for Cleft Lip to shake.

More stoked, Cleft Lip shook Key's hand while, at the same time, letting out a sigh of relief.

With perfect timing, Ruby shouldered her way past several lighting guys and riggers, who were hauling in equipment from the back of a truck parked in a loading dock, and approached Key from behind.

"Excuse me, sir," she said, pulling Key away from Cleft Lip, "you're needed in Marketing. Eleventh hour is approaching, and we need your feedback."

"Sure thing," he said, checking the time on his wristwatch. He left Cleft Lip and walked with Ruby to the "Bot Farm" room. "Let's make this fast, Ruby. I've got to check on Craley and make sure he's fully prepped. Last time I checked on him he was acting a little glitchy, if you know what I mean."

"Could be last-minute nerves?" Ruby suggested.

"They weren't trained to be nervous, Ruby."

On the way to Marketing, Key walked past a monitor displaying a video of a segment, which was going to be aired during the Telethon. The video showed a caller who appeared down in the dumps while sitting on a couch in a dark living room with the glow of the TV pressed against his face. Somewhat skeptical, he picked up the phone from the coffee table and dialed a number. Once the dejected man started to talk to the operator on the other line, his mood began to change and surprisingly, his spirits were suddenly uplifted.

While walking, Key said to Ruby, "Tell the Video Department to bring up the lighting in the promo shots. We want the callers to actually see each actor's reactions, not be left in the dark."

"You got it," Ruby said, typing in a MEMO on her eTablet. "Anything else?"

"Maybe add some music in the background."

Ruby typed in "Add music" to her MEMO.

Passing by several more staff members, Key and Ruby finally arrived at the Marketing room. The sign outside the room said, "BOT FARM."

Bracing herself for the unexpected, Ruby cautiously opened the door for Key, who immediately wrinkled his nose due to the foul, pungent smell emitting from each one of the zombie-like creatures that were standing in slouched over postures inches apart from one another inside a humid and dimly lit room. The creatures' faces were slack and droopy and hung like oversized masks, each orifice on their face hollowed out. On the back of each creature suspended fleshy umbilical cord-like tubes attached to the callused nipples of a subterranean Hog Maggot, which was bathing in fresh manure.

Undistracted by Key's presence, the zombie-like creatures, these "Bots," had a smartphone in their hands. Their heads were hanging downward and planted in the devices as they mindlessly typed away a hundred tweets per minute.

"What's the problem, Ruby?" asked Key.

"It's nothing big," she said and at times, held her breath from the awful smell. "Well, it's just some of their tweets are suspicious in nature."

Ruby showed several "flagged" tweets on her eTablet device.

One read from **John Smith @IAMJOHNSMITH**:

@MidnightWorldOfficial The whole damn thing is a scam!!! **#MidnightWorld** #Tele-not

Another from **Claude Barnshed ⚑⚑⚑ @ClaudesKitchen**:

Don't believe whateva they be tellin u. **Midnight World** is not real. #MidnightGate

Then, another:

Melissa Kyle @BatshitCrazyBitch All u mouthbreathers r being played by these fools in charge of #FakeWorld. The telethon 2nite is the END OF THE F'N WORLD as we no it. You can all kiss ur ass goodbye ☮ ✋

More timid than cautious, Ruby hesitantly escorted Key to three of the zombie-creatures who were mis-tweeting. They were tweeting at a much more lethargic pace, Key noticed. He looked around the farm, saw the half-full water bottle in Ruby's hand, and asked for it. She handed over the water bottle to Key, who, in return, squeezed the bottle in the zombie-creature's face, dowsing it with water.

Key ordered Ruby to pull up John Smith's latest tweets. The zombie-creature was typing faster and doing so with more liveliness.

John Smith @IAMJOHNSMITH: So looking forward to **@MidnightWorldOfficial** Telethon tonight. Can't wait to see Zip Drive live in action!!! Going to be off the hook!!! **#MidnightWorld**

"There you go," Key said, handing the eTablet back to Ruby. "Get one of the interns in here. Make sure you tell them to keep the Bots hydrated."

"Will do, sir," Ruby said, following Key from the Bot Farm.

On the way out, Key's massive shoulders hit the sides of the doorway, forcing him to exit sideways from the room.

"DRENELLE'S GUEST"

As Ruby parted ways with Key, she ran into Drenelle, who was standing next to a line array speaker.

Dressed in orange tights underneath a tracksuit jacket, she was holding what looked like a script in her hand. Next to her was the scriptwriter, Calyx, who had written the speech for Drenelle.

Clearly, while rehearsing lines, Drenelle wasn't at all comfortable with parts of the speech.

She pointed at one line in particular: "How are people going to sympathize with. . . *being raised in a mental institution*? People have a nose for sniffing out bullshit. Besides, all my followers know I spent most of my adolescence raised in the city. It ain't me—"

Drenelle paused from the sight of Ruby, who flashed him a smile.

Speechless, Drenelle couldn't help but lose herself in Ruby's familiar face as she passed by.

Deep down inside, a part of Drenelle knew Ruby; strangely enough, in what felt like another life, she was, once, acquainted with Ruby and she'd go so far to call her a "friend" or even more than a friend.

"Drenelle?"

Calyx was chirping in Drenelle's ear.

Both Drenelle and Ruby shared eye contact. Ruby was skittish from the sight of Drenelle, being that she was in the presence of a notorious murderer known as The Snipper. Drenelle, on the other hand, found—if anything—great comfort in Ruby's presence.

Drenelle snapped from her trance and pulled her eyes away from Ruby's familiar face and while doing so, no-

416

ticed a pig with a leash being walked down the hallway by the pig's caretaker, a stout man dressed like the countryside.

She wondered what a pig was doing here.

Maybe it was part of the show.

A prop perhaps?

Nonetheless, Drenelle couldn't take her eyes off the domestic pig.

Overwhelmed with nostalgia, she handed the script to Calyx, who insisted that Drenelle finish rehearsing the rest of her speech.

Annoyed by Calyx, Drenelle excused herself and followed the man, who was walking the pig down the hallway.

She was more interested in the pig than the man.

"MANDATORY"

STAR, as well as the four other members of Five Fistfuls, or what advertisers were advertising as a "Not Your Everyday Coven," shuffled through the line in front of the spread of the most succulent food. On a silver tray sat a roasted pig with an apple in its mouth. Rhonda helped herself to a part of pig butt, which drew a look of disgust from Fay, who immediately recoiled and said, "I think I'm gonna puke."

"What's the matter, Fay?" Rhonda said innocently while placing a generous helping of sautéed green beans on her plate.

She kept the line moving by shuffling her way to a dish of sweet yams and helped herself to not one scoop but two scoops of yams.

"So, what? You a vegetarian again, Fay?" asked Carmen.

"You're one to talk, Carmen," Fay said sickly. "Self-proclaimed vegetarian who promotes herself as a 'vegetarian' one week while, the next, you're secretly stuffing your gullet with fucking meermaarms."

417

"So what's wrong with meermaarms?" asked Carmen, holding up the line for Star, who was waiting in the back of the line. "They're rich in protein."

"But they're so hard to catch—"

"—Not if you're doing it right."

"Gotta take whatever you can find, Fay," Mandy said in defense of Carmen's dietary indecisiveness. "After all, we're kind of limited in the desert."

"Quit your bellyaching, Fay," Rhonda said, piling on a slice of cheesecake with raspberry sauce on her already packed plate of food. "You need to eat something or else we're not going to perform to our best abilities." Rhonda's temper became more heated with every word she spoke. She grabbed a couple of glazed donuts and piled them onto the plate, as if the anger itself was driving the snake worms' enormous appetite. "There's a reason why we're called *The Five Fistfuls*. *Five Fistfuls*, meaning it takes all five of us to contribute to the act!"

"Yeah," Carmen said mildly. "Rhonda's right. You're being selfish, Fay. If you have to, force yourself to eat. You need your strength."

Fay turned to Star, who remained quiet in the back.

"Thanks for coming to my rescue, Star," Fay said, turning her attention back to the endless spread of food stacked on top of the table, which stretched across an entire room that was curtained off from the rest of production.

"Just shut up and eat something, Fay," Star said without a care in the world.

"Easy for you to say," Fay said, grabbing two vegetable spring rolls from the tray and doing so with disgust.

"If we blow it tonight," Mandy said, ignoring Fay's childish behavior, "millions of people are going to rip *The Five Fistfuls* to shreds on Tweeter. We don't need that kind of bad publicity."

"We?" Fay said under her snake worm breath. "You mean 'you.'"

"Besides, what does eating have to do with our act?" asked Fay.

"It has everything to do with our act, Fay," Mandy said, losing her cool with Fay. "You need to feed those little puppies inside you."

As of lately, Mandy referred to the snake worms as "puppies."

Which only made Fay sicker to her stomach.

As Fay was about to rush behind the curtains, Drenelle entered the room.

Standing in a frozen posture as if she got caught in the act of doing something she wasn't supposed to be doing—or better yet, sticking her nose in a place that was considered off limits—Drenelle's presence alone forced *The Five Fistfuls* to acknowledge her and, let's just say, her "unwanted" presence.

"Sorry to interrupt whatever it is you're doing, but. . . " Drenelle said, trying to make sense as to what exactly these five red-cloaked snake worms were doing, which, to Drenelle, went well-beyond just your average eating, ". . . have any of you seen this man walking a pig?"

Over the tense silence, Carmen said, "Excuse me?"

"A man," Drenelle reiterated for the members of *The Five Fistfuls*, "who was walking a pig on a leash, did he come through here recently?"

More tension built.

Misplacing sass for sarcasm, Mandy said to Drenelle, "No. But we got ourselves a pig right *her*."

The comment provoked laughter from the other members, except Star.

Over the laughter, Star said in a more serious tone to Drenelle, "No. We haven't seen him."

"Thanks," Drenelle said to Star, who replied, "No problem."

As Drenelle exited through the curtains, Mandy turned to Carmen, saying without any shame, "Weirdo."

"I know, right?" Carmen returned. "Can't believe that creep's going to be the main attraction."

"She's the creep?" said Star, releasing the pent-up frustration.

"Yeah," she said. "*She* is—"

"—When's the last time you looked at yourself in the mirror?" asked Star.

"Like you're any different?"

Feeling more at ease with the others' discomfort by Drenelle's presence, Fay said, "Face it, Carm. You're just jealous because you're not the main attraction."

"Whatever," Carmen said to herself.

From a distance, Drenelle could hear those "things" arguing behind the curtains. Normally, she'd be amazed how her presence alone created such contention among both sexes—but snake worms?

Who would've ever thought?

Drenelle picked up the pig's scent coming from down another hallway, which led her to cage where a werewolf snake was being held. From the rattling of the cage's bars, it was clear to Drenelle that the werewolf snake appeared agitated.

As Drenelle peeked behind the wall, she soon realized why it was so agitated.

There, only feet away from the cage, stood the pig's caretaker, who was teasing the werewolf snake with the pig.

The caretaker, who was anything but a caretaker, picked up the squealing pig and held it up to the cage, only inches away from the werewolf snake's reach.

As the werewolf snake swiped at the pig with its massive claws, the caretaker retracted the pig.

"Here, *Zippy Zippy*," the caretaker said more cruelly.

The werewolf snake reared back in a defensive position and made a low, guttural noise, which sounded like a cross between a hiss and a growl.

"Looks like someone's going to be supper tonight," the caretaker said to the squealing pig, who was trying to kick itself free from his arms.

Drenelle had no other choice than to act. She searched around backstage for a tool, anything sharp. She found an open toolbox next to a rig. She dug around the tools but couldn't find any scissors; however, she found a screwdriver.

She told herself that it would have to make do.

"A PING—OR LACK THEREOF"

WHILE Key was talking about the album *Flaming Skyline* with Eel-Baby from the band Eel-Baby and The Cuts, he heard a disturbance behind Eel-Baby. Key was in mid-sentence when he leaned past Eel-Baby, only to witness Stat rushing to the bathroom.

Key excused himself and checked on Stat, who appeared extremely fatigued as he exited from the stall. He went straight to the faucet to wash his mouth.

As Stat looked up at the mirror, he witnessed Key standing behind his reflection.

"Sup, Key?"

"Sup with you, Stat?" Key asked, as if his question was more appropriate.

"I ain't feeling too well," he said honestly.

"Well," Key said, "you know I need you for the show, right?"

"Yeah," Stat said, drying the corners of his mouth with a paper towel. "It's just. . ." he waved his hand, ". . . Never mind."

"Out with it."

"It's just strange. That's all."

"What's strange?" asked Key.

"I was making my rounds through the building when, all of a sudden, I had this feeling come over me. It came out of nowhere—"

"—What kind of feeling?"

"It's hard to explain," Stat said, thinking. "It's like I felt. . . nothing. Like an emptiness, you know?"

"I see," Key said and drifted off for a moment.

"What's going on, Key?" asked Stat.

Lightning flashes lit up the dark skies in Key's mind.

The sound of Stat's voice forced Key to snap from his trance. He told Stat to stay close; and together, the two exited from the bathroom.

"COLD FEET"

IN the dressing room, Biff Craley was closely watching old videos of himself—or his former self—on the monitor.

The footage displayed on the monitor was a scene from the flick, *The Shallowing*, where ole Biff played a savvy marine biologist named Mark Riddlehouse, who was studying the reasons as to why the ocean waters were drastically receding across the entire East Coast.

He'd carefully study TV-Biff's body gestures, facial expressions, and movements. Then, while looking back and forth from the vanity mirror to the monitor, he'd mimic TV-Biff, starting with a smile, which looked as though the corners of his lips were being pulled by strings.

Frustrated, Biff turned off the TV with a remote and snatched the script from the vanity and looked over his speaking parts but could only get through a couple of lines of the opening monologue before giving up.

Saved by the *knock*, Biff turned to the door where Key was poking his head inside the dressing room.

"Just checking in," Key said, carefully studying Biff. Standing next to Key, away from Biff's range of sight, was Stat. Without Biff noticing, Stat was listening in on the conversation in order to detect any irregularities in Biff's voice. Key asked Biff, "How's everything going?"

"I don't know if I can do this, Mr. Warrick," Biff said unsurely.

Clearly, based on his insecurities, he wasn't like the debonair actor but rather a far cry from the man who once possessed a supernatural-like charm, which had ladies from across the entire world swooning while moaning his name with a faint tremble in their voice.

"Sure you can, ole buddy," Key said, stepping into the dressing room. Key placed his hands over Biff's shoulders and began to massage them. "Just remember your training and you'll be fine." Biff appeared more disheartened by Key's reinsurance. He slapped Biff on the back. "Smile, Biff. This is your comeback."

Distracted by the sound of *knocking*, Key pulled his eyes from Biff's reflection in the mirror and turned to the door where Paige, one of the PAs, was muffling the speaker along her headset.

"What is it now, Paige?" asked Key.

"It's Drenelle," she said, pulling down the headset.

"What about her?"

"She's missing," Paige said, bracing herself for Key's wrath.

Key asked, "Have you checked the other dressing rooms?"

"Yes," Paige said. "I can't find her anywhere. Also. . ."

Key found himself clenching his teeth from that word *also*.

"There's one more thing. . . " Paige said, as she struggled to finish the rest of her sentence.

"CUT, PASTE, COPY"

PAIGE escorted Key and Stat to the werewolf snake's cage.

Immediately, Key knew something was terribly wrong when he saw the puddle of blood outside the cage, as well as inside the cage where the werewolf snake was curled up like a coil. Extremely protective of its kill, the werewolf snake was obviously in the middle of consuming its meal, and all that remained of the caretaker was one of his tennis shoes.

Stat picked up the bloodstained shoe, which was lying outside the cage.

Key called out to Stat, "Help Paige look for Drenelle."

"Where are you going to be?" asked Stat.

"I'll be in my office," he said.

"WHO REPLACES THE REPLACEABLES?"

BIFF returned to the script and was enthusiastically reciting his lines for tonight's telethon, "*And now, without further ado, it is my honor to introduce the talented, the haunting—*", when he was caught off guard by the *squeak* of a closet door behind him.

Biff set the script down on the vanity and checked out the noise.

As he reached the closet, which was partially cracked open, a black rat about the size of Biff's foot, suddenly darted out of the closet!

The black rat scurried underneath Biff's feet, causing him to dance around a bit.

Startled by the pesky rodent, he followed the black rat back to the vanity but ended up losing it underneath the table.

As he stood up, he noticed someone standing behind him.

In the reflection, he witnessed another reflection staring directly back at him. The reflection looked identical to himself; in fact, it was a mirror image, the only difference being that this man—this stranger—was dressed in more casual attire, opposed to a suit and tie.

Biff rotated around until he was face-to-face with the look-alike.

Stupefied, Biff asked, "Who are you?"

"Death," the look-alike said and before Biff could respond or even make any attempt to flee from this darker, sinister presence before him, a stinger withdrew from the tip of the look-alike's finger.

Once Biff spoke, it was all over.

The look-alike already had the stinger jammed directly in Biff's ear.

Biff's eyes swelled outward, mouth gaping, screaming.

His screams were soon cut short as the stinger violently thrust its way farther into Biff's head.

By the time Ollie, one of the several makeup artists who was helping out the Wardrobe Department, entered the dressing room, the talent, Mr. Craley, was sitting in his chair, casually rehearsing lines.

Ollie picked up the tie off the floor and placed it on a clothes hanger.

As she tended to Biff by first making sure his face was properly powdered before he appeared on camera, she stopped what she was doing and further examined the piece of loose skin on the back of his neck. A couple drops of blood ran down the strange-looking cut—or burn, Ollie couldn't tell which. Ollie excused herself from the dressing room, grabbed a first aid kit from another room, and by the time she returned to Biff's dressing room with a band-aid, as well as gauze, the loose piece of skin was no longer there; in fact, all that remained was a couple of drops of blood that had stained part of Biff's white collar. Ollie was stumped, but she didn't think anything of it.

Right now, she'd take any break she could find.

"A CONVERSATION"

BOUNCING his leg up and down along the floor in a state of anxiety from the domino effect of mishaps, Key was sitting in a high back leather chair inside his office when the door unexpectedly opened.

With the back of his chair facing the doorway, he didn't bother spinning the chair around to acknowledge or even make eye contact with the visitor; yet, somehow, based on Stat's "feeling" or his *lack of* feeling earlier that night, Key had a pretty good idea who was creeping up behind him.

"Have a seat," he said and spun the chair around until he was facing the desk. There, sitting stiffly in the chair on the other side of the desk was none other than his host of the tonight's telethon: Biff Craley.

"What can I do for you, Biff?" asked Key, who was pretending that the handsomely rugged yet debonair man sitting in front of him was, in fact, Biff Craley.

"What can you do for me. . . " Biff responded, his voice somewhat raspy as if he had a glob of phlegm stuck in the bottom of his throat. He momentarily paused to massage away the grittiness. He used his hand to straighten out the vocal cords, as if, in a way, he was tuning them. As Biff's voice returned to normal, he finished saying, ". . . there is one thing you can do for me."

"Oh yeah," Key said, sitting upright.

Biff kept a surprisingly fidgety Key waiting as if he received pleasure in watching his boss squirm and wiggle in his seat.

Just as Biff was about to respond to Key, he said, "I saw what's her name? Is it Drenelle?"

Key barely nodded.

"I saw Drenelle storming from the studio," Biff finished. "Now that she's no longer part of your show, who's going to replace your final act?"

"I don't know, Biff," Key said, going along with Biff's game. "You tell me, since, clearly, you know more than I do."

"It sucks, doesn't it? When things don't go your way—"

"—We'll find a replacement," Key said, bleeding internally.

"I'm sure you will." Biff turned his head in thought. "Your whole plan was to 'humanize' a man, now woman, for the viewers who were going to tune-in into tonight's show, am I right? As the talking heads call it, play the 'sympathy card.' It's not a bad strategy, though. What better way to gain more viewers than to exploit the media and how *they* tried to ruin and destroy a human being's life? 'Call 'em out,' as they say. All for what? Ratings? Most people, who won't be tuning in, are well aware of Drenelle's past crimes. But it doesn't matter, does it? It's all about the clicks. More clicks means more revenue. More revenue means more advertising. More advertising means more revenue. Round and round we go," he moved his hand in a circle, "the money keeps pouring in. Did you ever think that you, Melanthius, the son of the great Drómia, has a story worth telling?"

"I haven't been called that name in," Key said finally, not thinking about his story but rather his last encounter with the dark, manipulative entity sitting before him, "I dunno," he uttered, "seems like centuries."

"Hello, Thius," Biff said, confirming Key's suspicions.

Key pulled himself from the office and mentally found himself back on Dark Mountain, confronting Black Death. *Lightning flickered all around them. The air was electric and it felt as if something incredibly wicked was about to happen—a sort of calm before the storm. Right before Black Death was about to pounce on Key, that wickedness, the storm, was upon them; however, it wasn't like any other storm that neither one of them ever expected. A warm bright light flashed in the corner of Key's eye, forcing him to shield his face. The once dark sky lit up with an array of orange, red, and purple colors. The flickers of lightning muted from a distant explosion. Directly above Key, the great beast, the serpent known as Sheik disrupted the dark sky, coiling the very clouds that protected them from the other, more hostile worlds. Coiling and slithering in and around the swollen clouds, Sheik wrung out the rain, which provided the nutrients to the life below. As the radioactive rain turned to an all out downpour, each and every life form below started to change and mutate. Key readied himself to attack Black Death when it was the most vulnerable; however, before doing so, Black Death had already fled from the summit of the mountain, leaving Key with no other choice than to seek refuge back in the neighboring world.*

"What did you say to Drenelle?" asked Key.

"I didn't say anything," Biff said innocently. "She left on her own *free will*." Biff studied Key and the contours of disappointment forming underneath his face. "No matter how hard you try, Thius, you can't control people."

"And you can?" said Key.

"No," Biff said, narrowing his eyes. "I have no interest in controlling them, Key. I'd rather kill each and every last one of them. But I agreed to live up to my end of the deal. . . "

"Deal?" said Key. "What deal?"

Key was well aware the entity that sat before him, the one that wore the face of a man named Biff Craley, the one who was the former advisor to Drómia, the one that innately spat on Deals of Man, would strut to the edge of oblivion in order to stop the manufacturing of Neuvak's new "soul-controlling, award-winning" drug, Quidaquin, or Q, for it felt as if its greatest competitor was gaining the upper hand.

Biff said to Key, "You thought she was just going to stay out of your way as soon as you got her the votes she needed to win the White House? All you are to her is a failsafe. A woman like Avanti Washington would risk wiping out half of humanity, if it gave her a greater lead in the polls, which, by the way, are sliding the wrong direction despite the death of her son, whom, by the way, I've heard is making quite a name for himself. You, of all the travelers, should know that there can only be one cook in the kitchen."

"You think I didn't know she'd try to take me out after she got elected president?" Key asked but didn't expect Biff to answer. "Surely, I thought she would at least send some low-grade assassin after me: Lil' Grim or the Darker Angel, the Russian Bot, even the so-called 'Cosmic Vigilante,' the balancer of good and evil. Hell! The fuckin' Corrector. You and I both know that genocidal maniac is always looking for work; *but*, the fact she sent you after me shows me how desperate she really is."

"What can I say, Thius?" Biff said arrogantly, displaying a crooked smile. "I am good at what I do." The smile grew wider and wider into the side of his face. "Ask Narcissus," he said, evoking a reaction from Key.

"Curious," Key said, as he attempted to put the remark about his loyal right-hand man behind him, "What do you get out of this so-called 'deal' anyway?"

"Every few years or so I get to unleash a disease onto the world without wiping out humanity in its entirety."

"Thought your ass worked alone."

Biff held up both of his hands while holding his shoulders in a shrug. He said foolishly, "Gotta make ends meant somehow."

"She obviously doesn't know what she's up against, hiring a piece of shit like you who piggybacks off fleas."

Biff shrugged.

"I'll take that as a compliment," he said, smirking.

"You might want to consider updating your name from Black Death to something a little more modern, don't you think? I mean," Key said and paused as he dug through an entire list of names that Black Death had used throughout the past millenniums, "you can always go back to *Creode*. That name suited you well."

The sound of the name "Creode" wiped the smirk right off Biff's face.

For Black Death "Creode," Key learned over the millennia, it was its button. The creature, as powerful as it was, despised the name for it bore so many stereotypes. Throughout print, the name was associated with insignificant hearsay, lies and conjectures, conjured as a drawing of a slender-looking silhouette which possessed no gender, an advisory being completely void of the "be" in *being*, a stick figure that lacked any detail whatsoever, no background, no origin story, nothing more than an ink stain standing in the shadows of legends. Yet, the imposter sitting before Key happened to be one of the deadliest creatures to ever share the same air as him.

Biff shrugged off the comment and said freely, "I'm open for suggestions."

Not at all interested in giving Black Death any suggestions, Key watched Biff closely and waited for the perfect opportunity to make his final move.

"However," Biff said, "this story isn't about me, Thius, nor is it about Drenelle. Don't you think people would like to know what's it like living the shadow of such powerful entities? Me, personally, I'd think people were more inclined to hear your Mommy and *Daddy* issues than op-posed to—you know—the misguided host of a nuclear kid in embryo."

Biff was right to the fullest extent, Key understood. Drenelle's story was one worth telling—like the real Biff, it was a comeback story, more or less. However, he was weighed down by insecurity, as well as the notion that human beings—the modern human being that is—as arti-ficial as they might sound on paper or appear at times with their techno-crafted judgments and hacked brains, wouldn't find any relevance or similarities in the story of an Individual who was forged by the hand of a blood god. Even though his flesh was no different than their flesh, his blood was not of this world.

Key envisioned himself pulling back those curtains and walking on stage and telling his story to that world be-yond the lens of the camera.

What would they think of me?

Biff said over Key's thought, "It's just too bad you skipped the one gene that would've ultimately saved you from your own demise."

"And what's that?" asked Key.

"Immunity," Biff said.

Not at all shocked by the comment, he glanced down at his hand on the armrest and witnessed a couple of fleas biting at his flesh.

"Wrong again," Key said with a checkmate-type vic-tory. "You think I didn't know your ass would show up here? Little do you know we now have a vaccine to stop the spread of your disease. It looks like we both wound up on the wrong side of the deal. . . "

Key moved his eyes upward at Biff, who was sitting across from him. Millions of fleas were pouring from each one of Biff's orifices on his face, most of those fleas coming from his gaping mouth, as well as the piece of torn flesh peeling along the side of his neck, revealing the veiny, plated blackness underneath.

Key nodded at the place on Biff's neck.

"Check yourself, *Creode*," he said. "You peeling, boy."

While Biff was adjusting himself, Key reached below the desk and hit a dime sized "Red Button" located underneath the table.

Once Key pressed the button, a bookshelf along the side of the wall slid open, revealing a dark chamber.

Out of the darkness, a werewolf snake darted from the room and charged directly at Biff.

With its mouth open and its dripping-wet fangs ready to dig into Biff's body, the werewolf snake leaped at Biff.

At the last second, Biff threw up his arm and held it as straight and stiff as a sword and while the werewolf snake was in midair, stabbed the werewolf snake in the head with the stinger protruding from his index finger.

With its slack mouth hanging open, the werewolf snake slid from the stinger and dropped dead to the floor.

Biff turned to Key and asked, "Anymore tricks up your sleeve?"

The sight of the dead werewolf snake caused Key to tremble with rage. The walls all around him started to drip with blood. Blood seeped from the molding, past the corners of the ceiling, down all four walls, soaking them with blood.

As the blood flooded into the office, the beads of sweat along his skin turned to blood. Like the walls, eventually, Key's entire body was covered in thick, rich blood.

In return, Biff used the sharp stinger to slit open the skin along his forehead. He ran the stinger down his entire face and peeled away the skin suit that Black Death was wearing.

As the two squared off against one another, Key pulled yet another trick out of his sleeve. He summoned the great serpent. Sheik burst through the floor below, causing Key's desk to explode with tiny fragments of wood.

With its fangs exposed, the massive serpent let out a sharp hiss right before it struck at Black Death. . .

"BREAK A LEG"

THE chaos lasted for only a few seconds before falling to silence.

The door swung open.

Key exited from the office as victor.

He gathered himself by adjusting the oversized shoulder pads of his suit and made sure he looked presentable for the show. He stopped next to a reflection on a massive clock, which read "11:53 PM." Using the reflection, he wiped a couple of smears of blood from the corners of his face. He resorted to licking his fingers and using the saliva to wipe away tougher spots where the blood was caked on his skin. He checked the ticker at the end of the hallway, which read the time counting down to the airing of the show. The time read "6" minutes and "37" seconds.

As Key made his way toward the main stage, many of the crewmembers were scurrying around backstage. Among the crew was a disturbed Stat, who immediately tracked down Key.

"Did you just feel that?" asked Key, who was calmer than Stat expected him to look after the recent rumble.

"No," Key said nonchalantly.

"It must've been an earthquake."

"Well," Key said, grabbing Stat by the shoulder, "it's nothing we haven't experienced before, am I right?"

"Are you okay?"

"Do I not look okay?"

"Nobody can track down Biff. . ." Stat paused, ". . . did Ruby not tell you?"

"Of course," Key said. "There's been a slight change in plans. I'm going to be taking over for Biff."

"You are? When did you decide this?"

"Just now," he said, again remaining nonchalant despite having only six minutes, going on five, to prepare before the show began.

Stat looked into Key's eyes and saw nothing behind them.

As the fear crept in, Stat backpedaled from Key and trailed off, "I'll catch up with you later."

Key left Stat and made his way to the curtains but was stopped by Ruby, who appeared way more uptight than Stat.

"I can't find Biff anywhere—"

"—Don't worry, Ruby," Key said over Ruby, as he adjusted the jacket's collar. "I'm going to take Biff's spot—"

"—But what about the promo—"

"—The show must go on, Ruby," Key said, putting Ruby in her place.

Ruby stared at Key's face, studying it.

Key acknowledged the strange expression on her face.

"Is there a problem?" asked Key.

With her eyes widening, Ruby reached forward and grabbed a black speck of what she assumed was an insect on the side of Key's chin.

"There," she said, smothering the tiny insect between her fingertips. "Got it."

"What was it?"

"A flea, I think."

"Thanks," Key said and made his way to the curtains.

Ruby said from behind, "Break a leg."

"THE DENOUEMENT/ 'GET DOWN WITH THE DARKNESS!'"

KEY pulled out a pack of Coffin Nails from the breast pocket of the jacket. He lit one up; and as he was passing a crewmember, who happened to be a middle-aged man from the Lighting Department, he took a drag and blew a cloud a smoke in the man's direction. He walked right through the cloud of smoke, breathed in the smoke, and took a couple of steps forward before stopping dead in his tracks. He rotated around and faced Key, who, like Ruby before, was studying his face. All of a sudden, the middle-aged man barked.

Then, as though his brain was on autopilot, the man walked away.

Amazed, Key glanced down at the cigarette in his hand.

"Nice trick, Thius," he said and continued walking toward the main stage.

He arrived at the red curtains surrounding the stage; and just as he was about to step through the slit in the curtains, he heard the sound of a *squeak* below him. A rat crawled between his feet, causing him to take a step back. The rat acknowledged Key's interest. What stood out were the eyes of the rat. They were cloudy and gray, familiar.

Without hesitating, Key lifted up his foot and stomped on the rat, causing the rat to let out a high-pitch *screech*. He removed his foot from the bloody squashed rat, whose entrails were lying on the floor, took yet another drag from the Coffin Nail, and dropped it to the floor.

He meticulously smothered the butt with the sole of his purple wing-capped shoe and more energetically walked through the curtains. He took his position at the center stage. To his left suspended a countdown ticker, which read "10" seconds to airtime. To his right dozens of actors and actresses were seated in a raised booth, waiting to take the upcoming calls from viewers, as well as listeners from around the country.

During those final remaining seconds, a couple of makeup artists patted down Key's face with cotton pads, preparing his face for the camera.

The cameraman held up five fingers, representing one second for each finger. By the time he was down to three fingers, the overhead lights came on and shined down on Key.

Two fingers.

One finger. . .

"GOD SAVE(D) THE PIG(S)"
(FOUR DAYS LATER)

DRENELLE lost count of the number of "Mystery" bill-boards that she passed about forty-something miles after she crossed the state line of Arizona. Each one of the billboards, as enticing as they were whenever they rode past them along stretches of vast, empty desert, had a hoax-like vibe to them based on the goofy font, the S in the word *Mystery* spelled in the serpentine-pattern of a snake. Each one would provoke certain enticements like "You have to sssee it to the believe it!" or "Find out the myssstery behind The Mystery!" or "What is The Mystery?" She pointed out the upcoming sign on the side of the highway to the rescued pig named Runt, who was sitting in the passenger seat of the beat-up powder blue Grand Caravan.

After what was perhaps the sixth or seventh billboard, Drenelle was left with no other choice than to fall for the possible gimmick and make the detour to Interstate 10 where the great "Mystery" would be revealed to weary travelers.

Feeling the hype of The Mystery, Drenelle spent the past thirty minutes of the detour making guesses as to what they were about to witness. Runt sat there and listened to Drenelle rattle off guesses, each one sharing a common theme of extraterrestrial life forms. For sure, she thought it was an alien or some kind of alien artifact. After all, the so-called Mystery was located in the small desolate town of Sopalm, Arizona; and once she made her way into the town, which known as "Da Palms" by locals, her deepest suspicious started to come true. Main Street, or "Mystery Way," as the mock street sign read, was literally about the length of two blocks. Drenelle spotted only few businesses, one being a small 1960's style diner called Annie's, a bar called The Watering Hole where outside perched three cartoon-like blow-up dolls of bright green colored aliens, as well as silver saucer-shaped toys of UFOs hanging from the windows, a

435

corner building with the sign "Kross Real Estate," which, to Drenelle, was strange considering the population of the town of Sopalm must've been under a hundred, then, a boutique-sized town hall which shared the same building as the police and mayor.

Driving more cautiously, Drenelle passed more signs with large arrows pointing her the way to the great Mystery.

"I have to say, Runt," she said, more doubtfully, "I'm a little nervous."

Finally, Drenelle and Runt arrived at a gift shop, as well as a museum, where a large yellow sign with red lettering read "Mystery Inside!"

Drenelle pulled up to the roadside attraction. The sight of the parking lot being half-full relieved Drenelle.

After parking, Drenelle used a leash to walk Runt to the front of the gift shop. The sign on the door read, "No dogs allowed."

"I think we good, Runt," she said to Drenelle. "You ain't a dog, is you?"

Drenelle and Runt walked into the gift shop. Behind the counter was a slack jawed man who was wearing glasses and had what Drenelle referred to the classic "eye problem." Drenelle immediately recognized the purple "Washington 2020" T-shirt with the sticker "I Voted." On the TV above the counter displayed the results of yesterday's election, which Avanti Washington won by a landslide. The clip showed last night's highlights of Washington's victory speech.

In the back of the shop hung the sign "The Mystery is Here!" along the top of the black curtains. Giant arrows were pointing to the curtains.

On the way to the attraction, Drenelle couldn't help but look around the shop. She didn't notice one single shopper in the vicinity. Except for that strange clerk sitting behind the front checkout counter, she didn't see anybody for that matter. No shoppers. No *weary* travelers. She told herself that maybe they, too, wanted to see what the mystery was about and that they were already inside the attraction, taking selfies and posting and doing whatever trend people did these days. Honestly, she didn't know what to think of the atmosphere for it felt as if she was in a different reality and everything around her was nothing more than props.

More mindful of her surroundings, she reached the front of the black glittered covered curtains where yet another man was standing behind a podium. As with the clerk, he was wearing a purple "Washington" T-shirt. The features on his face appeared like abstract art. His bird-like nose didn't fit properly and was way too big for his face; one eye was bigger than the other; his eyes long and saggy and hung like damp towels along the side of his shrunken head.

The man, whose name was Braille, glanced down at the pig on the leash.

Lethargically, he looked back up at Drenelle.

"Five dollars," he said in a child-like voice.

"You take credit cards?"

The man, Braille, looked confused by Drenelle's question as if, somehow, he didn't how to respond to the question.

Drenelle awkwardly smiled and dug her hand into the red leather fanny pack worn around her waist. She pulled out a crinkly five-dollar bill and handed it to Braille, who, in return, handed Drenelle a ticket, which looked more like a bookmark with the words "*Mysterious World.*"

"Enjoy the mystery," Braille said to Drenelle.

After giving a nod of thanks to Braille, Drenelle stepped through the curtains and entered a dark and narrow corridor, which was covered in neon-colored snake tracks along the walls and ceiling.

She walked to a sign that explained the discovery of "The Mystery." Benjamin Winslow Nahum had discovered "The Mystery" inside an abandoned mineshaft. Locals who knew Benjamin called him "Cannon," because he was said to have an "explosive personality." Legend said that Cannon went mad and wound up in a mental institution and blamed his mental decline on spending years trying to solve the origins of The Mystery.

Intrigued to uncover the mystery surrounding The Mystery, Drenelle and her pig, Runt, continued down the corridor until they reached an exhibit hall basking with black lights. Inside the hall were artifacts that were collected from a place called the "Nether Realm."

The artifacts included misshaped skulls caused by mutation, shrunken heads, a special sparkling log of driftwood, which was taken from Resurrection River, as well as volcanic glass-like rock known to foresee one's fate.

Drenelle and Runt left the hall and walked down yet another corridor covered in snake tracks. Not once seeing another visitor or traveler in sight, they followed the dimly lit corridor, which zigzagged into the main attraction, "The Mystery of the Mysterious World."

Those snake tracks led up to the unveiling of The Mystery, which was lit up by a bright yellow spotlight.

Displayed inside a glass enclosure was the great "Sheik," which was a giant mummified snake. The snake was three times the size of an anaconda and said to have been a great "king" who had slithered its way from "The Void." According to the engraved description along a gold plate, the serpent, Sheik, was discovered by the artist, Benjamin Winslow Nahum, inside a mineshaft. The artist, Cannon, also discovered over a dozen of hatched eggs, each broken, cracked, and chipped shells being roughly the size of footballs, which were displayed on a bed of wheat straw in a glass case next to Sheik.

After reading up on this "Sheik" character and how this so called "Cannon" fellow believed it had escaped from the Nether Realm, Drenelle drew the conclusion that all of it was smoke and mirrors. One giant hoax. A big fat waste of time. Simply fake. And the money she spent to see such bogus nonsense!

She was, in fact, duped.

For a moment, she actually contemplated storming through the curtains, confronting Braille, and demanding her five dollars back.

Drenelle smacked her gums and glanced down at Runt.

"Come on, Runt," Drenelle said, putting aside her disappointment. "Let's get outta here. . . "

Once Drenelle left the gift shop with a bookmark as proof that she had braved the journey and finally, after miles of passing one enticing billboard after another, could say that she unveiled the great mystery along Interstate 10, she walked back to the van and laughed off the recent experience. She helped Runt into the passenger seat; and then, once Runt was all buckled up, she walked around the front of the Caravan and took her seat behind the steering wheel. First, she buckled her seatbelt, making sure she was secured in the driver's seat. Next, she rerouted the GPS along the dashboard to her final destination, which was mapped for Loganson, West Virginia. She wasn't entirely certain of what that next chapter of her life was going to look like, even though she carried around images in her head of the dangers—and adventures—that awaited her. Those images were only images, Drenelle knew, and dare she say, it was useless trying to understand the origin of their inception. And maybe, just maybe, that was the best part of life: not knowing how things came to be or where she was going to end up; and in essence, traveling into the dark without a flashlight. What better way to discover the light?

www.ingramcontent.com/pod-product-compliance
Lightning Source LLC
Chambersburg PA
CBHW030928020726
47498CB00001B/158